ARCANE KNIGHT

AN EPIC LITRPG FANTASY

ORDER & CHAOS
BOOK 3

TIMOTHY MCGOWEN

ILLUSTRATED BY
RICHARD SASHIGANE

RISING
TOWER
BOOKS

Fantasy / LitRPG / Gamelit

OTHER BOOKS BY THE AUTHOR

Haven Chronicles
Haven Chronicles: Eldritch Knight

Short Stories/Novellas
Dead Man's Bounty
Exiled Jahk (https://dl.bookfunnel.com/c10uz8peaf)

Last Born of Ki'darth
Reincarnation: A Litrpg/Gamelit Trilogy
Rebellion: A Litrpg/Gamelit Trilogy
Retribution: A Litrpg/Gamelit Trilogy

Order & Chaos
Arcane Knight Book 1: An Epic LITRPG Fantasy
Arcane Knight Book 2: An Epic LITRPG Fantasy
Arcane Knight Book 3: An Epic LITRPG Fantasy

Arcane Knight Book 3: An Epic LITRPG Fantasy

Order & Chaos

Ebook ISBN: 978-1-956179-18-7

First Edition: April 2023

Published By: Rising Tower Books

Publisher Website: www.RisingTowerBooks.com

Author Site: AuthorTimothyMcGowen.com

REVIEWS ARE IMPORTANT

Every review matters, get your voice heard.

Follow me on Amazon to get informed when my next book is released!
https://www.amazon.com/stores/Timothy-McGowen/author/B087QTTRJK

Join my Patreon for early Chapters!
https://www.patreon.com/TimothyMcGowen

Join my Facebook group and discuss the books
https://www.facebook.com/groups/234653175151521/

SPECIAL THANKS

I wanted to give a special thanks to those that helped bring this book to its current state.

Candace Morris - Alpha Reader, Beta Reader, Editor, and Proofer

Dantas Neto - Editor, Proofer

Sean Hall - Proofer

I would also like to mention my patreons and thank them for their extra support!

Bobby, John Matsinger, Brad Gibson, FlOdis, Eric Letcher

Thank you.

Thank you to all my readers and fans. As long as you keep reading, I will keep writing.

CONTENTS

PROLOGUE

"South Den mines have fallen," I said, repeating what I'd just learned from the most recent scouting reports.

"Damn Variyn, that sneaky bastard," Lord Blalor said, his words coming out as a growl. "For too long he's stayed idle, I should have never weakened my borders or allowed him to buy up the Eastern mines. I ignored reports of his treachery and now look where we are. Sanel, have we any reports from the King, will he send us troops?"

I shifted uneasily in my seat not wanting to give additional bad news. "Though we promised favorable deals, all requests have been met with silence," I said.

"What say you, Kelter?" asked Lord Blalor.

Kelter, the spy master of house Blalor cleared his throat, but did not respond. He was a slimy piece of a man, slick black hair, sickly skinny, as tall as an oak and as a wiry as a branch.

"Out with it Kelter," Lord Blalor said, his eyes suspicious of the man.

"I have it on good authority that," Kelter said, pausing to stroke his wispy thin beard before continuing, "King Newaliyn has put his support behind House Variyn."

I pinched the bridge of my nose, the aches coming in waves now. "I've heard nothing of this," I said, flipping through scouting reports for any mention.

"I know that look," Lord Blalor said, flicking his hand at Kelter in an annoyed manner. "Tell me what else you've heard."

Kelter's oily smile flashed across his face, and he continued. "Even now he sends a legion of his best soldiers mixed with Gilfoy's abominations. Runeforged, I think they're called. I recall I suggested that we purchase several thousand to bolster our forces last winter as they became available. I fear it will be too late now, as rumors already spread that Gilfoy will be pulling out of House Blalor as to not anger the King. We will face this threat alone."

Lord Blalor nodded; his attention suddenly fixed on a report in front of him while he digested everything he'd heard. I was having the same trouble believing the news. Surely the King wouldn't so easily be swayed toward House Variyn in this matter? What did they have to offer that House Blalor could not? Because of Lord Blalor's shrewd dealings with the elves, House Blalor stood at the height of wealth and prosperity.

"Get me General Fain," Lord Blalor said, his resolve hardening along with his eyes. "Sanel, I want the Adventurer's Guild reports on all native *Awakened* and a report on able-bodied men. Begin work on a call to arms. We may be standing alone, but I won't give in without a fight."

First all this mess with Chaos monsters threatening our borders, and now an invasion stands at our doorsteps. House Blalor already operated with far less noblemen than other houses, nearly half of three hundred keeps throughout House Blalor stand empty and unguarded.

This coming winter would be a difficult season and I feared for my Lord. But there was one thing House Blalor had in abundance above all other Houses, and that was raw materials. It was true that nearly all our supplies of ores were sent to the elves, who always seemed ready with more coin, but we'd stockpiled plenty. The smiths would be working long hours in the coming months to get arms and armor for the massive army Lord Blalor would need to field in order to deal with the coming threat.

Just as I was about to leave, a thought struck me, and I opened my mouth to suggest it before I could think better of it. "What of the elves, Lord Blalor? Surely, they have mercenary forces that we could employ?"

The light of hope sparked in his eyes as I watched him, and he shook his head. "Perhaps, yes, they owe us a fair bit of goodwill and the elves are known for keeping a battle-ready army at all times. But how willing will they be to go to war after the losses they've dealt with some ten years back? It is worth exploring. Send our emissary to the elves, call in every favor we have, raise the banners of war!"

I didn't have the heart to tell him that it was unlikely

that the elves would ride to war for something as mundane as a House War, no matter the stakes to our survival. My mouth moved faster than my mind but the light of hope in his kept me from correcting my mistake.

CHAPTER 1
SATHERGORGAN

W arrick laid in a grand four poster bed, resting his body while his keen mind worked on a way for us to proceed. He'd grown quiet in the last few minutes, so I stepped away and looked out a window into the sea of red sands. Life in the Southlands didn't look like it was for the faint of heart, very little life could be seen unless you focused hard on small patches of land. Doing so, I could make out a section of sand that shifted as something beneath moved unseen below the surface.

It had been at least a day since we'd arrived atop this tower, I knew now it was a creation of Warrick's—a variation to my Arcane Asylum perk that allowed for the placement of physical anchors to hold a transdimensional inner location that somehow existed in several locations at once. Or at least that is what Warrick had said and I didn't pretend to understand all of it.

Suffice to say that we are inside of his tower now, but

in the Southlands. The room I stood in the window in wasn't a place I'd been before but that hardly meant anything with how the rooms shifted around in his tower. It was fairly expansive and decorated with fineries that I wouldn't normally attribute to someone like Warrick, a man of simpler and straightforward tastes.

"Water," Warrick said from behind me. I grabbed a cup of water from the nightstand beside the bed and handed it to him.

"Are you feeling better?" I asked, but I felt like I knew the answer. As soon as we'd passed through the portal he'd summoned, he'd fell forward and passed out. Kora helped me move him through an open door and down a staircase before Warrick snapped back to consciousness, directing us where to go from there.

"I'm somewhat better," Warrick said, saying each word slowly as if tasting them for their truthfulness.

"What happened to you?" I asked. He'd talked very little about his ordeal and I was beginning to worry that our trip here might be one way. I didn't know much about the Southlands but without Ares with me—she'd been off hunting when I'd gone to see Warrick—I had little way of getting anywhere fast.

"We have much to discuss but let us start at the beginning of my capture," Warrick said, his voice tired but firm.

He went on to tell me that after being captured he was set into a machine of Ordu making. He didn't know how but it was able to pull free essence that had long been solidified into levels and attributes. It drained him of years of essence, but his high thresholds saved him from the worst of the attribute loss. There was something about thresholds that the machine couldn't undo. He wouldn't tell me what level he'd been reduced to but assured me that he was still a force to be reckoned with.

I'd be more willing to believe him if he hadn't then coughed up some blood a moment later. When asked why doing a teleport spell had brought him to his knees, he told me that portal spells were tricky and required massive amounts of mana, so much so that he'd pushed himself too far, too fast after recovering. Earlier the day before, he'd set Kora to task on finding various items in his tower, tonics and such that he claimed would help him.

In turn, I gave him a watered-down version of my life story since leaving his side. He smiled in all the right places and cursed when the situation merited it. Telling Warrick of my journeys felt good in a way that I hadn't experienced before. It was almost like sharing my successes with my father, almost.

"Which brings us to now," I said, my thoughts turning sour as I considered my father. "If he is truly alive and in the Southlands, where will we find him?"

"I've had time to think," Warrick said, a saddened look on his face. "While I do believe your father might very well be alive, I don't know if that is why he sent us here. Your father, if this is his work, has a way of being frustratingly mysterious when he wants to be. I fear we will find nothing of your father here, but I could be mistaken."

"Then why are we here?" I asked, my anger rising

despite trying to keep it in check. The idea that my father could be alive sent all sorts of mixed emotions through me. I knew one thing for certain, I wouldn't be sharing this information with my mother or siblings. I refused to put them through what I was feeling unless I discovered the truth of it all.

"We shall see soon," Warrick said, smiling. "I worked a fair bit of sneaky magic that should be returning within the hour."

As if on cue, a black raven appeared and landed on Warrick's bed, then shockingly it faded away as if it were just a construct of light. I recognized that bird as the ones that had been following me throughout my adventures.

"You've been watching over me?" I asked, smiling at how tricky Warrick must have been to get that spell working while being stripped of his power.

"What's that?" Warrick asked, a puzzled look on his face.

"That bird," I said. "I've seen them following me here and there since I began my adventure. Surely that was you watching over me?"

"Curious," Warrick said, his eyes filled with puzzled bemusement. "I dare say another piece of a complex puzzle has been set into place."

"Are you saying you didn't? Then who?" I asked, my thoughts went to one other, but I couldn't dare to wish.

"I learned this spell from your father, who learned it from a beastkin tribal leader, his name escapes me, but it isn't well known. Sure, there are similar spells, but the

Seeking Raven is unique. Are you certain you've seen them before, it wasn't just a passing bird?"

Doubt crossed through my mind as I remembered each encounter and the many times that I'd seen them and paid no mind. "I can't be certain, but it certainly felt odd at the time. How common are black birds, that I've seen them on every leg of my journeys?"

"It would be like your father to watch over you if he could," Warrick said, smiling deeply. "I would say there is no harm in us believing that they are sent by him. Further proof he is hanging on somewhere and still has a few tricks up his sleeves."

"What did you learn from the Raven?" I asked, still processing how I felt about my father possibly watching over me. Surely there must be something preventing him from coming back to us, but whatever it was it didn't stop him from casting spells. My stray thoughts came to an end as Warrick answered.

"It is as you said in your tale of your adventures," Warrick said. "I know why the Southerners are fleeing the Southlands." Warrick paused to pull himself up, with great difficulty, to a higher sitting position on the bed. "I was able to detect at least a dozen Mana Shrines turned to the side of Chaos. The delicate balance is in danger."

"So why don't the Southerners turn them back," I said simply. "I've done it before, and while it takes a lot of Mana, it is possible. Unless they destroyed it like that Chaos Knight did."

"Don't remind me of that wretched woman," Warrick

said, shaking his head. "What she did is a greater threat to us than any simple turning of the Shrines. But it will take much time or further destroyed Prime Mana Shrines before it will cause any direct issues. It is an issue that must be resolved, but you aren't strong enough to deal with it yet."

I had so much that I needed to accomplish, the quest to retrieve a Blade of Order from the isle of Avalon—a task someone at my level couldn't hope to do without significant help. My main goal had to be to grow stronger so I could face off against the impossible tasks that stood before me. I needed to get stronger, I would get stronger!

Warrick cleared his throat, looking at me with a wry smile. "You are much like your father, getting lost in your own head. I answered you but you didn't hear me. I believe that Southerners don't turn them back, because they can't. A force from the Eastern lands must be taking root down here, it is the only explanation. There is a city nearby, a fairly large one, where we might find more answers. Give me another day or two to recover and we will seek more answers."

I was alone in a room of my own now, Kora was tending to Warrick's needs. It was time for me to go over my quests and growth I'd accumulated over the past few weeks. The first thing I noticed was my class assigned quest had been updated, giving me essence and a new ability.

Restoring the Balance Part 2

As a Defender of the Balance, it falls onto your shoulders to investigate and restore the planet's equilibrium. To do this you must first understand why it is out of balance. Seek knowledge and understanding anywhere you can find it.

You have encountered an Agent of Chaos who has been instrumental in disrupting the balance between Order & Chaos. She has poisoned the very blood of the planet and must be dealt with. Purify the Ley Lines and Slay the Agent of Chaos responsible.

Objective: Purify the Ley Lines, Slay the Agent of Chaos.

Rewards: 1,000,000 Essence, New Perk 'Third Eye Open'

Third Eye Open: Gives you the ability to Open your third eye. While third eye is open your spells are ten times more effective and powerful. You also gain the ability to perceive the true nature of the Cosmos.

I checked the description of my new ability from Part 1 of the quest and was impressed.

Restoring Light: A spell that can be used to remove Chaos corruption and heal a target for 255 Health over 10 Seconds. This spell has a cooldown of 5 seconds and a cast time of 3 seconds.

Comparing that against my other heal spells, I decided

it wasn't too bad after all. Taking a quick look at the rest of my spells and skills I felt confident in my abilities. My titles hadn't changed and neither had my Perks, so I switched over and looked at my Profession's progression. I was progressing decently enough as a Gem Inscriptionist, with a good variety of recipes at my disposal.

Finally, I looked over my Attributes page, I was still wearing my armor and it reflected as much.

Name: Caldor Miles | Classification: Arcane Knight | Species: Human

Level: 20, 66,150 Essence to Lvl. 21 | Essence: 143,597 | Reputation: Rank 2, 79%

Health: 1,150/1,150 | Mana: 1,210/1,210 | Stamina: 1,020/1,020

Health Regen: 95 Per Minute | Mana Regen: 44 Per Minute | 82 Per Minute

Constitution: 95 (40 Base) | Intellect (50 Base) | Endurance: 82 (40 Base)

Core: 31 (31 Base) | Concentration: 40 (40 Base) | Strength: 100 (50 Base)

My items and gear made up a large chunk of my attributes, but they wouldn't raise me above thresholds unfortunately, so I needed my base attributes to hit those marks. Either way, I was close to hitting my next thresholds, but I'd want to bring my Core up sooner than later. It would be a shame to lose out because I couldn't hold any more essence, especially now that I had ways of gathering additional essence. Then the thought occurred to me, and I laughed. I could always fill a gem with essence if I got close to my limit, then retrieve it later.

After thoroughly going through my quests, attributes, perks, titles, and more I checked on my armor, items, and rings. I was ready to go, but unfortunately Warrick was not. So instead, I flopped onto the bed and pulled out a book to read.

It was a full week later when Warrick finally said he was ready. His color had returned, and he had a pep in his step. He'd dressed in thick grey robes and leaned onto a gnarled staff with a gem set into the top. All he was missing was his signature conical hat with the large brim and we'd be set to go. But he surprised me by lifting a hood over his head instead, a look I couldn't ever remember seeing on him before.

Kora wore her usual long cloak with a deep-set hood to hide her identity. I tried to tell her it was likely not needed but she insisted on wearing it. In her hand she had a polished wooden dueling cane, an old-fashioned thing that she'd found somewhere in Warrick's tower, and he'd given her permission to use it. It had a rounded top of polished wood and was half the length of Warrick's staff, except where his was gnarled wood hers was a polished smooth shaft wrapped with leather strips for a handle.

I wore my Basilisk Armor, Black scaled Cloak of Negation, and my various other dungeon drop items. My dimensional cube and storage ring held any other supplies we might find ourselves needing, or at least that is what I told myself as we exited out the lower entrance of the tower and into the southlands.

A circle of lighter colored stones that barely stood out against the red sands had been arranged around the tower, something told me that after walking even a short distance from the tower we'd find that it was missing. Warrick's magic was wondrous, I just hoped he still had some kick left in him if we encountered resistance out in the wilds.

"This magic feels similar to that used by my kind for our dungeons," Kora said, regarding the tower and the circle surrounding it.

"Is it now?" Warrick said, smiling. "I'd always assumed a dimensional shift of some kind was used, but without the advanced lessons in portal magic and the perk that became available because of it I would never have been able to accomplish such a feat."

"How much control do you have on the nature of your dungeon?" I asked, suddenly curious, as this was the first time Kora had brought up the subject. She'd been quite reserved about being a dungeon core and I hadn't wanted to press her into uncomfortable details.

"There are two parts to every dungeon, and I am but one," Kora said as if that answered my question. After a minute of silence where Warrick and I both allowed her to gather her wits, she spoke again. "I'm hesitant to share all of my secrets, but my memory is vast and my lifetime ever more so. Since taking this form however, the more time that passes the harder it is to remember certain details."

"Like a dream," I said, nodding my head that I could understand that much at least. I'd had so many dreams that still felt important but looking back it was almost impossible to recall what had been so important about them.

"I think you are rather unique, Kora," Warrick said, putting a hand on her shoulder and steadying himself. "I've never heard of a liberated Dungeon Core that didn't break upon leaving its pedestal. The fact that you've been turned into a golem of sorts with limited access to your summoning abilities is downright baffling. Very unique indeed."

Kora and Warrick must have been talking while he was meant to be resting, it almost seemed like he knew more of her and her abilities than I did at this point.

We continued on with our conversation for another three hours before we needed to rest. Warrick huffed and puffed from the strain of walking. I wished that I had Ares nearby to carry him, but wishing did nothing and our bond wasn't so strong as to reach across a continent.

"Are you sure you can make this journey?" I asked for what felt like the tenth time. As with the times before, he merely nodded and took a long pull from an orange potion he kept in his front pocket.

"I'm not as weak as I appear," Warrick said, coughing all the while. I wanted to believe him, I really did, but from what I could tell he was on death's door. "My body is adjusting to its new limitations, but when I'm needed, I will be ready."

A determined gleam in his eye told me that he meant what he said, I just hoped that was enough when the time came.

CHAPTER 2
VENSHTI

The time to prove himself came a week into our journey. We traveled down a dusty road in the cool of the evening, the best time of the day temperature wise. So far, we'd encountered no monsters of any kind and a part of me wanted to believe those circumstances led to our lax nature, but I didn't know for sure.

As if in answer to my need to do something, I felt the stirring of magic, but from where I couldn't tell. Warrick perked up as well and held a hand up to forestall us.

Suddenly out of nowhere, a figure stood before us, a long sword out and pointed in our direction. A moment later, my own sword was in my hands and my instant cast Lightning Strike spell released, cracking the air in front of us. The lone swordsmen slashed at the air in front of him, intercepting my magical attack without any visible harm coming to him.

Suddenly I realized that I couldn't feel the normal

structured power coming off him as with any *Awakened* I'd encountered before. In its place was an ebb and flow of energy, like the waves of the ocean against the shoreline.

I thought perhaps we were encountering a Chaos Knight or something, but this swordsman didn't have any of the taint that I felt from the last one we'd encountered.

"Careful now Caldor," Warrick said stepping between us and the swordsmen. "He's a *wild-spark*, the eastern kingdoms answer to their sparked. Very chaotic magic and extremely deadly. Allow me to handle this."

The last few words lost a bit of their confidence when a blade crossed in front of his throat, held by a shadowy figure that swiftly appeared.

"Quiet now, or lose your tongue," a scratchy voice could be heard from the figure behind Warrick. I began to step forward only to find a staff with a blazing red gem atop it, pressing into my chest.

"I'd be happy to blow you into several pieces, but if it is all the same, I just washed these robes," a nasally voice said from right in front of me.

"Stand down for now," Warrick said, turning enough to catch my eye. He didn't look scared, if anything he looked curious at our sudden change in fortune.

Two more figures appeared, a bow-wielder and a bald-headed woman dressed only in cloth wraps.

I dropped my sword, willing it to return to wherever it was stored when not being used, before it even touched the ground. The wizard snorted and reached down to the ground. To my utter surprise and astonishment, he pulled my blade from the ground, reaching through a shimmer of light.

"I'll hold on to this for now," he said with his nasally voice.

We were in trouble.

"Warrick," I whispered as they finished tying the three of us up and sitting us down together. "Do you have a plan?"

"It is fascinating the control over magic they have while not following any recognizable patterns or flows. That staff wielder, obviously some sort of mage or wizard, reached into the remains of your temporal displacement field and retrieved your sword like it was a trifling thing. I'd need to study the spell for weeks before I'd feel safe attempting something like that, but he just reached in and grabbed it."

"Quiet down," said a new voice, the ranger type with leather armor and a bow. He had a smooth baritone voice, and his rebuke held a commanding yet kind tone to it, almost like a parent scolding a child.

I took his command to heart and focused in on the bald female speaking to the swordsman at the edge of the light. They'd built a campfire and seemed to be getting ready to make camp for the night. What a strange encounter this was becoming.

With effort, I got my ears to focus enough to pick up their conversation.

"Then we should kill them and take what rewards their corpses offer," the bald female said in a harsh whisper.

"I took this job because I wanted to explore unknown lands, not give into the dark one's rhetoric or become their murder hounds. Of all my party members, Kriss, you were the last I expected to be so ready to end a life for being different," the swordsman's voice was low and gentle even in its rebuke.

Kriss paused and looked our way. I averted my eyes in time and the words continued, lower but still loud enough for me to pick up. Looking at Warrick I could tell he was listening as well.

"It's their wizard," Kriss said, shaking her head. "He isn't what he seems. I feel enough power moving through him that he could snuff each of us out without a second thought. I don't know what they are playing at, but I don't like our odds if we wait to find out."

I looked away again as both sets of eyes turned to Warrick. He however did not look away, instead standing without the aid of his staff, the ropes holding him falling free at his feet.

"I'd hoped we could talk and perhaps find common ground, but now I'm worried that has been spoiled," Warrick said, cracking his neck to the side.

"Sit back down you tired old fool," the nasally wizard said, lifting his staff up as if to strike him in the chest. The wizard let off a fireball from the tip of his staff, it reflected off Warrick and slammed into my chest, knocking me backwards and scorching my face. Warrick turned his eyes on the man and suddenly the nasally wizard's red robes blew backwards as if by a great wind. His body disintegrated into dust before it hit the ground.

I broke my own bonds; the ropes weren't much for someone with my strength attribute. Brushing off the smoldering bits from my chest, I stood. If we were going to do this, then I was ready. With a stray thought I summoned my sword, it came as quick as ever, forming in my grasp.

"The last great conflict," Warrick said, leaning forward over the fire and warming his hands. "Your people stayed out of it, why now are *wild-sparks* joining with the Chaos Knights?"

On the edge of the firelight, barely visible, a vein on Kriss's forehead bulged and her fists tightened. I thought I caught her saying, 'I told you so' or something to the swordsman, but I couldn't be certain. I walked up to the fire's edge and took a page from Warrick's book, warming my free hand and playing it as casual as I could under the circumstances.

"Peace, friend," the swordsman threw down his blade and stepped into the light where I saw his face for the first time. "My name is Jared Nullspar of the Nullspar clan. You have shown your power and ended the life of my friend. It is not often that I find myself so outmatched and I would humbly request you allow my people to flee and take my life as your reward."

"How noble, Jared of Nullspar," Warrick said, his voice still filled with his trademark humor. "But you've failed to answer my question. Please sit and let us speak like civil beings."

Jared Nullspar sat across the fire and with a wave of his hands, so did his remaining party. He wasn't what I expected when his cloth hood came down. He wore plate armor over loose dark blue cloth, the same made up his hood and his cloak. When his hood went down, my eyes went wide in surprise. While the rest of his companions, the ones I could freely see, appeared to be human, Jared was an elf or at least had the ears of one.

Elves tended to be much more slender than he appeared, but that was just a generalization as they did vary as much as humans did. His skin was the color of white porcelain with scars tracing over every few inches of space, giving his face the look of marbling. His flesh was so white that he made Zander seem tanned in comparison.

"He called us *wild-sparked*, it is a crude name for a Venshti but I've heard it before. If I answer your questions, will you permit my men to leave here alive?" Jared asked, still not answering Warrick's question.

Warrick sighed and produced an apple out of nowhere, taking a bite. After chewing on it for several long and uncomfortable seconds, he answered. "Yes, I think that is agreeable."

Jared visibly relaxed and in doing so I noticed a measure of tension release from all the party members but one, the one known as Kriss.

"Kriss, heal the injured one in a show of good faith,"

Jared said, Kriss immediately stepped forward but I held a hand up.

"I can heal myself," I said, placing my hand on my chest and casting Restoring Light for the first time. The phrases and focus for the spell came as easy as if I'd studied them my entire life, as did all abilities learned through the system of the Ordu. Three seconds later my spell went off and I felt the cooling effects of the spell wash over me. It had a distinctly different feel than my other healing spells that I attributed to the removal of Chaos corruption.

"A trio that never ceases to amaze," Jared said, looking at me like I'd just turned water to wine or something.

Even Kriss looked at me with new eyes, instead of fear and distrust I saw amazement and curiosity. Her features were narrow and her eyes hard, but as she tilted her head to regard me, I saw a beauty there that had been hiding beneath her anger.

"You don't see many healers?" Warrick asked, seeing how amazed they all looked by my simple casting.

"It is the rarest of all the mysterious arts, Kriss is one of only three healers I've ever met," Jared said, not hesitating to answer this question. As if he realized he was staring, he finally blinked several times and looked back at Warrick. "You wanted to know why the Venshti have entered the conflict of the dark rulers?"

"Indeed, I do," Warrick said, his warm fatherly smile infusing me with a measure of comfort. I realized then that he must be weaving some spell to help calm the emotions of all those present. How many times had he used such magic on me? It mattered not I decided, instead relaxing and listening to Warrick and Jared talk.

"For as long as my people can remember, the dark mountain has reigned over our tribes, only the Venshti has freedom to ignore their laws and mandates. When armies were gathered, never did any of our kind who hadn't taken on the mantle of Chaos join the fights. But these past few years have been different. Our people, the dungeons we rely on for supplies, and the harvest lands of monsters have all begun to fall under the banner of a new force."

He took a moment to stare into the fire, obviously reliving some unseen memory.

"It became apparent that an old enemy, the ones the dark ones speak of, had finally come for our land. So, the Venshti fight not for the killing of others, but to seek new dungeons and turn more waystones to our path. The monstrous men who fight like the fiercest of beasts have been stemmed at Hiddles fall, but it won't last. We need to take more ground if we are going to keep our tribes fed. We fight because we must."

Warrick listened to his words, nodding along as he spoke.

"It is as I feared," he said, turning to regard me. "The Beastkin nations have overstepped and begun to overrun the Eastern lands. This imbalance will have more conse-quences that even I foresaw if the Venshti have entered the battle."

Then turning to Jared and his team, Warrick sighed.

"How many Venshti are there and how many are here fighting in the Southlands?"

Jared paused, but a sudden movement from Warrick made him jump and he answered. "I can speak only from rumors of the other clans, but my own clan, Nullspar, numbers at one thousand and nine at last count. Although, that will be eight now. The others claim similar numbers, but we estimate they are several hundred less."

"No more than three thousand in total?" Warrick asked, surprise evident in his tone.

"The spark of power is a cruel mistress that only one in ten survive," Jared said, speaking solemnly. "Surely your kind numbers around the same?"

Warrick nodded his head, then said as if it were nothing at all. "Awakened number at least ten thousand continent-wide, if not twice that by now. The elves don't share their census numbers and I only had access to outdated records from Newaliyn, and then there is the south to consider. No efficient record has ever been made here."

I watched Jared's expression as the information sunk in. It went from casual confidence to confusion and landed on utter astonishment.

"You can't possibly expect me to bel-"

Unexpectedly, Jared went stiff, and his eyes shut, falling over to the side. I watched in concern as all other party members did likewise, until I saw Warrick weaving his fingers about in the workings of a spell.

"I need a moment," Warrick said, taking a drink from

his orange potion, draining the remainder of it. "Fetch me my staff, I will clear their minds and set them back where they came. I so wish I could question them further, but I haven't the strength to keep this facade going. My disintegration ward took a considerable measure of my stored strength. We will need to travel for another week before reaching our destination and I fear I'll need my strength for what is to come."

I watched in astonishment as Warrick went to work over each of the adventurers, weaving spells so advanced that I couldn't begin to understand their meanings. When he was finished, he put the fire out with a wave of his hand.

"We will need to move stealthier, otherwise they'll find us again," I said, wishing my armor would hide me better in the shadows as it was meant to.

"Nonsense," Warrick said. "I allowed them to find us when they roamed within a few miles of our path. I am maintaining a decent enough warding that not even the local monsters have happened upon us. Though I worry that we will still stumble upon one or two before our journey's end."

Of course, Warrick had been keeping us safe this entire time. Pity he didn't trust me enough to tell me what he was planning, but I imagined his train of thought easily enough. Can't fail at acting surprised if you were actually surprised, right?

We'd attracted a fair bit of Sand Worms in the past few days. Most were around level ten, but just yesterday I killed one that was level 20 and as big as all the prior ones combined. Warrick barely seemed worried when they showed up, and I dispatched them quickly to ensure that he wouldn't have to use any of his reserves.

It was the middle of the second week of our travels and the sun beat down as harshly as ever; my feet struggled to keep a decent pace against the thick sand. Whatever road we'd been following before had been lost to the endless sea of red sand that now took over the entire horizon. Occasionally, through the heat and shimmering of reflected sunlight, I swear I saw villages, war bands, and once a keep, but each time a second look proved my sight to be unreliable.

"Can I defeat the next one?" Kora asked, speaking for the first time in nearly two days.

"I don't see why not; you feel strong enough?" I asked, she hadn't shared her level or how the 'leveling' Rune-forged body interacted with her Dungeon Core and the power laying within her.

"I am stronger than my current form and level would suggest," Kora said, tilting her head to the side just slightly before continuing. "I've reached level 12, the latent essence and collecting from fallen foes bolstering me enough to improve my overall strength. I will reach a limit eventually, but until then this body will do fine."

Another 2 levels already! She must know her way around the use of essence to level up in a way foreign to me, because I definitely hadn't increased by any significant amount fighting sandworms.

"You should be up to the task then," I said, patting her gently on the back. She looked up at me, her porcelain white armored plates contrasting against the fierce blue glow that filled her eye sockets.

"I'm eager to test the three summons I've gathered, but could I ask you something?" Kora asked.

"You just did," I said, chuckling at my own little joke.

The humor fell flat, and she stared at me for several long seconds before I amended my response. "Sure thing, what would you like to ask me?"

"Will you train with me? Your sword against my body? I wish to test the limits of this physical form I have, and I think you are a suitable subject to test myself against," Kora said, her delicate porcelain lips curling into a smile that wouldn't be possible on any other Runeforged.

I nodded my head and took Warrick sitting down as a sign that he wanted to rest, so we could do this now. My sword appeared in my hand, and I rolled my neck, cracking the bones and stretching the stiff muscles.

"I will do my best not to hurt you," I said, deciding I'd stick to completely martial attacks and no abilities of any kind.

"I will not make such a promise," Kora said, her cloak falling free from her shoulders. She wore the leather armor I'd gotten her early in her creation and though it was low leveled, it would offer some protection. Her arms were free of any armor and as she raised her left arm several hundred small runes glowed on the surface.

The arm shifted suddenly, morphing into a bladed point. She smiled, rushing forward with speed way beyond that of a level 12 Adventurer.

I caught her strike against my sword just in time and shifted my weight back, throwing her off balance. Then as she fell forward, I hit her in the back of the head with the pommel of my sword. A soft clink sounded, and she fell to the ground.

"I am struggling to adjust my body's speed potential, allow me to apologize," Kora said, standing and brushing off the dust from her armor in a very human way. I'd noticed that throughout the trip she'd been purposely picking up human quirks like that.

"I'm ready when you are," I said, smiling as she faced off.

This battle was going to be interesting if she could master control of her body. She lunged forward, moving at speeds that would be hard to track if I hadn't passed my thresholds already. I caught her obvious attack, but with a flash of light she nearly struck me with a shorter sword arm to the back. I spun to the side, having to make a conscious effort to not activate a skill to parry her attack.

The dagger like strike from her right hand glanced harmlessly off the back plate of my armor, but I felt the pressure of it and knew that she was going full force.

What followed was truly an amazing dance of skill and learning. With every strike Kora became smarter in her movements throughout our three-minute duel, and she wasn't wasting a single step. It was towards the end of this exchange of blows that she got me twice, but I healed quickly, until I finally caved and used a skill to block a backstab.

"I have endless faded memories of your kind using channeled power like that, could you teach me?" Kora asked, stepping back to speak.

"Honestly?" I asked, bemused by her sudden appreciation of my skill Swift Strike.

"Yes, I wish to learn," Kora said, a hint of her innocent earnestness coming out in her words.

I thought about it and realized something. "I don't know how to teach the use of skills, I mean, I can try to explain what I do, but the system put in place by the Ordu provides the knowledge directly, so I didn't really need to study it or anything," I said. I'd had some success learning spells but oddly I'd never heard of skills being taught, though I wouldn't be surprised if that was just one of many gaps in my study.

"It is possible," Warrick said from where he lay back resting in the sand. "Skills aren't so unlike their spell counterparts. Focus on the knowledge the Ordu placed in your head, walk her through the steps of using the skill. She's a quick study, I'm sure she will work the rest out."

So, I did just that, starting with the smallest of feelings or impressions I had regarding Swift Strike. I told her what it felt like to activate, to expend Stamina instead of Mana and how it left me feeling afterward. For a solid ten minutes we went over it, but she couldn't grasp the concept of Stamina. We began our trek again, but I continued to explain other stamina-based skills. Still, nothing I tried to teach her over the next day was sticking. It wasn't until that evening, after a day of no monster attacks, that Warrick weighed in on why he thought she was struggling.

"I don't think her body has stamina," Warrick said simply. "It appears to be burning a mix of Essence and Mana to do all of its basic functions. Kora, what size Mana pool are you working with?"

Kora gave Warrick a strange look but seemed to understand a moment later when she said, "I have access to 2,150 Mana at any given time. Though you are right, my basic movements are fed by this resource in as much as they are offset by my rather high regeneration rate. This was a necessity for stabilizing my Dungeon Core."

"What's your regen rate?" I asked, curious when she didn't actually say.

"10 Mana per second," Kora said.

Warrick and I shared a surprised look over the campfire.

"That is more than even I can manage, you truly are a modern marvel," Warrick said, taking out a pipe from within the folds of his cloak and lighting it with a flick of his fingers.

It smelled of Felweed, a common relaxing herb smoked in the Creeshaw area. I'd never known Warrick to partake, but I'd done so on many occasions when offered. It was an expensive and rare plant that took care to prepare properly so up until recently it would have been outside of my financial reach to expect to buy my own. Warrick offered it to me, and I gladly took it.

Pulling in a great breath and holding it, I felt the effects immediately. A gentle calm reverberating over my entire body, while I felt my mind sharpen and my ability to perceive increase several notches. This was different from the times I'd tried it before, but I enjoyed it all the same. Normally, the body relaxing calmness overtook the mind as well, but that wasn't the case this time.

I took another pass on the pipe before handing it back and getting comfortable.

"It isn't quite the same after *Awakening*," I said.

"Felweed is one of many pleasures you will find being *Awakened* alters," Warrick said. Embers from the tip of the pipe lit his face and I saw he'd closed his eyes in pleasure as he inhaled the smoke.

"Not just Felweed or food, nothing is the same," I said, my mind wandered over the events of my life since everything changed during that fateful fight against the boar.

I'd always wanted more out of life and now that I had it, there was a certain overwhelming quality to it that I was doing my best to ignore most days. Something about the effects of the Felweed gave me the clarity to confront the difficult choices I'd made.

So different was my life now that perhaps I needed to readjust and rethink my path forward. Obviously, the threat of the Chaos and maintaining the balance wasn't something I could ever ignore, but how I went about growing stronger and facing the threat might need some adjustments. I had access to unfathomable wealth now and I was still doing dungeons the hard way, with people lower leveled than me.

What is stopping me from gathering the strongest, or at least stronger adventurers to battle at my side for simple gold? I barely posed the question to myself before I knew the answer. It wasn't enough for me to get stronger if left my friends behind. It wasn't enough to just battle the Chaos or maintain the balance, I needed to stay true to my core self.

I would stay true to my oaths, honor my friends by assisting them in growing stronger, and live a life worthy of the powers I'd been given.

Warrick had spoken while I gathered together my thoughts and I looked up just in time to see him try again.

"It is common for those who've had greatness thrust upon them to yearn for the days past, but you are not a common man, Caldor, and I have no doubt that you are worthy of the challenges you will need to face before the end," Warrick said. He took another long pull and added, "Good stuff, this Felweed."

I smiled and promised to take first watch before Kora reminded me that she didn't require sleep, so instead I slipped into my bedroll and fell asleep to the sound of the fire crackling in the night and the wind trailing sand through the lonely red desert of the Southlands.

The fight between Kora and a level 16 Sandworm progressed wonderfully. Kora had yet to do anything but dodge the Sandworm and it was becoming increasingly agitated by its lack of success. Warrick and I stood to the side, a globe of power around us shielding us from their fight.

As was always the case, the sandworm fought from the side of a medium sized sand dune, the full length of its body hidden beneath the vast desert. It had a curious design about it, its skin looking scalier and more snake-like than that of a worm, but its face and head was everything you'd expect from a 'sandworm'. It had no visible eyes, instead a mouth big enough to swallow the three of us whole opened to show rows of rotating layered teeth.

The mighty maw seemed to open to an endless darkness within, but I knew by experience of fighting them that a throat formed about ten feet into it. I made a note that killing a sandworm from within is not the best option, despite the heavily armored scales on the outside.

Sand swirled around the rotating form of the giant worm as it struck out like a snake at the porcelain white form of Kora. Her bladed left hand cut deep into the sandworm's scaly hide, adding black blood to the light brown scales. It screeched in response and flung its body to the side, throwing Kora off balance and tumbling several feet away.

I clenched my fist, every instinct I had wanted to be in

this fight and ending it as fast and safely as possible, but Kora wanted a chance to fight alone, and I'd owed her for all the nights she'd stood watch. Though a part of me wondered if it were necessary at all, as I was positive that Warrick was setting up wards of one kind or another. I also caught him, at least three times now, watching Kora when she wasn't looking in his direction.

Did he trust her as readily as I did, or was he more reserved in his feelings? I knew myself enough that I trusted and forgave perhaps too readily, but knowing this wasn't the same as flipping a switch and changing. Should I trust so readily? Maybe not, but it was hard not to if I had the right feeling about a person. Should I forgive people like Zander who literally tried to kill me on at least two occasions that I was aware of? Probably not.

But the bonds that form in battle are sturdy and more than once he had proven himself a worthy team member. It didn't stop all my animosity towards Zander, but it went a long way. Then there was his budding relationship with Ismene. That was something I hadn't yet examined my feelings on, and I wasn't quite ready to do so. I shifted and watched the fight as Kora seemed to be doing something other than dodging now.

A blue light flared around her and suddenly she wasn't alone. It happened so fast that I didn't even have time to see or feel the mana when she enacted her summoning. Warrick must have noticed more because he let out a surprised noise.

"Oh, how fascinating," he said. "It even looks a bit like her."

I had to do a double take before I saw what he meant, but sure enough, the Disruptor Cat—one of three of her possible summonses—had a faint white pattern I recognized from Kora across its skin. This Disruptor Cat was smaller than the one I'd killed to get the Core, but it looked no less able to dish out destruction.

As if to prove the point, it snarled and leapt at the sandworm, the tentacles on its back slashing against the skin of the worm a moment before its front four paws landed, claws first. The worm spun, flinging red sand up and temporarily blocking my view as the two fought. Kora stood to the side; her hands returned to normal as she watched them fight.

They kicked up enough continuous dust that it was hard to see what was happening, so I leaned onto my other senses instead, including being able to sense their mana. The cat was a weaker source of power, that much I could tell without trying, but the worm was having trouble dealing with its physical strength. Between the little glimpses I caught and the feeling of their energies, it was obvious that the cat would lose eventually.

Kora must have made the same determination, because suddenly she started to glow and this time, I saw a bit of the spell or abilities she used. Her power distorted the air around her and it was almost as if a portal was being opened, then the next moment an Owlbear appeared beside her. It was the first one I'd seen alive, and it looked fearsome.

All the physical power of a monstrous bear and the predatory hunting glint in its eyes like an owl. Besides the raw physical strength, I knew them to have, one also had to watch out for powerful mana infused abilities. They were well known to be creatures that balanced raw physical and mystical abilities.

It had grey feathers with a blueish tint to them and an owl-like head ending in a sharp beak. The face had familiar white lines around the eyes and along the beak that again reminded me of the patterns Kora had over her white metal plated form. Sparking blue claws dug into the red sand as the owlbear opened its beak to make the most unnerving roar mixed with the sound of a bird call. Instead of being one or the other it seemed to reverberate between the two as it let off its battle cry.

Then, just as sudden as its appearance had been, it fired off blue energy from mouth, three twirling balls streaking right at the sandworm. The sound was muted by the sand, but three thumps followed, and it was the sandworm's turn to cry out.

Between the two of her summoned creatures, the sandworm stood no chance. Each time the worm changed its focus, the other opponent would be there with a devastating attack. The cat flickered in and out of sight, going to wherever it went when it disappeared. Meanwhile, the owlbear traded heavy blows and magical attacks at every opportunity.

With a final mighty slash of glowing blue claws from the owlbear, the worm fell still, halfway out of the sand dune it fought from. I felt the shield around us flicker away, but I kept my distance, waiting to see what Kora would do now.

She walked up to the owlbear, it ruffled its feathers but made no move to attack her, only lowering its head at her approach. I watched as she placed her hand on the crest of its forehead, then in a flash of blue light it was gone. She repeated this with the cat, before turning her attention to the sandworm.

So far, we'd not recovered any intact monster cores, except the last few times I'd decided to let Kora take over the search. She was proficient and even if it were cracked, recovered much of the core that could be used as dust for binding enchantments. I watched as she turned her left hand into a short blade and began to cut away towards the sandworm's center, black blood marred her perfectly clean white metal with its intricate blue lines.

She reappeared out of the monster's guts minutes later, a wide smile on her face. Her hands had shifted back to their normal five-digit fingers and in her left hand she held up a familiar sight. An intact monster core!

CHAPTER 3
RUELOCK CITY

We reached the city with very few interruptions, all of which were sandworms that Kora dealt with by herself. With the core she recovered, she gained the ability to summon her own sandworm, which made the battle a fair bit more interesting to watch, but after two weeks of killing sandworms, I was mostly over it. It was a welcome sight to see an actual city cresting the horizon.

Several roads set with black stone were like lines pointing to the city entrances. Following one of the wider ones, I saw that we'd been traveling adjacent to one of the larger roads, just a mile or so off to the side. I wondered why we hadn't just traveled on the main road but didn't question Warrick's wisdom. Surely, he knew how close we were to a road that would have been much easier to travel.

"Well, I'll be," Warrick said, his gaze following mine. "That explains where the road got off to."

I facepalmed and stifled a moan of frustration. Instead, I took out one of our few remaining water skins and took a long drink. One of the first things we would need to do was replenish our food and water stores, a task that should be simple enough with how much gold I had in my storage ring.

The city walls were surprisingly well made and large considering the desert nomad existence I assumed all Southlanders lived. It stood at least twenty feet tall and taller in places where square sections had been cut out, hanging out like little divots cut loose. The closer we got, the more I understood the design. Long straight openings on the bottom side of the tower extrusions would allow for things like boiling oil, water, or even arrows to be shot down at attackers.

The entire section of wall ran the length of the city that ran up the side of a red colored rock facing up into the sky like a pointing finger. The height of the walls continued along with the natural raised area of the city, connecting into the red rock from which the stones were likely strewn.

"See the crenellations?" Warrick asked, pointing at the walls. "They have such an effective design."

I saw what he meant, the walkways that ran between the little tower-like sections—I didn't know enough about wall design to say what they were for sure—had a large section that overhung and would allow the same kind of defensive attacks throughout the entire line of the wall. This wasn't a city that would fall easily.

On the outskirts of the walls and for half a mile all around, tents and wagons were lined up haphazardly. People moved in and around the encampment outside the city, but Warrick took us on the main road and straight towards the walled city.

I eyed the enormous gate, a stream of people coming and going passing through seemingly unchecked, but as we neared and fell into step with those around us, I saw a few armored orcs that must be guards of some kind. They stood on either side of the twenty-foot-wide gate opening. I indicated them to Warrick, and he smiled, changing course to speak with them. Massive iron banded gates that must have weighed thousands of pounds loomed over us as we approached.

I was surprised by the general hum of conversation, half of what was being said was definitely in common speech. And what was more, no one really cared that humans walked among them. Kora had taken to covering herself again to avoid undue attention, but Warrick and I had our hoods down and walked in full sight of the crowds.

The two orcs we approached wore iron armor that covered their entire body, but in sections and not a full suit of enclosed armor. A red tabard with a wolf's head depicted in the center and two swords crossing behind hung over each of their chests. One was a good seven feet while the other stood hunched over and couldn't be more than five and a half.

The taller one wore a helmet that covered his entire

face right up to the mouthline where a strap held the helmet in place, and a mohawk of red feathers split the top of his polished metal helmet. The hunched over one had a simple metal cap, no feathers and it didn't cover more than the top of his head.

Warrick stepped up to the larger one and the orc stiffened in response, his eyes meeting ours for the first time. I noticed then the front part of the faceplate on the helmet was cut in a way to almost look like the top part of a wolf's face, snout down, but it didn't quite get the look.

"We wish to gain entrance to your fair city," Warrick said, his words seemed a bit terse and sharp, but I trusted in his choices. "Does Chieftain Ruelock still rule here?"

The taller orc let out a string of words that I couldn't make heads or tails of, but Warrick took it in stride, responding back with words of the same tongue. After a few minutes of back and forth, Warrick motioned us away and we began walking past the city gates and into the city proper.

After a minute of silence, I couldn't take it anymore and I cleared my throat loudly. When that didn't get Warrick to spill the beans, I spoke. "So, what did he say?"

"Oh, he told me about how ol' Ruelock had his head put on a pike and his wife's brother took the city, but then in a strange turn of events the wife, Gerralak, put a knife in her brother's back not long after. Then Ruelock's brother appeared with an army and liberated the city by killing Gerralak. The brother, also took the name Ruelock—I think it was a title of honor or something—well, he died the next week from a bad case of diarrhea. So now someone named Ruelock the third, no relation to the prior Ruelocks, is in control of the city and has been for the last twenty years."

I blinked several times as I strung together what he'd said in my head and gave the only proper response I could think of. "What?"

"You meat bags are perplexing creatures," Kora said.

I'd forgotten that she was walking so close behind me and it took a greater deal of control than I would like to admit to keep myself from jumping.

"Meat bags?" I repeated, I'd told her several times that wasn't a good way to address others, but I think she liked getting a bit of a rise out of me. For someone so old and ancient, as she claimed to be, she had a certain naïve innocence that I couldn't help but want to protect.

"We should gather supplies, I don't know about you Warrick, but mine are getting low," I said. It wasn't worth mentioning, so I didn't, but the reason I'd been burning through my supplies is because Warrick ate twice as much as me and only consumed my supply of drink and food.

Of course, food really wasn't an issue, I had hundreds of small snack food items that would stay preserved, but water was a big problem. I drank twice as much as I normally did under the heat of the desert and Warrick might as well be a bottomless pit with how much water he has been consuming.

Warrick looked down at me and said, "Speaking of water, give me some would you? I'm parched."

I handed over our last water skin and watched in horror as he took it from half full to only drops left. My throat itched already, and I wanted a drink.

Looking around I tried to make sense of the sprawling city and what purpose the buildings had. The construction had a very hobbled together appearance, mixed with reinforced metal.

It was like someone made several hundred stone and wood huts, then added some atop, carving stairs on the outside, then kept doing this until most buildings were five stories high. At some point there must have been an abundance of metal supplies, because everything was framed and reinforced by metal bars fused to each other by some miracle of magic. It even extended to the streets, which had metal rusting gutters set into the stone.

As I scanned the buildings, I saw one with a crew of short green men with large heads and big ears working, goblins no doubt. We were walking that way, so I tried to get a look at what they were using to connect some of the thin metal bars to the surface of a lower story building, but it was like trying to look into the sun and I had to turn my eyes away after only seconds. They were using some kind of metal wands attached to a bulbous construction the size of a small carriage. It smoked and steamed, making extremely loud burping noises every few seconds.

I was glad when we got far enough away from them as to not hear it any longer. Warrick looked back several times, clearly as curious as I was about the goblins' clever magic.

Eventually we found our way to an open street market of some kind. All around were the sweet and spicy aromas of food and drink. I took it all in and savored the moment. For my trouble, I was jostled into roughly, then cursed at in a language I didn't understand.

Warrick had begun speaking to a vendor some ten feet away that sold an array of uncooked red meats. I decided my stomach wasn't up to the task of smelling that particular vendor's goods, so I roamed over to one that had large casks of some type of drink that people were buying by the barrel full.

"Good afternoon," I said, speaking slowly and hoping this green skinned orc with the scowl on her face understood me.

She growled and adjusted an already precariously thin shirt so that it nearly exposed her breasts. I blinked and averted my eyes.

"Barrel of grog, 3 gold," her voice rolled over the words, a mix of a growl and a sing song voice.

"Do you know where I can buy water?" I asked, risking a look in her direction and happy to see she hadn't further exposed herself. She did however have a wry smile on her face and I wondered suddenly if she had done that on purpose to throw me off guard.

"No water, only grog. 3 gold per barrel, how many do you want?" She asked, leaning forward and tilting her head to the side. For an orc, she had quite a beautiful form, not to mention the crimson in her eyes matched the deepest reds of the sands, like sparkling rubies.

"I suppose I'll take a barrel then; do you speak common often?" I asked, handing over the 3 gold and getting a small cask that I stored into my storage ring.

"Many tongues are spoken in Sathergorgan, Ruelock is no different," she said, her lack of interest in continuing to speak with me apparent by her deliberately looking past me and calling out her wares in a language I didn't understand.

I held up six more gold coins and asked, "What's your name? Also, I'd like a few more casks of grog."

This drew her attention back and I realized something while her eyes glinted with greed. I would be willing to bet I'd overpaid for the grog by a substantial margin, as if the world wanted to confirm this for me, a goblin came up and threw down a few silver on the table in front of the grog seller. She looked nervously at me, then shrugged and handed over a small cask of grog to the goblin, who barely got his hands around it and waddled off into the crowded square.

I purposely put back all but two of my gold coins and set them on the table.

"Five gold coins for three casks and information, it is the best deal you'll be getting today," I said, my jovial mood turned a touch dark, but I made a point not to scowl.

She didn't seem too concerned about me and just chuckled, grabbing the coins and giving me two casks. "Name's Ge'oluk of the Ugk'luck clan. I'm not much for gossip, so make your questions quick and be gone."

Her sudden ability to speak clearer common and without the struggle of being a growly singsong from before made me smile, it had all been an act.

Finding myself suddenly on the spot, my mind cleared of any useful questions. After a solid ten seconds of awkwardly looking around the square I had an idea, perhaps I'd see something on the map that would be of interest. I looked at my map and saw that the city was now marked on it, as was a path leading through the desert back to a tower that remained unnamed, Warrick's tower. Around the city were several symbols that indicated, when I looked deeper into them, that a silver mine and an old abandoned Mythril mine were nearby.

"How long has the Mythril mine been empty?" I asked, putting on my best smile.

Ge'oluk narrowed her ruby colored eyes at me and growled. "There is no gods' metal mine in all of Sathergorgan. Why do you waste my time?"

"For five gold I'd think I have paid for a bit of time to waste," I said offhandedly and for whatever reason this response made her laugh. It was a loud boisterous sound and after a second of hearing it I too started to laugh a little.

What was I playing at? I was no good at interrogation or pulling free useful facts, hell I didn't even know why we were here if I was being honest with myself. Warrick brought us here on the pretext of finding my father, then abandoned that as being possible days later. Now we've walked two entire weeks through worm infested sands to a city filled to bursting with trolls, orcs, goblins, and if I saw correctly, even a couple of elves and humans. My eyes followed what was clearly an adventuring group as they walked through the busy square and down the road we'd come.

"Is the city always this crowded?" I asked, an obvious question occurring to me.

"No," she growled the words but cleared her throat and spoke in a clearer tone. "We've taken in more refugees than the city can stand, they are forced to sleep outside the protection of the walls and without the eastern trade routes being active I fear supplies will run out."

"What happens when the supplies run out?" I asked, prompting her to continue as she'd stopped to scowl into the distance.

"Old promises will be forgotten, and clans will fight clans for the scraps left. Not even the word of Ahn'pulaka will stop us then," she said, her head shaking slowly side to side.

"Why aren't the eastern trade routes being used?" I asked, it took her a moment before she answered, as if her mind were living through the future that she suspected would be upon them soon.

"You know nothing of the threat that washes over Sathergorgan?" She asked, a perplexed look on her face.

I shrugged, I had an idea based off what little intel we'd recovered from that wandering group of Easterners, the ones that called themselves Venshti, but I was curious how much the general population knew.

"An army from the forbidden lands marches down the Paugmook River, their numbers so vast that they occupy the space between the great river and the endless waters. The clans squabble and flee while precious resources fall into the hands of an enemy that would rip us from our ancestral lands."

"Then fight," I said, before thinking over the words. It just seemed so simple an answer. The orc people, even the common folk, were bigger and stronger than your average human. I imagined that even for *un-Awakened* fighters they'd be fierce opponents.

"You would have us rebel against the word of our most high god? This city," she looked around with her arms out to gesture to the people and places around her, "is a refuge unlike any other in Sathergorgan. Our god sits in his throne overseeing us. It is my belief that when the time comes and the enemy is at our doorstep, Ahn'pulaka will call us to battle. I just hope we aren't killing each other from starvation by then."

Someone else appeared at my side, a troll standing a staggering eight feet, and he asked for grog in very broken common. Ge'oluk shot me a look that said our conversation was over and I took the hint. Thanking her with a nod I turned to find Warrick. Despite the oversized population of Ruelock City, I found him remarkably easily. He was entertaining several children in a large circle that had formed by making little sparks explode all around them. I smiled, remembering Warrick doing silly tricks like that for me when I was younger, back when my father had been alive.

My life had become complicated, emotionally difficult to navigate, and tiresome at times. But as I stood among a sea of strangers in a land that few humans got the opportunity to walk, I felt alive in a way I wouldn't trade for all the coin in the world.

"We need to see about meeting this chieftain Ruelock," Warrick said, scratching absently at his beard. A windstorm had kicked up and even inside the gates of the city, enough sand was being blown around to make seeing more than ten feet difficult.

Despite the sand bombarding Kora and I, Warrick leaned hard against his staff and the sand parted around him as if he were shielded by it somehow. That was Warrick for you, always working a few simple spells despite his claim that he needed to rest or recover his energy. How much of that energy had been expended so he could show a few kids a wondrous light show?

I wasn't upset at him, just worried that he was overextending himself. Even now, a month since his release from the vile Chaos Knight and her wretched machine, I didn't understand the full extent of what she'd taken from him or why. Had it been just a means of torture or something else? Where did the power go that she took from him? Did she funnel his power into herself, and that is why she became so drastically stronger after retreating to her machine?

If Bren hadn't been there, it was possible that Zander and I both would have fallen that day. My stomach turned thinking about Bren's death, and I knew all too well what Zander would be going through. A more callous and practical side of my mind tried to tell me that I shouldn't worry so much about Zander, as he'd tried to kill me several times, but somehow my trusting side was warming up to him. I was mostly sure he wouldn't attempt to kill me again. I mean, how would that look if he killed me and tried to still court Ismene? Surely, she wouldn't go for it.

I had to shake my head at the ridiculous path my mind was taking while we stood in an alley, blocked from the worst of the sandstorm.

Finally, I acknowledged Warrick with a nod and spoke.

"The storm is dying down, or at least it sounds like it has calmed," I said, peeking out into the main street where people still went about their business as if they weren't being covered in red sand. "Let's ask around and see if we can find our way to this chieftain."

It took over an hour to find someone willing to talk and another to get someone to lead us through the maze-like streets to the throne of the gods, which was said to be where the chieftain could be found.

The higher we got in the maze-like city, the thinner the sandstorm became. There was a notable change in the aesthetic of the buildings the higher we went as well. Where the lower buildings were made of stone blocks clearly cut from the very finger spire rock that traveled up, these buildings here were literally formed into the rock. Sharp clean edges unworn by time made up homes, businesses, and even a few larger public buildings whose use I couldn't determine.

Along with the cleaner buildings, unmarred by the metal construction of the goblins, was a noticeable uptick in color variety. Even the population this high in the city was noticeably smaller, with more than double as many guards patrolling in their full plate armor and tabards.

We followed a tattered dressed goblin, we'd paid him a gold coin to walk us all the way to where we needed to go. He stopped and pointed forward.

He said some words in a language that Warrick understood, very guttural and terse. Warrick responded and the goblin left.

The place the goblin had indicated was a sudden wall of red stone, the surface of which had a barely perceivable line cut into it where a door must be hidden and had two guards standing on either side of it. As I examined the flat exterior, my eyes went up and up until I noticed windows cut into the stone above. This entire keep must be cut into the very stone, just like the houses. That would mean the size of the keep could be enormous, as this section of the finger rock formation was thick and rose steeply on all sides.

"We'd like to speak to Ruelock, Chieftain of Ruelock City," Warrick announced as we walked up to the two heavily armored guards, each holding a tall halberd with wickedly sharp looking ends.

"No," the guard on the left said, his eyes flicking over us and dismissing us in the same second.

"Please?" Kora added, and I couldn't help but smile.

The guard looked at Kora, her hood was low but if you wanted to, you'd see that she wasn't a normal flesh and blood being. He seemed taken back by her appearance and he stepped forward, slow and steady.

"Lower your hood," he commanded.

"Okay, but don't be afraid. I'm Kora, what's your name?" Kora asked, lowering her hood.

I could just barely see into the orc's helmet, his eyes gone wide. The next thing I knew he had taken a knee before Kora and his partner, the other guard, jerked his head in response. He too looked at Kora and after a moment's pause, took a knee as well.

They spoke a language that I'd begun to attribute mostly to orcs, guttural but with a flow to it that goblin speech lacked. To my surprise, Kora answered back in a perfect match for their language. Warrick joined in a moment later and I was really starting to wish I knew how to speak this language.

After a few minutes of back and forth, the two guards got off their knees and one of them went inside the door—which turned out to be more magical than physical. He touched the door and spoke a word, it swirled and moved like sand atop the dunes, and he walked straight through it. Several more minutes of conversation continued until

Warrick finally decided to clue me in just as the second guard returned.

"They are going to allow us a meeting with Ruelock, and they mistook Kora for a god," Warrick said, elbowing me and stepping forward through the sandy doorway before I could respond.

Kora shrugged and smiled before following him through. The two guards scowled at me, and I hurried through before I got left behind. The sand felt like a warm blanket being placed over me on a cold winter day, then suddenly pulled away as we entered into a wide entryway with several dozen guards lined up with halberds at the ready. At their head was an orc dressed in furs and fine silks, she had shoulder length black hair and purple eyes that sparkled in the low light of the cavernous room.

The high ceilings, at least five times my own height, held large burning pans, the flames of which tickled metal pipes running the length of the walls and ceiling. What purpose it had was lost on me, but I traced the many lines of white metal with amazement.

Mythril.

No Mythril mine indeed, I thought back to the encounter I had with the grog merchant. Kora spoke just above a whisper as the purple-eyed orc approached us with arms outward and a warm smile on her face.

"Unrefined but decent purity," Kora said, her glowing blue eyes tracing the pipes of Mythril.

"I assure you, honored guest. This Mythril is as refined as any you will find in Sathergorgan or dare I say the northern wastelands," she winked at me as she said the last bit and I frowned. "You may call me Lawkspector, I am the speaker of this keep and I will see that you are taken to Ruelock. If it isn't too much, I'd ask of you a few questions while we walk."

Her voice was beautiful and her common sounded perfect.

Warrick leaned down and whispered in my ear. "She's using a translation charm, see that pendant. I wonder if I can buy it from her," Warrick said, raising his eyebrows at me when I gave him a look of mild frustration.

I assumed she'd be able to understand him and thus he'd be spoiling our first impression, but one look at her told me that wasn't the case. She looked confused and reached down, pulling a triangular rock charm on a golden chain out from under a fur covering and gave it a shake.

"Can you understand me?" She asked, finally letting the charm fall loosely to her chest, one of the furs fell to the side revealing an exposed chest and upper bosom. Perhaps it had been a while or that two-week desert walk had scrambled my brains, but these orc women were far more attractive than I remembered them being at Blackridge Keep.

"We can," Warrick said, smiling at her. "Is your charm working to translate our words as well or should I speak in-"

"It is fine, I can understand you perfectly," Lawkspector said, with a friendly smile. "Follow me and please answer my questions as best you can."

"How much to buy your translation charm?" Warrick said, hurrying to be the one standing beside her.

"It is not for sale, Wizard," she said rather tersely. Then turning to Kora she asked, "How is it you walk among us, Uhralt?"

Something about the last word didn't translate and it sounded throaty and different from the words before it.

"Uhralt, god, ancient one, spirits of the makers," Kora said, listing off names while dropping fingers down. She kept going for a few seconds more, listing at least two dozen names, and then answered Lawkspector's question. "A servant of Chaos attempted to sever my bond instead switching my allegiance as has been done for life untold. They succeeded, but I was recovered by this agent of the balance, and he has been kind enough to provide me with this form." She gestured to her body as they walked.

"Time will come that I return to my duties, but for now I am content to explore the lives of you mortals," Kora said.

"What is your opinion on the matter of Ruelock's insistence that the great Ahn'pulaka wishes us to remain inactive?"

"I don't know Ruelock or Ahn'pulaka," Kora said simply.

"Are you not connected?" She asked, slowing to turn and regard Kora with a speculative look.

"I am alone in my mind, much as you mortals must be," Kora said. "I admit that it was unnerving at first, but I have grown accustomed to it."

The questions continued, all of which were targeted at Kora, so after a while I tuned them out and studied the elaborate carvings and paintings on the walls. We were being led through very clean-cut stone passages, each one had depictions of battles or powerful monsters cut into the very stone. The carvings were painted to stand out more, some places the paint had faded, but most were fresh and must have been recently tended to.

We passed guard patrols, five in each group, as we walked, but the hallways we passed through and stairs we took were all built wide and so we could easily pass by each other. It wasn't until we reached a grand spiraling staircase that we had to stop walking shoulder to shoulder. It was wide enough for three of us to walk abreast, however we transitioned to a single file line, Lawkspector in the lead, Kora behind her, Warrick directly in front of me, and I took the back.

I noted that several slits about a fist wide had been carved into the outer edge of the staircase, arrow slits was my best guess. I couldn't imagine the force it would take to capture this city, much less the keep. Perhaps the Ahn'pulaka everyone spoke of had the right idea. Hunker down and wait for the enemy to come to you. I didn't know much about warfare, but I had enough common sense to know that the person with the high walls and keep would be safer than the ones out in the open.

The climb lasted a solid twenty minutes and really cut into my stamina, luckily my regen was decent enough that after a minute of rest at the head of the stairs I was all topped off again. Warrick and Lawkspector didn't recover as quick.

"You okay?" I asked Warrick, putting a hand on his shoulder and catching his eyes.

The glint of humor was still there, strong as ever, but around his eyes I saw the sign of exhaustion. Whatever that Chaos wench had done to him, his Stamina was worse for wear. He slipped out the potion he'd been sucking down for the last two weeks and drank deeply. Where he stored them or how many he had left, I didn't know. He put the empty vial back into his right robe pocket from whence it came, but I heard no clink of glass on glass that would indicate that he had more than one vial in his pocket.

"I will announce you, and have the harem withdraw," Lawkspector said, bowing to Kora and inclining her head to both Warrick and then myself.

Her fine clothing and furs shifted around her as she glided off towards a ten-foot-high wooden door banded by white metal, Mythril. At the head of the door stood a single guard in the same white armor. He had an entire enclosed suit of armor, each piece connecting and protecting every inch of his body. It was the kind of armor that few adventurers wore, as they tended to limit mobility when moving several times faster than a normal person.

However, for a non-*Awoken* being it wouldn't likely be a limiting factor at all. In fact, such craftsmanship would make them extremely hard to kill and be a reasonably deadly threat to even a stronger adventurer.

I didn't know enough about Mythril's conductive

properties, but I really wondered what would happen if I struck that man with a Lightning Strike. Would it react like iron or steel, sending the shock throughout the surface or perhaps Mythril acted differently?

I got distracted looking at a particularly grand carving all around the door about a battle with a massive dragon, and when I looked down again, I snorted in surprised amusement.

Warrick and Kora were taking turns moving the arms and helmet around on the guard at the door. I hurried over and looked at them with a muddled grin on my face.

"What are you two doing!" I hissed.

"This is a golem," Kora announced. "I name him... Tank, because they've locked him away in an enclosed tank of metal. Well, armor obviously, but who knew it could be so air tight!"

Kora was really enjoying herself, and I turned to Warrick to see what he had to say about this silly turn of events.

"Don't look at me," he said raising his hands while keeping his staff tucked into his elbow. "It was her idea; I thought a person was inside."

Golem or person, I stepped back, pulling Kora and Warrick with me. It didn't move, only righting itself into a standing position once more. Could it speak, I wondered. Last time Kora had given a name to a golem, it was one of mine that she'd named Ventus, a wind spirit turned Rune-forged. It had done something to his voice, making him sound like a natural baritone instead of the standard monotoned Runeforged.

A smaller door set into the bottom of the larger door swung open and Lawkspector appeared in the doorway.

"Ruelock will see you now," she said, moving aside and bowing her head.

CHAPTER 4
RUELOCK CHIEFTAIN

The room before us was circular in shape with massive pillars set seemingly randomly into the floor, one of which obscured a full view of a throne made of white metal at the other end of the room. Moving to the side as I walked, Warrick and Kora next to me, I got my first look at the chieftain and the throne he sat upon.

I'd seen a great many orcs in my day and this Ruelock the third, no relation to the prior ones, looked like no orc. He had green skin, but it was deeper and a richer color than the others I'd come across. His teeth had the signature tusks jutting out the side of his mouth, but instead of a single pair like all the others, he had two pair of twisted fangs. His ears were pointed like others of his race, but longer and lined with white gold hoop earrings.

The oddest and most non-orc feature had to be the horns he had growing out of the top of his head and twisting back with his flowing mane of black hair. The same-colored hair, save for a few streaks of white, filled a beard that would make any dwarf proud. Then of course there was the fact that he was easily twice as big as the biggest orc I'd ever encountered. It wasn't that he was unusually tall, muscled, or thick he was just double the normal size but otherwise built similarly.

I felt waves of power emanating off of him and I knew he was an *Awakened* orc and from the little I could feel, a strong one. The throne he sat upon was rather simple yet striking in its pure Mythril construction. It looked like an oversized dinner chair, with a tall back and four simple legs. Ruelock sat upon a purple and gold pillow, his only clothing a much too small loin cloth barely managing to cover his sensitive bits.

As we finally got within speaking distance, I opened my mouth to speak, but Warrick beat me to it.

Warrick laughed suddenly and asked, "Uk'blat is that you?"

The chieftain spoke in perfect common. "Warrick the not so wise?" Ruelock or Uk'blat said, his voice deep and rumbling. "I thought I recognized your devious presence, glad to learn I haven't lost my touch. I go by Ruelock the third, or just Ruelock these days. Appearances are important, as you know." Ruelock laughed again, this time a much deeper and fuller laugh.

Warrick turned to me and gestured to the orc with his staff. "Uk'blat or erhm, Ruelock and I used to run together many years ago in my youth. The Southlands, at least back in the days I traveled them, had the best roaming monsters and if you had a good tracker, it was faster essence than dungeons. Ruelock is the very best tracker I've ever encountered."

"Nice to meet you, Ruelock," I said, bowing slightly. Kora did the same but remained quiet. "My name is Caldor. It is good to meet one of Warrick's friends and I have a pressing question that I'd like to ask you."

Ruelock's sapphire eyes rested on me, and he smiled, showing many sharp pointed teeth. "A friend of Warrick's is a friend of mine, speak your query, and I will do my best to answer it."

"Do you know of the one they call Elkor Miles, the Arcane Knight?" I asked, hoping beyond hope that Ruelock, as a tracker, might have some insights.

"I've met him once before and by the smell of you," Ruelock paused to take a deep breath through his nose before letting out a slow sigh of air. "You are his kin and have followed in his footsteps. Caldor Miles, Arcane Knight."

"I am!" I said, my excitement getting away from me. "How does your ability to track work exactly? What I mean to say is, have you sensed my father in the last ten years or months even? Or perhaps you can reach out and try to sense him?"

Ruelock sunk into his chair a bit and a concerned look flashed across his face before being replaced by a kind but gentle smile. "It was my understanding that Elkor fell many years ago in battle?"

Warrick shifted next to me and spoke before I could

answer. "We have reason to believe that he might have survived. I was there the day he supposedly fell and there was no release. Someone as mighty as Elkor would have released a fierce wave of essence on his death, but nothing happened. Just ash left of my dearest friend."

Ruelock shook his head, and I could tell he didn't want to say what he was about to, but I listened anyways. "Chaos can introduce unexpected variables. I would say it is more likely that his release was displaced and felt by others. But I will say that I have not felt his presence and I would have remembered if I had. Like you, Caldor, he burned like a dozen stars ready to ignite the sky and burn down all around them. My ability to track is directly related to sensing the power and potential of those I encounter. You will be great, as your father was great, there is no doubt in my mind."

I wasn't here for affirmations of my potential, I just wanted to hear news of my father! I held my tongue, but it was disappointing to say the least. There were other matters that needed tending and my life would go ever forward regardless of the fate of my father.

"We do have other matters to discuss," Warrick said, looking over at me and likely sensing my mood darkening. "I have sent out many a messenger to check on the Mana Shrines to the east and found only a handful that remain on the side of Order."

"Yes, an unfortunate reality we've had to deal with, but what brings you to Sathergorgan and my fair city of Ruelock? Is Warrick ready to join the fight once more? It is some months off I fear, but eventually they will come. That is if we don't starve by then. This influx of refugees has been crippling. We have more mouths to feed and throats to quench than I have supplies. But with your portal magics, perhaps you can help to ease that burden?"

It was Warrick's turn to look uncomfortable. "I could certainly try, but I've undergone some limiting changes in the past month. It is likely that I am weaker than the last time we met, however I'm an old dog with many more tricks than I knew back then. I'm sure we will be able to help move supplies; you'll be able to provide the funds? Because as ever with me, coin eludes my grasp. But tell me friend, what do you plan to do about the corrupted Mana Shrines?"

Ruelock looked Warrick right in the eyes and leaned forward just a bit in his seat. "Nothing."

***

After a full minute of silence and confused looks traded among us, I spoke. "What about the balance?" I asked.

Warrick put a hand on my shoulder and spoke then. "You know of the threat that approaches? An army from the East with Chaos Knights among their ranks will not be an easy foe when they've dug in."

"And like a gnarled old root neither will we," Ruelock said, looking almost bored at the exchange of words now. He looked to the side, and I saw a smaller orc attendant appear from a curtained section of the wall, perhaps a servants' nook. This orc was female and fairly beautiful, but what really caught my attention was the fact that, other than a small loin cloth around her waist, she wore nothing else. In her arms she carried a colorful variety of fruits, and she presented them to Ruelock, who took three in his enormous hands and threw one straight into his mouth, chewing it to bits within moments.

I noticed that Kora was staring at the topless orc, and I shot her a look. She didn't notice and instead raised her hands up in a cupping motion over her chest then shrugging she positioned her cloak tighter around her chest.

"What will it take to have you see reason?" Warrick asked, waving his hand and a chair appearing behind him. He sat, and I looked on astonished at his casual show of magically summoning furniture.

"It isn't just my reason you'd have to sway," Ruelock said, finishing off the last piece of fruit and summoning the orc female back. "I'm merely a puppet leader set into place by our god, Ahn'pulaka. If you wish to sway his mind, please be my guest and walk into his domain. My only request is that you leave this one," he pointed at Kora who had gone back to examining chest sizes between herself and the orc servant again, "to speak with me. I have never seen a god walk outside of their domain before and I am eager to hear her words."

Kora spoke then, but more to herself than anyone specific. "I need larger breasts." She nodded her head as if to add emphasis to her words.

Warrick looked critically at Ruelock, or Uk'blat as he

knew him in the past, and waved me over. I leaned down and he spoke to me in a whisper.

"They worship dungeon cores as gods. You will need to challenge the dungeon alone and I will rest here. Good luck."

My eyes went wide, and I regarded Warrick, but he just looked at me and gave me a reassuring expression mixed with a nod. Then to top it all off he gave me a thumbs up and said, "You got this."

CHAPTER 5
DUNGEON GOD

The dungeon entrance was in the throne room, on the farthest wall behind a lavish curtain depicting a battle between a three headed dog and a man with golden feet. On Ruelock's urging, I'd entered alone and weapon ready.

The standard dungeon staging area laid within and I drank deeply of the fluid. I checked my health, mana, and stamina, making sure all were topped off. I cast my buffs and looked down at the translucent blue Arcane Armor that settled over me. I was as ready as I could be, so sword in hand I stepped through the swirling portal alone.

A sudden cheer from above and the brilliant light of a noon day sun struck me all at once. Pushing through the disorientation, I blinked my eyes against the light and forms blurred into view. I stood on an arena floor surrounded by walls, and above those were hundreds, no, thousands of arena seats filled with every race imaginable.

Orcs, humans, elves, delvish, and several dozen I had no names for.

A quick scan of the arena floor told me I was alone, but I counted eight metal gates, each one obscured in shadow beyond. Above, a voice echoed over the cheers of the crowd.

"You will be challenged, and your worth determined. Be ready, a challenger approaches." Its voice was melodic but firm. I caught sight of a larger box set apart from the sea of people in the stands and thought I could make out three figures looming above it all. The middle figure was the most striking, as it had the head of a wolf and the body of a man.

The steady clink of a gate being raised pulled my attention away and I looked up to see who I'd be fighting. I Inspected it as it flapped its wings furiously to stay afloat.

Winged Kobold, Level 10.

I waited for more to appear to even out the fight, but the gate slammed behind it. Stepping forward I raised my hand, ready to cast Lightning Strike. The kobold flinched and a fireball appeared in its hand. The little guy was about a third of my size and looked like a scaly child with a draconic snout. Nothing about it really screamed threatening, so I didn't even try to dodge the fireball. Instead, I used my free hand to bat it away, trusting in the magical protection of my Arcane Armor to shield me, which it did just fine.

The fireball careened off course and exploded in a small puff of smoke on the arena wall. I'd heard of kobolds before and despite this one being able to fly, I had always heard they were pack creatures and rarely fought alone.

"Die from the might of Fak!" A screeching high-pitched voice called out from across the arena. I'd looked away from the little guy and it must have upset him.

"Sorry, Fak, time to die," I said, raising my hand and unleashing a Lightning Strike. Poor little Fak literally exploded, or his wings did at least. Each one exploded into a few pieces and the poor little Fak found himself face first in the dirt, bleeding out.

I didn't like to see him suffer, dungeon creation or not, so I hurried over to stick my sword into the base of his neck. Before I got there, I heard words rumble through the arena.

"Enough, you will spare him and ready yourself for your next challenger."

I looked toward the gate he had entered from and suddenly, five more flying kobolds zipped out and scooped up their now still comrade, shooting me dirty looks all the while.

The moment they'd left the field of battle, I heard the gentle clink of another gate opening behind me. Turning, I saw what I faced next, a trio of goblins.

They weren't much different than the previous dozens of goblins I'd seen, except that they were all wearing outfits befit an adventuring party. The biggest, which meant the one that was maybe a few inches taller than the rest, wore full plate armor that enclosed his large head and ears completely. While at his side, one goblin struggled to wind the crank of a crossbow and the other waved around a staff twice his height.

The lead goblin raised his spiked mace in my direction and shouted words of challenge that I couldn't understand. Instead of saying anything back, I let my magic do the talking for me, lashing out with Lightning Strike and Arcane Missile.

I Inspected the armored goblin as my spells smashed into his little round shield and, surprisingly, he stayed on his feet.

Goblin Keeper, Level 19.

I didn't know what a keeper was, but this had to be the beefiest goblin I'd ever had the pleasure of fighting. The other two goblins sprang into action as the armored one began his long charge, little legs pumping.

The staff wielding goblin sent forth a sparking ball of raw energy, just as the leather armored one got his crossbow in place and took aim. Diving to the side, the magic ball of energy threw up dirt all around me, but it missed. However, as I rolled and lifted my arm to send a Firebolt into the crossbow wielder's face, red hot pain flashed through my side. I looked down to see a barbed bolt sticking out of my armor.

Painfully I stood and threw down a quick Mending Touch just as the Keeper reached me. Spinning to the side I ripped the barbed bolt from my side and clenched my teeth from the ensuing pain. Slashing downward I got the Keeper to stay at bay while I held my blood in with my other hand. As one did when they'd passed enough thresholds, my body healed, and the blood stopped pouring free. I'd need to mend my armor later, but first I had to take care of that crossbowman before he got another shot off.

I raised my sword, parrying a blow from the Keeper and delivering my own in return. My blade clinked harmlessly off the surface of his full plate armor, but the blow did drive him back a few feet. Doing a quick scan I caught sight of my target, still struggling to get the crossbow reloaded—it was nearly the same size as him. Pushing my power as hard as I could I formed a Fireball, keeping an eye on my surroundings.

Before I could get a ball of significant size together, I realized I could no longer see where the caster goblin had gone. A moment later, something hit me in the back of the leg and all my muscles seized up at once, sparks running all around my form. It was then that the buildup of my spell went off, blowing me backwards and into something directly behind me. I heard a grunt and what could have been goblin curse words from behind.

With pain from my own spell backlash reverberating through me, I turned on my side and saw I lay atop the caster goblin. He screamed in surprise, trying yet failing to get to his staff. I swiftly pulled free a dagger from my side and plunged it into his neck several times in quick succession. The brutal efficiency of daggers was something to be admired.

While in the act of ending the caster, the Keeper must have recovered his wits because suddenly I was cracked upside the head with a blow that sent my helmet careening off in the direction of the strike. Seeing stars, but utterly used to pain at this point, I rolled quickly and let off another Lightning Strike just as it came off cooldown.

My spell's strike lit up the arena with white light and cracked the air as it struck the Keeper and took him off his feet. Just as I stood and found the crossbowman, I heard his painful attack release. I dove, but I wasn't fast enough to dodge such a viciously swift weapon. It slammed into the exact same spot, going even deeper from the lack of armor. It must have hit something important inside of me because my legs quit working mid-roll and I had to steady my breathing so as not to panic.

Goblins shouldn't be this difficult to deal with, I told myself, but I knew in dungeons, goblins could be whatever the dungeon wished them to be, which in this case turned out to be fairly effective adventurers.

I wasn't down and out yet, legs or no legs. Restoring Light was only a 3 second cast, so I struggled through, taking nearly 5 seconds before I got it off properly. The heal over time effects began to work and with water in my eyes from the pain and knowing to expect more in a moment, I clenched the end of the bolt that hadn't gone inside of me. Ripping it free I screamed in pain and let the blood flow, a puddle slowly forming around me.

Instead of covering the bleeding, I immediately grabbed a health potion from my storage ring and pulled the cork free with my teeth, sucking free the contents. Immediate and refreshing healing coursed through me, my legs tingling and finally movement returning just moments later. I really needed to end that crossbow wielding goblin.

The Keeper was back on his feet and stood protectively in front of the remaining goblin, he obviously anticipated my next move. I rushed to my feet and began channeling Fireball. It would take the crossbow goblin some time to get his next shot ready and I wasn't going to give it to him. When my attack reached what I considered significantly enough power, I lifted the torso sized blast over my head and threw with all my might.

The ensuing blast, as it connected with the Keeper's shield, forced me back a step or two. I averted my eyes from the flash and shot off a Firebolt a second later for good measure. It reached the two or where I guessed they would be, as the area was all black smoke still, and pierced a line through the smoke before hitting the far wall.

Just when I thought my victory was assured, a whistling sound from behind the wall of smoke made me curse. A third stupid painful barbed bolt hit me, but this time it went into my left arm and out again, leaving me a painful hole but no bolt to deal with.

No more of this shit, I thought to myself summoning back my fallen blade and rushing forward. I was bloodied, bleeding, and angry as hell. The goblin must not have seen me coming because the smoke cleared moments before I arrived and he stood in the same place, the ruined corpse of the Keeper beside him.

Activating Power Strike, I felt my Stamina deplete and infuse into my strike, slashing down with deadly intent.

The goblin dropped his crossbow and daggers appeared in his hands. He caught my blade, but he obviously underestimated my strength because my sword continued onward and slashed through his leather armor, leaving a bloody gouge in his chest. He cried out, but I hadn't waited to see what would happen next. My downward slash turned, and I thrust forward into the wound I'd just opened, before activating Swift Strike to flick my weapon up, spilling out his guts and killing him instantly.

His body became suddenly heavy on my blade, and I let it slide free, his blood flowing out to soak the ground along with his comrades. I nodded my head to him; he'd been an annoyingly effective opponent for a minute there. But like all those that stand against me, they will taste the bitter sting of defeat.

"A final challenge awaits you." The voice echoed again above the boisterous cheers and jeers of the audience. "You are not prepared. Make yourself ready."

The gate clinked open, and a new team of goblins appeared carrying stretchers made of thick cloths suspended between two wooden poles. They carefully scooped up the remains of all three goblins, treating them with more respect and care than I would normally attribute to their race. I caught sight of a thinner goblin, a female I guessed by her proportions, and suddenly I felt guilty. She held tightly to the crossbowmen's hand and tears fell freely from her face.

Just as they disappeared back into the darkness of the gate she looked back out at me, and it hurt. The real anguish and pain that I saw reflected in her devastated expression told me all I needed to know. For her, this hadn't been just a dungeon. Did dungeon creatures live real lives inside of dungeons? Had I just cut short her lover, her husband, or perhaps her brother? This entire challenge lost its excitement, and I suddenly just wanted it to be over.

Instead of an immediate gate opening to usher in my next challenger, I was met with silence. Standing in the arena, waiting, I became aware suddenly that the cheers had stopped. Looking out among the faces I realized I couldn't make out any details anymore, the arena stayed crisp and clear, but something was off about the arena crowd.

I looked around the arena floor and saw enough blood to empty a goblin or two, but most of it had come from me. My Stamina regeneration would suffer for several minutes while my body worked to heal not only the external wounds I'd received, but the damage inside, and the job of replacing my blood. Lately, I often found myself laying wake at night wondering the limits of my healing and my body. Soon those limits would be pushed further as I took the plunge into my next thresholds with Constitution and Endurance.

My Strength and Intellect had already peaked over their second threshold, a fact I was always readily aware of, as it left me feeling a bit out of sorts. But without those increases, I doubt I'd have had the strength to push through the deadly bolts or deliver powerful enough spells to end the fight as quickly as I did. No, it was worth it, I told myself for the tenth time just today.

The silence suddenly broke and raucous cheer from all around sounded in my ears. I looked up and suddenly the sun had shifted, and I had to look away, the west no longer safe to look if I wanted to see anything. Looking instead to the east I saw that each of the individuals in the crowd once more had distinct features. Whatever had happened it was over.

Clink, clink, clink.

I turned toward the sun and squinted against the light, raising my hand to shield my eyes. A lone figure, wearing armor I recognized and grasping a sword that couldn't be what I was seeing.

Remembering my helmet, I turned from the fighter and ran over to retrieve it. The buckle had busted but I put it atop my head anyways, if this fight was what I thought it was, I was going to need every bit of an advantage that I could get.

The fighter that stood before me, was me. Whether this dungeon version of me would have the same strength and skill as myself, I did not know, but this was taking 'fighting your inner demons' to a whole new level.

"Behold your doom, you arrogant fool," my copy said, as blue translucent armor—my spell Arcane Armor—appeared over his identical basilisk armor. His voice had a darker sneer to it that I know for a fact I didn't have, but I couldn't let myself be distracted.

I had to think. What would I do first, how could I dodge it or prevent it, how much of a copy was this figure? As the questions poured through my head, I saw my copy raise his hands and make a sign I recognized.

Throwing myself to the left, I narrowly avoided being struck by a Lightning Strike.

Everyone has a plan until you get the ever-loving shit shocked out of you. Fine, fuck it, I would fight him by instinct alone, plans be damned.

I cleared the thoughts from my head and went to work. First, I unleashed a Lightning Strike of my own, quickly followed up by a Firebolt. He slashed downward, his blade—an identical match for my Shell Blade of the Sea Witch, iridescent light reflecting off its surface—glowed with the light of 'Light Blade' and an arc of damaging energy sprang forth.

As much as I tried not to think and focus on not being hit, it occurred to me that I hadn't used that attack in here so how had the dungeon known to give it to my copy?

My moment of hesitation cost me; the arc of light threw me back a step but otherwise caused me no damage. I returned the favor, sending an arc of light back in his direction with an extra couple modifications. The combined might of Light Blade, Force Wave, Power Strike, and Swift Strike hissed through the air as it went off, and for some reason my sword grew hot in my hands.

The sudden use of 405 Stamina all at once had me

staggering backward a step before I caught myself. I hadn't done something like that in a while and the increased cost of Rank 2 skills were a fair bit more than I realized. With my Stamina only at 483 out of 1020 I decided I could hold off using Stamina Surge for another few seconds.

My attack moved at the speed of a deadly barbed bolt and like I'd hoped, my copy wasn't able to dodge in time. What I didn't expect him to do however, was scream and cut downward with his sword, straight through the attack. I saw energy lance through his sword and knew he'd used a skill, likely Power Strike or Swift Strike, maybe both, to enhance his speed and power. It cut through the attack, severing my arc of energy into two pieces, one of which smashed into his shoulder and sent him spinning off in the other direction.

It would hurt like hell but there was no way that attack would be enough to finish me off, so I let off an Arcane Missile before he even stopped rolling and followed it up with a Firebolt, before rushing forward with my sword ready.

My copy rose to a kneeling position, his hand movements and words told me all I needed to know about what he was doing, and I let off a Lightning Strike just as it came off cooldown, but he got his cast off first, the effects of Mending Touch washed over him and the blood flowing from his arm stopped.

I'd taken myself to 490 mana already and would need to be more conservative if I wanted to survive this fight. I felt it slowly tick upward, but it wouldn't be fast enough to keep up my barrage of spells.

Swinging downward, I aimed for my copy's neck, hoping to end the fight in a single deadly strike. Suddenly blue sparks erupted around him, and his sword appeared in his hands. An ability infused the blade, and he parried my attack with such strength and power that I was thrown backwards.

He had my ability to Essence Infuse!

The sparks died down around him as he stood, sword up and ready. I cracked my neck and stepped forward, thinking he was ready to fight sword to sword when suddenly a Lightning Strike slammed into my chest. My muscles cramped and tightened, but I managed to stay standing. Or at least I did until a Force Wave struck me in the chest, and I fell backwards on my ass.

I used my only spell not on cooldown that didn't technically have a cast time, only a channel time. Putting a quick fifty mana into a Fireball I launched it into my copy's face, using the time I bought to get to my feet. I unleashed an expensive Lightning Strike just as it came off cooldown, bringing me to only 208 mana. Then, following his example, I unleashed a Force Wave from my sword.

My attacks weren't as effective as his had been on me, something that made me think I wasn't fighting an exact copy after all but someone stronger than me. The lightning hit him, staggering him just a step and he put his shoulder forward into the Force Wave, taking the damage but not falling over.

I infused Essence into my Stamina Surge skill, the five second recovery becoming only two. Then, rushing forward, I infused Swift Strike with Essence, knowing that I had to give myself the upper hand somehow. My skill allowed me to change the direction of my sword after I'd normally be committed to the swing's direction, and I scored a critical strike on my copy's chest, ripping several scales free and spraying red blood over the both of us.

My copy raised his sword, ignoring his bloody wound and we fought sword to sword. His blows came swift and deadly, but I kept up and recognized Michael's and Fran's teaching in the way he moved and searched for openings. We matched each other in strength, blow for blow, until I saw his sword flash with sparking blue energy, and I knew what was coming. I did what I really was trying to avoid doing, I used Essence Infusion directly on myself, infusing my muscles, bones, and blood.

I jumped backward, springing with impossible speed and agility, but it wasn't fast enough to dodge his infused Swift Strike/Power Strike combo. Hot red pain ran down my belly and I felt the warmth of my blood seeping onto my pants, but my guts remained inside so I wasn't out of the fight yet.

Infusing my Restoring Light spell, I began the three second cast. My copy looked right at me, his eyes the same sparkling blue as mine. I saw a glint of something there, worry or concern, but I didn't read into it, instead focusing on getting the spell off. The healing washed over me, and I released my gut as the blood stopped. Why hadn't he rushed me during my downtime? I'd have done it, he's just a dungeon monster, so what did it matter?

My copy raised his blade in a high striking position, and I copied him. Slowly circling each other, our breath coming out in a fast steady rhythm, we readied ourselves for another furious exchange of blows. Just before I stepped forward, I saw him scrunch his brow in concentration and his tension seemed to ease just a fraction. I guessed he'd just expended his Stamina Surge, meaning we were both operating at nearly full Stamina now.

We clashed in a lightning storm of sword impacts and sparks. Each of us taking the opportunities we saw to infuse essence or use skills to give us the upper hand, but the more we fought the more in sync we became, our attacks mirroring each other.

I took damage, he took damage, but the final straw came when he went for a combo strike, and I saw a fatal opening. It was something I must have done a dozen times and each time it caused me to pause in a state of focus as I applied the Stamina, leaving me open for attack. I twisted to the side, dropped my sword, and stabbed him in the gut with a dagger just as he activated his attack. It happened so fast that I wasn't sure I'd finally put a stop to him until he dropped his own sword and fell to a knee. The long dagger's blade must have hit something vital, because he could barely keep himself up on his knees.

Panting and sweating, I materialized my sword into my grip and placed the edge against the back of his neck. He was basically me, and I knew he would be a threat even now, so I had to take no chances and end him for good. So why was I thinking about it, why was I waiting?

I looked up into the stands, the multitudes of people continued to cheer and chant, but I was looking for the three figures in the box separate from the rest. Finding it, I looked up to see if they had anything to say as they had on the first fight. All three stood at the edge and I could see clearly that not a single one of them was normal, a female with a birdlike head in a flowing green dress, the wolf headed man shirtless but with a golden loincloth and jewels set all throughout his body, and finally a hairy man with a boar's head and large tusks.

The boar man spoke, and I realized it had been his voice I'd heard with each announcement.

"What will you do, Caldor Miles? Is your opponent to live or die?"

Why was he asking me? Was the fight over, did I not need to kill him? He was just a dungeon monster after all and what was more, he had my abilities, which I didn't like. What else did this thing have of mine? I gripped my sword tightly and raised the blade, ready to take off the head of my copy.

I dropped my sword, letting it clatter on the ground and took a step back.

"Fine," I said, yelling as loud as I could but sure that the trio wouldn't be able to hear me from so far away. "I spare him, but what is the point? Is this not a dungeon where I'm meant to kill and gather essence? Why do you taunt me with moral quandaries, are you testing me? I'm done with this farce, just show me the exit."

I'd worked myself up and now I just wanted to leave. To be as far from this fake me and this dungeon that had the ability to replicate a person so thoroughly. A voice I hadn't heard before sounded from behind me, a smooth baritone, and I turned to see the wolf headed man standing there.

"Is there no benefit in fighting yourself? Could it not lead to you gaining insights to your weaknesses? Would you like a second chance to fight yourself?"

I turned to see my copy was back on his feet, helmet off and smiling in my direction. I could just see a few lines of scars rising up his neck and realized he'd been given my limitations as well. It was eerie as can be and I wanted no part of it.

Taking a careful step backwards that allowed me to see both the wolfman and my copy, I answered. "No, I'm done here, I think. Please show me the exit."

The wolf headed man frowned and waved his hand. My copy began to shimmer and then a moment later he was gone. "Speak with me a bit, you did finish my little challenge after all. I am called Ahn'pulaka. What is it that you hoped to ask of me by challenging my domain?"

Before I could respond, I felt a wave of essence hit me. I quickly drained my essence bracelet, but it was too late, the wave had stopped so I only got as much as the gem could hold.

I blinked, trying to remember why I had come here

into the dungeon in the first place. Then it clicked back together, and my mind started to work once more. I was here to get the southlanders working on taking back Mana Shrines and maybe even fight the coming army from the East instead of fleeing. I wasn't a tactician, but I imagined that dying a slow death behind walls wouldn't be preferable over fighting and dying in glorious battle. From what little I knew about their culture, they normally didn't shy away from fights, spending as much time as the Human nation houses did at war.

"I want the nations of Sathergorgan," I said, using the name they did for the Southlands, "to rise up against the threat they've been fleeing and turn back the tide of Chaos that threatens to overrun them."

"Your request is the wrong one, however I am bound to hear and consider as you've proven yourself worthy," Ahn'pulaka said.

I looked at him expectantly, but he just stared at me.

"What is the right request what question should I ask you?" I asked, growing frustrated.

"The right question has to do with the balance. Is the balance being maintained by taking back these Mana Shrines or are these eastern invaders doing the same task you've been given, Defender of the Balance? Perhaps they are maintaining the balance by reclaiming lost land? Had you considered that?"

I hadn't but I wasn't about to tell wolfman that. "So, the beastkin have begun to invade the Eastern lands?"

"And the next question you should ask," Ahn'pulaka

said, ignoring my previous question. "Is, will any of it matter if someone doesn't purify the infection that is slowly taking root in the heart of the planet?"

"You mean the corrupted Ley lines," I said, nodding. "I've been set on a path to do that, but I don't know where to go next. I have a spell that purifies Chaos corruption, but I don't know how to use it on a Ley line. I thought maybe if I got a Blade of Order, I might be able to work it out, but I'm nowhere strong enough to challenge the isle of Avalon yet."

"You are correct that you are on the right path," he said, nodding his head knowingly. "I will encourage you to gather powerful allies and find the shard of the Ordu that you seek, wield it as you may, but it will amplify your power and the means to purify the Ley lines will become clear. As to your first request I would say this, I will give them leave to do which they desire. May their enemy quake in fear. However, I cannot suggest they convert the Mana Shrines back, instead they must accept the loss for a time."

"I will relay your message, but what proof do I have to give them that you have spoken?" I asked. Ahn'pulaka held out his hand and a scroll appeared for me to take.

"This will act as my word. These people have allowed me to thrive for over a thousand years. I tell you this so that you might understand what a terrible request you've made of me. I do not relish the idea of losing a single soul to those Chaos mongers, but your presence here speaks of change and the need for drastic actions."

"I understand," I said. Whether or not that was true was questionable, but I knew I had tasks that needed to be done and would do my best to accomplish them. But war has a way of destroying the best laid plans, a fact I was sure I'd learn in the future.

Shifting uncomfortably, I had a very dungeon centric thought. Before I could ask the question that was building on my lips, Ahn'pulaka looked at me and smiled.

"You are wondering if you are going to get loot?" He asked.

"I am wondering if I'll get loot," I admitted with a laugh.

"I am first and foremost a dungeon, you will find your loot in the chest just there," he said, pointing at a large golden chest that hadn't been there a moment ago.

I smiled wide and walked past the dungeon who fancied himself a god, to collect my well-earned loot.

Inside the chest was a velvet red pillow and a single golden ring sat upon the top. It was remarkable in its simplicity of design. Just a simple golden band, but when I picked up and Inspected it, my jaw dropped open. A freaking Core attribute item!

Ring of Anubis

Enchanted with 'Elite Protection' Enchantment.

Elite Protection – This enchantment places a thin layer of physical protection around the skin that will repel a vast amount of damage once per day. Also grants a passive defensive bonus of +10 armor.

+10 Core (Grants +1 for every 2 levels bearer has achieved)
Durability: 25/25
Rarity: Legendary
Weight: 8 Grams
Item Level: 30, Level Required to use: 15, Gifted by: Ahn'pulaka

"This is unbelievable," I mumbled. According to Ismene, items that added to your Core attribute were ultra-rare, but what was more was that the Core attribute was the only one that could benefit in terms of passing thresholds. That meant I was now only 9 attributes away from my 2nd threshold for the Core attribute.

Moving it around in the light I saw the barest of engravings in the inner ring, but I didn't recognize the language. I could only use three rings at a time, until I raised my Core to its second threshold, so I quickly pulled off my 'Ring of the Sea's Might', losing 3 Strength and 3 Intellect. I slipped on the ring of Anubis and felt something expand inside of me. It happened so suddenly that I fell to a knee, my breath coming in jagged gasps for a solid ten seconds.

"The first step is always the hardest," Ahn'pulaka said. He'd walked to my side and placed a helping hand under my arm to assist me in rising. I welcomed the help, not sure what had happened to me, but whatever it was it was passing.

"Thanks," I said, pulling myself free from his surprisingly iron grip. Looking around I noticed the crowds had gone and one of the gates had opened. "Is that my way out?"

"It is. Good luck in your adventures. Remember, grow stronger and seek powerful allies," he said, then just like that he was gone. One moment I was looking right at him and the next, I was alone.

Turning back to the golden chest I tried to do something I figured wouldn't work but I had to give it a chance. I grabbed hold of the chest and attempted to put it into my storage ring. It didn't work, but again I told myself it was worth trying. What was the point of having dimensional magic storage items if you didn't try to take everything not nailed down?

"This is for you," I said, handing over the plain and ordinary scroll that the dungeon had given me. It was a simple thing, a wooden post in the middle with a leather wrap that was held closed by simple twine and a button.

Ruelock took it from me carefully as if he were holding the most precious item in existence. Respectfully and slowly, he unlatched it and opened the scroll. For a full two minutes he stared at the words, unmoving and with absolutely no reaction. Then, as carefully as he unfurled it, he put it back and turned to his maidservant, gently handing it over.

"Put it with the rest and call my council together," Ruelock said, his voice firm and resolute. The servant woman nodded her head and carefully took the scroll before disappearing through a side door.

"It went well then?" Warrick asked, getting my attention. I looked at the weary wizard and nodded. He remained in the same sitting position I'd left him before entering the dungeon, but if it were possible, he'd lost a bit more color in his face and did not look well.

"I know what I need to do, just not sure I am up to the task yet," I said, taking a deep breath to steady myself.

Ruelock interrupted us by clearing his throat.

"Ahn'pulaka has given us leave to raise an army and push out those that defile our ancestral home. No longer will fleeing Sathergorgan be allowed by its people. All tribes will be invited to read of his words, and with a bit of luck, we will raise the required forces to make these invaders think twice about taking our land. But we have also been warned not to turn the Mana Shrines back to the course of the Ordu."

Warrick looked stricken. "What? Caldor were you not able to communicate the urgency to the dungeon? The *Awakened* will be weakened by such a course of action while their Venshti will be empowered. This doesn't bode well for our efforts."

I tried to respond but Ruelock was quicker.

"It is the will of the gods," Ruelock said, shaking his head. "I understand that doing their will does not always make sense but in this case, perhaps Caldor can offer explanation?"

I waited for them to stop talking and when they both had their attention on me, I made them wait another few seconds before speaking. "I do, actually." I cleared my throat, dragging it out in a small show of spite for not being allowed to talk. "The dungeon, or god, whatever he is. Ahn'pulaka said that if the balance is to be maintained, the shrines must remain as they are. The beastkin are taking Shrines from the Easterners and I guess they've decided it is easier to invade the Southlands than fight back? That's speculation but I can't understand why the beastkin would want to push into the Eastlands either."

Warrick nodded. "Many mysteries remain unsolved. But these tasks will not be accomplished in a day. I propose you return to Newaliyn and see to gathering allies and growing stronger. Perhaps your position in House Variyn can be exploited in some way to get support from some of the stronger adventurers?"

I groaned thinking about all that was happening back in House Variyn. A House war was brooding and if what I'd heard in rumors had any truth, my free time might soon be harder to come by than I cared to imagine. My oaths to the office I'd taken meant I would soon be called to service.

Now that I had the funds to start my own city, or at least it felt that way, I had often found myself questioning my need to stay attached to House Variyn. But as with each time I strayed upon those thoughts I squashed them,

I had made an oath and taken a responsibility. It would violate the very core ideals that I hold to be true about myself to break such a promise.

No, I would hold to my oaths and do what needed to be done.

"I can try to leverage my position, but like I told you there are rumors of a House war. If I get dragged into that, I don't see myself having much choice but doing my duty while trying to grow stronger all the while," I said, still unsure how I felt about what the future held.

"House Variyn has been relatively peaceful for many years; I wouldn't think Lord Variyn would be so quick to go to war. Even ten years ago when wars between the Houses were at their worst, House Variyn participated in very few of the conflicts. Not to mention who you say they are wanting to challenge, House Blalor. They are by far the richest of the Houses and if there are mercenaries to hire or armies to be paid, they will win that struggle," Warrick said, running his hands through his beard as he spoke.

Something occurred to me as he talked. "Could House Blalor be considered a threat to Newaliyn or the King? Perhaps I'm not seeing the entire picture, maybe these politics are about a greater scheme by the King to squash a potential rebellion before another Gilfoy situation arises."

"That is quite a bit of insightful and intelligent speculation," Warrick said, chuckling. "It could very well be that the plans of the nobles are as convoluted as you say, but I don't have the patience for their politics. Do what you feel you must, but don't lose yourself to their petty games."

"I wish to stay with you," Kora said, stepping out of the shadows.

"Are you sure?" Ruelock asked, sounding surprised.

"I am," Kora said, turning to Ruelock and inclining her head in a small bow. "Your offer is generous, but I feel drawn to see where Caldor's adventures take him. He has a great destiny and I wish to entwine my own with his."

I couldn't help but blush a little, I'm not sure I'd entwined my destiny with someone before. I was pretty sure I knew what she meant, but I couldn't help but smile.

"That's fine with me," I said, not even realizing she'd had other offers. As much as I tried not to think like it, a part of me saw her or at least her Runeforged body, as my property since I'd purchased it. I made a conscious effort to push those thoughts from my mind as she was clearly an intelligent being who could decide her allegiances on her own. Instead, I just felt grateful that she wished to remain at my side.

"If you are ready, Caldor, I believe I have the strength to open a portal," Warrick said, his color still didn't look great, but he stood easily and didn't appear to be leaning as hard on his staff as he had before.

My eyes flicked across the room, and I moved to stand beside Warrick. "You'll be careful, won't you?" I asked in a hushed whisper, trying and failing to hide the concern in my voice.

Warrick pulled me into a tight hug and patted my back. Then releasing me, he looked me in the eyes and spoke. "I'm much stronger now than I appear. I'm going to open a portal to the room we left a few weeks back, normally I'd connect to my home but as it was destroyed, I'll need to work on resetting the connection and manifesting a new tower location. That will take more time than I'd care to keep you."

I wanted to trust that Warrick would be okay, but it was hard. Instead, I trusted that there was little I could do to change his mind and that I needed to press forward on my own journey. "I'm ready," I said, matching his stare with a look of determination.

Leaning forward, Warrick spoke into my ear. "Don't obsess about finding your father. Now that I know that there is a possibility that he may be alive, I will see to it that he is found. But should you hear anything, do not hesitate to tell me."

I nodded, not sure what I could do if I wanted to look for him anyways. I'd been no good finding Warrick and was just lucky I'd stumbled upon him at the time that I did, costly as it had been to retrieve him. No, if my father was alive then he was out of my reach for now.

"I understand," I said, nodding.

Warrick stepped back and began to chant. A translucent area in front of us slowly formed into a swirling mass. After a minute of soft chanting and focus I began to see what lay beyond. Sweat dripped down his brow as a bed and an empty room came into view until he finished chanting and the portal seemed to snap into place.

"Be bold and take chances," Warrick said, smiling down at me. He was tall, much taller than I realized as I stood right up to him. And his eyes were kind, the blue orbs of someone I trusted and knew to be a friend. It hurt more than I cared to admit tearing myself away and take that step into the portal, leaving Warrick to the unknown and out of reach once more.

Kora followed behind me silently, but I noticed Ruelock from the other side of the portal lift a hand as if to motion her back to him. The Southlanders really had a thing about dungeons, so I could imagine having a dungeon in the form of a golem was like having a god walk among them. I wondered if that attention was something that Kora didn't like and perhaps that is why she chose to stay at my side, aside from her talk of destinies.

The portal shimmered and snapped away leaving Warrick behind in the Southlands. He would be amidst a war soon and depending on how things had progressed back here in House Variyn, I might be as well.

But Warrick was right, war wouldn't be won in a day, so I needed to get stronger and find allies so that I could make it to the Isle of Avalon.

CHAPTER 6
HOUSE VARIYN

I needed to meet with Lord Variyn, but I needed to get cleaned up first and I didn't want to do it here in the keep. Being as inconspicuous as I could, I slipped into the hallway with Kora right on my heels and moved through the halls, careful not to make eye contact with anyone lest they tell me about some important meeting I'd missed or perhaps that I was needed at this very moment. Luck was with me, and I made it to the door with barely a head nod from a guard or two.

It was mid-afternoon by the look of the sun, which was odd because I remembered it still being early morning in the Southlands. A thought occurred to me as I slipped out the keep, I needed to check something that was so obvious that it wouldn't work but I hadn't actually tried yet. Slipping to the side and following the path into the gardens I came across the remains of the Prime Mana Shrine.

The Prime Mana Shrine and the surrounding area were covered in a blackness so deep it seemed to whisper and pull in the light around it. The ground around it had snaking tendrils of the corruption reaching outward. I'd noticed none of this two weeks ago when I'd last seen it, so it was rather shocking to come across.

The old feeling that I used to get around it had dissipated into nothing. Two guards stood by, likely just a cautionary force set into place by Lord Variyn should anyone return or perhaps meant to keep people away from the corruption. What these two guards would do if the Chaos Knight did return, I couldn't say, but I ignored them after catching one's gaze and him acknowledging me. Despite being dirty and disheveled I was recognizable enough to the guards that saw me frequently.

"Has it done anything since you were set over it?" I asked one that I thought was named, Relk, but I couldn't be sure, so I didn't risk it.

He had dark hair and light-colored eyes with a five o'clock shadow. His partner looked sleep deprived, large black circles around his eyes and his brown eyes drooped. They both straightened when I addressed them with Relk speaking for them.

"It's spreading a few inches a day but otherwise it's been quiet, my Lord," Relk said, saying the words in a stiff reporting manner.

"At ease guardsmen, Relk wasn't it?" I asked, he nodded and seemed surprised I'd remembered his name.

"I'm going to touch it but if I start seizing up or acting weird at all pull me off it. You have my permission to knock me out if you can, just don't let it kill me."

The guard laughed, then must have thought better of it halfway through because he stopped and said, "Yes, my Lord. I will do as you ask."

I smirked at the guard and stepped up the cobbled ground toward the remains of the Prime Mana Shrine until I was close enough to place my hand on its surface. There were several things I thought might happen, but what actually happened took me by surprise. A warmth infused me, and a voice screamed into my head.

"The bonds are broken and the dragons approach! The bonds are broken and the dragons approach! The end is nigh, heed my words, the end is nigh!"

I jerked my hand off the surface and stumbled back. There was no doubt in my mind who that voice belonged to in that moment. The pain that was transferred to me while hearing the screams crack against my mind left me reeling. That had been the arbiter I'd met during my *Awakening*.

"You alright, my Lord?" Relk asked, putting a hand on my shoulder to steady me as my body swayed from a reverberating shock of the initial contact.

"Do not touch," I began to say but my lungs felt suddenly empty and Relk stepped back before I could finish. "Do not touch that thing." I said finishing my thought after catching my breath. I pointed weakly at the remains of the Prime Mana Shrine, unable to get my mind to calm down.

What I'd heard just then and the arbiter I knew before were one and the same, but the insanity that reverberated off him in waves was nothing like the quirky being I'd known. I came here to try something, and I wouldn't leave until I'd at least given it a go. With apprehension and a great deal of hesitation, I approached the stone once more.

"Is that a good idea, my Lord?" Relk asked, he and his fellow guard had moved an extra ten feet away from their original standing position beside the stone.

Instead of answering, I just raised a hand, waving at him to stay back while I went over the spell in my mind. I didn't need to spend any time examining the workings of a spell before casting it, but for this task having additional understanding would be key, so I spent the next minute going over the phrases and hand motions that were required. Then at last, I reached out and put my mind to task for what I wanted to try.

Casting Restoring Light a fraction of a second before my hand touched the stone, I focused on spreading the effects of removing Chaos corruption. The screams returned, but there was a distance to them this time that hadn't been there before. I could feel tendrils of something reaching towards me as I touched the stone, but a light ever present and powerful kept it at bay. What didn't happen though, was that light, the power that would remove the corruption, refused to go any farther than a few feet into the stone.

"You must unite the world against the real threat! The balance has been broken!"

I heard the new words and oddly I felt as if these were directed at me, not just ravings of a mad man any longer.

"Can you hear me arbiter?" I asked, speaking as clearly as I could while maintaining the focus of my spell. It had already grown difficult to maintain and I doubted it was meant to be maintained like I was doing.

I received no response, so I removed my hand and let my spell fade. There was a final trick I had left to try, Essence Infusion. Taking a deep breath and clearing my head of all distractions I held my hand out, ready to place it. Using Essence Infusion, I sunk as much as I dared into my Restoring Light spell, close to a thousand. Then I cast the spell and slammed my hand onto the Prime Mana Shrine.

Where before, my spell had created a small light that held back the darkness, now it was like I'd harnessed the power of a roaring bonfire. Light flickered and ripped deep into the stone, grabbing hold of tendrils of darkness and rendering them into ribbons. But even still, my light barely penetrated the surface area of the Prime Mana Shrine and didn't travel more than a foot into the ground.

"Direct your light toward my voice! Free me by ending the corruption that has inflicted my mind!" It was the Arbiter again, this time closer and stronger than before.

I focused my mind on his voice and shifted what light I had left toward him. His pleas had held more than just words, there was a feeling in them that pushed me into action. The least I could do was to help free him from the ruined prison that bound him and rotted his mind.

All at once, my light hit upon a vast consciousness riddled with blackened Chaos rot and sickness. Like a moth to the flame, the Chaos was drawn out and consumed. It took a matter of moments for all this to happen. What was left afterwards spoke only a few words before it fell to tatters, ceasing to exist.

"Take up the mantle, free the world."

I released my grip from the stone and examined it while my head did its best to drive me insane with pain. The black rot that had covered the base of the ruined Prime Mana Shrine and had slowly been reaching out from it was gone. I'd done enough to stem the spread, but I knew that just below the surface and deeper in the Ley lines, that corruption still spread. My task was far from complete, but I felt encouraged by what little success I had been able to achieve.

If only the arbiter's words hadn't shook me so thoroughly, I might even be relieved at my accomplishment. What mantle did he mean and how was I to free the world?

"It should be safe to be around, but I wouldn't risk touching it," I said, the guards nodding their acknowledgement as I turned and left, my mind set on finding a bath at Miles Manor.

I made it perhaps a mile into the city before I had to stop and see what the crowds were all about. This one, in a slightly poorer part of town, was the biggest gathering I'd seen yet, and my curiosity could only handle so much.

A crowd of at least thirty people were gathered around the main street plaza listening to someone yell about one thing or another. There were two obvious divisions in the group, ones booing and jeering at the speaker and a quiet thoughtful looking bunch that seemed genuinely interested.

I decided to plant myself right in the middle of this natural division and hear what the announcer was going on about.

"Soldier pay will be provided to kin for a period of three months after death, should you fall in the service of your Lord. Those who sign up for service now will get the bonus I spoke of earlier, a single gold coin. Those who wait will instead be given the weekly pay of two silver and a week's time to get their affairs in order."

I stopped listening as more jeers came from the crowd when a young man, couldn't be older than eighteen, stepped up and approached another man behind a booth that was set up behind the speaker. He spoke to them but was too far away for me to catch any words. He was obviously signing up and that had angered the opposing side to the point where even hearing the announcer had become impossible.

The table now had a small group of four young men lined up to sign away their lives to serve in a war that shouldn't be. Flanking the table were three city guards, one of which I thought I recognized as the fellow Alayna had rebuked all those weeks ago. They did not appear happy that the crowd has getting louder and beginning to push each other.

The announcer went suddenly quiet, and I looked over to see he'd been hit by rotten fruit thrown from the crowd. A wave of laughter ensued and several more fruits were thrown, not all soft. The man was dressed well enough that he might be a low nobleman or at least a footman to one. He shrunk back from the attacks and the guard stepped forward to block him.

"That'll show them to steal our young men for another stupid war!" A grizzled old man spoke from just beside me. I nodded and pulled my dirty cloak around my armor as to hide what I was, whether or not it worked I don't know, but he kept talking.

"We work and we work to keep this damned House going and all we ask is peace. Ten years of it, but now his Lordship decides he's not happy with our borders. He wants more and more; they always want more!"

He was shouting at this point and no longer were his words directed at me, if ever they were.

His words got the crowd going even more and several stepped forward as if to challenge the guards, one old timer walked forward and tried to pull a young man out of line. They must have known each other because they spoke, and the young man nodded his head. The old man looked dejected and turned to leave, but a guard was there blocking his way back.

Swifter than I'd have expected from a city guard, he punched, and blood spurted out of the elderly man's nose, dropping him towards the ground. I don't even remember beginning to move, but I was there before the man hit the ground grabbing him. The crowd suddenly went silent, only the yells from the guards to disperse continued.

Using Mending Touch, I laid a heal on the man. I didn't know the exact methods of healing non-*Awakened,* but I'd been healed before *Awakening* so I knew it would at least work. Sure enough, the blood stopped, and the old man blinked back to consciousness.

"Are you alright?" I asked as his eyes focused on me. He nodded and I helped him to his feet. Then turning to the guard, who stood in stunned silence as what I was became undeniably apparent.

"You will disperse," he said, but his words held no confidence that his orders would be followed, and I detected the smallest bit of a quaver in his voice.

"I don't have the patience for you," I said, mostly under my breath than to him but he heard me. I decided it was only fair to return what he'd given the old man, so I lashed out with my fist. I caved in his nose and sent blood splattering over my arm and his chest.

He fell to the ground in a heap, knocked out cold but clearly alive.

This didn't go over too well with the other two guards, who instantly lowered halberds and marched forward. I hadn't meant to get in any exercise before bathing, but I guess I could be tempted into it.

"Are you sure you want to do this?" I asked, cracking my neck as I spoke.

"By the authority of the city Guardsmen's Guild you are ordered to stand down and allow yourself to be taken into custody," the one I recognized from before said. His name was Veltrees and he'd been a Lieutenant, but the rank markings on his armor had less bars now, so perhaps he'd been demoted.

"Listen Veltrees, I won't be taken into custody, but I am willing to teach you a lesson that I wish I'd been able to teach you last time we met," I said, smiling as I saw recognition flash over his face.

Instead of him backing off or thinking twice about attacking me, my words enraged him. He lunged forward with his halberd, using some kind of guard skill it flashed with deadly speed. However, I was level 20 and had attributes of someone much higher. I side stepped the attack, purposely not summoning my sword yet, instead smacking my palm against the flat of the weapon and sending him stumbling.

His partner didn't stand idly by, slashing down in a deadly chop. The vast difference in facing guards while being just a Sparked compared to being a Level 20 Awakened that had passed a few second thresholds, was insane. I side stepped the attack by instinct alone and had to squash the urge to hit back with a Lightning Strike. Instead, I rushed forward and hit the guard with an open flat palm.

Though I thought I'd measured enough force to stun him and not throw him completely off his feet, I'd been wrong. He flew backwards and smashed into the announcer who squeaked as he went down.

"Behind you!" An elderly voice cried out and I turned just in time to see Veltrees thrusting for my gut. I might have had enough time to spin out of the way, but I didn't feel like it. Instead, I activated Power Strike and punched the flat side of the halberd, the metal dented and flung out of his grip from my strike. Without slowing, I reached down and snapped the thick wooden shaft of the weapon, before kicking it toward the crowd. The pieces of the weapon skittered across the cobblestone, well out of reach of Veltrees now.

"You'll be imprisoned for this!" He yelled, taking a step back. "The Adventurer's Guild won't stand for one of its members going rogue and attacking guardsmen!"

I could tell he believed his words, but I didn't see an outcome that my new wealth or my position as a Knight of House Variyn and a land-owning vassal would result in me being imprisoned. Perhaps someone would give me a firm talking to, but it wasn't like I was acting out of spite. These men had taken the first step towards violence, striking a weaker opponent, and I was just showing them what it felt like to be completely outmatched.

"It doesn't feel good to be on the receiving end of someone so much stronger, does it? You abuse your power and the people you are meant to serve, and you think I will be the one to answer for my actions?" I asked him, a sneer on his face all the while.

"I was doing my duty to House Variyn and the city Guardsmen Guild!" He screamed the words, spittle flying from his mouth and his face going red. "You think striking an old man is bad? Without us this city would be a den of thieves, murders, and worse! You are the problem and those like you!"

Try as I might, I couldn't see things in his perspective. Was he trying to say that because the guards kept the peace in the city that they were due a little leeway when it came to abusing citizens? I must be too much of a country boy for the city, because when we saw a problem or an abuse, we stepped up and took care of it. So, damn them all and may the entire Guardsmen Guild come running, because I hadn't even broken a sweat yet.

As if my desire for a thorough job had cued their arrival, a half dozen more guards appeared, these with swords, spears, and two crossbows. Well shit, I didn't like crossbows. Reaching out my hand before the newcomers had a chance to determine what was happening, I cast Lightning Strike on the crossbow, hoping I'd not fry the wielder in the process.

It worked, the weapon exploded into several pieces and I followed up with a Firebolt to the other crossbow just as it rose up and loosed a bolt. The bolt was charred and sent off course by my attack. The final crossbow shattered, but the wielder went down groaning as well.

I wondered absently if these Guardsmen had any decent proxy levels or how they dealt with rogue adventurers. A seventh guardsmen arrived then, joining the remaining ones pushing back the crowd and attempting to encircle me. To my surprise, Veltrees and the others regarded him with a bowed head when he looked at them. I could feel something familiar coming off this one and suddenly I knew what I was dealing with, an *Awoken* Guardsmen.

I Inspected him and my heart quickened. He was level 23, and I was about to have a real workout.

He spoke then, his voice deep and solemn. "You are violating the Adventurer's Guild charter section 8 subsection 3b line 52. Further resistance will result in heavy fines, possible imprisonment, or death. It is your choice; will you stand down?"

"I stopped your guards from beating down a helpless man, believe it or not, but I am not the one in the wrong here," I said, holding out my hand and summoning my sword. I'd meant it only as a precaution, but he must have taken it as me making my choice, because he blurred as he went for the attack.

Him being level 23 should have given him an advantage, but it did not. I parried his first sword strike easily, and stepped around his side, delivering a punch to his ribs before withdrawing a step. The exchange took mere moments, but I could tell that my speed had surprised him. He'd likely Inspected me and thought he'd had a slight advantage with his higher level. What he couldn't know is I had the attributes of someone well into the upper 30s.

I felt a rush around him of energy that I recognized as him activating an ability. Suddenly he was fast enough to surprise even me, and I barely got my sword up in time to catch his strike with the help of Swift Strike. His sword got past my defenses and scored a hit on my arm, but at the last moment the tip of my blade cut a line in his guardsmen outfit as he attempted to disengage.

"You aren't a match for me," I said, my breath finally coming slightly faster than before. To prove my point I cast Arcane Missile, directing each strike to smash around his feet.

He'd arrived moments after my first spell castings and seeing my magic didn't dissuade him like I'd thought it might. He smiled while adjusting his guardsman cap on his head, red feathers in a mohawk waving in the breeze.

"You are a dual type, which means you are weaker than a pure martial class. I think I will fare just fine. Name's Bolten, by the way. Figure you should know the name of the man who kills you," Bolten said, a cocky smile on his face now.

"Best of luck," I said, tipping my helmet as if it were a hat.

Bolten screamed suddenly and his veins bulged along with his muscles in his neck. I lowered my guard for just a moment, thinking someone else had just attacked him, but then he lumbered forward breathing heavily. He was using a skill I realized, sensing a gathering aura around him that sparked and hissed in my senses.

When he came at me this time, he was an even match for my speed and what was more surprising he had strength that surpassed my own. Back and forth we traded blows, each of us skilled enough in the blade to avoid harm. I didn't know how long he could hold with this skill active, but I was finally getting a workout and I'd keep trading blows until he couldn't.

But it wasn't meant to be. I heard shouting and saw movement outside our little fight but couldn't spare a glance if I wanted to keep my limbs intact. But suddenly it didn't matter as a form crashed into the both of us, sending us to the ground.

Lying beside each other, I thought I might try and stab him just a little for good measure, but when I went to poke him, I realized I'd been disarmed and saw that Bolten had been as well. I looked up to see what or who could disarm two level 20 plus adventurers and send us sprawling so easily.

Galt stood where we'd been moments before, a sword in each hand and a smirk on his lips. "You mind telling me why you've assaulted a Lord, Guardsman Bolten?"

Bolten's face went red, and he looked over at me with a look of utter terror. Standing, he bowed his head and spoke. "I was unaware, yet I know that doesn't excuse my actions. Please allow me to submit for punishment and accept my apology."

"I'll accept nothing from you but your sword, which

you can get back by visiting me personally at the keep. Get your guardsmen and go. See to it no reports are written of this event and just maybe you'll get your weapon back in a single piece," Galt growled the words. When Bolten didn't bolt immediately, Galt narrowed his eyes at him, and he moved.

Standing, I held out my hand, my sword materialized out of Galt's grip and into mine, before I let it fade back to where it went between uses. Galt raised an eyebrow at me, looking down where the sword had been, but said nothing.

"You ruined my workout," I said, trying to lighten the mood with a joke, but it didn't have the effect I wanted. Galt growled at me, then stepped closer. The growing crowd and military sign-up table had been all but abandoned, so he pulled me to the booth with a hand on my shoulder.

"I heard you were back, and Lord Variyn sent me to give you an urgent message. You are to report to him and receive your orders. After which, I'd like you to find me. I've heard good things coming out of Blackridge Keep and I want to commend you," Galt said, his voice evening off from the angry growl he'd used against Bolten.

"You aren't going to lecture me about the city guard?" I asked, chuckling.

"Nah," Galt said, shaking his head and shooting them a look. "Everyone knows city guards are assholes."

"Seems that way," I said, smiling at Bolten and Veltrees as they departed.

City Guards were definitely assholes.

With a great deal of luck and stealth, I made it to Miles Manor and into a bath without encountering anyone wanting my attention. Even though I'd been gone for several weeks, the guard and the Runeforged didn't try to stop me to inform me of Regina needing me, so that was a good sign.

Kora left to try and find Fred, a fact that made me smile as I thought about it. He'd been so obsessed over her that Fran had gone out of her way to joke about them being a couple at every chance she got.

But now, alone in the bathroom I was struck with other thoughts. The misunderstanding with the guards had left a bad taste in my mouth, and not only because of how fast it progressed but what they were guarding. I'd seen several little recruitment stations throughout the city after encountering the first one. It didn't take a genius to figure out what Lord Variyn must want to speak with me about. War had come to House Variyn and that meant I was going to be drawn into a potentially deadly conflict.

What did I think about war and potentially killing others for a cause that I didn't understand? To be honest, I was very torn, as I had to honor my commitments but at the same time, I didn't want to take the lives of others forced into service by the promise of coin for a conflict they couldn't care less about. I determined I would need to speak with Lord Variyn and try to understand why he felt war was necessary.

Perhaps understanding what was so important would help me get emotionally behind fighting in the war, perhaps not. I went back and forth, examining the options I saw before me while I finished bathing. By the end of it I was no closer to knowing what I would do than when I started, but at least I was clean.

Dressing and suiting back up into my armor, the self-cleaning function working like a charm, I found Fred, Fran, and Kora sitting alone in the drinking hall close to the rooms they stayed in.

"Fred was worried you'd left for good and taken his metal bride with you," Fran said, smiling my way as I entered the room.

"I said nothing of the kind," Fred said, shooting an angry look at his sister.

Kora smiled and chuckled.

"I'm heading back to the keep for a meeting, you staying here?" I asked Kora, her gaze had settled back on Fred and I wondered if they were getting a bit too close.

"I'll stay here for now," Kora said, not taking her eyes off Fred, who for his trouble began to blush red in the cheeks.

"We were thinking of going on a dungeon run soon, because I had an offer to take my brother and get a few levels worth, but it'll take a couple weeks at least, so I wanted to run it by you. Are you planning on leaving on a dungeon run soon?" Fran asked.

I thought about that for a few seconds before shrugging. "I honestly don't know. I'm level 20 with enough essence for 21, what level are you all at now?"

"We just made it to 15, I'm a bit ahead of Fred, but not by much," Fran said, taking a long pull on her drink.

"I'd say go do the dungeon run and catch up as much as you can, but before you go, see Regina and tell her Caldor requests you both be given essence bands, she'll know what I mean," I said, smiling.

If I knew Regina, and I think that I did, she'd be working on her own models and gems by now so she must have a few sitting around. It was time we get them out in the population and help people level faster. Plus, it never hurt to generate a little more income, not that I didn't already have more than I could possibly know what to do with in a single lifetime.

"Ismene told me that you'd given her something that's helped her progress, I'm guessing this essence band is that? If so, I'm ready for any advantage I can get my hands on. But it isn't going to like, blow me up or anything right?" Fran asked.

"It hasn't yet," I said, offering a weak smile as I poured myself a drink and downed it in a single gulp. "I'm taking off for now. Kora you can go with them if you want, but if you do, let someone know so I don't worry you've disappeared."

"I'll wait for your return," Kora said, Fred's expression went from excited to dour within moments.

"Fred, try not to, well you know, she's a Runeforged,

man, get a grip," I said, speaking a bit lower as I passed by Fred.

Fran laughed out loud, obviously I hadn't spoken low enough. Fred went beet red and pretended to be interested in something in a far-flung corner of the room.

CHAPTER 7
MEETING WITH LORD VARIYN

Lord Variyn sat across from me, wearing glorious armor of black and gold with a helmet set atop his massive oak desk. But despite his armored appearance, his eyes showed a deep exhaustion and sorrow. I'd been sitting across from him for nearly a minute, maybe two, but he continued to go through papers, making notes on them here and there. I peeked and saw that the one in front of him had to do with troop reporting numbers and recruitment efforts.

Apparently, we had a force of ten thousand recruited but another ten thousand were expected from outlying towns. At the bottom, was a list of vassals that would be required to bring troops of their own and I was surprised to see not only my name, but Zander's as well. When had Zander been appointed a vassalship? Much had changed in the last two weeks. As I finished reading it all upside down,

I saw that Lord Variyn had lifted his eyes and now regarded me with a curious look.

"Did you read all that you needed?" He asked, his voice firmer and less fatherly than I ever remembered.

"Sorry, I was just curious I guess," I said, my face growing a little hot from being caught.

"It's fine, as a vassal you will be getting reports to review soon enough, let's get started, shall we?" He asked but didn't wait for me to respond as he pushed his papers away and launched into it.

"I have thirty-one vassals who hold keeps within House Variyn. Each one is required to bring a legion to battle pulled from the population around their domain. Our legions consist of roughly one thousand soldiers: two hundred cavalry, five hundred men at arms, and three hundred bowmen. These numbers can flex as losses are incurred but it is a vassal's responsibility to maintain their numbers. When can you have your legion ready to report for training?"

I blinked several times as my brain slowly processed what was being asked of me. How in the hell was I supposed to raise an army of one hundred, much less one thousand! Surely, he knew I hadn't any way of doing such a task and the region around Blackridge was mostly abandoned, with those who had been joining our general area that wished to be far away from the hustle and bustle of the city life.

"I can't, I'm sorry I just don't have any idea how I'd be able to recruit so many people," I finally said, setting my jaw and ready for the rebuke that would follow.

Instead, Lord Variyn smiled at me and nodded knowingly. "I expected as much, which is why I've been recruiting from the general population. It is expected that half of my newer vassals wouldn't have the means to recruit or train a force, but you'd be surprised that few of my vassals admit as much. Even my nephew has sent word that he will recruit his numbers by the deadline I gave him. Poor boy is likely to get his head removed by an angry populace when he tries to recruit the numbers I require."

He shook his head and scratched at his beard. "I will require that you gather together a hundred men or women or in your case, Runeforged, perhaps. I've heard odd reports lately that you've bought up a small army's worth of Runeforged to protect a compound within my city. You are much more resourceful than I first believed you to be, young Caldor Miles."

"I believe that a hundred soldiers will be possible," I said, the wheels turning in my head as I tried to figure out how exactly I'd get even that many. "But I do believe my forces will be a mix of Southerners, Runeforged, and humans. Will that be alright?"

"If you can keep them under control and direct their bestial ways, then I wouldn't care if you recruited owlbears to fight for you. You will want to create squads of ten men each, with each squad focusing on a specific soldier type, be it men at arms, bowmen, or cavalry— though obviously you'll need to provide horses as well.

Supply trains will be important as well, so prepare your people on the logistics of bringing food. I'd suggest you create a squad of *Awakened* able to act as Commanders and logistics officers. Their ability to use storage items will be a great relief and something all resourceful armies must take advantage of."

"So, war is no longer a rumor, it is happening?" I asked, obviously I knew the answer, but I wanted to hear it from his lips.

"Yes, I have called House Variyn to war, and we won't stop until House Blalor is no more," Lord Variyn said, pinching at the bridge of his nose before continuing. "It might not seem like it, but this has been a long time coming, my brother's death was just the spark that ignited the fires of war."

"When must I have the force of a hundred men gathered and where do I bring them?" I asked, resolving to the fact that war was coming whether I liked it or not. I thought I'd have more to say about it, but now that I was being told I just felt ready to serve.

Lord Variyn went over the details, outlining where to bring the forces—a frontline encampment at the border of House Blalor and House Variyn—as well as when to arrive so that training could begin by General Busard, sent from the King himself.

"The King is assisting House Variyn?" I asked as Lord Variyn finished his informational instructions.

"He sees the benefit of fewer Houses and Blalor has long been a thorn in his side. I only had to offer him a twenty percent stake in all the means of industry in return for his support."

"Does House Blalor have a lot of industry?" I asked, going over what I knew of House Blalor, I was sure they had many mines and Warrick had said they had more coin than any other House.

Lord Variyn nodded. "They've got the most mines, the oldest forests, several high populous monsters to provide leather, and vast farms, both wheat and animals. It is one of the most abundantly rich areas in all of the continent besides maybe the elven lands, which King Newaliyn knows he will never take without such a great loss to make it impossible."

"How do we hope to defeat them if they have so many resources at their disposal?" I asked, not sure what reaction to expect from him, but the smile I got wasn't what I expected.

"They have all of their troops, which are only half as vast as what I hope to enlist, standing guard at twelve major keeps. Despite how well fortified they are becoming now that rumors of war have reached them, they've done a poor job at maintaining the defenses of all their keeps and soldiers, relying instead on mercenaries and bribes to maintain their defenses."

"So, if we can break the line, you hope that we can push in and take the capital, ending the fight?" I asked, trying to envision his plan.

"Not quite so straightforward as that, but I have ways to deal with them that they won't be expecting and have no counter to. I believe I will be able to end this conflict and take all of House Blalor within three, maybe four months. I do however require your service for that entire time, so do what you must to prepare and in a months' time I will see you at the Crest of Anul just as the snows begin to melt. Any additional instructions will be sent to you by priority messenger bearing my signet lock that can only be unlocked by one of the same." Lord Variyn handed over a signet ring and I took it.

"Is it magically enhanced?" I asked, worried I'd have to be rid of one of my rings.

"Yes, but not in a way that should interfere with your attributes, so feel free to wear it while equipping your other two rings...or three in your case. You are developing much faster than I could have expected. I can't wait to hear of your victories on the frontline," he said, turning his attention back to his paperwork. This one looked to be a list of supplies and harvest reports.

"I will honor my oath, but I have to say something before I leave and give you a report of what I've learned," I said, swallowing hard. "I do not think war is the answer or at least not this war. The Southlands are being invaded by Easterners and the beastkin nations have united to invade the Eastern lands, all of this I believe is the cause of our Chaos monster trouble, well that, and a Chaos Knight hellbent on destroying the Ley lines. We should prepare for war, but as a united force under the Ordu to face what is coming."

"And what is coming, young Arcane Knight?" Lord Variyn asked, his eyes lifting from his papers.

"I don't know yet, but the balance being as it is, there is a sense of foreboding that I can't shake. I would like to speak with the King regarding it, but I don't know how to go about it. So, for now I would warn you that unless we can restore the balance, I believe a threat to our entire world is on its way."

Lord Variyn nodded, asking me a few questions about how I knew what I did, and I explained my dreams, my adventures in the Southlands, and removing the corruption from the broken Mana Shrine, but in the end, he dismissed me without much more words on the matter.

I found Galt around the corner from Lord Variyn's office, and he pulled me into a closet to speak, his head snapping back and forth looking for anyone else that might see us but finding no one.

"You've heard the news now?" Galt asked, he stood uncomfortably close to me in what appeared to be a narrow linen closet with a window set into the far end.

"I'm going to war for House Variyn," I said, the words sounding strange coming out of my mouth.

"War is upon us all. I remember the last war and it wasn't pretty. All those I'd trained as guards were thrown into service alongside ordinary peasants and given proxy levels as soldiers. It won't be pretty, but I trust Lord Variyn is doing what is right. He never acts without forethought and has kept us in peace for so long while other houses continued to squabble," Galt spoke the words to me, but it seemed as if he were trying to convince himself of something just as much as informing me.

"He seems confident that he can end it before it becomes a prolonged affair. I just have to go tell my guards at Blackridge Keep that they'll be serving as soldiers now, something I didn't imagine I'd ever have them do," I said, wondering how this would make Galt react, but if it angered him it didn't show, instead he nodded along as if it were expected.

"Just remember that some need to stay behind to maintain order, you can't send them all off. In fact, I've heard good reports and it hasn't gone unnoticed that kitchen staff and others have left to join your keep. Because of this I've been asked by Lord Variyn to provide you with additional guards from our own forces. I've sent for ten more guards and two elites. I'd suggest you use them wisely and in the defense of the small settlement you've started."

I didn't know what to say, but I was suspicious as to why Galt was being so friendly. "I'll see that they are put to work. Why was privacy required for this conversation?" I asked, looking around the closet.

Galt shifted and walked over to the window, looking out at the street below. Then turning back, his face had a fierce look of determination. "If things were to go badly for House Variyn, I am under oath to die at the side of the

Variyn family and I will see my oath fulfilled, but I need you to take an oath as well."

I squirmed under the intensity of his gaze but nodded all the same.

"Caldor Miles, you will take an oath that you will do all in your power to see that Lady Alayna Variyn escapes harm. If House Variyn were to fall, you might be given a chance to help her escape and together with the resources I know you've amassed, you could cut from the land a safe place beyond the reach of war. Promise, no, swear to me that you will do whatever it takes to keep her safe!" Galt spoke with such intensity that I felt waves of power coming off him with each word.

I got a prompt from the system asking if I wished to bind the oath and I had to take a second to consider.

I wanted Alayna to be safe from whatever potential backlash could come from this war, but to take an oath that would be bound by the very system of the Ordu was something else entirely. My actions would be bound in a way that couldn't be stopped by merely changing my mind. I cared for Alayna though and I knew that oath or not, I'd do all I could to maintain her safety.

"I accept this Oath and swear to keep Alayna from harm as best as I can with all of my abilities and strength of arm and mind," I said, feeling the oath bind around me with powerful bands of essence and mana.

"I knew you to be an honorable man," Galt said, a new respect reflected in his eyes toward me. I thought for just a second that tears welled in his eyes, but he turned away and when he looked back, his eyes were as dry as they'd ever been. "I will see to it that Alayna knows that she can always turn to you in a time of need. Together we just might get her out of this stupid war alive."

"I won't let anything happen to her without my own blood being spilled to stop it," I said, my own intensity matching Galt's.

Galt liked this, nodding and pulling me into a stiff embrace. "Good on you son."

"Before you go," I said, putting a hand on his shoulder as he turned to leave. "I need help finding someone to train my siblings."

I went on to tell him how my siblings were going to *Spark* soon, and they knew nothing about combat, then told him that money was no issue and I needed the best. He said he knew just the person, but Lord Variyn would be upset at him for poaching his service, but Galt would be willing to obtain them. He didn't tell me who it was but promised to send him to Creeshaw and begin the training immediately.

Then just as fast as he'd appeared, he slipped from the room, leaving me alone with my thoughts of war, sacrifice, and my siblings' wellbeing.

CHAPTER 8
MANOR MILES

I t was several hours later that night and I'd found Alayna in the halls earlier in the day, inviting her to dinner at her favorite restaurant before leaving to tend to mending my armor and resupplying my food and water stores. Now she sat across from me, her mood somber, as we ate our food in silence.

"How's your food?" I asked, smiling across the table. She'd been unusually quiet since I found her in the hallway to invite her to dinner and I didn't know why.

"It's fine," she said, not looking up at me as she poked her meat with her fork, not having eaten really any of it.

My food was more than fine, each bite sending waves of euphoria through my body. I could feel the potential it lent me as my body went to work digesting it. These fancy places made for the rich and noble added an almost magical quality to their food that provided certain buffs depending on the meal you ordered. For instance, the chicken on a bed of vegetables whose name I didn't know, seemed to infuse my muscles with increased strength and endurance.

All of which was to say it was more than fine. I didn't know what was bothering Alayna, but I trusted her to tell me when she was ready, so instead, I tried to continue with mundane conversation.

"How's your leveling going?" I asked, remembering she'd told me her research had been providing her with enough essence that she was able to level a few times. Surely after all this time she'd gotten a good deal of essence.

"I'm progressing but at what cost," she said, shaking her head. This caught me by surprise, a certain venom in her voice that I wasn't used to hearing. I decided that now wouldn't be the time to press her, so I shifted the topic once more.

"I spoke with your father today," I said, this got her attention, and she looked up at me for one of the first times since we began to eat.

"He's called you to service?" She asked, her normally docile tone hard and filled with annoyance.

"He has," I said, giving a weak smile in response. "But I'm not required to field as many men as his other vassals, so that is a bit of a relief. It'll be hard enough to gather a hundred soldiers; I can't imagine trying to get three thousand men together."

"You're just going to go with it?" She asked, her tone angry.

"Go with what?" I asked, confused. Surely, she didn't mean the war, I had no choice, and she knew that.

"The war, the fighting, the needless death," she said, each word rising in volume and turning heads from just inside our balcony seating.

"I made an oath of service, I don't have a choice here," I said, trying to get her to understand.

"You can ask to be stripped of your titles, or just renounce them and be done with the strings my father has attached to you. I warned you that he wanted to use you and now you're going to be his puppet of war," Alayna said, her breathing coming in rapid heaves as she struggled to calm herself.

"No, I can't," I said, not sure I was believing my ears. "You know me better than that. I won't just give up on an oath I've made because it suddenly becomes inconvenient. That isn't to say I won't be careful and train my men to only take a life when necessary. War can't be all bad, I'm sure I'll find a way to get through it," I said, trying to get her to understand but by the look on her face I wasn't getting through to her.

"You don't understand war," Alayna said, shaking her head.

"And you do?" I asked, suddenly feeling defensive and angry. "You are a noblewoman, what do you know of war?"

Alayna grew quiet and looked up to me with hurt in her eyes. "I've read firsthand accounts of generals, soldiers, and peasants forced into battle during the last great war.

War changed each of them without regard to their station or lot in life. Sure, I've never experienced it, but don't assume that I don't understand if even in a small way. You think because you've been an adventurer and had to kill monsters that you understand what killing will do to you? The men and women you will face in battle won't be monstrous creatures out to kill for the sake of killing, they will be fathers, mothers, brothers, and sisters all doing what they were ordered to do for the sake of their home-land. Are you going to be okay being the reason some kid doesn't have his father return after this war is over? I would think that you, of all people, would understand that the most."

Her words hit me like a boulder rolling unchecked down a steep hillside. I hadn't thought about it like that, but surely, I would be able to keep enough control over my men to keep them from needlessly killing. A part of me wondered if I'd be able to stop all the killing by a show of force. Surely no simple soldier wanted to fight against someone who could literally call down lightning from the sky or hurl balls of fire big enough to consume entire squads.

But I was forgetting a very important fact, they'd have *Awakened* on their side as well. How did one balance the battlefield when a select few could kill waves of soldiers on their own? A sudden heavy weight began to settle on my gut as I realized how unprepared I really was for a war against other *Awakened* and soldiers.

"I don't know," I finally said, something in my tone or

my eyes must have defused her angry mood because she looked at me now with sorrow in her eyes.

"It is worse than you think, but I can't talk about it here," Alayna said, shaking her head and finally taking a bite of her food.

We spent the rest of the evening not speaking of anything really and eating in silence. By the time the food was finished, and they asked if we'd be willing to have dessert, Alayna declined, and we paid and left. She allowed me to take her arm, though she remained stiff, and I asked her if she'd be willing to come to Miles Manor for a drink so that we might speak in the privacy of my home. She agreed and we made our way to a carriage that took us there.

Fred and Fran were gone by the time we arrived, Kora informed me that they'd left for a dungeon run and that she'd been dodging requests to be 'examined' by several of Regina's Clan members. Alayna watched us speak in silence, but I could tell she was confused by the appearance and speech of Kora and I remembered I hadn't actually told her about Kora.

Before we got started I relayed everything she'd missed along with Kora's creation and our adventures in the Southlands. She listened without asking a single question, an oddity for her, but I understood her mood wasn't the best, so I let it be. Until finally, catching her all up and telling Kora that we were going to my room where privacy runes had been set up, Alayna finally spoke up, then saying Kora could come if she wanted. She did and so the three of us left to my suite.

On our way, I relayed to her about something I'd left out so far, the discovery of Essence Bands and how I was going to put them on the market soon. This seemed to break through her icy exterior finally and she looked at me with wide eyes.

"You've discovered how to capture essence just like a monster core?" She asked, her eyes filled with amazement. "You are going to create an entire new generation of powerful adventurers. I can't imagine what else gems like that could be used for. Maybe powering enchantments with a more potent source of power. I wonder if the..." Her voice trailed off and she looked over her shoulder as if expecting someone was listening to our conversation. She stayed quiet until we got into my room, then she took care to examine all the privacy runes that had been set up in the room. Finding them adequate she turned to me with a worried expression. "Sit down, I have so much to tell you."

I sat and awaited her explanation for what was bothering her.

"You remember the discovery I was working on that had me so excited?" She asked. She glanced at Kora, but she didn't even appear to be paying attention as she was currently examining a few books on my bookshelf.

"I do," I said, pulling free Advanced Essence Theory and handing it to Kora. It was a book I'd wanted her to look through and give me notes about what she thought but it kept slipping my mind. Kora took it, read the title, and opened to the first page.

"My father has perverted my research and discoveries by making them weapons of war," Alayna said the words in a rushed expulsion of emotion as if they'd been damned to secrecy all time and finally set free. She breathed heavily and looked to me for some measure of comfort, but I didn't know what to say.

Instead of trying to speak the right words, I pulled her into a hug. Her body was as warm and lovely as ever, but I didn't know how to help her now and it made me feel odd. I didn't like feeling vulnerable or not being able to help. "It'll be okay, tell me what he did," I said as I released her. She had tears in her eyes, but she wiped them clean before continuing.

"I discovered how the ancient Ordu had flying vessels, ships that could sail the skies. Now my father is building a fleet of platforms meant to carry troops behind enemy lines. He plans to catch House Blalor off guard by circumventing their strong frontline and causing mayhem close to their capital without the traditional need to maintain supply lines or troops taking keeps."

I kept my expression neutral as I thought about what this meant for the coming war and the battles that were likely to occur. I could see now how Lord Variyn thought he could end this conflict without a prolonged fight. Even the four months he claimed it would take seemed long to me after learning this new information. What would stop him from bringing an overwhelming force straight to the capital city and capturing Lord Blalor before escape was possible?

Alayna saw this as a perversion of her research, but I couldn't help but see the genius of it in how Lord Variyn planned to use it. I would not be telling that to Alayna though, she wouldn't be willing to speak to me if I couldn't show some measure of concern or empathy to her plight. So, I examined it from her perspective. She'd finally found something she felt would be used to better all of society and instead that discovery was being used as a way to further a war. I thought I could understand how that would make me feel, and I didn't like it either.

"I'm so sorry," I said, to Alayna, pulling her back into a hug. "It wasn't right of him to take away something you'd hoped would benefit all of society and pervert it into a thing of war."

"Thank you," Alayna said, crying into my shoulder.

I couldn't help but feel a little torn as we shared an embrace. These new weapons of war would ensure a swift victory and I welcomed such a swift end to hostilities as it would likely result in less death. But a part of me hurt for Alayna and the guilt she would carry for each life lost because of the work she did. I knew no words would heal those potential wounds, so instead I held her tight and let her cry.

A few hours later, Alayna and I had retired to bed, lying beside each other while Kora continued to read, out in the sitting room. The tears had stopped, and the conversation had returned to more mundane topics as we talked about nothing at all, but I enjoyed the proximity of it all.

I held her close as I tried to picture what life would be like a year from now, or even five. The war, win or lose, would be over. I'd be reaching levels and attributes that would put me on par with my father's strength. Perhaps Alayna and I would be engaged to be married, or even married already with a child of our own coming into the world soon. Five years could hold all manner of change.

"Where do you see us in five years?" I asked, pulling her body close to mine. She curled around me and rested her head on my chest.

"Let me think," she said, making a 'humming' sound as if thinking something through. "We will live together in Blackridge Keep, your influence will have grown so great that the King will want to name your territory a house of its own, but you will graciously decline. We will be wed, and our second son will be on his way into the world. Our first boy will be the spitting image of his father, with the fierce intelligence of his mother. I will be working to discover the mysteries of the Ordu while you fight to maintain the powers of Chaos and Order as the strongest Adventurer in the land. And we will be at peace, the people under us living lives of prosperity and safety."

"You've thought about this more than I have," I said, kissing the top of her head. I'd only recently even let my mind travel into the realm of the 'what ifs' but it was clear Alayna had traversed the idea many times over by her quick response.

It didn't bother me though. I couldn't know the future, but it was hard to imagine one that didn't involve her. She didn't respond to my comment and soon I felt her relax into sleep, so I decided to try and do the same.

The dreams that I met upon falling asleep made me wish I'd chosen to stay awake.

Great dragons of immense power traveled towards our planet, ready to extinguish all life. Darkness of a purple variety swirled in my head, and I saw the faces of beings twisted by evil. Great weapons able to scorch the surface of a planet from a distance were being readied and I felt panic grow in my chest as I saw them work. Chaos and Order would be extinguished, and nothing would remain of either if nothing changed.

In my dreams I walked the halls of an organic looking vessel and saw many thousands of beings inside. I felt as if I were being drawn to a specific place, each turn bringing me closer and closer until finally I entered a room that burned with power beyond any I'd felt before.

"This forbidden power is what must be extinguished," Mah'kus said, he stood suddenly at my side. He wore the same clothing I'd seen him wear the last time we'd spoken but held a somber look on his face.

"What does this mean?" I asked, the dreams were nothing but confusing images of people I couldn't hope to understand.

"If the time comes, you will be ready," Mah'kus said, his words cryptic but self-assured.

Then as quick as the dreams had come upon me, they

snapped away. I awoke to the calls of birds and rays of sunshine coming in from the window. Alayna still snoozed in my arms, but I wouldn't be going back to sleep anytime soon, not if it meant seeing those evil creatures again. Instead, I carefully pulled myself free and began writing in a blank book I'd acquired about my experience and all the others I could remember regarding Mah'kus and my odd dreams.

By the time I was finished, I was sure about one thing, there was more going on than I understood. More even than the balance between Chaos and Order. Somehow, I needed to get the people, all the people of the Wyrd, ready for the coming storm.

CHAPTER 9
IMPROVING MY PROFESSION

Alayna woke a time later and I promised to meet her for dinner again before she left. Today I planned to spend most of the day going over my profession and what I'd learned so far. I started by opening my menus and listing out in my head all the recipes I had. Then I looked at the basic stats in the menu, like levels and such.

Profession: Gem Inscriptionist, Level 14

Profession Abilities: Quality Check, Mana Infusion

Quality Check: Allows you to determine flaws in either the cut of a gem or the Runes inscribed into the gem. The more you use the ability the more you can learn by the careful checking of your work.

Mana Infusion: Gives you a controlled method of infusing Gems, Runes, or Rune Inscribed Gems with Mana.

Gem Recipes: Pearl, Square, Octagon, Baguette, Oval, Pear

Inscription Recipes: Lesser Amplify Attribute, Minor

Amplify Attribute, Standard Amplify Attribute, Essence Transfer, Essence Storage, Mana Transfer, Mana Storage

All in all, I'd progressed pretty decently on my ability to inscribe gems, a lot of that thanks to the examples I'd pulled from the gem Merlin had given me, but my studies had broadened my understanding a fair bit as well.

I pulled out several chunks of Fluorite and the rest of my tools and supplies. I'd found a book that covered specific gem cuts and alteration of other cuts that could be used to slightly change or affect how best to increase certain attributes. For instance, a pearl cut favored increasing Concentration, however if you did a Trillion cut it would get you the same Concentration attribute gains, but with Intellect as well.

Starting off slow, I worked on the shape, one I hadn't tried before until I got the basic rough look. Then taking my grinding wheel I flipped it on and began to put the edges into place. It was a time consuming and painstaking process, but I enjoyed it. With each little strike some of the fluorite came away until I'd done it. I felt the system acknowledge my success by adding a new type of cut into my recipes, the Trillion cut.

I must have been close to leveling up my profession as well because I felt a rush of essence as I passed to level 15 Gem Inscriptionist. The next step was to do the cut on a proper gem that would be useful to either sell or find a place on my gear. Concentration worked best when done in Malachite, or at least that is what my book on Gem Inscriptionist claimed. The way it presented the information throughout the book made me wonder how much of it was personal preference of the author, and how much was accepted fact.

It took longer and more pieces than I cared to admit before I got a passable gem. Malachite was a softer gem than many I'd worked with before, and getting the facets right took a skilled hand. But on my sixth try, I had a gem that ranked above poor quality.

Malachite Gem
    Gem Cut: Trillion
    Durability: 10/10
    Quality: Fair
    Weight: 7 Carats

Now I had to work on getting the Inscription I wanted onto the surface. Taking my tools, each one magically enhanced to make carving into the gem easier but also at the same time trickier, I got to work. A hair too much pressure would destroy the entire facet or ruin the entire gem altogether if I wasn't careful.

With practiced patience I went to work, one strike at a time, while also infusing the gem with mana, pressing my intent into the inscription. I began with a reinforcing inscription, which I got off without a hitch. Then I progressed to adding a Standard Amplify Concentration

Inscription, excited to see if it would increase Intellect as adequately as the book had suggested.

I made a mistake on the final stroke, my excitement getting the better of me, and I had to start again with cutting a new piece of malachite. It wasn't that I couldn't just do the rest on another facet, but I wanted to have the most perfect gem I could get to see the max potential that it had. Spending the time to make three more malachite trillion cuts, I went back to the task of trying to Inscribe them properly.

It wasn't until the second to last one, when I finally completed the gem without any mistakes that my semi-trained eye could see. Going over it with Quality Check once more, I determined this was likely the best gem I'd ever crafted and inscribed.

Reinforced Malachite Gem

Inscription: Standard Amplify Concentration (Bonus Intellect)

Reinforced

Gem Cut: Trillion

Durability: 20/20

Quality: Well-Crafted

Weight: 6 Carats

It had worked! Just using the Standard Amplify Concentration Inscription but with the right combination of cut and gem, had added additional benefits to the attribute gains! I could hardly contain my excitement as I fished out more gems, ready to try different combinations and gem cuts.

———

I continued working on my profession but let my mind wander to other topics. The one that kept coming back to me and pestering me to no end, was how I could use my wealth to better society or at least my own life. My mother and siblings still lived in a farmhouse, when I could afford to buy them a small town. Unfortunately, I knew my mother well enough that she'd never accept living some-place fancy and she truly enjoyed her life, farm and all.

I'd have to hire some guards at least to work in a full time capacity in order to watch over them. Taking a break from my work I made a note to hire some guards soon.

What were the chances that the other Houses would join this war? Was there a way I could help to push them out of such a choice? Surely the King being involved would be a pretty big incentive to not join with House Blalor, but what of House Athesh? They are Blalor's neighbors and, according to Alayna, had provided House Blalor with mercenaries pretty consistently, which in turn grew their economy to the point where it depended on House Blalor considerably.

But what could I do to dissuade them? Maybe I could talk with Regina about who is able to buy our goods and secrets. If we gave preferable treatment to those willing to stay out of the conflict, it just might be enough to make a difference if they were on the edge of whether to join or not. Did my discoveries really have enough weight to accomplish such a feat? I really didn't know if I were being honest with myself, but I'd be willing to try it.

Then a clever thought hit me. What if I hired someone to do this type of thinking for me? Someone that could lobby and use my ideas to dissuade others from joining the war. Without directly being involved, I could fund my desire to avoid war, while still holding true to my oath. It wouldn't be like I'd be outright opposing the war itself, just others from joining. What was more, what if I set up someone or an organization, to start preparing people for the evil that was coming?

A council meant to help hold the balance together and prepare the nations of all kinds to be ready. My mind raced with thoughts of who would be up to such a task, but I came up short. Whoever I needed to lead such an endeavor wasn't something I knew yet, but perhaps Regina knew someone.

Yes, I would make a change to this world outside the violence I was capable of doing, instead focusing on fostering change and preparation.

With that decided, my mind turned to my own path in growing stronger. Very briefly I considered Tim's offer to join House Attra as a way to get stronger, but the consequences of such an act wasn't something I could live with, so I dismissed it. How would I grow significantly stronger when I was called into the service of House Variyn? I needed to find a way to continue to gain significant essence while still holding to my oaths.

And then there was getting to the Isle of Avalon. Perhaps Merlin could portal me over and help me grab the sword? That would surely lessen my burdens and he had helped Ismene in a similar way. I thought back to the last time we spoke, and I felt like he was going through something I couldn't quite understand. A trouble that might prevent him from assisting me perhaps, but it wouldn't hurt to check with him regardless. I added it to my growing list of tasks to complete.

If we would truly be attacking in the heart of House Blalor using special skyships to gain an advantage, it might give us an opportunity to clear a large number of monsters, and that kind of task would fall to those like me and Zander. That would be one way to gain essence, but I was purposely avoiding the best source of essence during a war. The killing of other *Awakened* and soldiers.

Would it be right to take a life just to grow stronger, but also save more lives? It was a path I wasn't sure I was capable of walking down, but I needed to consider all angles if I were going to find a way to save everyone. But how did you measure one life against another? If I killed a thousand to save a hundred thousand, would that be justifiable? The very thought left me sick to my stomach, and I was forced to consider other options.

Dungeon runs while in the service of House Variyn might be possible. Surely, they want their Awakened soldiers to be as strong as possible, then might that mean we'd be allowed to take a few days off every week to do dungeons and grow stronger?

There was another way I could grow stronger, a way I'd just gotten a little bit of essence from that was clearly slower, but it was something. If I focused on my profession and just general studies, then I might be able to gain enough to level at least once. Alayna had told me that she'd progressed admirably from study alone, though she was discovering grand secrets whereas I'd just be learning something new to me. Did that matter, I wondered or was learning just learning and it generated essence equally? Possibly a question for Kora, she seemed to know a fair bit about essence, though she dodged my questions when trying to pry more specific information from her on the subject.

I decided it would be worth talking to Kora before heading out to dinner and see what information I could pry from her. After leaving my study I went to my sitting room where I found Kora, reading the same book I'd left with her the night before. She was near the end of the book, and I didn't want to disturb her reading. I understood the joys of reading a good book, however, when I entered, she looked up and set the book aside.

"Kora, can I ask you a question and have you give me a straightforward answer?" I asked, trying to be as direct as possible.

"Perhaps," Kora said, a sly smile on her porcelain white face. How a clearly metal substance moved well enough to display emotions made me beyond curious, but I needed to stay focused if I was going to get anything out of her.

"It's about essence gains for studying," I said, watching her for any reaction, but she gave none. "You seem to know more about essence than anyone I've ever talked to, and I was wondering if you could tell me. Does the type of study affect the gains you get when studying? For instance, can I study about shoes and gain the same essence as if I were studying or learning about advanced mana rune crafting?"

Kora tilted her head to the side and looked at me as if I had asked the dumbest of questions. "You gain essence when studying?" She asked, as if the concept were totally foreign to her.

"Stop playing with me, you had to have known this," I said, shaking my head at her games.

She smiled and shook her head. "Honestly, I didn't, but it makes sense. Latent essence is drawn to events, discovery being one of them. If I had to guess, it would depend on how the person doing the discovery felt about what was being learned or discovered. You see, the mind and the spirit realms aren't so far away. Essence, mana, thought, all reside well within the same realm of existence. Even basic matter can be adjusted with enough energy. Make sense?"

I wasn't sure she was saying anything really, but I nodded and did my best to piece it together. "So, if I think whatever I am learning is a great discovery it will attract a greater amount of essence?" I asked, trying to decide if I could adjust my way of thinking while studying to test the effects.

"To a certain extent," Kora said, tapping at her chin and pausing to consider. "You see, there is only so much latent essence around, so you can't get a considerable amount no matter what you study. Perhaps if you studied in an essence rich place like inside of a dungeon, then you'd see decent gains, but otherwise, I'd say the difference is so marginal as to be pointless. I also wouldn't do it while around me, because I pull in every available stray essence by design, and I won't be sharing."

This was news to me, and I wore a confused expression while I thought over what she'd said. She pulled in spare essence; did that mean she needed some to function or was she just using it to get stronger? I asked her as much and she laughed, something that sounded very forced, but I'd noticed she'd been trying to do more human centric emotions lately.

"I am constructed in a way that I can fuel my basic functions by Mana like most living creatures, however the essence and the compounding of it into levels, is required and uniquely beneficial to me as a prior dungeon," Kora said.

"So intent matters but so does the environment. Got it," I said. It was time for dinner with Alayna, so I bid farewell to Kora and thanked her for the conversation before heading out to meet Alayna.

CHAPTER 10
BUSINESS TO ATTEND

This dinner went better than our last and I woke the next morning feeling refreshed and revitalized. A few steps out of my suite however, I encountered Regina, her small form as fierce looking as ever.

"You've been avoiding me!" She said, her voice rising higher than I'd ever heard it before. "You are mine for the next few days, come, come along."

Before I could tell her a yes or no, I found myself being forcefully dragged along towards her office. It was easy for me to forget that all the work we'd been working on had essentially become her entire life. That could be clearly seen now by the state of her lab and her impatience.

"I haven't been avoiding you per se," I said, attempting and failing to wrest my hand free from her. She had a surprisingly firm grip when she wanted to.

Her lab had grown by four times its original size, she'd likely been knocking down walls and taking more space for herself over the last month. I didn't mind, with the coin she kept delivering I would let her turn this entire place into her lab. We weren't alone inside, she had a dozen other gnomes and even a few Runeforged inside, working away. The Runeforged moved heavy equipment and stood close to the gnomes, likely ready to follow out any orders given to them.

"I'm going to need twenty to thirty Runeforged in about a month," I said, an idea beginning to form in my mind, but I would need to speak with Kora first and see if she'd be willing.

"A small expense with our current platinum influx," Regina said over her shoulder. She stopped us in front of a small area that had been converted into a little bar and seating area. "Let's have breakfast while you catch me up on your life."

We had bacon, eggs, potatoes, and a side of kelt fruit. It was prepared, oddly enough, by a Runeforged. I watched it work, stripped of its armor and wearing an apron to protect it from grease splatter.

"Do we perhaps have too many Runeforged already?" I asked, motioning to the cooking one and the assistant Runeforged.

"Nonsense, I've done them a service," Regina said smiling. "Our new patents have allowed them to upgrade their design, so I bought out most of their old stock. These are strong and sturdy models, but they aren't as well made or able to grow as the newest models. Got them for a good price too, all two hundred and forty-three of them."

"Two hundred and forty-three!" I said, dropping a piece of fruit from my mouth. "We have a small army."

"And those inspectors better remember that. The Lord Variyn, your liege, keeps having them poke around looking for violations of one sort or another," Regina laughed. "I bet if you weren't a lord they'd have just taken the land back already. But I'm prepared to defend this little plot of land until it becomes necessary to relocate."

"You think it'll come to that?" I asked, I hadn't considered that we should move our business elsewhere. "Sure, there are benefits to being in a major city, but what more do you expect to learn or discover beyond what we've already done?"

"We've already made several improvements to our initial design and discovered a few potential explosive reactions that we've been keeping to ourselves, until I had a chance to go over them with you. This branch of research is new and exciting, essence transfer is the way of the future," Regina said, then frowning she added. "Let's not talk business now. Tell me of your travels and let's eat our fill."

So, we did just that. I told her what I felt she needed to know, without going too far into the rabbit hole of my struggle against the Chaos and what I felt was an end to the world if we didn't unite. I brushed against each topic, but she was bright, and I think she worked the rest out.

"Heavy weights resting on such young shoulders," Regina said, shaking her head knowingly. "And how is your profession progressing?"

I relayed all the discoveries I'd made and my most recent successes without filtering anything out. I was proud with how far I'd come and wanted to see if she felt I'd been progressing well. She nodded along in all the right places and when I finished, she smiled.

"You are progressing at a decent rate, but I do wish you'd spend more time studying and less time swinging that sword of yours about," Regina said, clearing something from her teeth as she did so. "You'd be a fairly bright assistant if you'd let me really train you. I dare say, it would be nice to have you on the forefront of learning about the discoveries that are making us such a fortune."

"Unfortunately, I have oaths and responsibilities to see to," I said, shaking my head at her silly suggestion, considering she knew what was required of me.

"You should see about being released from your titles as protector of the realm and give up vassalship of Blackridge Keep. You could be such a force for good if you weren't tied up with the nobles," Regina said the last bit as she finished her breakfast and pushed her plate aside.

"I can't just give up on it all," I said shaking my head. "I wouldn't even know how to if I wanted to."

"I've seen it happen plenty of times, mostly due to being disgraced and being stripped of your titles, but there have been plenty who have asked and been granted a release from their vows and oaths to pursue other endeavors. With how long-lived we can be, you didn't think you'd always be tied to House Variyn, did you?"

I didn't want to say it, but I did, actually. I assumed I'd

build up Blackridge Keep into a place everyone would want to live close to, prosperous and mighty. That being a Lord made it easier to see myself with Alayna, who I knew wouldn't give up her station anytime soon, which made things a bit easier. There were a lot of people thinking how best my life should progress, but what of my own path. For now, I would stick to what I'd decided and when opportunity arose, I would reexamine my path.

"I don't think that is the right path for me right now," I said, settling on the best way to communicate my feelings and coming up short.

"You need to think in broader strokes," Regina said, sipping at her drink now. "With the funds we've got, my House has already expanded its borders twice. You could purchase the land of Blackridge Keep and establish your own House from the King or perhaps if you could get in good favor with Queen Elsena, she'd grant you land rights for a good price. You have the world open to you, do not think that following a simple House Lord is your only option."

I felt the heat of anger rising in my chest and I pushed it down. Everyone had an opinion on how I should live my life. I would do what I thought was best and everyone else be damned. I was getting so sick and tired of feeling like things were out of my control. Regina's claim that it wasn't so and that I could just get out of it all, enraged me in a way I didn't quite understand.

"I'll consider all my options," I finally said after letting my anger cool. I doubt I was as subtle as I attempted to be, because Regina just shook her head at me, but she seemed to have decided not to press the issue.

"I have a few requests, ways that I think I might be able to make a difference," I said calmly, my anger had subsided, and I was more in control of my emotions now. It felt silly getting angry like that but for whatever reason I was having trouble controlling it.

"Do tell," Regina said, standing and motioning me over to a pair of comfortable looking red plush chairs with polished carved wood frames.

I stood, pushing what was left of my plate away and taking my drink with me. It was a chilled fruit drink that sent ripples of sensation through my body as I sipped it.

I started with my idea of lobbying against the war or at least others joining and then moved on to the idea of hiring someone who could help advise me on how best to spend my wealth, while making the most impact on those around me. She hadn't spoken yet, but I could tell by her expression that she was a fan of the idea.

"Always surround yourself with the brightest stars you can; my father used to say before he died. You are wise to seek out someone to help advise you on matters such as these and perhaps they will have better luck than I have, doing exactly that," Regina said, a coy smile spreading across her lips.

"So, you know of someone?" I asked, ignoring her dig at me.

"I would suggest a few people, but it will take some time to gather a council together for you. I know of a bright politically minded cousin of mine, but we will want someone local as well and perhaps a master of secrets to help spread your agenda. Allow me to champion this for you and next time we meet I will have a council together to assist you in whatever you wish," Regina said, nodding her head as she stared up at the ceiling, likely going through all the individuals she felt would be fit for the roles.

I supposed a council made more sense than a single person, but a part of me felt uncertain about forming a secret council to undermine the war. It felt very much like something Tim and his cronies had done or perhaps were still doing. But that wouldn't be the council's only task, I would need much assistance as my wealth grew and my time being stretched tight.

"Allow me to show you some of the advancements my team has made," Regina said, standing suddenly and motioning that I follow her over to a worktable. She handed me a leather armband, it looked much different than the one I had to gather essence, but I knew it for what it was before Inspecting it.

It was made of black leather, with two straps to hold it in place on your arm. The shiny black leather was debossed with a symbol of a griffin done in a traditional, wings up and claws out, position that I'd used on the banners at Blackridge Keep. Had I shown her my banners or even told her? I must have or someone else informed her.

That made me think of Ares suddenly. I'd reached out several times since arriving, but she hadn't been in range each time. Again, I reached as far as my mind would span and called out for her, worry pulsing through my thoughts in waves, but again no answer came. Just another thing to worry about. Where could she be?

Regina cleared her throat and called my attention back to the leather band. "Have you Inspected it to see the changes?" She asked, obviously eager for me to do so.

"I'll take a look now," I said, smiling at her. I Inspected the band and nearly dropped it from surprise.

Masterwork Tri-Essence Enhancing Band

3 Gem Slots: 3x Masterwork Diamonds of Essence Pulling.

Masterwork Diamond of Essence Pulling: This gem has been enhanced to allow the collection and storage of essence. (45,000 Capacity with a 10% Pull each.)

Durability: *450/450*

Rarity: *Crafted*

Weight: *16 Grams*

Item Level: 50, Level Required to Use: 1, Crafted by: Dinky Flizzerbag

"Dinky is one of the finest crafters in my House and he's used my latest research into branching essence flows to three times so far. This is a prototype, but I hear he is working on additional branches to test the limit of how many a single band can hold. Already this is a vast improvement to the ones I've prepared to bring to market.

I've got several hundred apprentices working on some 'Fair' crafted ones that contain a single gem that will hold 25,000 consistently, far more than I thought would be possible at the crafting levels of those we've got working on them," Regina said, proudly.

"Regina," I said smiling as I took off my own essence band and handed it over. "This is remarkable." I put on the new prototype, amazed at the capacity and pull capability. If everyone could pull 30% more essence, what would happen when we scooped up all the essence, leaving none to waste? The future was going to be an amazing place.

"So, you agree with my decision to keep the creation and patents in house for the Essence Bands? It wasn't something we'd spent the time discussing, but we've made Gilfoy richer than they've made us, so I figured we ought to corner the market in the next logical step to our patent. I've used our original patent to account for additional adjustments, so you won't have to sign again, but I would like you to attend a monthly meeting with our company."

"Our company?" I asked, raising an eyebrow.

"Yes, I've formed a small company under the name, Black Griffin Supplies, I thought it was appropriate considering what I've heard about you and your griffin, Ismene even told me you used the symbol for your banner at Blackridge Keep. We needed an official entity to begin sales and having you at the head will cut tax and costs by a fair bit, you being so unwilling to give up your noble title as you are. Will you be willing to meet with the company staff once per month?" Regina asked, she looked doubtfully at me as if knowing I wouldn't like the idea.

But truthfully, I didn't mind, I just didn't think it would be possible considering what my future held.

"With the war coming so soon I doubt I'll be able to pull myself away, but I will try my best and I'd like written reports sent to me regarding the use of my funds, the company's progress, and anything else you deem necessary that I must know. With Ares, assuming I can find where she went off to, at my side I should be able to leave the frontline and be back without missing too much, so I might be able to attend a meeting here and there. When was the first one meant to be?" I asked, seeing a devious look in her eyes.

"Today," she said, smiling wide. "I would suggest you clean up a bit, your hair is a mess, and I will gather the company in the main hall so that you can speak a few words to them."

Suddenly I didn't like the idea of meeting with a mass of people if it meant I was expected to speak to them. What would I say that wouldn't just sound foolish and stupid? But I did as Regina requested, disappearing back into my room and doing my best to tame my ever-growing locks of hair. My hair had grown over my ears and the curls were so difficult to get under control, I decided that right after this meeting I'd go find someone to cut it for me.

With enough water I got it all to stay back but the curls still stuck up at odd angles. I changed out of my armor for once, and put on a nice set of brown slacks, polished leather boots, a loose white tunic with a tight black vest over it. They were clothes I didn't remember buying but had been placed in my room. To my surprise I recognized the Arcane Knight's symbol over the heart and on the other side, the symbol of Blackridge Keep and now Black Griffin Supplies, a black griffin reared up as if ready for battle.

Kora watched me dress, but I didn't mind. She was very curious but her interests were purely academic and, despite the attention she gave Fred, I'd seen no physical type of attraction from her. Not that she wasn't beautiful in her own way, I thought as I watched her begin to change as well. She normally wore the same simple armor and a cloak that was a size or two too big for her smaller frame, but she'd stripped all that off and stood before me in her lithe porcelain white form with the barest bits of blue rune work able to be seen on the surface.

Whatever she had done when altering her form, I was suddenly amazed at the details she'd included, giving herself all the right curves. There was a simplicity to her design, each plate overlapping in a way that almost made it seem more skin-like than metal plates. Even her face and neck were covered in a way to hide her structure within. She was staring at me while I examined her body and suddenly it got weird, so I looked away. Behind me I sensed her moving and assumed she must be dressing finally, so it startled me when she placed a hand on my shoulder.

"You look nice," she said, her mouth right behind my head. "Do you think that I look nice?"

I turned to see that she had dressed, amazingly quick too. She wore a simple black silk shirt and tan pants, with a cloak that didn't obscure her as much. On the chest of the shirt was the griffin symbol, but otherwise it was without decoration.

"You do look nice," I said, taking a step back as she'd gotten close enough that it was hard to really look at her. "Kora, can I ask you a question?"

"Please do," Kora said, inclining her head to the side just an inch as she'd been doing lately.

"I want you to lead a few squads of Runeforged into battle with me, would you feel okay doing that?" I asked. I was curious what she'd say in response. She'd been ready to follow me so far without much question, but what would she think about Runeforged being used to fight a war of 'meat bags' as she so affectionately called us.

"I'd be honored to teach them," Kora said, she inclined her head as if standing proud at the idea.

"And you have no reservations?" I asked.

"Only that I get to pick the ones that come with me, and I be allowed to make any modifications on their structure that I wish," Kora said, her words coming out quick as if she'd practiced them before.

"You've been wanting to work with them for a while now, haven't you?" I asked, smiling.

"Yes, I have," Kora admitted, smiling back.

"Very well. Pick thirty to work with and get them ready for war. It won't hurt to have a few extra ready to go if we need them," I said. I'd have to tell Regina that Kora would begin working with them immediately and not in a month as I'd first told her.

Kora followed beside me as I moved to the door and left my suite. Apparently, she'd be coming with me today. At the end of the hallway Regina waited for me, dressed in her normal lavish clothing, despite the fact that I knew she'd been working just minutes before. Regina was a fancy lady, always dressed to go have drinks or explode something in a lab at a moment's notice.

"She is coming with?" Regina asked, eying the Rune-forged greedily. "Perhaps I can get a team to look her over and take a few parts off to see her inner workings?"

"I'd prefer my inner workings stay where they are, thank you," Kora said, smiling down at the gnome.

"You are such a marvelous piece of technology, it would be a shame if you perished at young Caldor's side before we had a chance to fully understand you," Regina shot back, a smile plastered on her face as well. Neither Kora nor Regina seemed genuine in their joy, but I stayed clear, letting Kora make her own decisions.

"Many of my secrets are meant for my kind only," Kora said, with a touch of reprimand in her voice that made me look at her twice. Seems like Kora wasn't going to take Regina's prodding laying down.

"I will discover your secrets," Regina said, with a

haughty attitude as she stepped a bit quicker, taking the lead.

"She's nothing if not persistent," I whispered to Kora.

"She worries me," Kora said, her voice lowered as well but not enough that Regina wouldn't be able to hear. "Are you sure we can trust her?"

"She's given me all the reasons in the world to trust her and none not to," I said, letting my own voice rise enough that it would be heard by her as well.

I meant what I said. Regina had been an amazing gift of chance that had set my life into a direction that I never thought I might reach, financial freedom.

We'd gone outside the main building and headed over to a western section that had several large buildings connected by narrow passages. We entered through large oak doors into a room filled with worktables. Lining the outer perimeter, were Runeforged in full armor and the tables were filled with a mix of gnomes, humans, a few elves, a beastkin cat, and even a delvish male towards the front. When she'd said a hundred workers, I had thought there would be a hundred workers, not nearly three hundred.

There seemed to be an assembly line of sorts going on and not just leather bands were being made. The worktables were small enough that as one person finished a specific task, they passed it over to the next person who did whatever the next step was and at the end was a larger worktable where the true craftsmen were at work. I could feel the surge of mana and workings of magic as they did the final step that resulted in the creation of a magical attribute infused item, or in this case an armband that could channel essence.

"We are exploring the creation of many other items, but nothing you should worry about just yet," Regina said, as she noticed my gaze. I'd been looking at some leather armor with an insane amount of runic stitching in it, a light blue standing out against the deep black leather. There were a number of craftsmen with longer desks, *Awakened* I assumed, that worked on a variety of other items, including some weapons.

I stepped up to one such craftsman who was examining his work on a sword that looked completely finished to me, every part of it polished and shining.

"Do you mind?" I asked, holding out my hand.

"Oh dear, you startled me. Yes, please have a look," the female elf said. She had strikingly dark purple hair and gray eyes that spoke of many years seen, yet her features remained young and vibrant. She gently handed over the sword, it was a long sword with a 'V' guard and black leather grip, as well as a triangular floral design for a pommel. The blade looked ordinary to the unsuspecting eye, but all over its surface and even in the leather were the barest of lines carved into it. It drew me towards it in a way I had never experienced before.

I held off Inspecting it, instead feeling with my senses what the blade told me. It had a force to it, like a funnel of energy that I couldn't remember feeling from other swords or any other weapons I'd encountered. As I ran my hand up the blade, I could almost feel it wanting me to infuse it with power.

"It's a blade very few can take advantage of," the elf said. I handed it back to her and she set it aside. "My name is Estranel and I'm very happy to have been chosen to receive the essence infusion skill. It has changed my entire perspective on crafting weapons. I'm a Blade Smith and before I joined up with Black Griffin Supplies, I'd have said I was a Master of crafting and enchanting blades, but now I feel like a child of sixty years of age once more."

"I'm glad to have you," I said, reaching out to touch the blade again and Inspecting it. She'd intrigued me enough that I had to see what was so special about the sword.

"I built this sword with you in mind, a wielder of essence, a user of both Strength and Intellect. It is the first of its kind and I'd be honored if you would accept it as a gift," Estranel said, bowing her head slightly.

Fulgar'vi'lectus

5 Essence Pathways (0/5 Charged)

Essence Pathways: Channels have been cut into the very fabric of the blade to allow for essence to be more artfully charged into the blade. For each Charge that is completed, the weapon will increase its effective Base Damage and Attributes. Charges will last ten minutes and cost 100/200/400/800/1,600 respectively while increasing at a rate of 25%/50%/75%/100%/125%.

35-53 Base Damage

+20 Strength

+20 Intellect

Durability: 200/200

Rarity: Masterwork Crafted

Weight: 1.7 pounds

Item level: 40, Level Required to use: 20 (Soulbound on use), Crafted By: Estranel Elladent'ah

I picked the blade back up and understood why it wouldn't be a blade just anyone could use, as my ability to infuse essence was still a rare skill. I infused the blade with a hundred essence and watched as the base damage and the attribute values rose by a few points. The runes covering the surface began to glow slightly in a greenish-blue light. I felt something else while channeling the blade, I could take the power back or release it. I chose to funnel it back and was surprised when almost all of the essence returned, only losing a dozen or so in the process.

"It's magnificent," I said, in awe of the sword and its potential. "Are you sure that you want me to have this sword? Fulgar'vi'lectus is an interesting name for a sword. I've never owned such a blade before."

"It is named after its potential to hold energy and grant the wielder the attributes of Strength and Intellect. You will find I stray from normally accepted naming conventions that list the craftsman quality and directly what the item is meant to be. Any fool can see that this is a sword and figure out what it is meant to do. But only someone learned in the ancient tongues of our ancestors will recognize what the name of your sword means. And yes, it was crafted for you, and I wish you to go test its potential. If only you could report back to me how she fares in battle, I will be appeased."

"I can do that," I said, nodding to her but not taking my eyes off the blade. The runes had stopped glowing but the pulling, and need to be used, still remained. Carefully I reached down and picked up an equally basic looking scabbard and slid the blade into it. I smiled at Estranel and nodded slightly to her in respect before letting the blade slip into my storage ring.

"That's enough sucking up to the boss," Regina said, ending the moment and getting my full attention back. "Mr. Miles would like to say a few words and then he has much work to be done, so enjoy the break and try not to let it affect your productivity!"

Regina was a taskmaster I realized, her words curt and all business. She required nothing less than perfection and I was just now realizing I'd been seeing her easy side.

She had gathered everyone's attention and now it was my turn to speak to them. My mind went a bit foggy but I started speaking, saying how glad I was to have so many hard working individuals here and then going into a bit about how I wanted to make a difference in the world. Looking back, it's all a bit of a blur, but Kora told me I sounded inspirational while Regina said my words were sufficient.

CHAPTER 11
ARES

Ares surprised me that evening, coming into range while the sun crested the horizon. The sky was a mix of purples and reds, and I strained my eyes outside in the courtyard looking for her descent. Long before I saw her, I could feel her approach. She sent feelings of joy, excitement, and a tiny bit of resentment towards me as she came. I expected a bit of the last, as I'd taken off for two weeks without her, but she'd been gone a few days without me, so I felt we'd basically evened things out.

She appeared as a speck in the sky, but swiftly grew to a recognizable shape and then with the swiftness that only a griffin could achieve, she gracefully landed before me. I rushed forward, arms out and ready to embrace her. She bashed me to the side with her head, the force of which sent me stumbling. I righted myself and looked her in the eyes, there was more hurt there than she was allowing me to feel and suddenly I felt horrible.

"I'm sorry," I said, reaching out with my hands until she approached. Memory after memory, I funneled to her everything I'd done while I was gone, so that she knew I'd been okay. I also really laid into the hot and not comfortable feelings of the Southlands to hopefully sway her feelings towards wanting to have been with me. It helped a little, and though she was obviously still upset with me, she allowed me to come close and hug her.

"I've missed you dearly, Ares," I said into her soft feathers. She sent me back emotions that communicated much the same. Then came something I hadn't yet experienced with her, save for once or twice with extreme focus, her memories—sights, smells, and more—funneling into my head. She was attempting to tell me where she'd been as well.

I saw a coast in a strange land that I'd never seen before. She was with someone, but I couldn't make sense of the emotions and memories she tried to show me, feeling only that it was someone she trusted greatly. Whoever it was, cared for her, but was in trouble of their own. I sensed worry but no form to it that would make any sense in words. Then as fast as they came, they shifted, and I was bombarded by memories of her hunting.

At some point she'd encountered a Chaos monster, but she'd ended it with the swiftness of a true predator. Good girl Ares, I sent the thoughts to her, and it interrupted the flow of thought. Suddenly I was back in the courtyard, my arms around her neck and her nuzzling into mine.

"Is now a bad time to begin training some Rune-forged?" Kora's voice spoke from behind me, startling both Ares and me. Ares squawked at her direction, but I turned to regard her.

She'd donned her leather armor once more and had a dark red wooden staff in one hand. Her cloak was a different one than the two I'd seen her wear previously. This one was more a sleeveless coat than a cloak, her white and metallic arms showing off her Runeforged form, but it still had a hood, which she kept up. The center was buttoned up, only showing a bit of her leather armor, and the bottom flurried out, flapping lazily in the evening breeze.

"I don't see why not," I said, smiling. "How will you go about it?" I was genuinely curious as I'd never had any experience training troops and would likely have to wait to see what training House Variyn provided.

"I thought I'd start by sparring with a few until I've picked out which ones that I'd like to be squad leaders. Then I will attempt to make alterations to their runescript and make them more like me. They are mostly elemental spirits, with a few using the captured souls of dire beasts, but if I help their true selves emerge a bit, I believe it will allow them to manifest abilities, making them magnitudes more effective in combat," Kora said it so plainly that I had to blink away my shock for a few seconds.

"You can make changes like that?" I asked, flabbergasted. I knew that she'd done that to herself, but that made sense in a very dungeon core kind of way. Whether she might be able to alter other Runeforged, was something altogether different. I wasn't opposed to the idea, but it was definitely something I wanted to see.

At first, I'd planned on mounting Ares after sensing her, and I was going to fly to check on Merlin to see if he'd be willing to make a quick—and hopefully safe—trip to Avalon to get the Sword of the Ordu with me, but that could wait for a few hours while I watched this unfold.

"I believe so," Kora said. "Do I have your permission to proceed?"

"Only if I can watch," I requested, not thinking that would be an issue at all. Kora seemed to consider it for longer than I believed was necessary, before shrugging.

"Only you and the bird, the rest of the meat bags should withdraw," Kora said, nodding her head along with her words.

The casual use of meat bags always made me chuckle, but the way she said it this time sounded far less 'funny affectionate' and more laced with hostile sarcasm.

"That works for me," I said. "Give me a minute to clear the square, and let's move over to the east side so people coming and going won't see us."

I raced away finding Lance Terook and telling him to organize the staff and Clockstein House members to stay away from the eastern courtyard for a while.

"Lance, just the man I was looking for!" I said, shouting the words from down a corridor. The severe looking man with his tightly buttoned black coat that rose to just halfway up his neck and ended at his waist, looked surprised to see me, but marched over hurriedly at once. Papers appeared in his hands, and he began to hand them over.

"I've spoken with Regina and here is the short list of candidates along with several more items that I need you to look over. I fear Regina has grown tired of my presence, but as I've had no one else around in authority I needed to consult her about several important factors, including an inspection request by several nobles of higher station than you. It is not required that we allow them entry but I bel-"

"Not now, Lance," I said, patting him on the shoulder. "I'd like all staff and, well, anyone for that matter, to be cleared from the eastern courtyard and prevented entry for several hours. I need privacy. Anything else you need me to hear, please submit it to me in writing and I will be sure to come see you before I leave tonight."

"You are leaving again?" Lance said, his cool exterior seeming to crack a little as one of his eyes twitched.

"Yes, I have much to do before I get called to service and spend several months at war. You have my full faith, Lance, take the reins and let's see where things go," I said, giving him a thumbs up.

"Please my Lord, I'd prefer you call me Mister Terook, or at least Steward Terook, but I will see that your orders are followed. Thank you, my Lord," Lance said.

"Thank you, Lance," I said, turning to go. I didn't even realize that I'd completely ignored his request that I call him by his surname until I was well down the corridor, and by the time I turned back around, he was gone.

I reached Kora in the eastern courtyard, standing beside a fountain that I didn't recall being there, but I'd spent very little time on this end of the compound. She'd already gathered eight Runeforged and appeared to be talking to one in particular that I recognized, once I heard his voice. The normal monotone having been replaced by a gentle baritone. It was Ventus, he'd been a wind elemental before being bound to the Runeforged form.

"I am grateful for any assistance you can offer to bring me closer to what I was before," Ventus was saying, his movements much more animated than any of the other Runeforged. "Since you named me, I have connected with many memories of being free to call the might of the storms and I've yearned to feel them once more."

"I can grant you the ability to channel the storms, but you must swear loyalty to me and fight as a Squad leader in the army of my meat bag, Caldor Miles," Kora said. I couldn't tell if she realized I'd joined her, so I just stood a ways away listening to the very odd exchange.

"I am bound to follow Caldor Miles and Regina Clockstein," the voice shifted to the monotone suddenly, but after shaking his head several times he added, back in his normal baritone voice. "I wish to swear loyalty to you, if I am allowed."

"That is enough," Kora said, patting him on the arm in a very human way and turning to look at me. "Does he have permission to make such an allegiance?"

What in the heck was happening here? I trusted Kora, or at least I think I did, but why was she trying to get them all to swear loyalty to her? Surely it was enough that they were set into following mine and Regina's commands. But I did tell her I wanted her to train and lead them, so I guess I could give her a little leeway.

"And you swear not to rise up against me?" I asked, half joking, but kind of not at the same time.

"I swear that I or any that I release, will not rise up against you, Caldor Miles," Kora said, an odd grin on her face as she spoke. The level of expression she could achieve seemed to be increasing with each passing day.

"That's enough for me," I declared happily, trying not to read into the way she phrased her swearing of loyalty.

"Come closer Ventus and I will attempt to upgrade you," Kora said, reaching out her hand, she pressed it against his chest. There was a pile of armor nearby from where they'd all stripped down to nothing but the gray metal plates of their bodies.

I watched with fascinated curiosity as energy began to thrum down her hand and into Ventus. He bowed his head as she worked and I saw the lines of Inscription on his body shift and change, much as hers did. Then I saw his vast power, the presence that all Runeforged had, begin to diminish. His plates tinted towards white, but not nearly as white as Kora's, instead the edges were mostly white with the centers being much the same color gray as they'd been before.

His facial expressions, because he had one now, shifted from confusion to joy to anger. He rolled his neck and looked down at his hands, then around the square and towards me. There was a sense of curiosity as he looked at me, his eyes a white glow with sparks of yellow. They'd been blue before, but he was no longer the Runeforged I'd purchased, she'd changed so much about him.

His profile was thinner, but not nearly as thin as she was, and between some of the color adjusted plates I could see the same white-golden energy flowing just under the surface. This was different from Kora as well and I wondered what she'd done to him.

"You have been set free, but for a time you must continue your allegiance. Do you agree?" Kora asked, placing a hand on Ventus' shoulder.

"I do," Ventus said, his voice was the same baritone as it had been before, so at least that stayed the same. "I wish to fight and test my limits. I feel that this frame is weaker than it once was, and I worry that I'm no longer a proper guard."

"You've gained the ability to level up and progress, but that required I use much of your stored essence to make the transition. With raw strength you are still equivalent to one of theirs at the 25th level," Kora gestured at me as she spoke and I sat on the edge of the fountain, shaking my head.

Somehow, she'd just turned our base model Runeforged into an advanced version of the more expensive type of Runeforged. Hell, I was curious to see what he could do as well.

"Dress yourself and take up arms," Kora commanded. "I will test your battle capabilities."

The other Runeforged stood as still as statues during this entire exchange, not a single one of them moving or showing any interest.

Kora twirled her Bo-staff, a weapon that I didn't see holding up well against the sword that Ventus had just armed himself with, but I gave them room, walking to stand beside Ares who didn't seem even slightly interested in the actions of the metal creatures.

Ventus kept rolling his shoulders and looking at his hands as if he were still getting used to his body. Finally, after a solid minute of waiting for him to be ready, he squared off against Kora. She'd been waiting patiently, her staff held in her left hand and pressed against her back. With her free hand she waved Ventus forward.

He didn't wait any longer, shooting forward with intense speed. If I didn't have such high attributes, I doubted I'd be able to even follow what happened next, but as it were, I just barely made out the quick exchange. Ventus came in fast and low, sword out and ready to strike. Kora took a single step to the side and smashed her staff across his face, throwing him awkwardly in the direction of the strike.

Ventus wasn't fazed by the strike at all, regaining his balance and rushing back for another strike in the same second. Back and forth they went, Ventus was faster but Kora moved just enough each time to avoid his strikes. It was like a master facing off against his pupil. Kora had obviously found a way to channel her vast experience into an effective fighting style. She hadn't even tried to use a summoning or anything else, just dodging and striking when the opportunity presented itself.

After nearly three solid minutes of this, one side of her staff had begun to splinter from the powerful blows. But then something changed. Ventus began pulling his punches and yelling as he did so. At first, I thought perhaps he was being parried, but I squinted in the low light of the evening and still saw nothing. It became apparent seconds later what he was attempting to do, as a gust of wind slammed into Kora and threw her backwards.

As he channeled the power of wind, his form had flashed a golden color between the plates of his armor. He was a wind elemental, and he was using his elemental powers!

"Good," Kora said, smiling. But Ventus didn't stop, rushing forward he screamed again while punching in a very odd looking double fisted punch. The air flashed as lightning cracked around him and struck a surprised Kora.

I rushed forward then, grabbing hold of Ventus and with a surprising show of strength lifting him from the ground. "Stop!" I commanded, and he went still.

"I'm alright," Kora said, standing and rubbing the scorched section of her leather armor. "Good work Ventus." She added as I let him down to his feet.

He turned to me and tilted his head to regard me, but said nothing, his eyes flickering like the lights in a thunderstorm.

That wasn't creepy at all, I thought as Kora told Ventus to go stand with the others while she began talking with a new Runeforged. At first, I thought she'd be making changes to each of them, but instead she spoke with them all, named three of them and invited them all to return to their posts. She pulled Ventus aside and they shared a whispered conversation that didn't help the uneasiness I felt under his gaze.

With that bit of fun over, I went to find Lance and get the most boring part of having money over with, reports and meetings.

―――――――

The wind whipped through my hair and sent my cloak flapping behind me as Ares soared through the air. As I blinked against the fierce speed of a dive, I thought, and not for the first time, that I ought to get some goggles for riding to protect my eyes and make seeing easier. As if to punctuate the point, a bug flew right into my left eye as she leveled off above the forests below.

I recognized the trees below, we'd already made it half of the way to Creeshaw, my home. Or at least it *was* my home. With the funds that I had now and my two other residences, I could call any place home that I wished. But my mother and siblings were back at our orchard farm in Creeshaw and that is part of what made it home. I wondered suddenly, if Galt's instructor that he had chosen to help train the youngins had made it to town already. It had been a few days, but depending on the urgency of the person they might not have even left Variyn city yet.

Ares caught the scent of a monster suddenly, and she veered into the trees to pursue it. I was about to ask her kindly to call it off as I wanted to get home and see about speaking with Merlin, but then I felt it. Down below was more than one Chaos monster. My mind sharpened and I prepared myself to fight whatever it was we encountered below.

I could feel three of them, now that we neared and they knew we were coming, each of them seemed to disappear from Ares's senses at once and I was left blinking in confusion. She slammed into the ground, throwing up dirt and flapping her wings wildly right where they'd been moments before.

A flash of movement to my left and I turned in time to see a giant weasel, all brown except for black streaks running down its body starting from its eyes. Each eye had a crazed reddish glow to it that reminded me of my encounter with the boar. I didn't jump off of Ares at first, sending her a mental message that I'd cast from atop her until an opportunity presented itself for me to strike out. Ares acknowledged me but kept her focus on the big weasel. My Inspect failed to give me any information, as was common when dealing with Chaos monsters.

Instead, I held out my hand and cast Lightning Strike, my signature opening move. The flash of light and crack of the strike hit the giant weasel right atop its head, stunning it. In all, the weasel had twice the length and stood a full foot taller than Ares. If I were being honest, such a large monster would make a formidable ground mount if it could be tamed. I made a mental note to tell Ismene to tame one that hadn't been corrupted by Chaos.

The weasel lunged forward, but Ares was quicker. She flapped her mighty wings and slashed out with her claws, connecting with the weasel's face and causing it to scream out in pain. That is when the other two weasels appeared out of the forest like ghosts in the night. One bit hard on Ares's wing and I felt something snap, while the other headbutted me off Ares while clawing at her back.

Letting my body roll until I could transition into a kneeling position, I immediately readied an Arcane Missile and smashed all four missiles of arcane energy into the weasel on Ares's back. My Rank 2 Arcane Missile was paying off, each one hit with deadly force, throwing the weasel back and off her.

Ares was in an animalistic fight for her life, one wing tucked in tight and injured while two of the weasels slashed and bit at her. Despite her injury, she held her own and I took the time to get off my most powerful heal spell, Mending Touch, immediately followed by a Restoring Light, in an attempt to stop the spread of any Chaos corruption that might be transferred to Ares.

Then an idea hit me. What if I used Restoring Light on the weasels? It would heal them yes, but it could purge out Chaos corruption and possibly return them to a normal state. It wouldn't likely stop the attack, but perhaps it'd be worth trying.

Before I had a chance to test my theory, the five second cooldown stopped me from acting immediately. The third weasel appeared in front of me opening its mouth and black nasty bile filled the open space as it prepared to spit on me. I grabbed the edge of my cloak and pulled it over me just as the biggest nastiest Chaos loogie came hurtling toward me.

I felt it impact my cloak, but then something happened that I hadn't experienced since getting the cloak, it grew warm and suddenly it flashed with power. Without looking, I knew the nasty Chaos attack had been negated, but I also remembered that this effect could only be triggered once every ten minutes. Wasting no more time I slung the cloak aside, summoned the Shell Blade of the Sea Witch—I hadn't the time or focus to bind my newest sword yet—and pointed it at my target, releasing a Lightning Strike as I charged.

The iridescent colors played across the surface as I reared the blade back and focused on activating a combination of skills. First, light danced across the surface, then the glow of my condensed Stamina crackled over the blade, then finally the entire sparking light show launched off my blade toward my target. My combination attack of Light Blade, Power Strike, and Force Wave resulted in a hefty two hundred plus Stamina loss, but it was worth it.

The giant weasel reared back as blood poured down its face from the slice that I'd taken off its face. The left side's whiskers, part of an eye, and its ear had been sliced completely free of the face, revealing white bone, red blood, and a sticky looking black substance. Suddenly the weasel was atop me, it moved with speeds beyond tracking.

My shoulder screamed in pain as skinny sharp teeth pierced easily through my armor and into my flesh.

How this thing had gotten on me so fast I didn't know, but what I did know was that I was a match for it. With the full weight of the weasel on me I couldn't properly wield my sword, so I tossed it aside. A dagger fell into my grip from my storage ring, this thing was a lifesaver. I plunged the dagger into its side, but the weasel's hide proved to be a match for the length of my dagger. No matter how much I stabbed, it just continued biting and shaking its head while I clenched my teeth against the pain.

It wasn't even that this weasel was that much stronger than me, if it was at all, but it had several hundred pounds on me and was taking full advantage of it. Spells were out of the question, I couldn't focus my mind enough to get anything off, not even Lightning Strike if it weren't already on cooldown. So instead, I focused on my skills. Another second passed and my Power Strike came off cooldown.

Activating Swift Strike and Power Strike at once I plunged my dagger deep, so deep that it went all the way to my elbow. This attack missed the heart, as it didn't die instantly, but it got the giant weasel's attention. It released me to nuzzle at its wounded side and squeaked in pain. I rolled away in the moment it took to stand and check on itself, leaving a trail of blood as I went.

Ares was having a much better time of it I saw, checking on her for the briefest of moments. She'd taken one weasel down and battled beak versus tiny thin-toothed snout, while I felt she'd been injured further, my heals had helped to give her back the upper hand. I snapped my focus back to my opponent as it went low, likely preparing for another leap. Wasting no time, I threw myself to the side, just as it zipped past in a show of incredible speed.

I let loose another Lightning Strike, my mana finally cresting below a thousand. The sheer power of my Intellect based spell attacks left the weasel dazed, so I took the opportunity to rush forward, blade appearing in my grip as I went. The weasel raised its muscular arm to smack at my sword, its entire arm seeming to become reflective as if made of metal. I unsummoned my blade and resummoned it a moment later as I passed through the arm.

The resulting strike from his unblocked arm sent me flying, but before I'd been hit I had sunk my sword deep into the gut of the giant weasel. My back smashed hard against a tree, sending splinters out all around me as the force of it compacted a section of the trunk. But I wasn't just a farm boy any longer, it would take more than that to bring me out of a fight.

My bravado proved to be unnecessary. Looking up, I saw the guts of the weasel had been spread out before it. It was dead, it just hadn't realized it yet. Hot and steamy breaths escaped from the weasel, and it squeaked in my direction, cold black eyes blinking rapidly as what little life it had left drained from it.

I rushed over, my back aching a bit from the impact with the tree, but Ares had finished off her last opponent. Instead of going to help with the fight I began casting my heal spells on her, a choice I could tell she agreed with. When I was sure she had recovered enough I hit myself with a heal, the many dozen needle-like holes closing up and scarring over.

It was a pity I didn't get to try to purge out the Chaos corruption from one of them while they lived, but I still had a duty to do. Walking to the first one I cast Restoring Light and watched as the blackened corruption burnt up into a trail of smoke, dispersing all around us. Working on each of them until all signs of their corruption was gone, I spent some time gathering reagents like teeth, eyeballs, and livers. While doing so I was surprised to come upon a fully intact monster core.

I'd let Ismene and Kora fight over who got it, as I had no need for a core with only a mere five thousand essence. Sure, every essence helped, but I still had over a hundred thousand that I needed to distribute and hadn't due to the Prime Mana Shrine being destroyed. I knew that much essence was likely to get me to level 21, but no more than one or two additional attribute points as they continued to grow ever more expensive.

Either way, I put in the required essence to level and would check my map for the closest Mana Shrine. After cleansing the meat, Ares went to it, eating up a good portion of the remains. I was trusting the spell had leached away any toxins or corruption, otherwise the reagents I'd collected, and the meat Ares was eating wouldn't be sitting well with us soon. In a small bout of paranoia, I used my spell to cleanse Ares after she finished and cast it on the reagents I'd collected. I saw nothing like before, so we had probably been fine.

On our way again we made a small detour for me to visit a nearby Mana Shrine. I leveled to 21 and assigned all three points I got into my Constitution, bringing the base up to 43, then to my surprise I had enough essence to purchase 2 more attributes, raising Constitution up to 45, with plans to get it to 46 before leveling again. Paragon attributes like my Constitution, Intellect, and Core, were much cheaper to raise up than say Concentration, Endurance, and Strength. Looking at the math and focusing on seeing the tables that worked behind the scenes, I saw that I'd have paid double what I did for two attributes if I'd gone for Endurance instead of Constitution.

It was enough to make me think that once I'd passed this next threshold, I might need to focus on just bringing up my Paragon attributes as a way to further outstrip myself against my opponents. However, I hadn't been lucky enough to get Strength as one of my Paragon attributes, so that would leave my class out of balance. There had to be more ways to gain additional advantages. My father had done something to burst ahead of his peers, perhaps if I found him alive, he could give me some fatherly tips on the best ways to progress.

He must be a Paragon like me, or at least have two Paragon attributes, nothing else would make sense. Thoughts of my father had a dual effect on my mood, both angering me and bringing me a sense of excited hope. I squashed both feelings, mounted Ares and got ready to finish the trip to Merlin's pub and then possibly to the Isle of Avalon.

But as we flew, my mind wasn't on the Isle or the mission ahead, instead, I couldn't help but ponder whether or not it would be right to tell my mother and siblings what I'd learned about father. It wasn't as if I'd really learned anything hard and fast about whether he was still alive, it was more rumor and hope than anything right now. Perhaps Warrick would say differently, but I couldn't bear the thought of giving hope to my family only for it to be dashed months later when nothing came of it.

As we descended into Creeshaw I made a choice to keep the news to myself. I'd share with them only what they needed to know and only what I could prove.

CHAPTER 12
HOME

The evening had settled on the quaint town of Creeshaw and only the lights of a few businesses and the dozen or so street lamps lit it from above. After spending so much time in the city it really put Creeshaw's size into perspective. I counted maybe two dozen buildings, not counting the several dozen houses on the eastern side of town or the expansive Major's Manor.

From this height, even in the waning light, I could see miles of farmland mixed between the trees as well as orchards—which were far more common of a product that Creeshaw exported. I knew little about the workings of a small-town economy, but I had been learning due to my time in Blackridge Keep. It took a surprisingly large amount of food to keep a population of even a town the size of Creeshaw going.

We were lucky to have two fully functioning pubs, a

nicer dinner place, and even on occasion, a traveling food merchant with a cart that sold meat on a stick. I was sure that much of the meats used were of the monster variety. Adventurers could make a decent profit just providing towns with meat and other supplies that were difficult or rare, like specialty spices that grew mostly in dungeons.

The lights inside Merlin's pub shone brightly and a couple of adventurers leaned by the outside door. If I had to guess, they were both casters, one wearing billowing robes and the other with more of a bodysuit, but just as loose and flowing as the robes. The dark haired one, with the bodysuit-like robes, stumbled backwards in surprise as Ares landed right in front of the pub. I hopped off as both stared on with slack jaws.

Ares knew to go to the stables and await the golem that Merlin had affectionately called 'old rusty butt' for a thorough pet down. I pushed past the stunned adventurers and entered into the warmth of Merlin's pub. Music played in the corner, a single string instrument accompanied by the smooth baritone of a bard singing the ballad of some grand adventure or another. The fireplaces roared at full strength, filling the room with an abundance of light and heat. I felt my armor begin to adjust the temperature for me to keep my body at its optimal condition, I really loved some of the comfort enchantments you could find on the market.

I looked to the bar, thinking to find Merlin staring about the room as he had a tendency to do, but instead, a woman with curly black hair and sharp features stood in his place. Several barmaids walked among the room, filling drinks and taking orders. Very rarely had I seen Merlin's pub so busy.

I recognized a few people, Mayor Ghoft was in attendance at one of the larger tables with several business owners, including Mr. Fawlkner, the magic shop owner that had been thinking about moving his business. Joe Heddal sat with his wife and daughter at another table, a rare sight to see Mrs. Heddal out to eat someone else's cooking. I caught their eye and waved, Mr. Heddal recognized me immediately, but Mrs. Heddal squinted her eyes until her husband leaned over and a sudden look of recognition washed over her face.

I smiled but headed towards the bar to greet the unfamiliar lady doing Merlin's job.

She had a black gown, simple and straight with long sleeves that overlapped lace black gloves. A simple silver pendant hung in between her breasts, the tops of which were exposed due to the dangerously low-cut v of the neckline. She filled the space well, but her style was different enough from any I'd seen in the last few months that it caught my attention.

"Do you see something you like?" A velvety smooth voice spoke as if it were right in front of me. I looked up and saw the lady smiling. Had she said that? I was still a good fifteen feet away and despite looking around for someone else that might have spoken the words, I found only men at the tables beside me.

I closed the gap and regarded the woman, noticing

that she had purple eyes, a common enough color in these parts. But she'd done something I'd only seen a few noble-women do, adding some very heavy purple and black makeup around her eyes, making them stand out against her pale skin. And she was pale, so much so that I thought perhaps she might share a relation of some kind with Zander.

"Was that you?" I asked, thumbing behind me to where I stood when I heard the voice.

The same voice as before, spoke, this time out of her mouth. "Just a little trick I picked up," she said, setting down the glass she polished and pouring a frothy liquid into it. "Care for a drink?"

I looked pointedly at the glass but didn't drink. "Where's Merlin?" I asked, keeping my tone inquisitive, despite my growing sense of worry from this mysterious lady's appearance.

"Merlin has taken an extended trip to explore his heritage, my name's Mab and I'll be running his establish-ment during his absence," Mab said, her expression some-where between a smile and a sneer.

I took the drink she offered and downed it in a single long pull. "Do you know when he'll be back?" I asked, after catching my breath and putting the glass aside.

"Shouldn't be more than a hundred or two years, really depends on him," Mab said, tapping her lower lip with her index finger. She had a wild look in her eyes as she stared into the distance. It was like she could see something that I could not.

"How did you know Merlin?" I asked, unsure now what my next move would be. It would have been just too perfect to have Merlin ferry me through a portal to Avalon and help me retrieve the sword.

"Very nosy little boy, aren't you?" Mab said, filling my drink again with the same honey ale as before. "Just be rest assured that his place of business is in good hands. I've been planning on visiting this," she gestured around the room, "place for some time. I've set his metal man to tending to your griffin, by the by, but I think that means you owe me some form of compensation. Will you be paying via favor or gold?"

I looked at her hard, trying to figure out why she reminded me so much of Merlin when they looked nothing alike. They both had the aloof odd mannerisms and said words that felt like they meant more than what they first appeared to be. "I'll buy it with gold," I said, doing my best to put a fake smile on.

It was obvious I'd get very little information from her, but I had to at least leave a message. "Can you tell Merlin, if you see him, that Caldor Miles was looking for him. I need a way to get to Avalon and if he could help me retrieve an item, I'd be eternally grateful to him."

"Eternally grateful, hah, what a wonderful choice of words," Mab said, laughing. It was a high-pitched cackling sound, very out of sorts in the pub filled with the sweet voice of the bard behind me.

I looked at her, waiting to see if she'd truly acknowledged what I'd said, but she just smiled at me and stared with her wild wide eyes. I dropped a gold coin and asked for a key to one of the rooms. It was late and I wanted to give Ares a chance to rest in the stables from our battle.

"Enjoy your stay and stay to enjoy," Mab said, waving at me with her fingers. To me she looked like a child who desperately wanted to tell a secret she was holding from you, but just wouldn't for one reason or another. I tried to get her out of my mind and think about other ways I might get to Avalon as I lay in bed, but it wasn't until I began to dream that an idea presented itself.

In my dreams, I stood at the bow of a great elven ship, like ones I'd seen while hunting for the Sea Serpent. It sailed among the clouds and launched fireballs at circling sky monsters. The dream ended suddenly, as a great tentacled horror appeared in a dark cloud, destroying our ability to stay afloat in the sky. It fell with us pulling the ship and all those aboard into a wet death among the sea below.

I woke up the next day, both frightened at the idea of sky travel into the unknown and resolved that I'd found my way to the Isle of Avalon.

Ares dropped me off just outside my family home, she had a fierce hunger and wished to go hunting. It had taken all of my pull with her to get her to drop me off first. I finally settled to have her drop me off a little ways out so she could get to her hunt. I was beginning to learn that you didn't get between a hungry griffin and her meal.

The early morning coolness permeated the air, winter was upon us, but the thin layer of frost was nothing to be worried about today. It was in a month or so when the heaviest snows came and travel for people not flying atop a griffin would become difficult. I cut through the trees, taking a path that would let out right behind our house and give me a chance to surprise my family.

As I drew closer, my view blocked by the house and the barn, I heard grunts of frustration and then a high-pitched yell that I recognized as Grace. Suddenly my feet took on a speed beyond any that I'd known before, essence pulsing through my body and pushing me beyond my limits. I reached the area of disturbance within seconds, instead of minutes. My panic faded instantly as I realized what I was interrupting and I released the essence I'd been holding inside of me, most of it trickling back into me.

Michael the swordsman, trainer to the guards of House Variyn, and occasional torturer of mine, stood amidst Grace and Gregory, training them.

Michael stood tall, with willowy legs and arms. As I remembered from before, nothing about his physique spoke of brute strength or fighting power. His orange eyes flashed in amusement when he saw me, and he flourished his wooden sword in my direction.

"You and I must speak regarding compensation, but not now. You will spar with me and perhaps show these two complainers a bit of what I taught you," Michael's words were sure and confident.

"With a wooden sword?" I asked, looking at the one he pointed in my direction.

"No need, you may use whatever sword or weapon you wish, but no skills. There will be no shortcuts for their training, so neither will I allow you one."

I shrugged, used to his oddities from the trainings I'd endured. Honestly, I was surprised to see him teaching them the sword already. I'd have thought that with how he spoke of weapons training when I first met him, that he'd start with something like the spear or halberd.

Last night I used my Blade Bond class skill to bond my new weapon. With just a thought, I summoned Fulgar-'vi'lectus into my grasp. It appeared like such a simple design compared to my other two swords that I owned, but it was by far my most powerful weapon I'd owned yet. I didn't worry that I'd cut Michael or destroy his wooden stick of a sword. Without him telling me outright, I knew this was meant to show his skill to the twins and perhaps get them to take him more seriously. Even knowing what was coming, I wasn't fully prepared for the beating that I knew would follow, but I did my part.

Circling him, I meant to wait for him to attack first, but when he didn't, my patience eroded and I slashed downward, pivoting the strike into a piercing thrust aimed at his gut when he backed away. My attack was abated away easily by his wooden blade, and for my trouble I received two strikes to my head. Happy that I hadn't stripped off my armor or helmet—a requirement he'd given last time I'd trained with him—I shook the dizzy strike from my head.

Taking a fighting stance Fran had taught me, I patiently waited for his strike. When it came, I parried it and delivered one of my own. He sidestepped it, dancing away as if I were moving in slow motion.

This continued with me being hit several times and my own blade not coming close to striking flesh and barely making an impact on his wooden sword. Grace and Gregory ooo'd and aww'd at all the right places, being thoroughly impressed by their expensive teacher. We ended the bout after ten minutes of strenuous Stamina leeching practice.

"You've improved," Michael said, not out of breath at all. "I can also tell you've increased your thresholds in Strength, but clearly not Endurance. You of all people should know that balance is key. I suggest you fix your main imbalance at your first opportunity."

"You almost had him!" Gregory said, coming to my side. He wore a snug fitting gambeson along with a cloth cap, knee guards, and sturdy leather boots. A wooden sword hung from his grip lazily and a look of pure enjoyment graced his face.

"Sure did," I said, pulling him into a side hug and dismissing my sword. "How do you like your new teacher? He's the best weapons master you'll ever meet, I'd wager."

"Flattery doesn't lower the bill," Michael said while rifling through a large sack on the ground.

"How are you enjoying it, Grace?" I asked, as she slowly sauntered over.

Her face was red, as if the exertion from ten minutes before was still bothering her. She wore a similar gambeson and cap but looked far less excited about it. I pulled her into a hug and gave her a tight squeeze.

"It hurts," she said, holding her arm. I pulled up her gambeson sleeve to find her peppered in bruises and red marks. How long had they been at this training?

"I'll ease those for you," I said. This got Michael's attention, but he didn't stop me as I began to cast Mending Touch on her arm. He scoffed but otherwise remained quiet as the spell went off.

Grace's frown turned upside down and she hugged me with as much force as she could muster. "Thank you! We've been at this for two days and it's just so painful."

I looked at Gregory, but he purposely pulled his sleeves down lower so as to not show any signs of whatever damage he'd taken. I smiled and turned back to Grace.

"It won't be easy training but trust me when I say Michael knows what he is doing. With his help, by the time you spark you'll be ten times more powerful than I was when it happened. You both need this, just stick with it," I said, locking our gazes and watching the resolve take root in her eyes.

"I can do it!" She said, the defiance I knew she had inside of her shining through.

"So can I," Gregory said, then added in a mocking tone. "And I don't need healing."

I cut my eyes at Gregory, then purposely cast my Mending Touch spell on him as well when it came off cooldown. "There, we are all even now. But I will say this, unless Michael asks me to, I won't be doing anymore healing. We learn just as much from our pain as we do our victories."

Grace and Gregory gave me solemn head nods. I noticed that Gregory was more relaxed, the pain must have really been getting to him as well.

Walking over to Michael we spoke of their training; he praised them both but said they had a long way to go. We discussed price and I was pleasantly surprised at how affordable he came, until I realized he was saying his daily rate, not weekly. Despite the cost, it was something I could cover without any effect on my money flow, so I shut my mouth about it and paid the man for four months of service.

This caught him a bit by surprise, but when I told him I'd likely be off to war soon and unable to pay him, he accepted the coin.

"Why is it that you've become available at all?" I asked, now that we got the business of payment out of the way. I was genuinely curious as to why House Variyn would let such a powerful asset such as him go.

"I have fought in my last war and refuse to participate in any further," Michael said with an unusual amount of steel in his voice. "I officially resigned from my position the moment I was told that I'd be training soldiers and not guardsmen. I will not fault you for taking up your banner, but I would advise you to understand why you are going to war. If it is for another man's squabble, then you ought to rethink your plans. To kill another for the whim of some high Lord sitting far from the battle is murder, plain and simple. Do not let yourself become a murderer."

A chill ran up my spine at his words and I had no response. I'd examined my choices from all angles, and I would be going to war, but to call killing others in a war murder seemed a bit harsh. When it came down to it, I expected I would do what needed to be done to keep those around me safe. It was going to be more about keeping my troops and friends alive, than anything else. But I could feel his conviction and wouldn't try to challenge his words.

Instead, I thanked him for the training and left him to work with the twins while I sought out my mother.

I found her in the kitchen, cutting kelt fruit up into a large bowl. Our crops must have flourished if we still had fresh kelt fruit to eat. In the winter it was common to store a good measure away in the cellar, but the ones she cut didn't look diminished by time at all. If I didn't know any better, I'd say they were freshly picked.

"Those look fresh," I said, startling her and making her drop one of the fruits.

"Just like your father," my mother said, scowling at me playfully. "He was always sneaking up on me without trying."

"Sorry," I said, walking over and plucking some fruit out of the bowl and into my mouth. "What do you think of Michael?"

"You mean the man who showed up unannounced and declared that he needed a place to stay and that he was going to train my babies to fight properly?" She asked, her voice laced with sarcasm. I could tell just by looking at her that it bothered her that I hadn't given her a heads up. It also probably bothered her that Grace and Gregory were being trained, but she had to know it was important.

"Uh yeah," I said, rubbing at the back of my neck. "I honestly thought I'd beat him here, so at least part of that was an honest mistake. The training to fight part we talked about though."

"I know, I know," she said, putting the knife down and shaking her head. "I just don't like the idea of my babies having to go out and fight monsters. It's bad enough that I have to worry about you going out to try and be a hero. I just don't know that I want to accept that all my children have to be heroes. I've been talking with Grace, and she really likes the idea of getting into small town politics or shop ownership. As an *Awakened* she'd get certain added benefits outside of proxy levels, wouldn't she? You should talk to her about it, maybe you can set her on a path of non-violence."

I couldn't help but bend to the will of my mother, her gaze being enough to break my most steely of resolves. "I'll talk to her about her profession and maybe see what I can find out for her. I came here for another reason that if I don't get to now, I know I will conveniently forget to tell you about."

My mother looked suddenly serious and went still. "What is it, are you okay?" She asked, her eyes traveling over me but not finding any signs of injury. "Did you lose one of your friends? I told you being an adventurer wasn't for you, my poor baby."

"Mother, please," I said, grabbing hold of her hands. She was on the verge of tears, and it wasn't making this any easier. "My friends are alive. Together we have faced impossible odds and come out on top. It's about House Variyn and the rumors you might have heard. We are going to war, and I've been called into service."

I didn't know what her reaction would be, but I wasn't prepared for the silent tears and shaking head. "No, no, no, baby you don't have to go to war for that selfish asshole. You love your father and the example he set for you, I know he meant so much to you, so you listen here!" Her voice was suddenly full of force and I reeled back a little. Tears poured down her face, I'd rarely seen her so emotional so fast.

"It is my duty as a Knight of the Realm, as a vassal of Blackridge Keep, I am required to field troops and answer the call," I said, trying to get her to understand.

"Your father refused their petty house wars, and you should too. Even when given stupid titles from those haughty assholes he had principles he refused to bend on. If it involved saving lives or stopping monsters I would understand and so would he, but war, especially house wars weren't something he would stand and neither should you!"

Why did everyone have such negative reactions to war. What was I missing that turned people so against serving their House Lords? Didn't she know I'd given oaths, made promises when I accepted my titles? What kind of person would I be if I stopped being faithful when it became difficult? What kind of person only follows a path when it is easy.

I pulled my mother into a hug, and she wept into my shoulder. It wouldn't be so bad, but I just couldn't understand why she was so upset. I hadn't even had the chance to tell her my plan yet. How was I going to save the lives of all my men and ensure that no lives were lost needlessly. My power as an *Awakened* would give me enough of an advantage that no one would be able to stand against me. I understood that most other *Awakened* wouldn't be fighting on the frontlines, so surely, I could do as I imagined.

But I didn't say any of that, instead I let her cry and told her I was sorry, but it was something I had to do. I didn't want to tell her that it was likely we'd lose some farmhands to recruitment. She didn't need to hear that right now.

I left her in the kitchen, her eyes red and puffy and a frown on her face. Suddenly I realized that I shouldn't have told her. She'd have assumed that I was off adventuring, a much more dangerous pastime, I thought. But instead, she knew the truth and it hurt her just to know that her son would be off killing other sons. If only she'd let me explain my plan, how I'd kill no one, but save so many. If she'd understood that, then perhaps it would have made things easier.

CHAPTER 13
BREANNA THE DONKEY

"How is the winter treating you, Breanna?" I asked my father's favorite donkey. She was my buddy as well, but my father had even gone so far as to bring her on an occasional adventure, though now that I knew about his Arcane Asylum I couldn't imagine why he would.

Breanna the Donkey rubbed her head into my hand and accepted the fresh kelt fruit I fed her. My mother must have gained a new perk for the storage of produce, because we had several bushels all packed away outside the cellar. Perhaps she'd found herself with more stock than she'd been able to move, despite her tales of selling all we had to a city vendor.

"You don't judge me for wanting to go to war, do you?"

She brayed in response, and I could tell by the twinkle in her eye that she didn't judge me.

"I think she's missed you," Grace said. I turned to

regard her as she entered the barn. Her cloth cap was off, and her blonde curls fell on either side of her face. I'd heard her come; she was never one of the sneakier ones.

She would be fourteen at the end of winter, but she was already beginning to look like she'd reached adulthood. With her cloth cap off she really looked like a little woman and not my kid sister anymore. So much had changed in the small amount of time since I *Sparked* that it was hard to keep track of some days.

"How do you figure?" I asked, scratching Breanna behind the ears which made her shut her eyes in joy. She loved that particular spot. Perhaps I should take her to Warrick's old tower location and see if there is any mint left for her to pick at. The rubble had covered most of it, but mint was resilient, perhaps some had survived.

"I can just tell," Grace said, her smile warming my chest. "Michael is letting us take a break, but I already have two new bruises." She said lifting up two fingers to punctuate the point.

"I shouldn't heal you, but if it gets worse come see me and I'll see what I can do," I said, pulling Grace into a hug, her back damp with sweat. "I think I'll stick around for a few days. What do you think about that?"

"Yes please!" Grace exclaimed.

I missed seeing my siblings, all the annoyances aside.

"What do you think about becoming an adventurer?" I asked, but followed up before she could respond. "Mother says you want to open a shop or get into local politics? That doesn't sound like the sword fighting Grace that I remember."

"I don't know," Grace said, groaning. "She wants me to be safe and this training has been fun, but also so painful. I never expected being an adventurer to involve so many bruises."

I shifted uncomfortably, feeling at least a dozen new small scars forming on my chest from the battle with the giant weasels on my way here. Pain was a big part of being an adventurer, but I didn't want to scare her off by saying as much.

"I know it sounds crazy, but you kind of get used to the pain," I said, shrugging and picking at a few broken pieces of my armor. "See this here," I pointed at the many holes in my armor, "I barely felt it and it's already healed. Our bodies change after being Awakened, so much so that you really shouldn't let pain be the thing that holds you back."

"I guess," Grace said, tugging on her curls and looking torn in what path to take. That much I understood.

"You don't have to decide now, but I do want to drop off a few books on general professions and different trades where *Awakened* individuals, whether adventurers or not, can excel." I had several tomes I'd picked up that I needed to off load some of them.

"Really?" Grace said, looking excited.

"Really, really," I said, smiling wide. She giggled in response.

I joined them for some training, Grace and Gregory sparring together or doing conditioning drills, while Michael beat the ever-living crap out of me. The good news was, I convinced him to let me use the trick I'd been working with, summoning and unsummoning my blade. He said he enjoyed the extra challenge, but I think he was just messing with me.

Time and time again I tried to sneak a strike through, but he just anticipated where the blade would reappear, and my strike was wasted. This continued into lunch, my mother brought out food but said very little to anyone. Grace followed her back inside and likely had a one on one with her, finding out about my plans. She just as much confirmed it when coming out and glaring in my direction. I caught her eye, and she just shook her head.

She said something to Gregory, who came to talk to me during one of the few breaks Michael gave us.

"You're going to war, that's so cool," he said, looking up to me with wonder in his eyes.

I face palmed and shook my head. "It isn't cool, it is necessary," I said, not sure I was happy to have a reaction so completely opposite either. "By my honor, I gave my oath to serve and I will, but I doubt it'll be cool. You know what is cool." I leaned in as if sharing a secret with him.

He leaned in as well, eyes wide. "What?" He asked.

"Being an adventurer is pretty freaking cool. Have you thought about what type of class you'll want to take or what role you'd like to cover in a dungeon?" I asked, studying his face to see his reaction. He smiled wide and I could tell he'd thought about it, likely looking over some of the books I'd already left behind.

"I think it would be epic to be a frontline Tank, maybe like a paladin with magic too, but all-around defense. Make me so strong and unmovable that no one could take me out," Gregory said, shaking his head and biting his lip.

"Good tanks are hard to find, so I fully support that decision. But remember that you might not get the exact choice you want, so be prepared to take what is given to you and just know that you will excel at it if you give it your all," I said.

His expression fell a little, but he recovered quickly. "I don't care what I become; I just know I'll be awesome!"

"Break's over," Michael declared, pulling us back into his hellish idea of conditioning.

Michael took over my room, so I slept out in the newly constructed workhouse that, funnily enough, was in better condition than parts of our house. I'd need to get a crew out here to build us a new bigger house, perhaps a fancy manor and place a few servants to help my mother in her daily tasks, like cleaning and cooking. When I arrived at the workhouse I was greeted by the ever-enthusiastic Ferdel.

"Want a drink?" He asked, his voice a deep even tone.

"Sure," I said, seeing that three other men sat around a fireplace burning brightly on the far wall. Two empty wicker chairs sat nearby, and I took one. Ferdel grunted to get my attention and handed over a small cup with a very alcoholic liquid inside.

I gave it a sniff and considered whether to drink it. Ferdel took a long pull on his own cup, so I figured 'what the hell' and downed the entirety of the contents. It burned on the way down, but I'd need three times as much as a normal man to begin to feel the effects.

Not wanting to drink poor Ferdel and his crew of workers out of their liquor, I searched inside my dimensional cube at my side until I found a cask of strong kelt ale I'd acquired in Variyn. The look on the younger of the two workers' face when I pulled out a cask as big as my midsection from seemingly nowhere, made me smile.

"Anyone care for a drink?" I asked, pulling out a larger mug and handing back the smaller cup. I filled mine to the top, foam cascading over the edge. Kelt ale had an interesting effect on *Awakened* in that it seemed to ignore your body's natural resistance to getting intoxicated, making it easier to relax with a warm ale.

"I could go for a mug," a light-haired man said. He had deep brown eyes, light blonde hair cut short, and a strong jawline. His clothing choices were simple, tunic and brown slacks, but he had a ring on his hand that spoke of marriage.

I poured him a large mug and caught his eye. "How long have you been married?" I asked. It might seem like an odd question, but he couldn't be much older than me and I didn't see myself truly settling down for at least another ten years or so.

"A few months," he said, smiling at me and taking a deep pull on his ale.

"I should know this, but I don't," I said, wiping foam from my upper lip. "Give me your names, I'm Caldor if you didn't already know." That got a chuckle from the lot of them.

"Name's Cam Castle," said the married man.

"Dan Lion," said a dark-skinned man with very handsome features and piercing blue eyes. He was the most physically built looking man of the entire lot, myself included.

Ferdel just grunted and I chuckled.

"Dred Bone," an older man said. He had weathered skin that looked as thick as a cow's hide and a voice to match. He couldn't be any older than Ferdel, but time hadn't been kind to Mr. Bone.

"Well met," I said, my gaze gliding across the small group. We had more workers, but the workhouse we'd built was decently sized and most appeared to be sleeping already.

Winter was an easier time for laborers, but I knew Ferdel would keep them busy enough, he was a hard man to please. Even so, winter was the time that many of the laborers could go out into town and enjoy the pay they've been earning up to this point. That might explain why so few were up at the fire now, but it also made me wonder something.

"Why aren't you home with your wife, Cam?" I asked, the younger man blushed a little.

"We are saving up to buy a little cottage not far out of town, till then, she stays with her parents, and I stay here. Plus Mr. Ferdel requires all work hands to stay on site until harvesting season ends. Soon I will have enough and finally get a little land of my own," Cam said, beaming with pride. I had to ignore the urge to hand him over several platinum, thus fulfilling his dream with coin I wouldn't even miss.

Luckily, I had more sense than that. Cam wanted to earn what he got, and the sense of accomplishment wouldn't be the same if it were just handed to you. Even more fortune, though it felt like a windfall at times, was something I had to discover and work hard at to bring the essence discoveries to the world.

"Harvest season isn't over?" I asked, confused at what kind of harvesting could be going on this late in the season. It was easily a month and a half past the latest I'd ever been able to harvest.

"Not over till we get all the fruit down," Ferdel said.

"Do we need to hire some temporary workers? Ferdel, I'd have thought you of all people would understand the importance of getting the fruit picked before it goes bad," I said, annoyance clear to be heard in my voice.

"Not going bad, Perks are keeping it fresh," Ferdel said.

I remembered the Perk I'd picked before I *Sparked* and finally understood.

"The Longevity Perk," I said, nodding my head knowingly.

It must be working better than I originally thought, as it had surpassed the month-long extended harvesting period. That could be somewhat explained by the vague explanations that came with Perks, nothing was ever clearly lined out in them, only vague mentions of extended periods of time or harvest bonuses. They were all well-known enough by local orchard farmers that I'd assumed what others had said was right, that it would extend harvest by a single month.

"How long until you finish?" I asked, an idea coming to me as I basked in the heat of the hearth.

"At least a week," Ferdel said, taking another sip at his drink.

"I'll be here for at least another few days," I said, deciding that it was worth sticking around for a few days and checking to see if Merlin had returned before leaving back to Variyn. "I'd like to help harvest, at least during the day. Wake me in the morning with the others."

"Fine," Ferdel said, nodding.

We spent the next few minutes in silence until Dred brought up some local gossip and conversation resumed. For nearly an hour we talked about everything from our favorite drinks, prettiest girls in Creeshaw, to local prices finally coming down for a multitude of items. Then the topic turned when Cam mentioned talking to a man at

Merlin's pub who spoke of a coming House War like nothing Variyn has seen before. They all looked to me at the mention of it, somehow knowing I would know more on the subject.

"It's true," I said, simply.

"That fellow I met, Grayson, said they are recruiting in the city and might be coming to smaller towns like Creeshaw next," Cam said, I couldn't tell if he seemed excited or not by the rumors, but he didn't seem as opposed to it as others.

"Being a soldier paid well in the past," Ferdel said, surprising me. Had he served as a soldier before and if so, how had I never heard of it until now?

"You've been a soldier?" I asked, watching his reaction to my question for any cue that I should back off.

"Twice," Ferdel said. "Fed me well, good pay, and learned a few useful proxy skills." Before I could ask what skills he might have learned, he produced a knife out of his belt and did the impossible. I felt the activation of a skill, weaker than any *Awakened* skill but still, it pulled from the ambient essence and mana in the air. His knife thrust forward three times in rapid succession, much faster than a normal human ought to be able to make it move.

Ferdel grunted as he put his knife away and shook out his arm. Whatever he'd done it hadn't felt good, he had a grimace on his face now.

All the men looked awed by that little trick, and it almost prompted me to show off one of my skills, but I decided not to be a showoff.

"Maybe we ought to sign up," Dan said, nudging Cam with his elbow. "You could make enough to buy up a few trees yourself and start your family off right."

Cam seemed to consider his words, growing quiet. He sat there for a good minute before nodding his head. "Yeah, I probably could, couldn't I?"

This was such a different view and reaction to war than I'd been used to getting from people, that it stunned me a bit. Finally, among people that looked at the practical side of things I figured I'd share my own lot in the war.

"I've been called to raise a few squads myself, so I might see you all on the frontlines if you end up signing up," I said, watching their faces for any adverse reactions. But the opposite happened, they smiled, or at least Dan and Cam did.

"Hey, maybe we can join up under you," Cam said, excitedly.

"Yeah, I bet you'd treat us right, what do you say? Can we join under your banner?" Dan said, leaning forward. His intense eyes boring into me.

"I'm Lord of a place called Blackridge Keep, I'm not sure how it works for recruiting, but I can request that you be transferred to my squads and see what they say," I said, shrugging.

"They keep you with people you know," Ferdel said, he'd finally stopped shaking out his wrist. "Makes you less likely to run and more likely to fight to keep your brothers alive."

"Maybe I can get the entire Creeshaw region troops

transferred under my banner," I wondered aloud. "I'm not going to have the legion I'm meant to because of the low population at Blackridge so I'm sure troops will need to be moved around. I'll see about having it done." I was more speaking for my own thought process and benefit, but Dan and Cam nodded along becoming more enthused by the idea.

"You know how to fight?" Cam asked Dan, looking him up and down with new eyes.

"Who me?" Dan said, flexing his considerable muscles. "I've been known to get into a scuffle or two."

I smiled as the night devolved into a jovial exchange of stories about fights and obviously fake tales of surviving monster attacks. I even shared a few stories of my own, but they sounded so fantastic as to be unrealistic as well. It was rather amazing how my life had changed over the last few months.

I found myself wondering if I could help Cam and Dan more in the upcoming war, if they truly signed up. Cam hadn't even run the idea by his wife and I'm sure she'd have something to say about it. What if I used the monster core I'd collected or my ability to move around essence to Spark both of them? I immediately dismissed the thought, remembering how it had gone with Ismene. I'm sure they valued their lives more than a small chance at becoming an Adventurer.

CHAPTER 14
RETURN TO MILES MANOR

I landed in the courtyard of Miles Manor in the early evening, happy to be back in the city. It hadn't been physically grueling work to help finish the harvest, but Michael took his training very seriously and drilled me late into the night as punishment of missing his earlier trainings with the twins. I'd tried to explain to him that I had responsibilities to help where I could, but he just hit me back with a 'know your place' response that shut me right up. So the last five days, since I wanted to stay until I could finish the harvest, had been spent working all day then training all night.

Finally, I could take a break from it all and have some drinks with my friends. It wasn't that I didn't enjoy the company of folks like Dan and Cam, both were becoming fast friends, but they saw the world differently than I did. My view on what was best to do next was driven by my sense of honor and the slow passage of time, whereas they saw things in a more narrowed sense, seeing as they didn't have the benefit of long natural life.

Cam had convinced his wife that going to be a soldier would be the best for them and had even spoken to a recruiter that came to town on my last day. He'd promised to report to duty, alongside Dan, two weeks after harvesting ended, so at least they had some time to themselves before leaving to be trained. I had a few words with the recruiter, a man who served directly under a Lord Fairmount—I learned he was over several towns and maintained a keep a day's travel away.

The recruiter seemed skeptical that troops raised outside my own boundaries would be transferred over, but when I told him Lord Variyn himself had said my troop numbers I needed to bring were far less than the norm, the recruiter changed his tune. Suddenly he seemed enthused by the idea, saying he was certain he could get his Lord to agree as long as I told Lord Variyn how helpful he was being. I'm sure there was some politics involved that I was missing, but I agreed to do so.

I didn't know how many troops the Creeshaw area would provide, but the surrounding orchards and farms did have a fair bit of youth my age and above. It was rare for a family in the area to have less than three or four kids, so I imagined that at least a hundred or more could be recruited if the pay was right. Of course as I wasn't directly recruiting them I had no control over the wages being provided, nor did I have an idea of what they should be paid.

I encountered Kora shortly after landing, two other Runeforged with similar light-colored armor plates flanking her on either side. I raised an eyebrow at her as I realized that neither of the two newcomers were Ventus, so she'd converted at least three in my time away. Did she mean to convert all the Runeforged under her to this new upgraded version? I decided to ask her as much when the opportunity presented itself.

"I have a complaint to be lodged against Regina," Kora said, her tone terse and upset. "She has taken Ventus apart and I fear that his sense of being will be lost along with it. She claims to have his elemental spirit captured but will not allow me entry to see him."

Now wasn't the time to ask, I decided, instead I shook my head and began to march towards Regina's office. I didn't have to say a word, Kora and her two new converts followed behind me, each of them held grimaces on their faces that wouldn't have been possible before the changes Kora had made.

I passed through the common area where food and drink w served. Ismene, Emory, Creed, and surprisingly Zander, sat eating and drinking. Ismene saw me and waved. I waved back but yelled over that I'd see them in a bit. She got the hint and smiled as I slipped down a hallway towards Regina's reinforced office.

Two normal Runeforged in full armor and spears stood outside the door. I noticed that the door had been further reinforced and a peephole installed. I knocked on the door as hard as I could. The thickness of the door became more apparent by the low thud it made when I knocked, and I wondered if anyone would be able to hear it.

I didn't have to worry, as the peephole darkened and latches began to be unlocked, clicking along as they went. One by one until it sounded as if nearly twenty bolts had been unlatched, and finally the door swung open. It wasn't Regina that answered, instead a Gnome I didn't recognize in a white coat and goggles.

"What do you want?" He snapped, lifting his dark lensed goggles onto his forehead.

"I need to speak with Regina, now," I said, my patience growing thin by the rudeness of the gnome's tone.

"She's busy, come back later," he said and began to close the door.

I had other plans and pushed on the door, causing the startled gnome to take a few steps back in surprise. Then he did something that surprised me, he pulled out a metal rod and swung at me. I didn't even have to dodge as he was a solid three feet too far away, but to my surprise I felt a jolt of electricity slam into me. If it had been any stronger it would have locked up my muscles, instead it just hurt and pissed me off more.

Mana began to course through my arms and into my hands as I instinctually went to use the Lightning Strike spell, but a voice cut me off and I let the spell fizzle out.

"Enough of that! Damn you Bindlewheel, you realize who you just attacked?" Regina yelled from across the room. I saw her climb out of a stool and make her way over.

Bindlewheel wore a confused look on his face and shrugged. "Some nosy human, one of Caldor's friends I figured," he said, indifferent to the fact that he thought he assaulted one of my friends.

"That *is* Mr. Miles you dolt," Regina said and suddenly Bindlewheel went a shade of pale white that made me smile. It wasn't that I wanted people to treat me differently, but it sure was nice seeing this asshole feel a sudden surge of regret for attacking me. I'd want him to feel the same if he'd attacked one of my friends, but this was enough for now.

"I uhh, that is to say that I, uhh," Bindlewheel struggled to get any words out of his mouth that sounded like a coherent sentence. Regina came over and smacked him on the back of the head, then hissed at him to go back to work. He apologized and turned to go to a nearby workstation.

"I will deal with him, please don't feel the need to dismiss him," Regina said, shaking her head as she looked over at the flustered gnome. Then she saw the three Runeforged behind me and her expression changed.

"What are they doing here?" She asked with more venom in her tone than I'd ever heard from her.

"Kora says you took apart a Runeforged named Ventus?" I asked, trying to maintain my cool after the odd interaction between the Bindlewheel character, but failing to keep all the frustration from my voice.

"They are our property and some of the runic formations he had on him have already done so much to further our research. You can't possibly expect me to ignore a resource like that?" Regina asked, tapping her foot impatiently and looking up at me with a no-nonsense look.

"Is he going to be the same when you put him back together?" I asked, pinching the bridge of my nose.

"He should be, I've been personally handling his deconstruction, but there is a certain risk as there is with all things," Regina said, her tone remaining serious.

"You will finish with what you are doing and immediately return him to his proper form. Kora is gathering a squad of Runeforged under my command, and any that she uhh" I searched for the right word to use to describe what she was doing to them and found it a moment later, "converts to their upgraded states, you and your team will leave alone. From that point on they are solely my property and should be treated as such."

I knew that she'd used exclusively my funds to purchase the Runeforged, Lance Terook had confirmed as much in the many reports regarding my funds and expenditures. It wasn't something I cared to press her on, but it meant that I had full control when it came to their care, in my mind.

"I'm nearly done and had planned to return him to his precious Kora this evening, had she just waited an-"

Kora spoke over her suddenly. "I must be allowed to oversee his construction!"

Regina began to answer, and not in a way Kora was

going to like I figured, but I beat her to it, by speaking louder.

"Kora will oversee it but will remain at a distance. Is that agreeable to everyone?" I asked. Seeing Regina sneer I knew it was not, but she surprised me with her response.

"I would love to have Kora present during my research, perhaps she could answer a few questions along the way?" Regina's voice had taken on a sweetness to it that I remembered from our initial negotiations all those weeks ago in the office provided by Gilfoy's Emporium.

"Fine," Kora said, crossing her arms and straightening her back. Everyday her mannerisms became more and more human like. I hoped she wasn't changing too much, as she was beginning to remind me more of a moody teenager than a timeless dungeon core living out her life in a golem construct.

With that little bit worked out, I left, leaving Kora with Regina, and the other two Runeforged turned to follow me out. I wondered if they'd continue to follow me when we reached the outer door, and then one of them spoke to me.

"Permission to go train by the eastern fountain?" Her voice was extremely feminine and sweet. I turned to regard her, before nodding.

"Go ahead," I said, watching her go. She swung her hips a bit more than the other and I wondered where she'd picked up that particular mannerism. These new versions of Runeforged were much like Kora in how they patterned their actions to match those around them. What did that mean for the future I wondered, would these new Rune-forged be able to give other Runeforged this expanded upgrade or was Kora alone able to do such a thing? The world would be a different place with a few thousand of Kora lookalikes in it.

"We doing a dungeon run or what?" Ismene asked, the moment I sat down.

I turned my gaze on her and let out a tired sigh. "I think I have time to run a dungeon," I said. Looking to Zander I added, "What do you think? Do we have time to run a dungeon before we are sent to report to the front line?"

Zander looked away from Ismene, it was clear he'd been drinking—his cheeks red and his head turn a bit more erratic than normal. "I've got three weeks before I'm set to arrive, but I'm not in the mood for another dungeon run," he said simply, then went back to staring at Ismene, who blushed under his gaze.

"What level has everyone gotten to now?" I asked, looking around the room I saw Emory, Zander, Ismene, and Creed all sipping at their drinks. It was late in the evening now and a fireplace that was set into the middle of a massive stone column was the only source of light, none of the lamps having been lit yet.

Creed had reached level 15, Zander level 20, Ismene level 17, and Emory sat at level 18. It was amazing what some focused power leveling could do for someone like Zander. He'd powered through enough levels to catch up with me, which meant he must have been running dungeons pretty continuously up until this point. Either that or he'd spent a fortune on Dungeon Cores and ignored extra attribute gains.

"I can always heal, but I won't be as effective as you," I said, directing my words at Zander. "Any chance you would reconsider?"

Zander sighed and turned back to me. "Only if I get to pick the dungeon and you have to tell Ismene to consider joining me on the front lines," Zander said, smiling drunkenly.

"I care for you, but hell no," Ismene said, sending a harsh look his way. "I refuse to be a part of some stupid war between houses. Right, Emory?"

Emory was completely taken off guard, he'd been looking at a cute little female gnome who was making eyes back at him. Turning to Ismene he stumbled over his words, until finally saying, "What'd you say again?"

How long had they been drinking before I arrived, I found myself suddenly wondering. "She wants you to agree that war is stupid," I said, offering my best explanation with a healthy measure of sarcasm.

"War isn't much different from what we do, just killing people, which are basically another type of monster," Emory said with surprising clarity.

"You can't believe that," Ismene said, looking askance.

"Nah I'm just fucking with you, war sucks," Emory said, laughing.

"Would you have us do nothing in response to my father's death?" Zander asked, his words casing away any remaining laughs.

"It's not that," Ismene said, reaching out and touching Zander's face. "I don't judge you for doing what you think is right, I just can't make decisions for my life based off the beliefs of another. You understand, don't you?"

Zander pressed his face into her hands but said nothing. They'd grown surprisingly close since I'd last seen them together. Watching them be affectionate made me miss Alayna. She'd likely be mad at me for missing several dinners and leaving for nearly a full week without any word, once again, but I'd go find her tonight and see if I could apologize before taking off to do another dungeon.

Then an idea hit me. If Zander wasn't willing to heal for us, then maybe I could get Alayna to come. I decided to test the waters and see how unwilling Zander truly was towards going on a dungeon run before I gave up on him entirely.

"You can pick the dungeon, does that mean you'll go, or should I ask your cousin if she's free?" I asked, shifting in my seat to lean forward.

"We should stay and spend some time with your mother," Ismene said, her words a low whisper but loud enough that my *Awakened* ears picked up on them.

Zander looked her in the eyes, then leaned forward to kiss her on the lips. I turned away, not needing to add that mental image into my memory. When they finished their passionate kiss, Zander spoke.

"I'm going to sit this one out to spend some time preparing. Try my cousin, but good luck, last time I talked to her she wasn't happy with you. Something about ditching her repeatedly," Zander said, a devious grin on his face. He was enjoying Alayna's anger for me a bit too much for my liking.

Ismene cleared her throat and added. "I think I'm going to sit this one out too, I promised to help Zander's mother with a few things this week."

Well, there went our fifth party member. Maybe Creed knew someone that could fill in, or maybe I could take Kora. That was, if I'd be able to pull her off training new Runeforged, a job she took to with much more vigor than I expected her to.

"Creed you've been awfully quiet, do you know a fifth person we could bring on a dungeon run or maybe a healer if I can't convince Alayna?" I asked, bringing my attention fully onto Creed. He had his cloak back just enough to show his pale skin and his features shadowed by darkness.

"I got a letter from my father," Creed said, his words barely audible. I got up and sat a bit closer, Emory joining me.

"What does it say? Are you doing alright?" I asked, seeing his face more clearly it was obvious he was in distress. I'd been so caught up in my own business that I hadn't even noticed.

"He's called me home. A new threat is rising in the

Southlands and the Southern Houses are banding together to march against it. He didn't say any more than that really, but I don't understand what he expects me to do," Creed said the words slowly and carefully as if each word were something he couldn't quite believe.

"The southern houses are going to war against the Easterners' armies," I said, swallowing hard. Would four Houses be enough to challenge such a large force, and what about the Southerners, would they try to fight them as well, not knowing the full extent of the threat? "When you get back, tell your father to seek out Warrick in the city of Ruelock. If he works together with the armies of the Southlanders, they might stand a good chance of holding back the threat."

"I don't know if I am going back yet," Creed said, looking ashamedly toward the ground.

"Wait, you're a noble too?" Emory said, shaking his head. "Can't take a piss into the wind without hitting one of you lot. Am I the only normal person around here?"

"You're not helping," I said, giving Emory a flat look. He just shrugged and took another deep pull on his drink.

"Do you feel like going on a dungeon run?" I asked, not knowing what else to offer Creed to help him work through his issues. We'd already had so many heart to hearts, and normally Ismene would step in here to give him an encouraging word, but she was distracted at the moment.

"I think," Creed said, never lifting his eyes off the ground. "I just want to take some time to work through things. Is that alright if I just hang out here while you all go?"

"I'll figure something out and you let me know if there is anything I can do to help you decide what to do next. Also, Ismene should be around, and she always knows what to say, right Ismene?" I raised my voice at the end, so she heard me, unfortunately she was mid-kiss when I did so.

"Sure am," Ismene said, holding her thumbs up but looking like she clearly didn't have a clue what we were talking about.

I finished my drink and stood.

"I'll find us a healer and two more party members," I declared to no one in particular.

"Find a tank so I can actually practice being a damage dealer for once," Emory said, adding a level of complexity to an already daunting plan.

"Of course," I said, nodding along as I walked off. "Find a tank, a healer, and another damage dealer, so basically an entire team. Shouldn't be too hard."

"I'm ready for dinner now," I offered, but Alayna didn't seem amused.

"You are sending me mixed signals, Caldor," Alayna said, from across the table in her favorite library, the one with the massive skylight. "Do you want to try and make this work or not?"

It took me longer to respond than it should have, but not because I had to think about it, I had just been caught off guard. "Ares had just come back, and I only thought I'd be gone a day, but after visiting my family I felt like I needed to spend a little time with them."

"So, you weren't off running dungeons or slaying monsters just to avoid me?" Alayna said, her words teasing, but her tone said she hadn't completely forgiven me.

"I promise I will tell you if I plan on disappearing again," I said.

"It isn't like I need to keep track of you or anything," Alayna said, letting out an exasperated sigh. "I just know how little time we are going to have together in the coming months and figured you'd want to spend as much time together as possible while we still can."

"I do," I said, reaching across the table and putting my hands atop hers. "I have a way that we can spend a week together if you are willing."

"Let me guess," Alayna said, shaking her head. "It isn't taking me to introduce me to your family, or inviting me to hang out with your friends, you want to do a dungeon run and you are short a healer because Zander wants to spend time with his mother before going off to the front lines."

Had he come and talked to her first somehow? No that didn't make any sense, I'd come straight to the keep and she was in the very first place I'd checked.

"Good guess," I said, showing a toothy grin.

"What level are you now?" She asked, sighing and rolling her eyes.

"I just hit 21, you?"

"I'm only 17, but I know of a dungeon that is supposed to be loads of fun," Alayna said, a devious smile that was a match for her cousin's, appearing on her face.

"Which one?" I asked, trying to remember if I'd told her all the different ones I'd been to or not. I wouldn't mind hitting up the Crimson Crusaders Dungeon again or even the Great Maze, both of which I'd basically streamlined the paths to the most essence.

"Most people call it the Murder House, but I like it for another name, Murder Mystery House," Alayna said, she seemed way too excited to be talking about a 'murder' house.

"That sounds," I tried to find the right words, "dangerous."

"No, it is a really fun dungeon themed after a dinner party and a murder mystery, where you have to go through the house, fighting monsters and finding clues to solve the murder. And each time you pick the wrong murderer, the real one gets stronger, so that means you have to really focus on figuring out the puzzles!" Alayna was practically giddy at this point, and I resolved myself to our next dungeon, a murder mystery.

"Where is it?" I asked the next most important question. If it were too far it might throw off what I had planned for after the dungeon and I was working with a limited time-table before I was expected to have troops ready to fight.

"Two days ride on horseback south towards House Thouca, but right on the edge of House Attra lands. I can ride Vash now; he's gotten big enough and he is faster than any horse. If it were just you on Ares and me on Vash, we'd probably make it in a day."

"So far it is Emory, me, and you, so if you know anyone else let me know," I said. She made a show of screwing up her face in a look of concentration before shrugging. With how little she went dungeon diving I doubted she had many contacts for Adventurers.

"Probably find a few willing volunteers outside the dungeon, it is fairly popular, but I'm sure I can use my name to get us to the front of the line. Speaking of which, we should leave tonight, just in case my father decides he has a new set of runes he wants me to decipher, so he can exploit my discoveries for war."

Her smile remained but her tone was anything but happy at that moment. It really was a shame what her father had done to her. She'd been so eager and ready to make a difference. It was something that filled her with joy and gave her meaning, then he swoops in to turn it into something perverse, at least in her view.

I was undecided how I felt about it as it would likely make my life easier and be the answer to how I'd get to the isle of Avalon. But this wasn't so much about my feelings towards it and had everything to do with how it affected her. The longer I knew Lord Variyn, the more I didn't care for him. He hadn't seemed so bad at first, but he truly showed his colors as the days passed. It was like he was willing to use anyone to get what he wanted, but to do that to family? To betray their trust like that? It was unspeakable, and yet he did it without so much of a thought towards how it made her feel. Or at least I assumed that was what had happened, as I only had what Alayna said to go off of.

"Let's get Emory and head out," I said, standing and putting my hand around her waist to pull her close. I leaned down and gave her a passionate kiss on the lips. "Thank you for being so amazing."

Alayna raised an eyebrow, giving me a cute look until I smiled. "I am pretty amazing, aren't I?" She quipped.

"You are." I agreed, and then we disappeared into the moonlit city, taking the long way to Miles Manor. Emory was knocked out drunk, so we made the last-minute decision to leave first thing in the morning. But instead of Alayna going home, we snuggled in close on my bed and enjoyed a vigorous and enjoyable night together.

CHAPTER 15
MURDER MYSTERY DUNGEON

"I'm a druid tank, I specialize in turning into a goat, like a really mean one and I use my horns, cause I'm a horny goat. I've got like, a lot of horns," Pan, the obviously stoned tank, said.

"And what about your buddy, what does she do?" I asked, the incredibly smelly man with his green robes and gnarled staff.

He took another long pull on a pipe nearly as long as my arm before answering, smoke wafting up out of his nostrils.

"She's a uh uhm, babe what is your class called again?" Pan asked, turning his bird-like features towards the scantily clad woman in the silliest leather armor I'd ever seen. It barely covered her at all, acting more like a leather bra and panties than anything else.

She didn't appear to be stoned, or at least not as much as her partner, but she still took a second to answer. "I'm a

Ki Archer," she said, smiling at Emory when he happened to look over and giving him a playful wave.

"She has my vote." Emory said. I could practically see him drooling at her.

"How long have you done dungeons together?" Alayna asked, she kept looking at Artemis and then to me. I got the feeling she was checking to see if I was staring, but I'd clued in on the need to focus on Artemis's eyes about two seconds after meeting. She'd failed to adjust herself soon enough when we were first getting names and she'd had a little slip from her leather bra. I wasn't sure Alayna liked the idea of us teaming up with these two.

"Pan and I have been on and off again dungeon buddies for as long as I can remember," Artemis said, winking at me as my eyes barely strayed off her face.

"What does a Ki Archer do?" I asked, before Alayna could tell them no. As a tank and archer combo they were exactly what we needed, and I saw no reason to throw away an easy group up because one of the party members had an aversion to clothing.

"I use Ki, a special focused kind of mana to fire arrows at things," Artemis said, leaning hard on her companion Pan and closing her eyes. She continued to talk but didn't open them. "We are both level 21 so slightly out of the optimal range for this dungeon, but I just love how each mystery is different, so we've ran it a dozen times already. We even have a spot saved, just couldn't find anyone else that wanted to run with us. Be a dear and let us help you, help us."

I looked to Alayna, and she shook her head indiscreetly. I gave her a look that said, 'come on it should be fine' to which she closed her own eyes and threw up her arms in defeat.

"When is your spot for, because we have noble clearance so we might be able to get in a bit quicker," I said, realizing both Pan and Artemis appeared to be sleeping now.

But despite how they looked, sitting on the ground, Artemis answered. "In about an hour, I've got to meditate and condense some Ki, but we will meet you at the entrance. Thanks a bunch, noble boy." Then she did a kissing face that made Alayna roll her eyes hard enough that I worried they'd pop out.

An hour later we stood outside the dungeon portal, buffs all out, my Arcane Armor set, and everyone filled to the brim with dungeon water. As Alayna and now Artemis had explained, we would be forced to fight some random party guests to get an invitation to the party, but what abilities they had seemed to change each time, so we'd have to be prepared for anything.

I stepped forward and through the swirling portal, ready for anything. What I found on the other side made me smile. We appeared at least a half a mile away from a grand house silhouetted by a moon at least five times as big as the biggest moon I'd ever seen. We were all hunched down at the edge of a little creek, the bank of which was enough to hide even Emory's large form.

He had asked for a sword, and I'd given him the

Hungry Blade of the Minotaur to use for the dungeon. What little he knew about using a sword, apart from what he'd picked up by watching me, had been learned in his futile year of leveling before Ismene and I joined him.

I found that I missed having Ismene at our side, growing stronger with us. I'd even gone out of my way to get some of the newer Essence Bands for Emory and Ismene but ended up giving the extra one to Alayna—a gift she thanked me for but didn't seem as overjoyed as I'd imagined she should be. Ismene had a calm chill manner that always helped to take the edge off things right before a battle, a sure calmness that I sometimes lacked.

However, I found myself unusually at ease crouched down beside Alayna and Artemis. Alayna gave me a confident smile and when I looked at Artemis to check if she was ready as well, Alayna decided to give me an elbow into my side. Luckily, my armor had been thoroughly patched up now. Artemis smiled at me and moved closer until her bare skin of her thigh pressed against my armored leg.

She whispered and pointed over the bank, each of her words overly breathy and seductive. "A carriage will break down just there and then we attack. Wait for Pan to engage before unleashing your load, otherwise we might pull their agro."

I felt uncomfortable unleashing my load so close to Artemis, so I nodded and pretended to adjust my armor before moving to crouch beside Emory and Alayna, leaving Pan and her to be next to each other. Looking up to Emory I saw that he was straight up staring at her chest now and not even trying to hide it.

"Get your head in the game," I whispered, punching him in the arm harder than perhaps I should. It worked, pulling him from his trance and he looked at me with a stupid grin on his face.

"Where do you think she keeps her bow?" He asked, raising his eyebrows up and down.

I glanced over at her and realized what he meant. She didn't have any weapon; I didn't even see any rings on her fingers that might be storage devices. Where did she keep her weapon? Before I had a chance to ask, I heard shouting across the way right by a crop of trees. Sure enough, a black fancy carriage had broken a wheel and several figures climbed out, while the driver worked on removing the wheel.

Before I could look over and check to see if Pan had seen them, he was up and running. Smoke trailed after him, he hadn't put his pipe down. His robes waved in the wind, and he held his gnarled staff in the air as he began to chant. Suddenly his entire form twisted and turned until the black wild hair of Pan the druid, had shifted into a gray thick coat of fur. A goat the size of a dire bear slammed into the carriage, making the entire thing go flying into the air.

One of the carriage goers had been in the process of stepping out at that moment and her small form went flinging up into the air followed by a surprised scream of alarm. I watched Artemis and waited to see when she'd act so we didn't get into the fight too soon and pull away the mob's attention from Pan.

I saw flashes of light and Alayna cursed, standing and readying a healing spell for Pan. Artemis took that time to stand as well, and a translucent bow appeared in her grasp as she loosed arrow after arrow in rapid succession towards the gathered carriage riders.

I took aim at the closest figure, a thin black-haired woman wearing a black dress, and let loose a Lightning Strike. To my surprise, the woman waved a hand and the bolt of lightning struck all around her, instead of hitting her. Emory screamed a battle cry that sounded a lot like, 'I'm hungry' but with much more ferocity and vigor.

We had our ranged damage covered with Artemis, so I sprinted after Emory to take the fight to the front lines. Pan the giant goat man, bucked his horns at random members of the group we fought, and I finally got close enough to get a good look at them.

I counted five, including a smaller female child who'd fallen from the sky and lay unmoving. The largest of the group was a green skinned behemoth of a man who was doing most of the work of keeping Pan from goring them to death with his three sets of horns. His hands were at least twice as big as they had any right to be and I thought I saw bolts coming out the side of his neck, but it was hard to tell with all the moving about.

There was a fat adolescent that kept producing fire from his fingertips and lighting fuses on small balls that then exploded as he threw them at Pan. The goat was covered in patches of burnt fur at this point, but he fought on as Alayna peppered him with heals. An arrow caught a sword wielding man with slicked back hair and an eerie smile, but instead of piercing his face where it hit, somehow the sword fighter caught the translucent arrow in his teeth. He smiled and spat it away.

That just left the tall slender female who had artfully deflected my spell. She sat towards the back, waving around a red rose and chanting words to a spell. It wouldn't be wise to let her finish that cast I felt, so I halted my advance, to fire off an Arcane Missile. Aiming each blast at different locations on her body to make them harder to deflect.

The first one caught her by surprise, she dropped the rose and faltered in her spell chanting. A moment later she'd locked onto me with an unusually seductive look and she casually diverted the remaining bolts of arcane energy with a wave of her hand. Reaching down, she picked up her flower and began to chant.

That is when Emory reached her, huge sword swinging for a death blow. Like lightning released from a dark cloud, the swordsman was there, his thin rapier flashing. Despite the weight and heft behind Emory's swing, the rapier turned his blade aside and he went stumbling backwards. But the swordsman wasn't done, lunging forward and putting several holes into Emory's chest, or at least he would have if Emory didn't have full plate armor covering his midsection.

Tink, tink, tink.

The swordsman seemed to realize his mistake, but he struck out once more as Emory struggled to stand. I released a Firebolt into his face, but it was deflected by the tall dark woman. The rapier pierced the space between his chest plate and his helmet, blood spraying out of him suddenly in a gushing stream.

I didn't wait to see if Alayna had seen, instead throwing down a Restoring Light as Emory struggled to stem the bleeding, while back stepping. Luckily for him, Artemis sent arrow after arrow into the fray, more than the silly swordsman could catch in his teeth. An arrow got past the defenses of the lady sorcerer, striking her in the chest and sending her to the ground. Suddenly the finely dressed man dropped his rapier and went to her side, a red aura beginning to grow around him.

I made it to the fight, throwing a Mending Touch on Emory as the blood finally stopped. He looked like a thing from nightmares now, covered in his own blood and his skin pale from the loss of it. He'd need time to recover fully after this fight.

Several pairs of hands reached out from the shadows, and I heard the faintest whispers of a chant. The young black-haired girl was on her feet now and shadows formed around her as she chanted. Just as we were held fast, the pudgy boy with his explosive balls took aim at us instead of Pan. But all wasn't lost, a spear of golden light struck the shadow clad girl through the chest and suddenly we were free.

I shot a thankful smile to Alayna before rushing

forward, activating Swift Strike to parry a thrown explosive back to its sender, then Power Strike as my blade fell down into his chest. His pudgy body fell bleeding to the ground, still as the corpse I'd just turned him into.

While Pan continued to trade blows with the giant of a man, a voice cried out in agony behind me, and I turned my attention to the swordsman.

"My Darling! Mon Cheri!" He screamed, between weeping sobs. His sorcery bride had gone down with a single carefully aimed arrow to the chest and now he was wreathed in a red mist.

He stood, a sudden weight in the way he moved that worried me. His rapier sword appeared in his hands, much like I was able to do, and he swished it through the air. With the blade perfectly splitting his face he looked past me towards Artemis.

"You will die by my hand," he declared and pointed his sword at her.

I readied my sword as Emory and I stepped between the swordsman and his prey. He narrowed his eyes at us and with a flash of movement came rushing in. Time to test my sword, I thought, as I flushed essence into it. The first charge filled, flushing me with increased Strength and Intellect, but I pushed it further charging another hundred essence and then four hundred.

My sword blazed with power, and I felt a hunger for more, but I resisted the urge to attack, instead waiting for my foe to come to me. When he did, moving as fast as he was, I was faster still. My sword struck aside his rapier and slashed into his chest, but he moved quick and only got the tip. The bottom corner of his jacket fell to the ground and he put his full focus on me.

His aura flashed brighter, and he came at me with even more incredible speed. I wouldn't be able to parry in time, so I activated Swift Strike, the nudge being just enough to get my blade in position. As he backed off once more, I sent out a Force Wave, slicing into his leg. I looked over to Emory to see if he was going to join in and he gave me a head nod as I looked, perhaps waiting for me to give him an opening.

Using his charge ability, he zoomed right up to the swift fighter and body slammed into him. The force and sudden arrival of Emory was enough to throw the light fighter to the ground and back several feet. But Emory wasn't done, he lifted the blade above his head and began to chop down like he was splitting wood. The first one missed, but Emory didn't stop, swinging again and again.

A scream from the frantic fighter trying to get to his feet sounded as he lost his foot to Emory's incessant chopping. That was enough to slow him down and Emory turned him into a pile of mutilated meat.

I turned my attention away from the pool of red just as Pan, the large goat, went flying past me. The final combatant had bloody holes and ripped clothing but stood tall and strong still. Artemis sent arrow after arrow into him, but they stuck and faded away, leaving tiny bloody holes. This did nothing but annoy the large beast of a man, as he slowly lumbered toward the goat.

I noticed that Pan had taken a hit to the back leg and wasn't getting up very fast. Getting Emory's attention, I nodded my head toward the large man, and we ran over to intercept him. He kicked at us as we entered into the space in front of him, but his movements were slow and lumbering. Emory and I took turns slashing and feigning back, our cuts only going so far into the thick hide of the monstrous man.

"He seems resistant to physical attacks," I said, as we both stepped back out of the way of his swinging fist. I cast Firebolt and was surprised when the small bolt of fire seemed to hurt him for the first time. He shouted and stamped at his shoulder where it had hit, his clothing igniting as fast as kindling.

It seemed he was weak to fire but resistant to basically everything else? In that case, I had the perfect spell for him. I began to charge mana into my Fireball spell, letting it grow to the size of my head before releasing it with an over the head throw. Emory jumped back just as my fireball slammed into the behemoth's chest and sent him teetering backwards into the carriage, breaking it into bits.

I wondered how he'd fit inside the carriage as it went aflame, and his entire top half was consumed in fire. Perhaps he was the driver?

"Totally spectacular fire show man," Pan said. He'd shifted back into his smelly human form and leaned heavily on me. I turned and held him up as Alayna hit him with another heal and he straightened.

Immediately he got out his pipe and began cleaning it

out, packing it, then lighting it. The foul-smelling weed hit my enhanced nostrils with the force of a punch and I had to step away while he indulged.

"You pack quite the powerful punch," Artemis said, walking up behind me and playfully smacking my butt. I flinched and shot her a 'none of that' look, but it appeared to be lost on her as she just winked at me.

Alayna was fuming again and marched over to my side. "Still think they were a good idea, stupid hussy," she hissed the words in a low whisper. I'd never seen her get so bent out of shape and it kind of made me smile.

"If it helps," I whispered back, low enough that Artemis wouldn't hopefully hear. "I don't appreciate her advances. But don't worry so much, let's relax and enjoy the dungeon."

"I'll try," Alayna said, abandoning the whispering volume and speaking loud enough that everyone could hear. "Let's all stay focused on the dungeon and keep our hands to ourselves."

Artemis did an impression of a cat pawing and hissing toward Alayna that make me chuckle before I could think better of it, and Emory laughed out loud.

"If that was just the introductory fight," I said, trying to get the subject changed before Alayna introduced Artemis to the end of her golden spear. "How difficult do the fights inside tend to be?"

"Oh man they are fun, but if I'm being honest, and I am always honest," Pan nodded along with his words as if agreeing with himself. "This fight was a tad bit harder than the previous twelve times we've been here. It's like the dungeon is trying to challenge us a bit more each time we come in here. Wicked smart dungeon, eh?"

He had a slow drawl to the way he spoke that messed with the tempo of his speech just enough to irritate me while listening to him, so much so that I had to think about what he said to understand it, as I'd been so focused on how he spoke and not what he'd said.

If that were true, then we likely had our work cut out for us, but I was excited to experience the differences that this dungeon had to offer. We collected our loot, which for me included an interesting broach that I immediately pinned to my armor. It had come from the largest man, despite his body being burnt to a crisp the loot had been fine. It was basically a weaker version of whatever ability allowed him to have such effective physical resistance.

Broach of Ancestral Protection

Enchanted with 'Pain Resistance' Enchantment.

Pain Resistance – At the cost of an additional weakness (Fire) you gain the ability to half all other incoming pain and one tenth damage reduction upon receiving any damage and for three minutes afterwards. Effect can be triggered once per day, double damage from fire-based attacks remains while wearing and regardless of cooldown.

+20 Constitution

Durability: 25/25

Rarity: Uncommon

Weight: 3 Grams

Item Level: 40, Level Required to use: 20, Dropped by: Lurdatch the Large

Other than the tickets we each got, the rest of my drops were trash, but Emory got a thin rapier that looked like a giant metal toothpick in his large hands. He said the attributes and special ability, an enchantment that allowed him to increase his speed three times per day, made it a tempting choice. I told him to hold on to my sword either way, as he might find the thin blade not a good fit for his style.

My own sword had lost its charges already, but the experience of using it had been such a rush. After the initial surge of power, I had adjusted, but I could see how taking it to the max would be something I'd need to ease myself into.

The warmth of the burning carriage was welcome in the cool night air inside the moonlit dungeon, but the smell that came from it made me wish I had an easier way to plug my nostrils. Dead burning flesh did not smell very well.

CHAPTER 16
INTO THE FRAY

In full armor and with weapons at the ready we strolled past a hedge maze, an ornate fountain with several sea creatures depicted, and upon a cobbled driveway. Several carriages passed by us as we approached, but as Artemis had promised, none of the dungeon people engaged us in combat. Apparently, there was an entire dinner party where we were meant to gather facts about the guest, before any killing even begun.

I didn't know how I felt about that, but this was likely to be my last dungeon for a while and I was determined to enjoy it, monster killing or not. The five of us got in line behind a group of six well-dressed individuals, three men and three women. The men had black coats with long tails and brightly colored vests, while the women were all wearing dresses that expanded out around them below the waist while remaining snug around their chest.

It wasn't completely different than the fashion I'd seen

in the more formal get togethers I'd attended, but different enough that I took notice. They spoke quietly among themselves, but I noticed that one of them—a blonde haired female that couldn't be much older than me with curly locks framing her face—looked in our direction and gave us a disgusted look, wrinkling her nose.

"Looks like we've got a snootier bunch of party goers this time," Artemis said, a fair bit louder than necessary. The same blonde curled girl turned and cut her eyes at Artemis, to which Artemis responded by doing kissy lips at her.

"These nobles, man, no offence though," Pan said, taking a pull on his pipe. "They like, don't want to talk to you and we have to like, talk to them a bunch, so it is going to be a drag that we got the ones we did. Man, I remember the first time we came through here, they were so nice man, it was great."

"Is that right, man?" Emory said, elbowing at me and chuckling.

"It is my man, it is," Pan said, not realizing that Emory was trying to tease him or perhaps not caring either way.

The house set before us had whitewashed exterior walls and neatly trimmed bushes all around. However, I did notice a tower built into the west wing of the house and it appeared to be rundown, the windows broken, and the wall covered in ivy. When I pointed it out to Artemis to ask if they'd been into that part of the manor before, she looked over with a surprised frown on her face.

"The manor changes but this is the first time I've seen

it so unkempt," Artemis said, squinting her eyes in the direction. "I'm going to go check it out while we wait in line. Every detail can be important to the mystery, you come with me," she said, grabbing my arm and pulling us out of line.

I looked behind me and Alayna was giving me a look, but I just smiled and followed after Artemis.

"What are we looking for?" I asked as we rounded the western edge to stand beneath the tower.

"Nothing and everything, just look around and make note of it all. Try to remember all you can just in case, but also don't stress about it because this could just be a misdirect," she said, running her hand on the side of the tower.

Beneath the ivy I could just make out signs of a fire, the wood scorched some time ago by the looks of it. I tried to look up into the windows, but the closest one sat on the third floor, and I wasn't going to try to climb it. Artemis didn't seem to share my qualm though, skimpy outfit notwithstanding, she grabbed hold of a lattice that ran up the side of the manor wall just beside the tower and began to climb.

"I'm surprised it is holding your weight," I called out to her, doing my best not to stare at her mostly bare butt. I realized how rude I sounded a moment after saying it, but it was too late to take it back.

Artemis laughed, a melodic sound, but said nothing as she climbed to the very top of the lattice, just outside the third story window. She peered in while I studied the ground for any clues and practiced not staring at the beautiful woman's backside.

It was because of my thorough study of the ground that I noticed large crystals spread among the gravel and onto the well-kempt grass all around the tower. Picking one up, I examined it closely and thought I knew what it was but had to test it. Wetting my fingertip I rubbed it on the edge before touching the smallest bit to my tongue. Yep. It was salt.

Why would someone spread salt around a burnt-out tower?

"Looks like someone might still be living in that burnt out room," Artemis said, from just behind me. I turned to regard her, but she turned her back to me again and examined the lattice. "I think I'm not the first person to climb this thing either. See how worn down some of the wooden openings are here. Very suspicious."

"I found salt," I said, holding up a fingertip sized crystal of salt.

"How nice for you?" Artemis said, giving me a look that seemed to say, 'why the fuck do I want to see your salt?' But instead, she just finished by saying, "Let's get back."

"So, what are the chances we bump into a soot covered lord or lady?" I asked, taking one last look at the tower.

"If any of our past visits to this dungeon are any indication at all, it'll likely have to do with the motivation to why one of them kills another," Artemis said, speaking of the murder as if it were the most mundane thing.

"So tell me again, the guy that gets killed is always the same but why it is done or what is taken, changes each time?" I asked, going over what little she'd told us about their many trips into the dungeon.

"That's right," Artemis said. "The last time we were in here his son killed him for impregnating his wife. We didn't figure it out until we'd angered like half the guests and had to fight them to the death."

"So, there is some fighting that happens?" I asked, letting myself get a little excited.

"Of course, and there are the servants and the inspectors, you get to kill lots of them," Artemis said, smiling.

We made it back to the group just as they stepped up to the doorman, an elderly gentleman with finely combed hair and his nose in the air.

"I am Master Black's Head Footman, thank you for joining us this evening," he said, taking each of our tickets and nodding knowingly. "Ah, I see you are the visiting family from Adamelsive? It is my master's great pleasure to host such a renowned family of monster hunters. He was overjoyed when the invitation was accepted, we've tried for many seasons to have your family attend. What changed your mind?"

I looked to Artemis, who just shrugged and walked into the Manor along with Pan, still smoking on his pipe.

"We heard you had the best booze," Emory said, offering what I can only assume was his best idea of an explanation.

"Yeah sure, why not," I said, smiling and taking Alayna

by the arm. Together, with Emory trailing, we walked into the entryway.

It was a grand entrance with many dozens of servants, all wearing suits and skirts, standing at attention. After walking through the entryway, we were led by a servant to a dinner table long enough to hold a hundred people. Toward the end were five spots that he indicated we take.

The chairs were highbacked and cut from a red wood with soft cushioned backs and bottoms. Each place setting had several spoons, forks, and knives—none of which I knew what to do with as I was more of a one utensil kind of guy. But I sat anyway, my body sinking into the surprisingly comfortable chair. The scent of food being prepared wafted into the room, spices aplenty.

"Do we actually get to eat or is this just play acting?" Alayna asked, looking towards the new group members, Artemis and Pan.

"Man, you won't believe the kind of spread they bring out," Pan said nodding his head enthusiastically. "Each bite is like, phenomenal, and melts in your mouth. You wait man, it is epic."

"He isn't wrong," Artemis said, shrugging. "They provide a lovely spread of food, and we are meant to start gathering information about the guests around us. Normally they seat us throughout the table, this is the first time I've seen it put us all together, rather odd really."

Just to the left of us was a chair much different than the rest, it had a back twice as big and stood at least a foot or two higher than the rest. It looked more like a throne than a chair.

The gentle ting of a bell sounded from somewhere close, and the chatter of the room went still. I looked around to see what was about to happen and noticed a grand door with golden accents on it slowly swing open. In the doorway was a man older than any I'd seen before. His skin a dusty white mess of wrinkles, his hands more skeletal than not, and cheeks sunken to the point that he looked more a corpse than the night's host.

Though I knew him to be the host, as all around the table guests stood at the sight of him, bowing theirs heads in respect. I followed their lead, as did my group, and we stood inclining our heads as the ancient man came to sit at the head of the table.

He wore a great fur lined cloak, the lining looked like it had once been white but was now covered in black spots of char as well as red spots that were stained by what was either wine or blood. The rest of the cloak was a velvet ret and wrapped so fully about his person that little could be seen of his clothing beneath. Despite his obviously ancient age, his eyes were those of an intelligent and sharp-witted man, dark and searching among the faces present. He wore the slightest grin on his face, as if he knew a secret that the rest of us didn't.

Walking up to his chair, two servants arrived to pull it out and once he'd sat, they pushed him into place. It was then that I saw he had a pet in one arm, it was a miniature dragon with red scales and spikes running up the length of its spine. The dragon belched and a ball of fire singed the cloak, sending the most foul smell into the air.

"My guests have arrived," he said, his words slow and plodding. A voice like worn leather, cracked and stretched too far. "All of you here are members of my family and as such, you leech off me like a bloodworm suckling at its mother's tit."

A round of nervous laughter for a joke I wasn't sure was meant to be a joke, ensued. We didn't join in, instead my group just exchanged glances. Artemis and Pan didn't look perturbed, so I imagined this was all part of the dungeon's little murder mystery.

"Who the hell are you?" Master Black demanded suddenly, looking straight into me with his cunning dark eyes.

"Uh, the visiting hunter family from, uh," I struggled to remember where the man servant had said the family had been from, but Alayna saved the day.

"Monster hunters from Adamelsive," she said, extending her hand to him in a very noblewoman gesture.

Master Black took her hand into his boney appendage and kissed it, before tossing her hand away with force I'd not expect from someone so old. "I forgot you were invited. No bother, the night will press on as I've intended. Sit with us, eat, and be filled. But be warned, there is a game afoot and someone will die this night."

CHAPTER 17
A GAMES WITHIN GAMES

"Is this normal?" I hissed the words past Emory toward Artemis.

"First time the old codger seems to know he'll be murdered, so no, not normal for us," she said, speaking loud enough that everyone could hear and turning a number of heads.

The old man, Master Black, had begun talking to a younger woman directly to his left, opposite of us, and so he didn't seem to hear Artemis's proclamation of his pending death. However, a middle aged gentleman with slicked back hair and a mustache that curled at both ends, cleared his throat, getting our attention.

"Allow me to introduce myself, I am Blake Binstone of the Furtherwell Binstones. I am a distant relative to the Black family. May I inquire two things from you?" He spoke in a very proper accent and looked almost apologetic as he spoke.

"Yeah man, hit us with your best shot," Pan said, blowing smoke into the gentleman's face.

He coughed, but quickly recovered to ask his questions. "First, I'd be pleased to know the names of Master Black's guests that he so conveniently forgot would be attending and as such we find ourselves at a disadvantage in the coming game."

We quickly went down the line and gave our names, with Artemis and Pan giving two fake names that I couldn't pronounce and made Blake grimace as he attempted to do so.

"Wonderful, quite wonderful, secondly, I would not want to be a bother, but did you say that Master Black would die this day? It was my understanding that he would play as merely an observer, not a participant."

"I'm confused," I said, honestly. "Are you all playing a game after dinner?"

"After dinner? No, dear no, I believe it takes place at the stroke of midnight," Blake said, a devious smile on his face. "Did your invitation not mention the night's festivities? I dare say that I would like to keep my mouth shut then, you all seem like a clever lot, and I'd dare not give you an advantage in the coming event."

"Is the dungeon setting up a mystery inside of a murder mystery?" I asked no one in particular as I strained myself not to face palm the entire idea. It honestly seemed like something Kora would find amusing. Perhaps I should have brought her along and she might have been able to talk it over with the dungeon, maybe let them know that they were being a bit on the nose with things.

No sooner had Blake Binstone turned himself away from us, did another person from across the table clear their throat to get our attention. I looked up to see an elderly woman with fine white gloves and a tightly set bun atop her head, waving over to me. She had a kindly look on her face that reminded me of my grandmother on my father's side, or at least how she'd been described, as all of my grandparents had either died or been killed well before age could put them through their paces.

"Are you as excited for tonight as I am?" She asked, her voice surprisingly boisterous for a woman of her age. She wasn't nearly as ancient as our host, but still, she'd aged to the point of her skin seeming more like fine paper than anything else.

I decided it was time to play along and see what I could learn. Artemis had reengaged Mr. Binstone in conversation and to my left Alayna was answering a question from our host.

"I am," I said, trying to think how best to get information from someone but failing miserably. Perhaps if I just kept her talking she'd share something worth knowing.

"My name is Madam Kreer and you introduced yourself as Caldor Miles, did I get that right?" She asked, her hearing was not lacking for her age.

"That's right, lovely to meet you Madam Kreer," I said, putting on a friendly smile.

Her expression turned coy suddenly and she leaned

forward a bit as if telling a secret. "Did you get promised an allowance for your participation? That's what I wouldn't have asked for. As it is, if I can identify the means and the killer, Master Black has so generously offered to raise my allowance by two-fold. It is dreadfully improper to speak of it, but the excitement has truly grabbed hold of me."

"Oh yeah, no I wasn't promised an allowance, but I sure am excited to get into the game and see what it's all about," I said, trying to match her enthusiasm but falling short. She gave me a look and shook her head, turning to speak to someone beside her.

Damnit, I was not good at this! Why couldn't we just skip all this and get to the killing 'dungeon made people' already, that I was good at. It gave me a sudden pause as I considered the parallels between my soon to be time serving in a war, where I'd be required to kill actual living breathing people, and the fun dungeon adventures where I sometimes killed living breathing people that weren't technically alive, as they were dungeon constructs.

There was likely a lesson in there someplace, but I wasn't learning it. I turned to my left and listened in to Alayna's conversation.

"I've gone all out on this evening's event, but I dare say some people are taking it a bit too seriously," Master Black said, his eyes darting about the table from one face or another.

"Whatever do you mean?" Alayna said, fluttering her

eyelashes. It took all I had to keep from chuckling at the show, but the old man ate it up.

"I've received a note just this evening in my study," Master Black said, eyes growing wide as he spoke. "It was written in charcoal and told me I would die today. But I know what they are getting at." He shook his head and scowled at his guests. "They are mad that I've decided to cut off nearly half of their allowances. They've sponged off me for far too long. This game will determine who is worthy of getting a taste of my money. But the audacity to use charcoal after we had that dreadful fire that took Rosy from us."

"Who is Rosy," Alayna asked, and I could tell she wasn't acting but was truly beginning to be pulled into the conversation.

"My great granddaughter, she lost her parents in the Trif war some ten years back. I built her an entire tower just so she could play at being a princess, but those damned fire fae. I still have to salt the ground to keep them at bay, all because I used a bit of their sacred wood. I've hired a dozen would-be exterminators to go slay their queen, not a one returns for payment."

"Is salt effective at keeping fae back?" I asked, trying to recall where I'd read that or heard of it before.

"What's that now," Master Black said, looking past Alayna and to me. "Don't intrude boy, and where is my DAMN DINNER!" His last few words were shouted, and servants began to move about all at once. As he leaned forward, I saw a pendant on his neck, it had a large red ruby at the center and seemed to swirl with light inside. But as soon as he sat back it disappeared into his robes once more.

Then, as if by magic, doors opened and servants poured out with silver platters of food, each one holding several bowls inside. Master Black was served first, his bowl filled with a thick hearty stew of dark gravy. After only a moment's delay, the rest were served their plate, but no one ate. All eyes were on Master Black who spooned at his meal, sniffing it. Finally, he took a bite and shook his head appreciatively at the servant that stood beside him.

Eager to try a bite for myself, I looked about the table to see which spoon precisely, as I had half a dozen, was the proper one to use for soup. Using Madam Kreer's selection as a basis of my own, I began the wonderful task of consuming my first bowl of dungeon soup. Words fail to describe the wonderful sensations that this simple stew evoked in me. But put simply, it was wonderful and close to one of the best meals that I'd had the pleasure to consume.

If that were all we ate that night, I'd be satisfied, but it was just the start. Six full courses were served, each one a mark above the last, yet smaller in size as well. There were meats I didn't recognize, and vegetables cooked in ways I'd never imagined. Then to top it all off, we were given a cake of such a sweet, delicious mix of cheese and milk as to make me forget all the prior meals I'd had that night.

I sipped on a glass of wine as the table began to fill with the chatter of voices again. The last thing I wanted to do right now was talk, instead I wished I could find a decent place to lay down and let the food settle. I'd overdone it, but the activity wasn't set to start until midnight —though I admit I haven't a clue what time it currently was or how long we had until midnight.

Master Black suddenly spoke up. "To the study for drinks and entertainment!" There was an extra bit of pep in his dry old voice, and I smiled as he nearly pushed his own chair out before the servants were able to wrest it back for him. As peppy as someone many years younger, he led the way through a side door which opened into a brightly lit room filled with lounge chairs, a small stage where a bard sung softly and strummed at his instrument, and a long bar staffed by at least three different bartenders.

The table slowly emptied, with our group deciding it would be best to take up the rear. Madam Kreer hovered back as well, then looking back at me said, "It's best to see where everyone lands, I find, then I know where my attention ought to best be spent."

"Good thinking," I said, but again she gave me an odd look before turning away. Whatever she expected me to say I'd obviously missed the mark, but I didn't care right now. We were one step closer to getting into some real action, just one more little social event of information gathering, and we were free to start killing off the guests.

"Normally after this drinking event is when the murder occurs, the old guy will excuse himself and then a servant screams," Artemis said, explaining the next little bit as planned. "Once the murder happens everyone is required to stay in the study, for a while, we usually use that time to go get a peek at the body for clues, kill a few dozen servants and get back just as the local investigators arrive. Then the questioning starts on their side, we get pulled off by a few of them for a fight. Then after we kill all the investigators, we'd go to whichever room we think is the killer and accuse them. If we get it right, they will confess and we kill them, if we get it wrong, they get angry, and we kill them. I have no idea how this game event will mess with any of this, so stay on your toes."

She was surprisingly all business for once and I was about to comment on the fact, commending her, when she went a bit off the rails. Entering the room, she pulled a drink from the first patron she crossed, downed it and sat on the lap of Master Black while he stroked his dragon. The red scaled dragon screeched and fluttered off to land on a perch set up by a bookshelf on the eastern wall. I couldn't help but notice how she pressed her body against Master Black and began to interrogate him with sultry whispers that I could only barely make out.

"Man, she is just great at these dungeons, you seeing this man?" Pan said, plopping into the closest open chair and pulling hard on his pipe.

He had such an interesting way of speaking that I knew it would be a while before I forgot about this dungeon adventure. Alayna hooked her arm into mine and pulled me with her. I looked over to see that Emory had gone to the bar and was ordering a drink while attempting to flirt with a beautiful woman who stood beside him. His 'flirting' face looked like a cross between someone who was constipated and drunk, but the dungeon created woman didn't seem to mind, she giggled along with whatever joke he'd told.

"Well met," Alayna was saying, and I realized she'd introduced us to a dark-haired couple with light blue eyes that seemed to glow in the lamp light of the study. She must have noticed my confused look as she helped me out with their names a moment later. "Caldor, meet Mr. and Mrs. Morris. They say they are distant cousins of Master Black and have recently gone into business with him regarding a favorable trade agreement. Isn't that interesting?"

I looked at each of the Morris's and decided that it wasn't as interesting as Mrs. Morris's beauty. She had wavy brown hair, an enrapturing smile, and a fierce intelligent kindness in her eyes. It was hard to explain, but I instantly felt drawn to her. Meanwhile Mr. Morris had the same keen intelligence in his eyes, but without the kindness his wife's eyes held. He was broad shouldered and carried himself with an air of confidence. If we had to fight these two later, I had no doubt the dungeon had made him a fierce opponent and her a keenly powerful one.

"Very," I said, lending almost nothing to the conversation. I smiled and waited to see where it would go next. I really needed to work on my social speaking abilities because they weren't great.

"How well do you get along," Alayna asked, gesturing

towards Master Black discreetly. "I hear he can be a bit tough at times."

I wasn't sure where she'd heard that, but I liked the question. Let's work out who has motive for wanting the old man dead.

"He's terrible," Mrs. Morris said, rolling her eyes. "I've heard things he's done to those who stay with him in the manor, if it weren't for the highly profitable business arrangements, I'd have told Teddy we'd never set foot in this wretched manor again. But here we are."

"But here we are," Mr. Morris, or Teddy I assumed, said, shrugging.

"How would you feel if he canceled your contracts?" I asked, remembering what I'd heard Master Black say about cutting people off. Unfortunately, even if it made them murderous it would likely have the same effect on each of these people who relied on him, so the point was a bit moot.

"I'd kill him," Mrs. Morris said without hesitating. "The old wind bag has wasted years of our life with very little payout and just at the end if he thinks he can back out, then I'd literally put a hex on him to snuff out the remainder of his life, Phoenix Stone or not."

"Phoenix Stone?" Alayna asked, taking a sip from a glass of wine a servant handed her. I took a glass as well, very fancy, and took a sip. Wine wasn't my favorite beverage, but this stuff didn't taste half bad.

"You really know so little about our host?" Mr. Morris said, his eyes suddenly suspicious. "Why'd he invite you?"

"Stop it Teddy, be polite," Mrs. Morris said, scolding her husband. "The Phoenix Stone is a rare artifact that grants the wearer the ability of rebirth. But what that truly means, no one knows, as there has only ever been the one for centuries and in its long history no one has died while wearing it."

"Though plenty have died after having it removed," Mr. Morris added.

"That is true," Mrs. Morris said, winking at her husband. "He has strings tied to each of us, that Master Black, but not you."

"Well, not yet at least," Alayna said, smiling. She was doing such a good job playing along that I was a bit frustrated when we were interrupted.

There was a tinging of glasses and I saw that Master Black had managed to extradite himself from Artemis long enough to get a drink. It appeared that he wanted to say something to the rest of the room. And as it happened, it took no effort at all for him to get the attention of everyone in the room. It would appear that he truly had strings tying him to everyone, as Mrs. Morris suggested.

"There are parts to this game that you have yet to be informed about, listen well, for your actions this day will determine the success of your future," his voice like cracked leather filled the room and silence from the crowd persisted.

"Each of you, leaches off me in some way and I tell you now that I've had enough." Audible gasps rang through the room, and I just smiled, so theatrical.

"As of today, all deals, allowances, favors, all of it is done. If you wish to be among the select few that will retain my services, then you will play my game and play it well. I am retiring for the night, but I have eyes among you and should anything unscrupulous occur, then good, you are learning."

With that the ancient old man stood and sauntered out of the room. Hushed whispers and even a few raised voices sounded as soon as the door shut. These people were not happy to be told they'd just lost their means by which they likely relied on. First to leave was Madam Kreer, storming out in a huff. Next went the Morris couple, Mrs. Morris did not look happy anymore. One after another departed, our own group took a seat as the events played out.

"Let's hear it, what have you all learned?" Artemis asked, laying herself on Pan, her barely covered breasts becoming a bit less uncovered in the process. I cleared my throat and pointed at her exposed chest, to which she looked down and shrugged.

When no one spoke first, she sighed and began talking again. "Fine I'll go first. I had a nice little chat with the soon to be dead old timer. I find you get the best clues if you can get right to the source. He told me about three suspects, Madam Kreer, the devious Morris couple, and his manservant Frankford. Since this dungeon has never been that complex, we can assume it's likely one of those and that the fire was just a way to throw us off the trail..."

"I spoke with Madam Kreer but I didn't get murder

vibes from her," I said, questioning the logic Artemis was presenting.

"Oh, she's a murderer alright," Emory said, chuckling. "I spoke with a guy, didn't get his name, and he said that she's had like twenty husbands. Each of them have died before their first year of marriage was up. She's been doing it all her life, and at her age that means a long time."

"Whoa man, that is some good insights," Pan said. "I like what you're putting down man."

To this, Emory just smiled a bit awkwardly and continued to stare at Artemis's exposed breasts. To which Artemis responded by finally adjusting herself and giving Emory a wry smile.

"Would you care for another drink?" A middle-aged servant said. I recognized him as the man at the door and the same one that personally attended to Master Black.

"I'm alright, thanks," I said, turning my attention back to the group.

"I'm afraid I must insist," Frankford said, pressing the drink into my hand and leaving.

I looked down to see a piece of paper around the glass with a sentence scrawled into it.

"You are in danger," I read it aloud, then looked around to see if I could locate where he'd gone, but the room was empty, like completely empty now.

"What's that mean?" Artemis asked, looking around she noticed what I'd noticed. "When did the rest of the servants and guests leave?" There had been at least a couple not long ago and several bartenders and servants continued to work, but now they had all left.

A distant scream brought us to our feet, weapons being drawn.

"What was that?" I asked, my sword materializing into my ready grip.

"A scream obviously," Emory said, he had the thin sword out and looked pretty silly, but I knew the weapon had decent attributes.

As we looked at each of the exits, another scream, then another, and another, filled our ears from distant places in the manor. Then came the heavy foot falls just outside the doors, as if someone were running the length of the rooms outside but never entering. Then as we stood, puzzled over the odd change of events, black thick smoke began to trail in from under the door that Master Black had left from.

"Is this normal?" I asked Artemis, who, based on her expression, I needn't have asked.

"Usually someone storms into the drinking room and declares the old guy dead, and three times it was that person who did it, but no this is new, this is bad," Artemis said, her voice cut off as she began to cough.

I looked to Alayna, but she was focused and ready to act, not any fear showing through her cool exterior.

"Let's get out of here," I said, motioning toward a door opposite of the smoke and toward the sound of the first scream. We turned as one toward the door, but suddenly there was a form there that hadn't been a moment before.

It was like a shadow of a person, all dark exterior but with a faint glowing orange that illuminated it ever so slightly against the shadows around it. Just behind it was the door we'd intended to exit from, but now black smoke filtered in from beneath it as well. The room we were in was fast becoming unsafe to breathe the air.

"Fuck this," Emory said, rushing forward as if he were the tank. His thin blade quelched into the form and it screamed, a sound that dropped me to my knees. Pan had transformed suddenly and charged the charred figure. I just made it to my feet when the figure went flying through the door, a wall of smoke pouring in after it.

A moment later it was back and now it looked mad. Its hands, which had been normal only moments before, turned into six-inch-long claws, slashing out at Pan and forcing us back into the room.

Finally getting a hold of my senses, I lashed out with a quick Lightning Strike, followed by an Arcane Missile when I saw how effective the first magical strike had been. The foe staggered back from each blow and Emory slashed with his new sword between my strikes, not giving the monster a chance to attack again. An arrow from Artemis smashed right into its forehead, but it only seemed angrier. Slashing out, it put several deep cuts into our tank and Alayna began to chant the words of a healing spell.

That seemed to catch its attention and suddenly a fireball formed around its hand, launching it towards Alayna. She got off her heal and ever-prepared, began a new chant, moments before impact a barrier formed between her and the attack, but shattered on contact, throwing her back.

I rushed forward as Emory jumped back out of the way of a slash. My blade glowed from the effects of my skill usage, and I hit the charred monster with a Power Strike, cutting it deep in the chest, and used Swift Strike a moment later to parry its follow up attack. Being forced to step back after that, I sent a Force Wave right down the center and staggered the thing further.

As I took a moment to assess what to do next, I used Inspect and stopped in shock.

Madam Kreer (Mutated), Level 22

"That's Madam Kreer!" I shouted, pushing off to the left to avoid colliding with Emory, as he backstepped to avoid a slash from the charred old woman.

"She's pretty spry for an elderly lady that's been burnt to a crisp," Emory said, laughing next to me. He was enjoying his chance to be a damage dealer for once and not focusing on tanking.

"It says she's mutated, whatever that means," Alayna said between her chanting.

I rushed forward, my blade clashing against the claws of the monster that used to be Madam Kreer, the odd old lady. She screamed in my face, and I staggered backwards, stunned. A sudden pain in my neck pulled me out of the stun and I slashed wildly in front of me, my blade cutting deep into something.

I heard a loud baaing sound fill my ears and I realized

I'd hit our tank with my wild attack. Pan, still in goat form, looked down at me and spoke.

"Baaa'd form man, baa."

"Sorry," I called out, taking a step back and throwing a Firebolt into the charred face of our attacker. What started as a casual attack, that I hoped would give me a moment to reset myself, turned out to be a killing blow. The fire pulsed and rippled across her after my Firebolt hit her and suddenly she screamed again, before falling into a pile of ash.

"That was new," Artemis said, her coughing had stopped as the smoke, at least on this side of the room, had cleared. "Let's go explore but be ready, the servants will attack, and they aren't push overs."

We collected our loot, I got nothing of value, but Alayna got a necklace that she said had decent attributes on it. I was surprised that none of the loot had a char to them, as dungeons usually loved to reflect the theme of the fight.

We stepped out into the hall, Pan leading the way in his goat form. What we saw first was at least four servants dead on the ground, bleeding from scorched wounds to the face or chest. Madam Kreer had done much of our work for us it would seem.

"Let's follow that trail," I said, indicating a line of charred footsteps that led to where Madam Kreer fell. "Perhaps we will find a clue as to why she turned into a charred monster."

"Good idea, babe," Alayna said, kissing me on the

cheek. I stopped and looked at her, she gave side eyes towards Artemis and I thought maybe I understood what was going on.

I'd notice Artemis had been keeping a good deal of attention on me and that must be annoying Alayna enough that she'd given me a pet name and felt like she needed to show that we were an item. I was all for this idea and turned to her, pulling her into a deep and passionate kiss. Let Artemis see this and know that I have eyes only for Alayna.

I think I surprised poor Alayna with my actions though, her face went a little red and she was blinking rapidly while catching her breath. "Thank you," she said, then looked to the side as if doubting that were the right thing to say. I just smiled and took her hand, letting my sword fade away. I had a strong enough command of the blade that I could get it back before anything attacked us.

Artemis harrumphed from just ahead of us and I smiled in her direction, to which she rolled her eyes. Pan continued on his way in goat form until we reached the steps, and he shifted back to a human.

"Man, this is so different than our last runs," he said. "Where are all the angry servants or the news of the dead old guy?"

"I don't know," Artemis said, shaking her head. "Let's see what we can learn from following these footsteps, then we can go to the places the old man was killed before to look for clues. Unless you all want to split up and half of us can check this path, while the other goes to find the old guy?"

In unison Alayna, myself, and Emory said, "No."

Everyone knew that splitting the party was always a bad idea.

We followed the footsteps up the stairs, encountering another dozen dead servants until we reached a door, charred completely black and half off its hinges. The stench of burning wood filled the hallway, but it was nothing compared to the odor that laid inside.

We'd traveled to a section of the manor that had only three doors down this hallway, two untouched by fire. Inside the burnt out room, was a sitting room and another burnt out door leading to what might have been a bedroom at one point. While the sitting room had only burnt footsteps and burnt up doors, the room beyond was a blackened charred mess.

Poking my head in for only a moment I was forced to pull it out. There was a heavy heat inside, mixed with the smell of something even more potent than burnt wood.

"Does anyone recognize that awful smell?" I asked, giving others a chance to look inside.

One by one everyone gave it a try, Pan being the only one to actually step inside of the room. He came out a moment later waving an orange feather in front of his nose.

"Man, that gnarly smell is coming from this feather, it's awfully stinky," Pan said, sniffing the feather deeply and sighing as if he enjoyed the scent. "Wonder if I could smoke this."

Artemis quickly pulled the feather from his grasp before he tried anything funny with it.

"It resists my attempts to identify it, why I wonder?" Artemis asked as she twirled the feather in front of her face, her nose wrinkled in disgust.

"Let me try," I said, grabbing the foul-smelling feather and using Inspect.

'Unknown Feather' was all the information the system offered. Thanks for that, I thought shaking my head.

"Okay," I said, handing the feather back to Artemis and taking a step away so I could think. "We have a burnt up charred monster that wants to kill servants and us, a feather that stinks but was untouched by the fire, and a warning from a servant about us being in danger. I've studied many monsters, including the mythical kind that exist only in legend, so hear me out." My attempts at building up to a big reveal were shattered by Alayna a moment later.

"It sounds like a phoenix. Fire rebirth, orange feather untouched by the fire. So how do we kill a phoenix?" She asked, smiling at me proudly. I frowned, I'd been excited to reveal what I knew because of years of study, but obviously Alayna had been trained and studied from birth to know this stuff just as much, if not more, than me.

"I can't say I've ever encountered a phoenix monster before," Artemis said, tucking the feather away into the folds of her clothing. It disappeared completely, despite there not being enough cloth for that to happen.

"Oh man, one time I swear I smoked this stuff that sent me into a cycle of death and rebirth where a bird was like, totally watching over me, and maybe a little bit judging me, you know man?" Pan said, nudging Emory as he spoke.

"I really don't," Emory said, chuckling.

"Let's just look for the old man," I said, a bit deflated after having my big reveal stolen away. "If it is a phoenix, a blade will kill it just as easily as anything else."

As quiet as we could, we moved out of the room and through the halls, not a single one of us really knowing what to expect.

CHAPTER 18
A SURPRISING TURN

W e didn't make it far out of the wing of the manor we were in, before the screams began again, this time closer and much less vigorous than those of Madam Kreer, but startling, nonetheless. We arrived first to check Master Black's private study, according to Artemis that is where he is usually found dead most nights. Traveling up and down staircases and through halls that were as much a maze as they were hallways, we turned a corner and got a face full of black smoke.

Alayna cast a spell, something I hadn't heard her chant before and a pulsing light traveled out before her, sending soothing heals up and around my body before pushing outward, taking the smoke with it. I wanted to ask her what spell that had been, but just then the cleared smoke revealed two blackened charr monsters. I immediately examined each of them, Mr. and Mrs. Morris.

Mr. Morris was several feet taller than he had been, a hulking beast that took up half of the hallway, luckily, we'd passed into the widest one yet so fighting wouldn't be terribly difficult. The floorboard creaked as the smaller Mrs. Morris went to all four and then scrambled up the side of the wall like an insect. She looked towards us, where her eyes were, instead sat two orbs of orange glowing magma.

"Man, that is creepy," Pan said, before shifting into his goat form, filling half the hallway as Mr. Morris had. There would be little room for both Emory and I to fight so I made the decision to pull out my bow and stand back with Artemis. She smiled a bit too much seeing me standing beside her and I looked to Alayna, but she was fully focused on the fight before us.

In unison, Artemis and I loosed arrows into the larger Mr. Morris. Each one had very little effect, other than angering him, his scream more a roar than anything else. Pan the goat lumbered down the hallway and smashed his mighty horns into the hulking form. Meanwhile, Emory slashed high, attempting to cut at Mrs. Morris, but she took to the ceiling, some fifteen feet up and spat out thick smoke all around Emory.

Artemis and I had the same thought I think, because we both turned our attacks towards Mrs. Morris. I led with a Lightning Strike, followed by an arrow, then using one hand I focused enough to let loose a Firebolt. Each strike staggered her back and as the Firebolt hit she screamed and fell from the ceiling.

The smoke cleared and a confused looking Emory found his surroundings enough to lash out at the fallen form of Mrs. Morris. As with Madam Kreer, her hands shifted and changed until each finger was several inches longer and had sharp pointed tips. She caught Emory's strike and with strength beyond what a small lady ought to have, she threw him backwards. He hit hard on his back and arrows smashed into her as she reared up.

It was enough to keep Emory from being gutted, but we couldn't fire fast enough to keep her at bay. A heal flashed down at Emory as he made it to his feet and he tossed the thin sword aside, reaching his hand into his dimensional sphere at his hip, he pulled free the larger sword, 'Hungry Blade of the Minotaur'. It came down on her with frightening speed, but she dodged, and the blow splintered wood as it connected with the floor.

Emory took a slash across the face, but his backswing caught the unexpecting Mrs. Morris in the legs, bringing her down right in front of Emory. Without hesitation he slammed downward, blade first into her head as his knee slammed into her chest. She went limp a moment later.

Mr. Morris roared in rage and suddenly Pan was thrown across the hallway, slamming into Alayna. I turned to see if she was alright, but a yell of pain from Emory brought my attention back front and center. He was being slammed by massive fists and I could tell he wouldn't last long. I cast Lightning Strike, then immediately started on my best heal, Mending Touch Rank 2.

For the cost of 300 mana, I finished the 2 second cast

and healing surged out of me. I began the longer cast time of Lesser Heal while Artemis pelted the monstrous Mr. Morris with arrows. Pan made it to his feet, and I heard Alayna up and chanting once more just as my last heal went off, sending a whopping 300 healing on Emory from my Rank 2 Lesser Heal. The immediate need of the heals was apparent, as Mr. Morris had beaten him to a bloody mess and currently, while Pan charged, picked up Emory and threw him down the length of the hallway.

The giant goat dodged Emory, his body slamming hard against the wall headfirst before tumbling to the ground. A red fiery aura had formed around Mr. Morris now and if it were possible, he had gotten bigger, now having to slump down to fit in the massive hallway. Pan gored him with his horns and Artemis did the first skill-based attack I'd seen her do so far.

She held an arrow in place and it began to glow, the translucent form of the arrow solidifying into a crystalline shaft. Then after a long two seconds, she released. I kept half an eye on her, but never slowed my own arrow shots, adding a Power Strike into one and a Swift Strike into another.

Her arrow hit with the sound of shattering glass and a spray of white dust. It didn't appear to do much at first, but slowly I saw crystals forming on the enraged Mr. Morris. Pan slammed into him, using his massive form against him by hitting his knees and buckling him backwards. Emory finally made it back to his feet, but the battle was in its final moments.

The crystal attack from Artemis spread with deadly efficiency. I couldn't help but wonder why she hadn't led with this attack. It made movement of any kind impossible for the massive Mr. Morris and Pan was scoring critical strike after critical strike with his horns. Letting my bow fall into my ring inventory I summoned forth my blade and sprinted forward to deliver what I hoped would be a killing blow.

Using the combined might of my Power Strike, Swift Strike, and letting my Light Blade ability immerse my blade, I leapt up and struck right at the behemoth's neck. He tried to swing for me, but the crystals prevented his movement enough that I got my strike off before kicking off his chest and back to the ground.

The roaring had stopped, followed by a thump as Mr. Morris lost his head.

"Nice arrow," I said, giving Artemis an appreciative nod. "And nice heals." I added seeing Alayna walking to my side.

"Hey man, you stole my killing blow," Pan said, laughing as he spoke. He was obviously not serious, but I went along with it.

"Gotta get those easy shots when I can," I said, slapping him lightly on the shoulder. The adrenaline of battle quickly faded, and we went to collect our loot.

I got an interesting trinket from Mrs. Morris that increased my constitution by ten but also could be activated to give me a surge of temporary health. It could be a decent item, but I had an idea of someone that could get more use out of it.

"Here Emory," I said, handing over the item. I didn't know if he had any trinkets currently in use, but regardless of what he pretended now, he was meant to be a tank and this would help him.

"This doesn't fit the build I'm going for," Emory said, giving me a flat look.

"It really should," I said, saying what I meant without actually having to say it.

He signed and rolled his eyes at me. "You are something special, asshole," Emory said, taking the trinket. I knew he wasn't truly mad at me, but I mocked offense to play along.

"You wound me," I said, punching lightly at his arm. He'd really been messed up that fight, but the heals had snapped him right back from the brink of death. How strange a life we led, where we walked the blade's edge between life and death. One moment away from utter demise, but always willing to come back for more.

It was this drive that all adventurers must share if they wished to be truly successful and the one thing I've had burning in my heart for as long as I can remember. Emory and Ismene had similar fires burning in their chests, but fate had nearly decided that it wasn't the path for them to follow or at least in Ismene's case, as Emory had sparked naturally just very late and had a weak core affinity. How many more are being kept from greatness because of inborn limitations that would fall away under the *Awak-*

ening process? Should I do away with my fear of helping others to join our ranks, at least give them the choice to walk the path?

It was something that weighed on my mind from time to time, but now wasn't the best moment to let my thoughts distract me. I checked Mr. Morris for loot but got nothing but junk items that I'd have to sell later. Artemis laughed at something she got, and I saw that she'd looted what looked like a charred hand.

"It's a trinket that gives me extra fire resistance," Artemis said, shaking her head.

"Oh man, that loot is really giving you a hand with the issues at hand," Pan said, giggling in a way that only he could, while pulling his pipe out to smoke some more.

"I got a book of spells," Alayna said, standing from where she was, bent over Mrs. Morris's corpse. "But it's all gibberish, runes, and a language that can't be real."

I walked over and took the book from her as she offered it up to me. It was a thick tome, perhaps five hundred pages if my guess were any good, and it was because I'd spent so long reading books that I could usually tell after seeing the paper what kind of length you were dealing with. It had a black leather cover with blue faintly glowing symbols in a circle on the cover. The edges had golden caps on them to prevent the cover from bending and it had the smell of an ancient book.

I cracked it open and sure enough I couldn't recognize any of the words or the obvious areas meant to be the spells. I flipped through a few pages anyways, seeing that each spell took up roughly twenty pages before a new spell form started. I could only know this by how the page was left blank afterwards like a new chapter or something, a common practice when paper became more abundant. Wondering what kind of attributes it had, I inspected it.

Grimoire of Grey Lady

+10 Intellect

+10 Concentration

Durability: 50/50

Rarity: Epic

Weight: 4 Pounds

Item Level 36, Level Required to Use: 21, Dropped by: Grey Lady

"Who is the grey lady?" I asked, looking at the slumped figure of Mrs. Morris's corpse.

"Maybe it was her, but I swear I Inspected her, and it just gave the name she gave us before," Alayna said, shrugging.

"Do you mind if I keep this," I said, leaning in close. "I want to have Kora look at it and see if she can translate any of it. Maybe there are actual spells here."

"Go for it," Alayna said, giving me a kiss on the cheek. "I would have just sold it."

I placed the thick tome away in my storage cube and focused back on the dungeon. We'd taken down three charred monsters so far, but no servants—as they'd all been dead by the time we reached them—and so far, we didn't even know if the old man was dead. This murder mystery was not playing out at all like I assumed it would, but I had to admit I enjoyed the fighting.

CHAPTER 19
DUNGEON WARNINGS

"We are almost there," Artemis said, she was leading the way alongside Pan. So far, we'd encountered more dead servants but no charr monsters. The house was eerily quiet once more and the clocks that we passed showed it to be a few minutes til midnight.

We stopped outside an ornate door with swirling patterns of fire, and an elegant bird with long tail feathers swishing through the flames.

"A bit on the nose," I said, gesturing to the door.

The party looked and Emory chuckled. "Guess that means we fight an old man or maybe a bird on the other side?" Emory sounded excited, as always, he was ready for a fight.

"Nothing has been what we expected so far, I'd wager anything could be behind the door," Artemis said, then sighing she looked back. "This door has always just been a plain wooden door with no engravings, so make sure you are all ready for action."

Pan went first, pushing open the door with his gnarled staff and still puffing on his pipe, the smell of it wafting to the back of the group. The man really never stopped smoking, but I wasn't sure I could blame him. The scent was strong, but the effects were calming, and I was just getting them secondhand. Pan must be as chill as a cucumber.

Books lined the wall of the massive study, a spiral staircase set into the far most left corner of the room leading up to a second balcony filled with more books. I noticed all of this after my mind passed over nearly a dozen kneeling charred figures and twice as many servants lining the top balcony with crossbolts pointing down.

In the middle of this mass of potential foes stood a young man with eyes that I recognized immediately. He held an amulet up in his hand, his fine clothing showing now that he'd taken off his sizable fur cloak.

"Master Black!" I called out, half in surprise and half to get his attention.

"You are just in time to see my ascension to the ranks of the immortal where I'll be able to gift life and death as I see fit," Master Black's voice hadn't changed, it was still as dry and cracked as old leather.

"Ideas?" I asked in a normal speaking voice, which, because of the sudden chanting of the servants, meant only my party were likely to hear.

"We need to retreat," Artemis said, her words coming

slow and measured. "Way too much to handle in this room right now."

"I think we can take 'em," Emory said, shaking his head with confident bravado.

My eyes ran the length of the servants, and I knew that with crossbows like that, there was no way. We'd be filled with so many holes before we got to the old man—who now looked more like a young man—and that wasn't even considering the charred people.

"I'm not sure what the dungeon is playing at, but there is no way we all make it out of this alive, unless someone has a magnificent plan," I said. Looking to each of the party, no one spoke up. Alayna looked fierce and ready to fight, but I knew her enough that if we had to run, she'd be all for fighting another day.

Our decision was made for us as the door behind us shut and a servant— Frankford—locked the door. He put the key in his vest pocket and I almost sprung on him to grab it, but he skirted wide around us.

"I warned you, but still you came," he said, shaking his head. Then he did something I definitely didn't expect, he walked through the charred figures and kneeled down before Master Black.

"I knew these prattling fools would try to kill me, so I lured them into thinking they had a chance to win my favor, and while they fumed over my news, I had each of them brought before me, taking my payment for so many years of support," he said, his words filled with confidence that only someone who'd already won could have.

Whatever he'd done to them, they'd become his loyal monsters and now he had youth. But was all that really worth losing everyone in his life? Sure, this was a dungeon, and it didn't matter how this ended, as long as we were alive to tell the tale, but these narratives usually had a certain reasoning to them.

That was when I noticed a body lying on the desk behind Master Black. From the side that I could see, it was a young girl, her face covered in red angry burns. She was so still that there couldn't have been a way she was still alive, but then she blinked at me, her purple eyes tearing up.

Master Black plunged the amulet he was holding against Frankford's forehead and a scream of agony filled the room. Orange violent energy pulsed around the pair and Frankford's skin began to char and blacken. Then to my surprise, all the servants began to scream, each of them dropping their weapons as orange energy slammed into them and funneling through Frankford's back. For a moment, the skin returned to its normal luster, clothing burnt away, but then as each of the other servants dropped into charred piles of dust, his skin began to turn again.

All the while we watched, helpless to do anything but stay away from the intense heat of the orange energy. Above Master Black, the translucent form of a bird appeared, feathers dropping free here and there, scorching wherever they touched.

Two of the charred figures rose and began to walk towards us during the entire ordeal, the time for waiting was over it looked like. Knowing dungeons for what they were, I was sure of two things: the door behind us likely wouldn't open no matter the force applied against it, and there was always a way to win.

"Stand fast and make ready!" I shouted. Emory nodded his ready at my side, Alayna stepped forward putting a gentle hand on my arm, a rush of power coming from it. Artemis and Pan looked a bit spooked like they didn't know what to do, but I stepped forward my sword raised. Casting Lightning Strike right into the lead figure's face, I followed it up by throwing my sword end over end at the same charred figure. Luck was with me, and it smashed point first into the slow lumbering figure, dropping it to its knees and eventually to its face, causing it to lay still.

The sword appeared back in my hand, and I looked to Artemis and Pan. "There is always a way to win, we got this." And I believed it. Without the servants to pepper us above, I knew we could do it!

Two more charred figures rose up when the first one fell, making a total of four coming at us at once. We'd need be fast and efficient while we fought. One of the larger charred figures stumbled into a beam of orange light and disintegrated, making me realize that we needed avoid that stuff.

The goat charged, catching the first charr monster in the chest, throwing it into a beam of orange and ending its sad existence. Perhaps this wouldn't be so bad after all, I thought. Four more rose up, bringing the total to six at once.

I let loose a Firebolt and stepped in beside Emory, slashing high at a nearby monster. It slashed down, but Emory blocked it skillfully on the flat of his blade, before kicking out using one of his tank skills. The monster flew backwards, hitting Frankford and puffing up in a ball of fire.

Okay don't touch that guy either, check and check.

The fight continued, until three remained and all had joined the fight. I slashed, cast, and bashed, but we were being pushed back. So much so, that we nearly had our backs against the locked door. The remaining three were lumbering figures that hit with more force than any we'd encountered thus far. One such monster grabbed hold of Pan, lifting him by his horns, and with a grunt of effort, picked him up and tossed him over his shoulder and toward one of the orange beams of light.

Emory appeared out of nowhere, literally charging through the air to hit Pan, grabbing him and then they launched back to where he'd started. A tank skill if I'd ever seen one!

"Two tanks?" Artemis asked, glancing over at me while between arrow shots.

"I guess so, as long as it works right?" I asked the question not expecting a response, as I cut and stabbed the opponent before me.

"A bit unfair I think," Artemis said, flatly.

Did she want Pan to get zapped or what? I couldn't

waste anymore focus on her, instead infusing my strikes with essence once more and bringing my blade to the fourth tier. Each strike split the air like thunder and hit with the force of lightning. Blue light danced across my form as I cut one of the closest monsters in half at the waist. Blood and guts poured out, making an absolute slippery mess of the small area we had to fight in.

In the moment of distraction from the flood of gushing blood, I didn't see one of the others slash down at me with huge claws. Alayna had and her lance of light slammed into its arm, throwing it off course just enough that it only slashed a few inches into my chest. As it was though, my armor had taken a beating and now my own blood soaked my chest. Before I could think to do anything but keep fighting, a heal washed over me and I sighed in relief.

Working together, the final two monsters were a challenge that we easily defeated. After the last one fell, I noticed that whatever Master Black had been doing was finally over, and in front of him stood the biggest, meanest, fiery looking charred monster yet.

"Buy me time to do my work," Master Black said, patting the huge figure on the leg as he was so massive as to only reach that high. Master Black turned to the burnt girl on the table and began to chant over her. Fire, orange and dangerous, flowed from him, consuming the poor girl. But I no longer could keep my focus on her as the lumbering thing headed our way.

Pan ran forward, but the charr monster backhanded

the giant goat into the far bookshelf like he was nothing. I opened with Lightning Strike, then tried to throw my sword again, but this time it was hit sideways and clattered to the floor.

Shit.

Summoning it back I stepped forward as Artemis unleashed arrows, one after another. Alayna chanted heals on Pan while Emory charged the giant monster. He wasn't immediately backhanded away but I wish he had been when the monster made his next move.

A maw of orange fire opened within his mouth and he unleashed a jet of flame atop Emory. Luckily Emory was a tank and had a massive health pool, because by the time the flames stopped, his skin was charred and ruined looking. I infused a Firebolt with essence and unleashed my attack, it ripped right through the monster's shoulder, leaving a large hole.

"You won't kill my friend!" I screamed, adding my heals to the ones Alayna poured down on Emory's moaning form. Using an Essence Infused Restoring Light, I could feel the heals rush into him more forcefully than ever before. Then as my heal went to work knitting my friend back together I decided I was going to end this fight.

A crystal arrow smashed into the hole I'd made and began to fill a section of the monster, but it moved slower than before. Either way, I was grateful for the help as I cracked my neck to the side and stared down the monster.

"Time to die," I said, infusing essence into my very muscles, blood, and bones. I rocked forward, my blade sparking as I cut lines into the monster. Each cut slid through like a hot knife through butter. The monster unleashed fire atop me, but I formed the sparking tendrils of magic around me and fired back. The lightning of my essence sparking about me turned back his attack in a sudden rush.

I could feel essence being drained from me as I worked, but there was nothing that would stop me from finishing this fight before I lost my friend. This stupid dungeon deciding to make this run much harder and more unfair than before, just added fuel to the rage that kindled inside of me. Nothing would stop me from killing everything in my way! Kill, kill, kill!

The edges of my vision turned black, and my muscles seized. I'd been fighting for longer than I realized, but my strikes hadn't been in vain. The monster was in pieces, literally a pile of neatly cut chunks of meat all piled up where he'd once stood. I fell atop the shaking form of Emory, his skin finally working its way to normal.

"Got that asshole for you," I panted the words and Emory smiled.

"Good, fuck that guy," his voice was rough, and the fire had likely burned his insides as well. I'd heal him some more after I could feel my limbs again.

"So man, do we have to kill you too or is this dungeon over?" Pan called out from above me while I was just getting some feeling back. I'd pushed myself too hard too fast and my body felt like it was in shambles because of it.

"My life is forfeit as will yours be," Master Black said,

his voice weaker than before. I managed to look up and see the image of a great red and orange bird floating all around him. He was lifted in the air and suddenly heat began to pulse off of him. Then with a wave of his hands, a pulse of fire starting on the little girl, washed over the room.

Alayna, quick as ever, began to chant and a barrier surrounded us, protecting us from the worst of the damage. It shattered from the impact, but most of the heat had dissipated outside the barrier.

Looking up, I watched as piece-by-piece Master Black began to burn up, his ashes falling on the girl and with each one she healed a bit more. She began to blink rapidly until she sat up suddenly, gasping for breath. Her entire form glowed with a golden light as piece-by-piece Black was being disintegrated and she was being healed.

"Thank you, Uncle Black," the sweetest of voices said. "I'll strive to live worthy of the gift of life you've given me."

Then just like that, Master Black was no more. His niece stood and regarded us in a little white night gown.

"I have no quarrel with you," she said, staring at me as I struggled to my feet. "You use power that you don't understand." She was obviously talking to me, and I felt small under the immense power of her gaze.

"I do what must be done to save those I care about," I said, panting all the while under the strain my body had endured. That last fight should have lasted a lot longer and been more of a challenge, but I'd basically said, 'nope' to that entire idea and overpowered it with use of my essence infusion. It was an ability that I needed to be careful with but all too often I find myself in need of more power, more speed, more force.

"Be careful that it is not your undoing," she said, then turned her head to the rest. "You have been witness to the rebirth of my avatar. This dungeon will be changing soon, and its doorways shut for a time. Please be kind enough to inform others of your kind. The power in the ley lines has been corrupted and I cannot keep up my responsibilities. Many dungeons will fail in the coming years, perhaps they will be wise enough to raise avatars as well, but I cannot be sure. Spread the word to those that need to hear it, change is coming."

And with that, the little girl faded away like a ghost or specter disappearing into the night. And in her place on the desk of Master Black, was a gold-rimmed chest. What possible loot would a dungeon give to her last dungeon divers before she shut the door for who knows how long? I suddenly felt a surge of greed as I reached down and started looting.

For whatever reason, I found I was able to loot Frankford's charred corpse, Master Black's dusty remains, all of the charred monsters we'd killed and the dead servants. Each one gave useful potions, gold, reagents, and a few good items, but nothing compared to what I found inside the chest.

Walking up slowly to the chest, each of us having done all the looting we needed but deciding to save the chest for last, I felt my pulse quicken and my palms grow sweaty.

There was no reason to assume that I'd be getting anything epic, but a part of me knew it to be so. Touching the chest, I slowly tilted its lid open and felt the light inside infuse me with a rush of energy.

It was then that the bulk essence for our run hit me, and I staggered back from the sheer amount of it. But that wasn't why I'd opened the chest, I reached in and grabbed hold of the item I'd received. It was a set of items, and I couldn't believe how lucky I was to get an entire set as a single dungeon drop.

Lord Black's Enchanted Armor

Set Items (6/6)

12 Gem Slots (0/12)

Enchanted with 'Reinforcement' enchantment.

Reinforcement – This enchantment will reinforce and redistribute the armored areas on a set of armor so that no one single point is weak to attack, instead the resistance will be spread out evenly.

+30 Endurance (+5 Per set Item)

+50 Constitution (Set Bonus)

Durability: 900/900

Rarity: Rare

Weight: 30 Pounds

Item Level 40, Level Required to Use: 19, Dropped by: Master Black

. . .

I had enough plus 5 strength and intellect gems to slot all twelve, which would bring my attribute gains for the armor up another 60 per attribute! This was an insane drop with an insane potential. Even the enchantment put on the armor would be useful as I'd no longer have to worry about weak points, and I could just focus on fighting.

It was good that it had the enchantment, because as I laid out the armor and got a good look at it, there were obvious points of attack that would be taken advantage of by my opponents. The chest plate was a solid plate, but raised high enough that it wouldn't obstruct my movements and a leather under armor went throughout the outfit, revealing openings in the arms, pits, stomach, crotch, and upper legs. However, the pauldrons, arm guards, and leg plates, all looked solid enough to take a hit from even the toughest of charr monsters.

I wanted to strip down immediately, but then I saw some of the other party members' drops and my jaw fell open. Half had gotten weapons, but Alayna had gotten a full set of armor just like I had but made for her class obviously. Artemis was frowning at her drop, a skintight leather suit of armor that would cover her from neck to ankle. Emory had a sword straight out of his imagination. It was three times thicker and longer than a longsword, with an extended handle to grip the unwieldy thing with two hands.

He gave it a test swing and I saw he could move it with ease, one of the benefits of being an *Awakened*. Heavy weapons, armor, and items just didn't have the same effect on you when you could naturally lift so much.

Meanwhile, the goat, Pan, had his gnarled staff replaced by the most ridiculous contraption I'd ever seen. It was half pipe and half-staff. At head level there was a mouth stem that he could suck in air and at the end a rotating bowl that could be packed with whatever he wished to smoke, then locked into place. He'd basically just replaced his staff weapon with a giant smoking pipe, and he was loving every minute of it.

"Oh man oh man, this makes me emotional," he said, and I swear I saw the smallest of tears form in his right eye.

"The sword lets me activate shield abilities with it, this weapon is beyond perfect!" Emory said, holding his sword out in front of him he slammed it forward in a motion I recognized as a shield bash.

"This dungeon really went out of its way to give us epic items," I said, looking around the room until I found the open portal to exit the dungeon on the far wall. "It's crazy to think that the dungeon is going to be going offline for a period of time. What do you guys think that means?"

I was partially concerned that Artemis and Pan would be freaked out by the announcement the dungeon had made. While I was unsettled, I'd wondered already what effects the Ley lines might have on dungeons operating, and now I had my answer.

"It means I'm going to have to move on to another dungeon and all the seducing I did to get a free pass into the dungeon whenever I wanted, is now wasted," Artemis said, her leather armor disappearing into the folds of her cloth outfit.

"Man, you were messing around with your cousin, that's heavy man," Pan said, lighting his staff pipe and taking a long pull. Smoke puffed out the top in a lazy trail leading up to the sky.

"What? No, eww, I only said that so you wouldn't be jealous," Artemis said, walking towards the swirling portal as she talked.

"Oh man, when have I ever been jealous, I honor you for your freedom my lady," Pan said, chuckling and disappearing after Artemis into the portal.

Alayna turned to me just as Emory followed through the portal and put a hand on my arm.

"Does the Ley lines and the dungeons shutting down have to do with what that Chaos Knight did when she destroyed our Prime Mana Shrine?" Alayna asked, concern clearly visible on her face.

"Yes," I said simply, watching her face for any reaction. She seemed upset, which was understandable, but there was something else there too. A determination to do something about it maybe? "I'll fix it." The words left my mouth before I could stop myself. While I did intend to fix the issue, I wasn't anywhere close to being at a solution.

"How?" Alayna asked, taking my hand and guiding me closer to the portal. "I mean, I don't doubt you Cal, but it seems like an impossible task."

"There might be a way you can help me," I said, a

sudden idea hitting me. "But it might technically involve you committing treason."

"I'm listening," she said, her face not faltering in the least.

To give her context, I explained my dream to her about the elven ships flying through the sky towards the Isle of Avalon, leaving out the bits about monsters assaulting the ship, as I didn't see how helpful that would be to our current conversation. Then, when she began to guess what I meant to ask, I asked her straight out.

"Will you find a way to get your research to the Elven nation in exchange for a vessel to take me to the Isle of Avalon? I can help fund the entire trip and some with my recent earnings, anything you need, just reach out to my head steward at Miles Manor. What do you say?" I asked, biting my lip in a nervous attempt to hide my anxiety about asking such a huge thing from her.

"If only a month ago you'd asked me this same question I'd have likely called you a fool and been rethinking our relationship, but now," Alayna said, her words trailing off.

"But now you are considering it?" I asked, finishing what I hoped her thought process had been.

"I think I can even do it without being a treasonous daughter," Alayna said, shaking her head as she thought things over. "Let me handle this, it might take a few months to get talks going, but I have a plan."

We shared a quick kiss and followed the others through the portal.

CHAPTER 20
BANDITS

W e said our goodbyes to Artemis and Pan, leaving them to inform the guild about the changes to the dungeon, a task Artemis readily agreed to. Watching her hips sway as they left and Pan's druid smoking pipe leave a trail of weed smoke, made me wonder what the future held for the pair.

The early afternoon sun couldn't diminish the cool air that lingered from winter, and I found myself thinking about the farm. What would I be doing if I'd never *Sparked*? Working the trees, scraping by silvers in the hopes that we'd survive another winter. My future had changed so drastically that when I took a moment to step away and look at myself, I often wondered if I was the same person that I had been all those days ago. Change was inevitable of course, but I found that in the wee hours of the night I often yearned for a life of action and adventure, but not so much change.

What would life be like if I hadn't accepted a place in the Lord's court? If I hadn't become an agent of the balance as my father had been? There was no changing my Paragon status, so while I'd likely have less advantages in getting into dungeons, my leveling would likely stay the same. Perhaps I'd have not gotten the infuse ability from the Arbiter, which would mean I wouldn't have come into so much coin. But even that wouldn't matter when put against my previous life.

It wouldn't take much coin to bring my family out of the poverty that we'd been in before. There was no changing Grace and Gregory's status as potential *Sparked,* so I'd likely would have taken time off from adventuring and diving dungeons to train them a little, giving them any advantage over my own would be helpful. Then a dark thought hit me that I couldn't push out of my mind.

What if I hadn't survived some of my first dungeon adventures or monster hunts without the benefits I'd gotten from all my choices and advantages? Though I'd been lucky, I knew that dungeon diving was a dangerous task that often left parties short of members. The fact that I hadn't really experienced that only increased the pit in my stomach that I might lose someone soon and perhaps someone close to me.

"Whatcha thinking 'bout, fuck face?" Emory asked, jarring me from my thoughts.

"That was rude," Alayna said, chastising my irreverent friend.

"That's Emory," I said, smiling. "As to what I'm thinking about, I was just going over what has changed in my life since becoming Sparked."

"I think about that too," Emory said, sounding surprisingly thoughtful, and then added. "I mean, so much has changed in my life since you Sparked."

We laughed, Emory being his usual silly self.

"No, I'm serious," he said, waving my laughter away and taking a drink from his mug. We'd sat down in the local tent pub to enjoy a drink before setting back out on the road. "I was struggling to level and now I'm a dungeon run away from hitting level 20."

"You and Ismene have really rocketed up recently," I said, looking to where I knew his essence band was on his arm. "I'm glad to see you improve, but make sure you are taking the essence needed to increase your attributes, otherwise your level won't mean much."

"I know, I know, I just wanted to catch up a bit and I'll dump some in later," Emory said, showing a very distinct lack of knowledge with how increasing attributes worked.

"Emory, listen okay," I said, trying to be serious with him was incredibly difficult. "The higher the level, the higher the cost of attributes. If I knew at level 1 what I know now, I'd likely have tried to do even more attributes at the lower levels when they were cheaper. But of course, it's much harder to get essence at a lower level so you can really only do so much."

"As long as you are doing two attributes a level, you'll

find yourself much stronger than the monster you face at your same level. That is why it is important, we need an edge over monsters," Alayna said, explaining it as if it were common knowledge.

I hoped that Michael was doing more than just conditioning with the twins, they needed to learn this kind of knowledge as well. "Too bad I can't pay for you to teach the twins, my siblings Grace and Gregory, some of that knowledge before they get *Awakened*."

"The twins are *Sparked*!" Emory said, slamming his mug down in surprise and making a bit of a mess. "Holy shit balls. We have enough adventurers that we ought to start our own clan, see if your noble status can be added to it and skip all those pesky fees. Speaking of which, I need to go pay my percentage, save my spot." Emory stood and left, hurrying off to pay his guild dues, wherever one did that. Another thing I didn't have to worry about because of my title and position in House Variyn.

"Where are we going from here?" Alayna asked. We'd originally thought we'd do a few runs, so it left a period of time open that we hadn't discussed yet.

"I was actually thinking about that," I said, making a show of doing my best 'thinking' face before cracking a smile. "I'm close enough to Blackridge Keep that I should go check in on them and begin the process of marshaling troops. I have no idea how to go about it but I'm sure I'll figure it out."

"Would you be okay if I tagged along?" Alayna asked, a rueful smile on her face.

I returned the smile and put my hands on hers. "You don't even have to ask, anytime you want come with me to do anything, the answer is always yes," I said, squeezing her hands gently.

"Even the war?" She asked, my smile suddenly disappeared.

"You don't want to go to war with me," I said, flatly. When I'd said anywhere, I never thought she'd want to come to the front lines with me. Obviously having a powerful healer would be useful but Lord Variyn wouldn't allow her to fight, would he? Or perhaps it would be expected. She was of course a powerful *Awakened* and title holder. Being an *Awakened* meant normal gender restrictions regarding strength and physical ability were out the window, so it didn't matter that she was a Lady of the House, she had abilities that would be beneficial to the war. My sudden flurry of thoughts made me miss whatever Alayna had said and she now stared at me awaiting my response. "Sorry, what was that?"

"I said my father already has a position set up for me," Alayna said. "I'll be working as the commander of the Medic Legion directly under his command. Unfortunately, that means I won't likely see you much, as my position is more of a lead from afar kind of deal. But I'll be sure to send the very best healers to your position."

Her eyes sparkled brightly in the sun, and I got lost in the purple swirls of color. "I hadn't even considered that your father would send you to war," I said honestly.

"I am the heir to his seat as Head of House Variyn, he

won't put me in any danger," Alayna said, pulling my head towards hers with the tip of her finger and kissing me gently.

After the kiss I just stared into her eyes, knowing that I'd do anything in my power to keep her safe and wondering if I'd be called upon to do so before the war ended. Did I trust her father enough to actually not put her in harm's way or did I think he would do whatever he felt was in the best interest to himself. He'd seemed such a nice and caring person when I first met him, but recent actions made me question my assessment. Perhaps I did truly give out my trust too easily.

"I had to sell that little toothpick of a sword to pay my taxes," Emory said, slumping into the seat across from us. How long had we been staring into each other's eyes, I suddenly wondered.

"I'm going to Blackridge Keep, you coming?" I asked Emory as he drained the warm remainders of his ale.

"Do you have a brothel there?" Emory asked, making Alayna scoff and ale to come out my nose as I spit my drink out.

"What kind of question is that?" I asked, I knew Emory was popular with the ladies growing up, but I never saw him as the type to visit a brothel.

"The kind this guy needs to know to make an educated decision," Emory said, gesturing towards himself with his thumb.

"Does Variyn city have brothels?" Alayna asked, her tone sounding concerned and confused.

"At least three that I've found," Emory said proudly. "They are heavily taxed and regulated, otherwise there'd be more. One day I'll open up the biggest and best one ever."

Emory's eyes glazed over as he imagined his dream, opening a brothel. Such an odd dream to have, I thought, but who was I to judge. Well, I was his best friend, so the least that I could do was tease him about it.

"You really so hard up with the ladies that you have to pay them for a bit of sex?" I asked Emory, making my tone as serious as I could manage.

"It isn't about the money," Emory said, shaking his head. "It's about the sex."

"Oh gawd," Alayna said, shaking her head again at the ridiculousness that was Emory.

"We do not have a brothel as far as I know," I said, finally answering my horny friend's question.

"Damn. I'll go anyways," Emory said.

I shook my head and took a deep breath, sometimes having Emory as a friend really stretched my ability to love the big ole guy.

We finished our drinks and enjoyed a quick meal before setting off. I found a place that let me change into my new armor with a bit of privacy and Alayna did the same. The golden armor, mostly soft leathers and cloth, but with golden pauldrons and fancy boots, made her look far more epic than I'd ever seen her. My armor fit well, as all magical armor seemed to, and we left the tent together, each of us admiring not only our armor but the view we got while changing. It wasn't that we weren't a bit crude like Emory tended to be, we just hid it better like proper adults.

Ares seemed annoyed with me since I had her walk on the ground with Alayna's mount, Vash, and Emory's warhorse, but I wanted a bit of conversation to help pass the time.

The road we traveled was well worn and according to my map was called Tellen's Highway. When it had been a highway I couldn't say, because now it wasn't much more than a well-worn dirt path that occasionally showed signs that it had been cobbled at one point or another. Snow or rain had wet the ground some point earlier, but the sun had reduced it to puddles. It was while we splashed through one of those puddles when I had my first encounter with a bandit group.

An arrow from an archer high in the trees that flanked either side of the road, whistled through the air and struck me in the chest. Luckily for me, it didn't penetrate and bounced off my impressive armor, despite hitting what appeared to be a leather spot between the shoulders. I was really going to like this new armor, I decided, as I followed the path of the arrow to a shadowed figure in the trees. Just as I released a Lightning Strike from atop Ares, a volley of over twenty arrows shot out from all around us.

Alayna began chanting and had a shield up, blocking them all. My spell strike shattered a branch and sent a figure sprawling to the ground. Looking closer, I saw that it was a goblin and inspected it. His name came up as 'Goblin Bandit' and he was only level 8.

"Goblins, and they aren't very strong," I called out, Alayna and Emory nodding that they'd heard me. Another volley of arrows went flying, still no match for her barrier. Finally, figures began to appear in the road, both in front and behind us.

To my surprise, they weren't all goblins, in fact, most appeared to be human. One such figure wore all black leather armor and a hood obscuring his face. When I tried to Inspect him, all it gave me was some oddly specific information about his role in this little encounter and his surprising level. 'Bandit Leader Ted' Level 31. Worried by his level, I Inspected the rest but was relieved to find he was the only one over level 10.

"Lower yer shield little lady and give us your gold, then you can go unharmed back on your way," Ted said, his voice had a growling aspect to it that sounded like he spoke a dialect of Common I wasn't familiar with but could still understand readily enough.

"You are outmatched," I yelled back, Ares screeching out her assent to my statement. Though she likely didn't understand my words completely, the meaning came across fine.

"You think so," Ted said, cracking his neck to the side and pulling a dagger from his belt. He threw the dagger at the barrier, purple light covering the blade as it flew through the air. The barrier shattered on impact and at least twenty arrows pointed right at us, ready to be loosed.

I struggled to think of what to do next. I had no doubt that I could beat each of these one by one, but with so many arrows pointed at us, it was almost as bad as our encounter in the dungeon before the servants got burnt up to ash. That gave me a sudden idea and I turned my head to Alayna and nodded. She took the hint, chanting up a new barrier as I began the process of powering a Fireball.

Only eight bowmen stood around Ted the bandit, with most gathered together behind us on the road. In fact, they'd formed a neat little cluster that I was about to take advantage of. You don't threaten my friends and get away with it! Just as my Fireball reached several hundred mana, I infused some essence. It sparked with greenish-blue lightning and Ares seemed to pull herself lower. Sending a thought to her to turn quickly, she repositioned just as the barrier shattered and arrows came down toward us.

I released the infused Fireball right in the middle of nearly twenty bandits, goblins, humans, and perhaps a few other races I hadn't noticed. The resulting blast would have taken me out of my saddle had I not been expecting it. Unfortunately, it did dismount both Alayna and Emory, the force also had the added benefit of blowing arrows away and keeping us from being filled with holes.

"You little shit!" A voice screamed from only steps away and Ares turned as Ted appeared from the dust cloud my attack had covered the road in, his daggers out and glowing purple.

Ares was not a regular mount though and she loved battle. With a slash of her claws and a flaring of her wings, she struck the surprised bandit Ted in the chest, slicing through his black armor and drawing blood. Suddenly he vanished and I felt a tingle on the back of my neck.

I summoned my sword and turned in my seat, putting my blade up I caught his dagger strike just as it came down for my spine. Using Power Strike while his blades were still against mine, I slashed outward, then activated Force Wave, sending a strike after him cutting through the air. He was quicker than I expected though and he jumped out of the way in a blur. He must have an ability that increases his speed in short bursts I decided, because a moment later he was within a foot of striking me again.

Activating Swift Strike, I put my sword into position to parry his attack and cast Light Blade. Ares turned and joined the battle, allowing me to stop tweaking my back in an odd angle. But the attack from the bandit Ted didn't come, he blurred and was gone. Looking around, I got a good idea why.

Those who hadn't outright died from my fireball spell were trying to flee to the forest edge, but they were all badly burnt. In front of us, Emory and Alayna had laid waste to the lower level bandits, half of them lay dead and the other half running for the tree line.

"I think Ted fled as well," I said, keeping my senses keen and waiting for a possible surprise attack.

"Bandits inside House Variyn," Alayna said, shaking her head. "I know we are close to the border and far from the capital, but I never imagined that bandits could thrive, even out here. This is news that my father will hear."

"I can't believe how weak they were," Emory said, laughing. He had an arrow in his arm but was currently ignoring it as he checked the corpses for loot.

Alayna walked over, dismounting Vash, who for his credit had blood dripping from where he'd likely ripped a throat out during the battle. What kind of idiot bandits attacked a group where one rode a griffin and the other an Astral Wolf. Perhaps that was exactly why they attacked, with our levels lower and them with a numbers advantage, they likely thought we'd pay some gold and go. Should I have just paid them and avoided the loss of life?

An alternative way this entire encounter could have gone, played through my head and suddenly I felt stupid. What if instead I had just paid them, then backtracked, killing them all afterwards in surprise? There was no reason to believe that they truly meant not to kill us though, as angering an adventurer and letting them live wouldn't be a good plan for any kind of bandit. Their actions only proved that they were worthy of their deaths, and I decided that I didn't feel remorseful in the least.

I pierced downward, killing the last of the retreating burn victims. It wouldn't be right to leave them to gather their forces or try for revenge later. On that same vein of thought, I called out to Emory and Alayna. "I think we should do House Variyn a favor."

"What's that?" Alayna asked, a confused look crossing her face.

"Let's hunt down the rest of the bandits and ensure they don't do this to anyone else," I said, rolling my shoulders and cracking my back.

"Yes, more loot," Emory said, smiling and rubbing his hands together.

Alayna took that moment to yank the arrow out of his arm and began a heal spell. Emory cursed but let her work. Pain really became something you could just deal with the higher level you achieved as an *Awoken*.

"Is it really worth hunting them down?" Alayna asked, I could tell she wasn't onboard with the idea.

"If we don't then they might cause harm to someone else and I won't take that risk," I said, catching her eye and giving her a reassuring head nod.

She sighed and said, "Fine, but I don't like it."

I thought bandits would be able to hide their tracks better, but that was not the case, especially when they are running scared for their lives. Alayna wanted us to gather up the survivors and take them prisoner and Emory wanted to kill them for essence and loot, I decided on a middle ground. We were a day and a half from my keep, so any that surrendered would be granted prisoner status and be allowed to be judged by the council I'd set up. So far, none had taken that option.

It might have had to do with the harsh penalties that were known to be thrown down against bandits, or perhaps it was Emory staring them down with his massive sword just waiting to get their essence, but in all cases so far, they ran instead of listening to my offer. It was late evening when we came across a camp set into the woods, there were a number of hammocks, tents, and even a start of a log cabin being constructed.

We'd taken to sneaking after we heard voices ahead, better to be prepared and see what awaited us than to charge straight into the fray. What we heard gave us all the intel we could have wanted.

"Jasper and his brothers are still alive, so that makes four, plus my two, and Ted," a voice said, it had been a whisper but with my improved hearing it was an easy task to eavesdrop.

"Ted made it back, why'd he let us get our arses handed to us like that!" Another voice, this one lower and a bit more gruff, but twice as loud."

"Quiet! You don't want to give away our position," the first voice hissed.

Then a voice I recognized spoke, it was Ted. "That's too late, the three of them are listening from the bushes over there and have come to kill us."

Seeing no point in hiding now, I stood up revealing myself. Ted stood among three other men and behind them were a group of six men, two of which were injured and laid out on the ground.

"We don't want to kill you," Alayna said, holding up one of her hands as if to calm them. "Please surrender and we will take you to be judged, if you refuse then we will have no choice but to kill you."

"I'm sorry boys, that curly haired boy is something else," Ted said, he eyed me harshly and I could tell he wished to kill me. "How are you so strong at level 21? I should be able to slice you up before you even notice me and where the hell did you get a griffin? Shit you are an impossible foe and I say fuck you I'm out."

Ted shimmered and disappeared; his voice rung out in the open camp. "Kill them boys, don't surrender!"

I readied my spell and sent an impression to Ares to be ready to swoop in and strike on my command. She flew high above us, meanwhile Vash circled around ready to capture any that ran away. I feared he'd have no luck against Ted, he was the one person I was sure we wouldn't be able to bring in if he wanted to hide. Rogue types were masters of staying out of sight and concealing their tracks.

Despite the command from their bandit leader, the three men—all remaining forces were human it appeared —set their weapons down, a bow, a spear, and a dagger. The six that were farther off did likewise, ending what would have been a quick fight. Emory growled at our quick victory and grumbled the entire time we tied them up. We scavenged for rope and found it aplenty in the camp, only having to use a small bit of my own supply.

Soon we had nine men tied up and tied together in a

row. I kept watch on them, confident in my ability to deal with them if the need arose, while Emory looted the place. He made a large pile of supplies, weapons, and even a good amount of coins. Ted had left a good little nest egg and Emory had found every little nook and cranny hidey hole. I worried that Ted might return for a sneak attack, but he didn't and soon we were ready to go.

"I don't think we have any chance of finding Ted," I said, leading the way with Alayna at my side and Emory taking the rear. The prisoners were tied to Ares, and we were ready to take flight should the need arise. I wondered how many Ares could lift but wasn't eager to find out as it was meant only as a last resort.

"You think he'll be tracking us?" Alayna asked, voicing a fear I hadn't had until she said it.

"I do now," I said, chuckling.

"If I were him and someone had taken part of my little group, I'd do it. Just wait until we are sleeping and slit our throats," Alayna said, her casual description of a brutal act made me smile and I wasn't quite sure why.

"Won't happen," I said, reassuring her.

"How do you know that?" Alayna asked.

"I'll keep watch and we are only one night away from the keep, he couldn't possibly find his way into the keep without someone noticing," I said, one of the prisoners behind me laughed. Turning in my seat I regarded him. "You have something to add, prisoner?"

"First things first," he said, shaking his head. He was

one of the brothers and had a nasty leg injury before I healed it. He spoke with a more refined voice than I expected from the lot and for whatever reason made me think he was likely a caster or a class that required a bit more elegance. "The name is Daniel, Daniel Marteese. I'd like to address your concern regarding Ted. He will not come for us and is likely halfway back to Attra city where we came from. My brothers and I, plus old Carter you tied up in the back, were a part of his original gang before he sold us on a plan to plunder travelers and adventurers that wouldn't involve much killing, if any at all. What I'm getting at not so quickly, is he has a very keen sense of self-preservation so you may sleep restfully. And I hope when our journey comes to an end you will remember how I kindly put your mind at ease when you pass judgment on us."

"That was a mouthful," I said, chuckling to myself. "Could have just said the guy is a coward and I'd learned just as much."

I turned back to Alayna; she was still looking back at the lot of them with a look of concern on her face. "What judgement do you think your council will pass on them?" She asked.

"Honestly, I don't know, but I imagine death isn't off the table. But we will have to see, I imagine my own word of the events will help sway their judgement, I'm just not sure what I think is the proper punishment. How many would they have killed, or have they killed already? Seems like death would be an easy answer to those who have killed for something so petty as a few coins," I said, surprising myself. There had been months when I'd have done just about anything for coin, but I doubted I'd go so far as killing another to take his gold. That took a desperation I couldn't imagine.

The ride went quiet after that and we traveled down the road much later into the night than we'd normally do, before breaking to make camp. I had enough food and supplies for everyone to sleep comfortable and eat a full meal. Some of them put down enough food that I felt a bit guilty only feeding them that evening and letting them starve during the day. I'd been so busy in my own thoughts and my stomach didn't empty as swiftly as a normal person's when not doing any activity, so it hadn't occurred to me.

After getting everyone laid down and both ends of their ties set into Emory's warhorse, I let Ares go hunt for a bit alone. I wasn't willing to leave Emory and Alayna alone with the bandits, because despite what the well-spoken one claimed, I feared that if Ted returned while I was away, they'd not be able to stop him.

But I worried in vain, because we went through the entire night where the only disturbance was several of the men needing to go the bathroom, which meant waking everyone and taking them all at the same time, I wasn't risking anything. After the third such trip where I put my shovel to good use and dug deep, the night finished off and

I didn't feel much tired at all, despite not using my sleep absorbing trinket.

We arrived at Blackridge Keep the very next day just as the sun set. I had guards take the prisoners with instructions that they be put in jail cells and watched closely. I didn't know how many were actual *Awakened*, and which had been benefiting from proxy levels beneath Ted.

CHAPTER 21
BLACKRIDGE KEEP

"Welcome back m'lord," Cron said, he wore a loose-fitting red tunic that had padding added in to almost resemble armor and he'd gained some weight since we'd last spoke.

What was more, Blackridge Keep and the surrounding buildings and wall looked as if they were brand new; some work was still being done and it appeared goblins were mostly in charge of doing the labor. I was surprised at the level of construction they seemed to be able to achieve when properly instructed, I'd have to congratulate or reward them in some way.

"Thank you, Cron, but I come bearing news that I fear you will not find welcoming," I said, trying to lessen the blow.

We'd retired to his office to speak in private and Mick stood outside as guard. Meanwhile, Emory and Alayna had been invited to take a tour of the city by Raphael, who recognized and bowed to Alayna immediately. She marshaled up a small force of human only guards and took them to see the various sites inside the keep.

"You speak of the war House Variyn has declared against House Blalor," Cron said, a clever smile spreading across his lips.

"Is it so public knowledge that even out here you've heard?" I asked, perplexed.

"Not so," Cron said. "I overheard a few of your guards speaking of the news after your new recruits arrived. I believe you will find the people of this keep willing to take up arms for you, if you but ask. Blackridge has been thriving with the influx of gold you've brought to us and the continued stream of supplies."

I'd almost forgotten that I'd had Lance make sure supplies and some of my gold continued to stream its way here. I regarded Cron, who had basically been the ruler of my keep, as I went off doing one thing or another.

"I'd like to get into the day to day of life here before I ask anything of them," I said. "I believe I have the time, at least a week before I need to start gathering troops and thinking about where to march them. What did you have planned today and how can I have a hand in it?"

"Well, I got word we have two more goblins imprisoned for stupid reasons and you brought that lot of prisoners, shall I call the council together? We can hear their complaints and judge some prisoners?"

Cron seemed more excited about this kind of work

than I was, but I was determined to see where I could help. "Yeah, let's get the council together," I said.

We discussed a few random items, including relations with the town which apparently had improved to the point that visitors to and from Valestein were becoming a common occurrence. The mayor had even come to share a drink with Cron on at least two occasions.

Walking from the meeting room I was greeted by Mick, he stood unusually stiff and saluted me, fist to chest. "Lord," he said, this was the second time today he'd seemed off and regarded me so stiffly. Had I done something to offend him or was life in Blackridge really changing him so much?

"At ease, Mick, what has gotten into you?" I asked, as we began to walk down the hall. I wanted to poke my head into my living quarters and get a chance to talk to Mick without all the informal stiffness.

Mick answered with a quick, "Nothing, Lord, all is well." But when we finally reached my sleeping quarters, a massive sitting room attached to two more bedrooms, I cornered him and just stared until he cracked.

"Sorry, mate," he finally said, giving me a weak smile. His yellow tinted hair and leathery skin cracked under his smile. "I've heard 'bout the war and I don't want you to think I can't be a good soldier just because I'm a bit of a shoddy guard."

I laughed out loud and slapped Mick gently on the shoulder—I had to be safe with my increased attributes.

"Mick, I don't think you are a bad guard, in fact I'd say you are the best I have."

"So, you will allow me to go with my men when you pull together a fighting force?" Mick asked, excitement overtaking him as he leaned forward.

"Well," I said, backpedaling a bit. "Because you are my best guard, I was kind of hoping you'd head off things here while I took a force West against House Blalor."

"Let Gabriel do it, he's basically running the entire lot of us as it is," Mick said, pulling out a thin piece of wood, possible a toothpick but it was a bit too large for that, and began chewing on it. "Man bursts a vein in his forehead each time he catches me and my men playing cards, like there is that much to do out here."

"Is it really bad?" I asked, plopping down on a chair. "The extra gold doesn't help?"

"It helps with my bets, but that Gabriel fool has made travel to the town forbidden for guards, so I've got squat to do on my off days," Mick said, he seemed legitimately perturbed which upset me a bit because he'd been a good friend to me.

"I'll be speaking with Gabriel, don't you worry about that," I said, shaking my head. "You are all sacrificing so much already, and he thinks it's a good idea to restrict visiting the town, likely the only place for you all to cut loose. Ridiculous."

"Well," Mick said, looking at the ground. "There is a reason, but it's stupid."

"What happened?" I asked, wondering if I had been too quick to anger.

"Well, you know Todd, he's joined us for cards once or twice. He got into it with a local and messed him up pretty bad, the mayor had to heal him up, but it was all explained and the mayor said that there were no hard feelings. You see this local had a bit of a temper and drank a bit too much so when he saw his sister in Todd's arms, it kind of blew up," Mick said, explaining the situation.

"And to keep further issues from popping up, Gabriel cut off access to the town?" I asked, finishing his thought for him.

"Exactly," Mick said, his air of confidence nearly all gone as he stared at his feet.

"I'm not sure I'd have done any different, at least for a time, but I will speak with him and see if maybe just Todd can be held back from the privilege until a proper amount of time has elapsed," I said, rubbing at my chin as I thought of the best way to handle the situation. I didn't want to step on Gabriel's toes so to speak, but it was important to me that my men remained happy, and that wouldn't happen if their only means to relax and unwind was taken away.

Mick and I left after that. There was going to be at least another hour before the council gathered and I wanted to walk among the people living beneath my rule, to get a feel for their mood. I told Mick to go find something to keep him busy when I spotted Gabriel, thinking I'd have him show me around.

"Guard Captain Gabriel?" I asked, getting his attention. He had his back turned and he began to respond before seeing who had addressed him.

"It's Commander Gabriel," he said, then seeing who he addressed he added. "My Lord, excuse me for my tone."

"You have made yourself commander?" I asked, raising an eyebrow.

"No sir, of course not. By order of Steward Cron and the council, I was given the position," Gabriel said, his face staying impassive as he spoke.

"We need to talk, Commander, walk with me while I stroll through the streets of my keep," I said, he nodded firmly and stood beside me ready to go.

We left out the front gate, a large metal door ready to be slammed shut at a moment's notice, it seemed. Walking over a short bridge above a moat built around the main keep as a defensive measure, we entered the main square around the keep. It bustled with activity, several stalls set into the walls and commerce being carried out all around. Leaving out the main keep gate we traveled into the inhabited structures built all through the lower section of the keeps enclosed area. A larger wall where I'd first presented myself against Cron, was a way's ahead, but I didn't go that way, instead choosing to walk into a busier area that had business springing up.

There was a pub, races of all kinds that lived within the keep entered and exited. I saw a shop, perhaps a general store I assumed, and I headed right for it.

There was a building just beside the shop that had

been burnt out, all the windows bare and blackened, and just in front of it was a small crater like blast.

"What happened here?" I asked, gesturing to the damage.

"Some goblin doing alchemical experiments lost control and did significant damage to the building and the street. I believe it is on a long list of places that need attention. Despite the improvements we'd had, thanks to Cron's perk choices in building out infrastructure, we remain unequipped for the growing population," Gabriel said, regarding the area and shaking his head at the damage.

Lots to unpack there but I'd deal with that stuff later, instead I decided to get to the real point as to why I had him come with me. "Tell me why my guardsmen aren't allowed to visit Valestein?" I asked, slowing my pace to give him a chance to answer before we entered the shop.

"Simple, Lord Miles, there was a disturbance and I wished to avoid any additional tension from building between the two settlements. You see, the orc, goblin, troll, and dwarf population are already doing that well enough on their own, I would not allow our own men to also set such poor examples," Gabriel said, his words sharp and frank.

"And why not just punish those that offended the rules or caused the trouble? Surely a harsh punishment to a single individual is just as effective a deterrent." I stopped altogether, just out of the way of the traffic coming in and out of the shop.

"I considered as much; forgive me but, I believe my actions were more effective."

"Effective immediately all guardsmen, except for those who had directly caused mischief, will be able to return to Valestein. However, you have a good point and I want it to be known that if and when another disturbance occurs, all guardsmen will be kept from returning to the town for one week. That ought to have the same effect we'd both like to see," I said, then another idea popped into my head. "Also, let's see if the Mayor wishes to have the aid of our guardsmen to police his town. Have we asked them as much yet?"

"You are wise beyond your years," Gabriel said, but his tone didn't change so it was hard to tell if he was being serious or having one at my expense. "The mayor has his own force of town's guards and when I requested as much, he refused."

"So be it," I said, sighing. "Let's see what this shop has inside."

I walked through snow fallen streets that bustled with activity, Gabriel still at my side as we finished looking into the various shops that had sprouted up. I was surprised at the variety that I found, everything from a bakery owned by a delightful orc female who had a delvish serving companion, to a leather goods shop, a pub that rose several stories into the air and likely had rooms to sleep in, and even two butcher shops. Blackridge was truly growing into somewhere worth living, but now I had to ask them to sacrifice, and I worried I'd be asking too much.

An argument between two goblins began to rise above the noise of the regular street goers, and Gabriel stepped forward and swiftly got between the two as one raised a hammer against the other.

"You will both spend a night in the dungeons if you keep it up," he shouted, and they cowered. "We have zero tolerance for petty violence, and you know it."

"Krek knows it, but Fek bit my fekking toe," the bigger of the two green goblins said, his common was horrible.

"Fek just likes you," Fek said, a bit of a blush appearing on its face.

"Oh," Krek said, dropping his hammer and biting Fek.

Gabriel let it happen and turned back to me, indicating we could move on.

"They have the strangest customs and I've been trying to let as much of it play its course as I can, but they are a violent lot for being so small in stature," he said, shaking his head.

This Gabriel really wasn't as bad as Mick had painted him, in fact, the council and Cron had done well to appoint him over them all. Mick was a fine guard, but he was a bit too lax to handle some of these situations, I felt.

"Are you enjoying your time here at Blackridge?" I asked as we passed a few guards patrolling together, and we continued into the keep.

Gabriel stiffened a little before answering. "Of course, my Lord," he said.

I smiled and shook my head. "You can be honest with me Gabriel, is it the money, the location, or the amount of work?"

"None of that," Gabriel said, his shoulders losing a bit of the tension. "My family is hesitant to come join us still, though I've told them I have a handle on the worst of it. I'm afraid they are a bit wary of other races, having only ever been raised around humans. Frankly, until the last few months I stood with them. These beings were used in stories to scare my children. But now I'm not so sure. Perhaps given more time they will join me, but that is not your worry, my Lord, forgive me for speaking out of turn."

All this formality really got in the way of easy conversation. "I'm glad you did and don't ever be sorry to speak your mind to me. If you think it would help, I could give you leave to go speak with your family in person? I'm sure we can manage without you for a couple weeks."

"I'm not so sure, but I appreciate the thought," Gabriel said, the first smile I'd seen on his face slipping into place.

The walls of the keep were lit with braziers hanging every ten feet or so, but even so, there was a shadowy quality inside the incredible structure. Guards, servants, and what could be council members, all walked in the same general direction that we did. Gabriel was leading me to where the council meetings had been held for the last several weeks, a newly restored meeting room.

We reached the door and waited for the traffic to thin enough to get through, based on how many servants slipped in and out I'd say we were a bit early, but I didn't mind waiting.

"Is this a dinner as well?" I asked, seeing the food platters being brought in.

"No, usually," Gabriel said, raising an eyebrow at the servants. "You there, stop." A servant with an empty tray stuttered to a stop with a 'yes sir'. "Who ordered food brought to this room?"

"Cron, sir, it is to be a feast," the servants voice was meek and quiet. He scurried off as soon as Gabriel gave him the go ahead.

"Let's have a look," I said, pushing past a servant and the line of people trying to get inside.

When we broke through the crowd, what I found was an arena style room that reminded me of my solo dungeon dive in the Southlands, where the arena seats rose up higher and higher with a pit in the middle. In this case, the seats were made of stone and there was a twenty paces wide space opened at the bottom like a flat stage. In that flat space a table was being set up and filled with food. Two dozen chairs sat around the table with one end capped with a throne-like chair that I was sure Cron expected me to sit in. To the right of the throne was a slightly fancier chair than the rest, but less so than the throne.

Cron must really like showing off with chairs, because the rest were all starkly plain in comparison.

"Nice looking chairs," I said, elbowing Gabriel to get his attention away from the servants he was eyeballing.

"Cron has an itch that can't be scratched when it comes to chairs," Gabriel said, confirming what I thought. "There is a local woodsman within the keep who makes items, but Cron refuses to use him and sends orders to the village to make all these specialty chairs. Wasteful if you ask me, but he was in charge."

"Maybe I'll mention it to him, but I'd hate to take away something so close to his heart," I said, chuckling at my weak attempt at a joke.

"Indeed," Gabriel said, humoring me.

Having seen all there was to see, I dismissed Gabriel to go about his duties, to which he replied he would be attending the meeting. I gave him a hearty pat on the back and told him I'd return in ten minutes and check to see if the meeting was getting started yet. I hadn't seen Alayna or Emory in our walk about, and I was eager to see if they'd returned.

I found them in the library of all places. The last I'd visited here, it had been half-filled with ruined musty volumes, but now it was a quarter filled with books that looked like they'd survive another few years at least. I'd have to see what was done about the older volumes as even in their ruined state perhaps we'd be able to have them transcribed if they were copies that had any value.

"You have you a pathetic library and only one," Alayna said, shaking her head. "I'm going to have a lot of work cut out for me when I move here. Perhaps we can restore one of the fallen towers into a spiral library? I know they are meant for defense or whatever but think of how amazing that would be!"

She was brimming with excitement, and I missed everything she'd said after the 'move here' bit. I stepped forward, ignoring both Emory and Raphael, and pulled Alayna into a deep kiss.

"You'd move here?" I asked, when finally, my lips released her.

"In the future, if all works out as I hope," Alayna said, blushing.

"I guess I could see myself living here as well," I said, really letting myself think about it for the first time.

Blackridge Keep wasn't so far away from Creeshaw or Miles Manor when on the back of a griffin. The entire world was open to me on the back of Ares. It was incredibly rare to have a flying mount, I knew of only two other species that could be used, Pegasus and hippogriff, each of them nearly as rare as a griffin. Most distance traveling was done by portal, or at least it had but ever since the conflict at Lynsteen pass many of the most powerful wizards, mages, sages, and sorcerers had fallen, leaving a gap of able-bodied casters strong enough to support the complex portal magic.

It was a type of magic that had to be learned the hard way, the system unable or unwilling to feed that precise knowledge straight into your head. It also required an ability to visualize where you wanted to portal to in vivid detail, so it went right along with the ability to use a scrying spell to locate areas before opening a portal. It was the main reason I hadn't even thought to ask Warrick to open a portal to the Isle of Avalon, he'd have to have been there or be able to scry the location, but it was much too far for even a complex scrying spell.

No, Merlin had been my best bet, he'd obviously been all around Avalon and could have taken me with ease, likely even fending off the monsters we found waiting. But like all things in life, it wasn't so simple. When I needed the mysterious wizard the most, he'd disappeared on me. His words from our last meeting echoed through my head and I thought perhaps I should have expected it. He'd spoken of regret and wanting to follow the path that his people had taken. It hadn't made sense then and didn't make much sense now. He spoke as if he were an ageless titan who'd been around since the dawn of the planet or at least the dawn of our modern civilization.

My thoughts shifted back to the freedom that Ares offered me as Alayna walked me over to some books to show the different titles we'd acquired.

A wild thought crossed my mind, and I shook my head at the ridiculousness of it. What if I took Ares and left everything behind, the titles, the oaths, the responsibilities. I could leave my money to my mother; she'd know how to manage it. I'd renounce my titles and with them the responsibilities. Without so much weighing down on me I'd be able to tend to my main focus, being a Defender of the Balance.

I could travel the land, killing Chaos monsters and

turning Mana Shrines back to the cause of Order. Perhaps I'd even be able to fly Ares all the way to the Isle of Avalon, but I doubted it. She could fly many miles without rest, but the isles were too far according to my map, being nearly the length of the entire Kingdom of Newaliyn across the great waters.

As wild as the thoughts were, they had a pull to them that I couldn't ignore, so I acknowledged them and set them aside. Not today, but perhaps someday I'd be free from such responsibilities.

"This is an early edition and I checked, it had the older versions of the Binding Runic Inscription, why they modified it I don't know but this has extra precautions that would actually make it harder, not easier, for someone to crack it," Alayna had pulled down a book and was showing me a runic formation.

"You want to be in charge of filling my library?" I asked, having a fun idea pop into my head. "I can provide enough funds that we can at least fill it with volumes from Gilfoy's newest line of cheaper printed editions."

"I've heard they've constructed machines that do the work of printing volumes. It requires specialty plates to be forged, but once they are made it can churn out hundreds, literal hundreds, of books a day. Or was it a week? I can't remember, but can you imagine every book you could ever want available for a few silver?" Alayna asked, practically bouncing in excitement.

"It will change the world," I said, nodding my head. It excited me as well, but I wondered how it would change how the common folk looked at the world. When volumes of magic runes, grand adventurers, legends, and all manner of knowledge was freely available for any who had an extra silver or two. The world was changing perhaps a bit too fast, but there was no stopping change.

"Not everyone reads books," Emory said, pulling himself away from the flirty conversation I'd been overhearing him have with one of my Elite guards, Raphael. She'd been whispering as many crude flirty words to him as he'd been saying to her, and it made me smile.

"No, but they should," I said, shooting back my reply with a wag of my head. "People who read are the best, because we like words."

"Not exactly a winning argument for us," Alayna said, giggling. "Books are doorways to new worlds of knowledge or adventure. Even if you aren't as enamored with learning as Caldor and me, there are more and more books written in a fiction style of adventure and action, even romance stories have been gaining popularity. I've read a few of those titles if you need a recommendation?"

Emory looked like someone had slapped him. "I have all the romance I need in my life, thank you," he said, trying to stealthily grab at Raphael, to which she elbowed him hard enough in the side to double him over. All the while she maintained a straight back and serious presence.

When I looked at her with a raised eyebrow she simply asked, "Sir?"

"Carry on, Raphael, you'll get no complaint from me," I said, smiling.

"Any mystery stories?" Emory asked after he'd recovered. "My parents used to tell us scary stories filled with mystery and monsters."

"I'm sure there are," Alayna said, tapping her chin as if trying to remember.

We continued to chat for another few minutes before I told them there was a feast and I'd like them to come. I also mentioned it was a council meeting, but that they could leave if things got boring for them. Heading back to the arena style room, we walked down the staircase and filled the chairs just as others were beginning to arrive as well.

CHAPTER 22
BLACKRIDGE WAR COUNCIL

C ron came and did as I expected, sitting on my right side. I had Alayna sit on my left, an action that caught Cron's attention. He leaned in and spoke to me.

"Seating is very important, and I'd suggest you hold your left side for Calgain the former Orc chief and lead council member. He won't speak against you, but I know his honor would be wounded," Cron said, giving me a very serious look.

Without me saying a word, Alayna stood and moved down a single chair. I caught her eye and frowned. "Sorry," I said, but it wasn't necessary. She smiled cheerfully and just shook her head a little.

"So, tell me Cron," I said, getting his attention back after he filled his mug. "Why are we buying so many chairs?"

"Ah, well you see in dwarven culture what one sits on

is as important as where they sit," Cron explained, stroking his beard.

"That may be so, but if we have such a great need of chairs to be made then why isn't the work going to a craftsman inside of Blackridge?" I asked, keeping my tone neutral, as I was genuinely more curious than anything.

"Oh that, well just a matter of politics, I don't like the dwarf who runs that place, and the village has a master woodcrafter whose skills can't be ignored. Plus, it helps to build relations with the town," Cron said, shrugging.

"Perhaps we can split the work?" I asked, but Cron just gave me a stoney look. "Are you at least giving them work in the repair of the keep and surrounding buildings?"

Cron suddenly became interested in something on the far wall but eventually looked back to me as I just kept staring at him, awaiting his answer.

"He's a lout of a dwarf and I can't be letting just anyone assist in such important work," Cron said, exasperated.

"I'll speak with him and if I agree then fine, but otherwise I'd prefer to make use of local craftsmen inside Blackridge as well, deal?" I said, giving him my best diplomatic look, which in this case involved me trying not to laugh at the ridiculousness of the situation.

"Bah, you are Lord here, so I suppose it's fine," Cron said, taking a long drink.

I hoped he understood my position and didn't think I was just doing it to frustrate him. But he had a grin on his face once more, the ale having that effect on all dwarves I'd met so far. Not that I didn't enjoy a good ale, but no one could put it away and enjoy a fermented drink like a dwarf.

One by one members of the council and a few guards joined us, guards taking positions by the doors and around the room, while the council members found spots at the table. I studied the guards, each of them wearing my sigil, a black griffin in a field of white, and armor that included a metal cap atop their heads. I saw humans, I recognized most of them, and each of the other races represented: orcs, trolls, and even a goblin.

The goblin stood taller than most I'd seen. He had the darker skin that reminded me of a Deep Dwelling variety I'd encountered before. I didn't want to be rude, so I didn't examine him. He noticed me staring and straightened, raising his chin to appear as tall as possible. When he checked to see if I was still looking a few seconds later I gave him a head nod and turned my eyes elsewhere. This had the effect of making him stand even taller, a proud look on his face.

The orc named Jrok entered last with an orc guard of his own wearing a more traditional orc outfit of furs and animal skins. Jrok wore pretty much the same thing he did when I first met him, furs and leathers. He had a stern look on his face and he scanned the table seeing the spot beside me open and nodded his head in appreciation. It was clear he cared, just as Cron had said, about the place at the table he was given.

I met his gaze and in orc fashion he glared me down, not bowing his head or showing any sign of weakness. I matched his intensity, not nodding my head or showing any sign that he might take as one of weakness. A grin spread across his lips as he stood there staring at me and finally, he inclined his head, ever so slightly, to me and I did the same. His guard took a place on the surrounding walls, and he came to sit beside me.

"Much learning have I done," he said. He hadn't spoken any common that I remembered last time, so this was a new development.

"I'm pleased to hear you speak in a tongue that I can understand, your efforts are appreciated," I said, speaking normally. I could tell he didn't catch everything I said, but he nodded all the same.

"We have translators during the council meetings and invite all who wish to join to enter after a certain point, so don't worry, he'll hear all you have to say after dinner," Cron said.

And then without any more fanfare, the meal began. Cron had organized a true feast. Birds cooked to a golden brown, steaks, and all other assortments of meats, including a few monster meats—they had an extra gamey taste to them, so they were easy to pinpoint. Along with the varied meats, he'd added an assortment of vegetables, fruits, soups, and at least three types of ale.

Bite after bite, I enjoyed the extraordinary explosions of flavor. I consumed a small amount of everything, not wanting to eat myself into a stupor before a meeting, when my attention would be required. I constantly looked over to Alayna to see how she was managing, but each time I did she was mid bite or sipping on some soup. When the table finally had eaten it's fill, chatter began across the table.

Alayna was having a conversation with Jrok, that sounded like it was going well. She spoke slowly but somehow without sounding like she was speaking with a child, which I tended to do when I slowed down my own speech to help someone understand my words. Cron was in a conversation with another dwarf sitting beside him, talking about new deposits of iron found in a mine nearby.

I sat in silence, just listening to everyone talk until, from a few seats down, Emory called out to me. At first his words were lost to the chatter of the table, and he sighed, loudly pushing out his chair and walking over to me.

"I'm thinking I'm going to take off," Emory said, repeating himself.

"The meeting hasn't even started," I said, turning in my throne chair to address him. "Surely you can stay for a bit longer."

"Well, thing is I was going to take Raphael with me, she's uh, said that she knows a local establishment that I might enjoy," Emory said, winking at me after finishing.

I didn't know if he thought he'd find a brothel in Blackridge but I hadn't seen one and I wasn't going to keep him here if he didn't want to attend the meeting, but I figured there was more to his ask. "Tell her she can leave too, but don't go pissing off one of my elite guards," I said, glaring at him so he knew I was serious. He just grinned and clasped my outstretched hand, shaking it.

I watched as Emory pushed his chair in and gestured to Raphael. She looked to me a question in her eyes, and I nodded my head. She straightened and saluted me, before leaving the room after Emory. That won't look suspicious at all, I thought looking about the room, but no one seemed to notice or care that they'd left, so I let it be.

A line of servants trailed into the room and began clearing the table, taking plates, platters, and bowls, but leaving drinks and ale containers. After another ten minutes, everything had been cleared and the door above came closed with a soft thud.

"Shall we get started, Lord Miles?" Cron asked, sitting tall and his voice loud and projecting.

I matched his seriousness and tone. "Yes, let's begin," I said.

I noticed two people, an orc and a troll, who had sat at the table were now standing and I soon realized why, as they repeated, one after the other, what was said but in two different languages. I wondered if the goblins spoke one of those languages or if, as per usual, no one thought to translate for the goblins.

Making a note in my head to ask as much, I realized I really should have something to take notes with. I pulled free some loose paper, a quill that auto-filled ink from within the feather—a genius invention of Gilfoy's Emporium—and made ready to take any notes.

It started rather mundane, going over food supply numbers, conditions of new wells that had been dug, more information on the output of the mine, then they transitioned into where money was being spent and how much was being collected in taxes. I hadn't realized we had been taxing so I paid attention to this bit. Apparently, we were taking in less than half in taxes than we were spending in the repairs, wages, and all the other workings of maintaining a small town and keep. Because really that is what the surrounding area inside the walls had become, a small town.

Then, each senior member of the council, there were four, spoke about the condition of their people and any major events coming up. It turned out that the trolls had made contact with another tribe living somewhere in House Variyn, I immediately thought of Tekicalla and wondered if it would be the same tribe. During their contacts, he said they'd been under near constant attack and wanted to relocate to Blackridge and be given a spot on the council.

This struck some very lively conversation and it ended in a vote that passed in favor of allowing them to join after a trial period, where the newcomers would prove their worth—which sounded vague enough to me but everyone else seemed to know what it meant.

Then finally, as discussion slowed, I decided I could wait no longer. I cleared my throat getting everyone's attention. All eyes were on me and my breathing increased. One thing was for sure, I enjoyed battle much more than politics.

"House Variyn is at war, which means so are we," I said, letting the words settle in. There was a noticeable stir among the council members and the guards. When the translator finished, I continued.

"I have been ordered to raise a force of five hundred," I said, stopping to let the translator get that little nugget out to everyone. It had about the effect I expected, several council members shook their heads and a few just cursed and slammed their fists on the table, knocking drinks aside.

"You expect us to give half our population to war?" Cron asked, shocked. I hadn't told him the exact amount before, but I was thinking that I should have, because he no longer sounded like he was on my side.

I stared at Cron for a moment hearing what he'd said, we had a thousand citizens now? Pushing the new fact away and deciding I needed to look at my Settlement tab once more after we finished, I cleared my throat. "Please let me speak," I said, my voice commanding. Surprisingly everyone stopped as the translations went out and I cleared my throat again. "You live under the rule of House Variyn and by extension Blackridge's Lord, me. But I do not expect that all these numbers will come from our small population. I will send out riders to all the villages nearby, including our closest neighbor. In addition, I have personally paid for two hundred Runeforged to fight alongside you. All who face the banner of Blackridge will learn to fear us."

This got an entirely new response, before the translators had even finished the guards around the room cheered at my words. Cron smashed his mug down and sputtered words lost in the commotion. When I looked at him, he spoke again, and I heard him.

"You have how many Runeforged? Those monstrous golems are worth ten or more men each! Oh, my Lord you have been hiding a king's fortune from me," Cron said, slamming his mug several more times while he laughed uproariously.

Jrok spoke then, his voice as confident as he could make it, considering his broken Common. "Jrok will fight. Jrok is through running." And then he slammed his fist against his chest twice in a salute that I'd seen the guards use many times.

Similar pledges went out and discussion opened to how to go about recruiting the numbers we needed. It started with a back and forth about the guards, Cron wanted them all to stay and saying we couldn't spare any, but the rest, myself included, wanted to draft at least half of them.

"With a reduced population a reduced force will be sufficient," I said, but Cron just shook his head.

"We lose our grip on crime now and we might never get it back. There have been talks of a thieving guild forming within our gates. This is exactly what they'd want to happen," Cron said, but Gabriel spoke up then.

"Those claims are overstated and while I do not wish to lose any guards to a war, I can and will maintain the peace of Blackridge."

Cron harrumphed but said nothing further. It went to a vote and passed to allow half the guard force to be added to the soldiers that would go West. Then it was discussed how many *Awakened* were in the city and if any would be willing to take part in service, for a substantial compensation. They couldn't be directly recruited, only the King of all Newaliyn could do such a thing, as he was over all Adventurer's Guilds, local or not. Not counting those participating on the council, we had an unusually high population of *Awakened*, including most of the goblins.

The goblin council member puffed out his chest at this, but the orcs were quick to add that the goblins were also the smallest population in the city with the highest number of current residents of the jail cells, which had apparently been overflowing recently, so our new additions were being held in lower keep storage rooms under guard.

In total, we had 62 *Awakened,* all of which were nonhumans. When asked the average level, most were less than level 10. The goblins for instance, had a high rate of being *Sparked,* but they only had a single warrior over level 10, and he was serving as a guard, apparently it was the one standing up by the door. While the other races had a higher rate being *Sparked* as well, they had lost many fighters. When I pressed why that was, they launched into a story about the greatest tribes refused to fight, wanting to follow the orders of the gods, but many chose to defend their land and perished for their efforts. Eventually they fled through old roads to the safety of the Northlands.

It was determined that we would approach all of them with offers to be more active in growing stronger, defending Blackridge Keep and the surrounding area, forming groups, and rotating two groups to the front line to deliver supplies and news. None would be required to fight, and all could turn down the offer. However, I offered to outfit all who agreed with basic gear and dimension spheres, they'd come down a good bit in price, and weapons to help them progress. I didn't know what I could do about getting them into dungeons, but I was assured by Alayna that she'd see to it that they were formally made members of the Adventurer's Guild.

This bit of news had cheered up the room considerably more than even the previous news. We finished talking about the war effort and what would be done, I assured them that supplies wouldn't be an issue and that I had someone already working on that. Lance was coordinating the purchase of enough food to feed four times the number I was meant to recruit and getting them stored in dimensional storage containers by trusted sources for safe keeping until they could be transferred over to my care.

I did, however, continue to encourage them to work to farm and cultivate the land outside the keep. I'd noted that several small farmhouses had been erected, but with the winter upon us the ground remained too stiff to work. There was a large amount of seed and fertilizer for the land the moment it was ready to begin farming. Because I thought about it, I even promised to pick a perk from the system Settlement menu to help with crops and encouraged the others do so as well. Cron would oversee assigning property rights in my stead, as I didn't have the know-how to properly do it, nor did I really want to do something so time consuming.

Cron informed me that we did indeed have a single Perk left, but as I'd left him in charge of all the previous ones we'd gotten when our population increased, they had gone to increasing and maintaining building infrastructure. Many of the buildings being made were assisted in some way by the system he told me, I had very little experience with it, but he explained in between bouts of discussion about one problem or another that didn't need my direct input.

Apparently, if you included specific materials in the building and you finished it then used the control crystal in the throne room—I hadn't even realized that was a thing until just then when he told me—you could select the building and have it be connected into the central keep's lines of power. Part of how these settlements grew stronger had to do with spreading the lines of power or more likely, just mana, through the ground naturally towards buildings that could then benefit from the magic.

It granted special perks and even visual changes to the buildings, which I guess he'd picked several perks that allowed us to have more buildings connected than normally would be allowed for such a small population, resulting in several Prime buildings that produced well above what they should. All but the woodworker's shop, a fact that made me shake my head at him some more.

Finally, the last bit of the meeting came, and at some point the room had filled with citizens who wished to listen, but honestly I hadn't noticed when so it came to a surprise when I heard a general roar of murmurs when the next topic was announced: prisoners.

It was interesting to me how they handled this portion of the council meeting. They'd read the name of the accursed, listed what they were accused of, and then asked if anyone in the crowd was willing to speak for them or pay reparations. So far no one had. I listened in to the next one, regarding a goblin just as the few before it had been.

"Stog has been imprisoned for eight days so far," a dwarf I recognized but couldn't remember his name, read from a scroll. "He is accused of public endangerment and destruction of community property. Is there any among you that will speak for him or pay his reparation in the amount of ninety-four gold."

I almost asked him to repeat himself, how had one goblin done so much damage and why? Could it have anything to do with the burnt-out building with the large crater in front of it that I saw during my tour with Gabriel. He'd mentioned that a goblin's alchemical experiments had gone awry but not that he'd been imprisoned for it.

"Crazz will speak," a scratchy voiced male goblin said, I turned to see that it was the dark-skinned goblin that was standing in his guard uniform.

"Very well, guardsman Crazz, you have the floor," the

announcer dwarf said, gesturing his hand towards the space in front of him.

Crazz looked around the room, his eyes skittish, but they landed on me, and he nodded his head towards me. I returned the gesture and he walked to the space in the middle of the floor where the dwarf stood.

"Crazz knows Stog, many years," Crazz said, his words very deliberate and slow. His common basic at best, but he was trying and despite his way of speaking, sounded a bit more even toned than Jrok. "Stog strong like Crazz but mind strong, not arms. Release Stog, and he fight his mind for you." Crazz was looking directly at me now and I got the impression his words were meant for me.

"And have you any gold to settle his debts?" The dwarf said, sighing as if he was already growing frustrated with the procedures.

"Crazz not have many gold, but master Lord can speak freedom and Stog be free," Crazz said, gesturing at me when he said the phrase 'master Lord'. I wasn't sure I liked the combination of those titles, but I understood what he was getting at.

"I'd like to speak for this Stog as well," I said, smiling.

"Very well m'lord, Crazz you may return to duty," the dwarf said, sending the large goblin away.

"I do not know Stog, but it sounds like he is intelligent enough to make a pretty big explosion and powerful enough not to die by it," I said, looking at Crazz all the while I spoke. He nodded along to all I said. "I will pay his reparations and would see him released if he agrees to receive training as an Adventurer." I paused, then looked to Crazz. "He is an *Awakened* isn't he?"

"Stog has traveled to stone, Stog spark mastered," Crazz said, excitedly.

"Good, that would have been embarrassing," I said, laughing. No one joined in, but Alayna gave me a pity giggle. "I'd like to extend the same offer to all *Awakened* prisoners who are willing to take an oath of service. It wouldn't do for us to have an untapped resource locked away."

This caused a stir among the crowd, and I couldn't tell if it was one of excitement or perhaps anger. Something occurred to me then and I added an addendum to what I'd said.

"This only goes for current prisoners; it is definitely not an invitation for *Awakened* individuals to go out and commit crimes with a free pass expected afterwards."

Some of the crowd quieted at that and I was glad to have thought about it. I stepped down after that and let the proceedings continue. After listing a few more names and surprisingly a few that had someone speak and pay for their reparations, that topic of business ended, and the doors opened.

Led by a chain and shackled together by hands and feet were the bandits that we'd captured and two goblins wearing surprisingly little, a female and a male I guessed by the bits that were covered.

This part I hadn't been looking forward to, but I knew that judgement must be passed. The lead member of the council would be the one to pass judgement after speaking things over with the council and the Lord of Blackridge Keep or its steward. Things started similarly as they had with the previous proceedings, the dwarf, whose name I couldn't remember, read off their names and the charges.

The humans were charged with banditry, attempted murder, and waylaying a Lord—this one surprised me but I just went with it. Then it got to the goblins, both of whom were being charged with public indecency. Cron leaned over and said they'd been caught going at it in a dark alley and two guards had caught them. I rolled my eyes, which made Cron laugh.

Then each of the prisoners were allowed a short period of time to speak on their behalf if they wished. None of the bandits, save the last, chose to take that opportunity. Daniel Marteese stepped forward as best he could and cleared his throat.

"I would speak to each crime individually," he said, standing as tall as he could and staring me down. "We are said to have been bandits, but we accomplished nothing other than getting ourselves slaughtered. In fact, you, m'Lord." He inclined his head slightly and continued. "You were our first attempt at such, and it failed miserably. To the second charge of attempted murder, while a few here wielded bow and arrow against these fierce warriors." He gestured to Alayna now. "Their powers out-matched us and never were they in any true danger. Also, I might add that I myself did not bring any force against you, as I am a Warlock of the 11th level and could have used my infernal fire on you but chose not to. Even now, I hold back my power to prove to you one simple fact."

"What is that simple fact?" I asked, startling him a bit as he likely didn't expect anyone to actually answer. He stammered for a second but caught his wind once more.

"That I can be of help to you and yours," Daniel said. "I know of the coming war, and you will surely need lieutenants or commanders or at least special forces that are *Awakened*?"

"And why would we trust you with such a task? You, who would turn to banditry and attacking the weak for profit?" I asked, my tone growing firmer as I considered this man's arrogance.

"I, ahh, I can only speak for myself of course, but I am very trustworthy. Surely you can find it in your heart to forgive a simple thing."

"Your time is up, I think. The charges stand and you will be judged," I said, watching his expression for any sign that he might try and attack.

"Don't worry," Cron said, leaning in and whispering to me. "Those shackles are enchanted to suppress an ability activation. We had them specially crafted after a dozen goblins used little tricky skills to break free."

The goblins didn't speak for themselves, but I doubted they needed to, as Cron was likely to recommend that they be freed with a fine or something. It was time to deliberate now, so the council got up and I followed a line of them into a room just to the side of the main chamber where another table was set up.

They went through each name and discussed what the standard sentence would be for each, starting with the goblins. As I thought, Cron spoke up on their behalf and recommended we release them. He also recommended that the guards be told to stop wasting council time by arresting fornicating goblins, otherwise we'd have to arrest every goblin in the city, he told them. I smiled but kept my opinions to myself, merely nodding along as he spoke to show my support.

When it came to the matter of punishment for the bandits, I listened intently. The dwarf read off the charges for each that would be recommended from a large tome. Where he'd gotten a book of law or who had drafted it, I didn't ask, but I made a note to give it a look afterwards.

"Banditry has a sentence recommendation of five years hard labor, a fine of ten gold per provable offense, or death. The charge of attempted murder is six months hard labor, five gold fine, or death. The charge of waylaying a Lord of the court in the pursuit of his duty is three months hard labor and one gold piece. As always, any fine can be paid by additional time imprisoned while doing hard labor at a rate of a month per silver."

No one spoke up immediately, so I decided I'd chime in. Standing, I stepped beside the dwarf, he ceded his spot before the table for me.

"I passed sentence to over a dozen of them when they failed to surrender," I said, choosing my words carefully. "With my blade," I summoned my weapon into my hand and looked hard at it, "they were killed. Put to death for the same crimes those that surrendered committed," I let my blade fall from my grip and it faded away before touching the ground, "but I think that death shouldn't be an option now. It seems a shame to waste life when an alternative is possible. I will cede the decision to you all, but I thought you should know my mind on the matter."

I took back my seat at the head of the table, letting the dwarven speaker of the council return to his spot.

"Has anyone else words to speak on the matter? If not, I suggest we vote on the sentences and return to deliver them."

Jrok spoke then, and I waited for the translator to give me his words.

"What of the offer towards *Awakened*? Didn't that human declare himself as such and should he and his kind be given the same opportunity?" The words were spoken by the most fluent orc I'd ever heard without barely a hint of an accent.

"I'm sure that Lord Miles did not intend for his words to be passed to those who do not live within his realm, these bandits deserve no such special treatment," Cron said, clearly aggravated.

A discussion broke out, whether or not they should be offered the same and we put it to a vote after much conversation. The majority felt they should be given the same opportunity and I went along with it, seeing in a small part the fairness of it.

"I'll require an oath from them, as I said before," I

said, reminding the group. Jrok nodded his head, likely thinking it was a good idea.

Oaths between *Awakened* and confirmed by the system were not things you could easily break if not released by the one you gave the oath to. It could literally cause death to those that knowingly break them. But it was a commonly accepted fact that if you gave an oath to someone who was *Awakened,* even non-awakened, could be affected by the consequences. It was more of a proxy type situation and acted more like a witch's curse than a death sentence, making you weak and sickly for a time.

Decision finally made, I followed the many council members out into the hall and back into the main room, where everyone waited, and the prisoners were guarded by a good number of guardsmen. Everything was as we left it and Alayna, who walked beside me still attending as if she were a council member, whispered into my ear.

"That was merciful of you, I appreciate it."

I turned and smiled to her, wanting to kiss her but not wanting to draw attention away from the proceedings. Instead, I reached out and squeezed her hand.

Things started much as they had behind closed doors, with the standard charges being read from a large book and the color draining from the faces of the bandits present.

The goblins were charged first, or rather they had their charges dropped and were released. Then it was time for the bandits and Daniel called out, his words filled with sorrow now.

"Please I don't want to die, I will take an oath of solitude and peace. Please, anything but to be killed with these numbskulls," he said, really laying it on thick.

The dwarven speaker turned to me and smiled, then gestured to me and I got the hint. I stood and took a place beside him.

"Before I pass down judgement, tell me, Daniel," I said, looking him right in the eyes. "Who else among you are *Awakened*?"

Daniel's expression relaxed all too fast and I saw how good at play acting he was when he spoke with a completely normally voice. "Why is that important?" He asked, a coy smile on his lips. "Awakened or not, we all die the same."

"It would be in your best interest to answer," I said, passing my eyes over the rest. Several of the prisoners, in fact, all of the brothers we'd captured and all but two of the nine, raised their hands. That made seven.

"Little Johnny at the end is the best healer I've seen, don't let him tell you he ain't one of us," one of the more dirty-faced bandits said. The smallest of the bunch, a man that looked no older than Creed, looked up from the floor and slowly raised his hand as well. So, eight out of nine then.

"If you are willing to take an oath of service and assist Blackridge in growing stronger, while staying clear of crime." I added the last bit as it seemed necessary for this lot. "Then you will be outfitted, armed, fed, and trained to enter dungeons and grow stronger. You will be in contract directly under me, Caldor Miles, and as such, anything you do will come under me and I beg you to remember the fight I had against your leader. If he'd stayed, I'd have slain him. Do not test my patience, for death is too easy a punishment for you."

CHAPTER 23
UNFORTUNATE NEWS

They all took the oath, except for the one that wasn't an *Awakened*. He was sent back to the prison cells to be added to the crews that worked the farms. It would take him time, but if he did his duty, he'd be a free man someday. I made sure the guards understood to keep a close eye on the bandits, but if they tried to flee and break their oaths the system would see to their punishment. With the council meeting over, I decided it was time to visit the village.

"Do you mind if I come with?" Alayna asked, fluttering her eyes at me.

I rubbed at the back of my neck as I considered it. "I don't know that it will be a pleasant visit, I'm going to be asking for them to give as many as they can to the war," I said.

"Perhaps you should wait to know how many troops you've gathered from Blackridge first," Alayna suggested.

I shook my head. "No, it needs to be now. I don't know how much time we have left, but it would be good to be on our way in the next few days, and I wanted time to gather them up and speak with them all," I said, confident that my way was the best path forward. Sure, there was a benefit to knowing numbers, but at this point I'd take what I could get and be all the better for it.

With that in mind, Alayna and I left to the village. Raphael, Mick, and Emory were tagging along. Raphael and Emory had returned as we prepared to leave and just fell into step beside the three of us. Mick of course, had been around the entire time, and couldn't wait to get a chance to go back to the village.

Ares reached out to me with her mind, she was happy and had found something to eat. I sent back thoughts of what I was doing and told her that I didn't need her at this moment, a thought that she appeared to be fine with as I felt her dig deeper into her meal.

The air was still of any sounds of birds or insects, the cold doing its part to keep them away. The night sky was lit tonight, both moons shining enough light to see by as we traveled a well-worn path towards the village on foot. We were nearly halfway there when Mick broke the silence with some conversation, a welcome break to the silence of the night.

"Have you thought about what I asked you about earlier?" Mick asked.

I knew what he meant, he was worried I'd leave him behind to stay in Blackridge Keep, but he'd already changed my mind. Gabriel was more than capable of running Blackridge Keep's security.

I made a show of pretending to think it over before looking him in the eyes and saying. "Only if you work directly under me. I don't know how the rankings, or anything work just yet, but I imagine I'll be able to appoint several of the guards into high positions over the legion we gather. You too Raphael, I'll need stronger soldiers like you."

"I'm a guard," she said flatly. "But I could be convinced to play soldier...for the right price."

I laughed, but stopped when I realized she was serious. "I'm sure we can work out the logistics of it later. You are already paid more than anyone else, you know."

"I know," she said, smiling ruefully.

The town came into view not long after. It was aglow with lantern light, and by the sounds of it, we would be interrupting a festival or something. We approached a palisade gate and a guard yelled down at us.

"No travelers tonight, it's the Winter Festival."

"I am Lord Miles, ruler of Blackridge Keep," I said, ignoring his words. "Allow us entry and fetch Mayor Valestein." It was rude, but I'd come all this way, and time was of the essence, so to speak.

The guard glared down at me but called down to someone to do just what I'd instructed. A few minutes later, the gate swung open and the mayor stood before me. He was a burly man with features weathered by time and age. His face mostly hidden from view by a thick full beard that a dwarf would envy. He stood alone and his low rumble of a voice broke the growing silence between us.

"Lord Caldor Miles, any other day you'd be a welcome sight, but tonight is our Winter Festival."

"If I could wait, I would," I said. "I don't need you to act on what I am going to tell you tonight, but I must speak with you in private for a few minutes."

The mayor looked at me with hard eyes, but eventually sighed and waved me forward. "You lot can join the festivities, but don't go eating all my food before I get a crack at it."

Walking through the gate, my senses were assaulted by smells and sights. Meats, sweets, and more wafted into the air inside the town. It truly was a town now, buildings that before had been half constructed or in ruins, now stood tall. As we walked towards the center of the town, the road curved around what must have been a woodworker's shop —it was twice the size of our own and every bit of it had been carved with swirls and floral designs showing off the skill of the one who did the work.

There were other shops, one that caught my eye was definitely a book store and perhaps a magic shop, it was hard to decipher the meaning. The mayor gestured for the group to continue onward and took me to the side, skirting the festivities. A large bonfire and many long tables had been set out. People danced, ate, drank, and the children played sword fighting with wooden sticks. I wasn't trying to notice, but I saw a good many healthy, strong men among those in the festivities. Then there was the number, at least five or six hundred people celebrated, half of that must be healthy able men.

The mayor led me to a building gated off from a street, just a stone's throw from the festivities. It had a black metal gate surrounding it, bushes growing healthy and strong around the base and a cobbled stone pathway leading to the front door. He pushed on through and into the two-story house. It was dark inside, but before I could cast Light, he'd muttered a few words himself and golden light sprung up in the center of the room. Using the new lights illumination he slipped to the other side of the cluttered room and lit a lantern set into the wall.

It was good he did it as fast as he did, because the spell he'd used, a healing spell by the feelings washing over me, had all but died out the moment he put match to wick. He proceeded to light two more lamps before sitting down in a well-worn wooden armchair and gesturing that I sit across from him. I picked up and moved several books off the chair and placed them gently aside, before taking my seat.

"Bout the war I'd wager?" Valestein said before I had a chance to open my mouth.

"I'm afraid so," I answered, meeting his hard eyes. He shook his head, and I could tell this wasn't going to be an easy conversation.

"I can't do that to them," he said, taking a deep slow breath before saying, "I won't do that to them."

"I'm afraid there is no choice, I will conscript them into service if I must, but it will be better if they volunteer," I said, suddenly wishing I'd waited to speak of this after all.

"We've had growth in our population, but we are still in need of every able-bodied man to work the field when winter ends, can you promise me they will be back in time for planting or even harvest time after that?" He asked. There was a sadness in his eyes that made my gut hurt.

"They will be paid for their time and I can arrange for that pay to come straight to their families," I said, my mind racing to come up with something to placate the man. "And supplies, seeds, food stuff, all of that can be provided through trade with Blackridge Keep." I knew enough not to offer charity. He was a proud man and they'd taken this ruins of a town from nothing, to a place so many could call home.

"Tell me, do you know Lord Variyn personally?" He asked.

The sudden change of topic threw me off a little but I nodded, indicating that I did. Deciding that wasn't a strong enough response I spoke, "I do know him personally and it is by his generosity that I've been ordered to only recruit half the amount all other Vassal Lords are conscripting."

"Because you've got no one to recruit most likely," he said, chuckling, his voice a low rumble. "Tell me why he thinks he can take on the might of House Blalor? I see none of my men returning from such a conflict. So why should I send them to their deaths?"

I took my time to consider his questions, I owed him

that much. "There are special circumstances that I can't reveal that will give us the upper hand. We will win this conflict and it will be a swift victory. I suspect your men will be returned within a matter of months, not half a year or even an entire year. I personally have a force of two-hundred Runeforged that will weather the front lines and ensure our people don't get cut down so easily. I promise you that I will keep these men as safe as they can be," I said, no doubt in my mind that I'd do anything in my power to ensure that each of them made it back alive.

"Which means not safe at all," he said, grumbling. "I've been in war, son. It is hell and it eats up honorable men with good intentions like hungry dogs. You won't save my boys, you might try, but I'll be telling them straight that to volunteer is death, but it's a death that might provide some coin for their families. I will pass on your message, but don't expect many volunteers. You never said by the way, how many men do you need?" He asked.

I bit my lower lip for just a second, before clearing my face of any reaction. "I'm still getting final numbers from my Blackridge Keep, but I suspect around a hundred men should do it."

The mayor shook his head. "You'll never get that many volunteers."

"I'll take what I can get," I said, clasping his burly hand and looking him in the eyes for one last time before getting up and leaving.

CHAPTER 24
COMMANDER TAB

I sat across the table from the respective leaders of each larger body of races, orcs, trolls, dwarfs, and goblins. Jrok represented the orcs, while Cron sat for his people, then there was a troll whose name was Pok'wu, and an enormously obese goblin named Baacs. We'd gathered to discuss what they'd learned about potential recruits, what I hadn't expected was how thoroughly they'd do their jobs.

"Out of the two hundred and thirty-nine dwarves living in Blackridge Keep, one hundred and thirty are able-bodied men but taking craftsmen that we will need out of equation, that leaves 95 Dwarves ready to serve," Cron said.

"Orcs have one hundred twenty-one ready to kill for Lord Miles," Jrok said in his broken common.

"Trolls are more committed and will provide one hundred and twenty-two ready to slay your enemies," Pok'wu said, his common much better than Jrok's but still with the troll accent that was common among their people.

"Baac make all goblins go, lots and lots," Baac said, shaking his head. Cron face palmed and looked down at a paper he had with notes scrawled on it.

Cron spoke after looking over the notes. "At last count they had a population of one hundred and eighty-four, but we need them for our most basic labor, so I'd wager we wouldn't want to take more than half their number. Say, ninety goblins to be fair?"

I did a quick bit of mental math to come up with the total. They were offering an amazing four hundred and twenty-eight troops when I'd expected them to be able to field maybe two hundred on the best of days. Their attitude had really changed since the first announcement went out. With my two hundred Rune-forged and a hundred men from the village I'd be arriving with seven hundred and twenty-eight men. Or I could cut back the recruits and come with the five hundred I'd been asked to bring, was there any reason to bring more? Sure, more men meant more potential soldiers to be able to be fielded and I wondered how many of those number were Awakened that would be needed to support the legion through supplies and logistics?

"Each of you will pick your sixty best men and I will go to the village where they will provide fifty men. That will give us all the troops we need while only having to take a small number from the guard forces that I can appoint as officers over the recruits," I said, nodding my head as I spoke, solidifying my own resolve.

"As you command," Cron said, making notes on his paper.

I left the council shortly after with plans to see the troops they'd gathered first thing in the morning to do some introductions. I made my way to the village, this time on the back of Ares so my trip took mere minutes. I entered the open palisade and made my way to the mayor's home. Ares flew above, keeping an eye on the surroundings for me, my own mind vaguely aware of what she saw. As I neared the town's center, I saw a bustle of activity and headed towards it. The smell of delicious breads being baked in the early morning filled the air, and I could see a crowd of townspeople surrounding a small raised platform.

"You live within the borders of House Variyn and will be expected to contribute!" It was the mayor, his voice echoing over the grumbles of the crowd. "I've it on good authority that the conflict will be brief and the pay high, think of this as an opportunity to grow in proxy levels and favor with your nation."

"What has House Variyn done for us other than tax us into the ground!" A voice cried out from the crowd of at least a hundred or more.

"Lord Miles has provided much of the food you eat, the stone we used to rebuild this mess of a town, and the iron you use all comes from Blackridge Keep mines and quarries. And at prices you'd never get from anyone else.

You may not like House Variyn or its Lord, but the man we've to deal with, Lord Miles, is a fair and honorable man. I'll have Tom Foundry outside the Kelly's bakery. See him if you are interested but heed my words. If not enough volunteer, conscripts will have to be made and I know which of you are able-bodied."

As he spoke, I slunk deeper into the crowd, trying not to be noticed. Unfortunately, I was wearing armor and a fair bit taller than the rest. The mayor noticed me but said nothing as the crowd began to disperse. There were mumbles among the people, but nothing so bad against me personally as much as House Variyn in general. Seems like they had a general discontent towards Lord Variyn, but not me personally.

When most of the crowd had cleared out, the mayor waved me over.

"I'd had only today and no, I've not got anything new to report," he said, seeming exasperated.

"I've just stopped by to pass some information, only sixty men will be required, and I'll be paying double whatever the standard soldier wages are. I figured maybe that will help it along," I said, watching his expression for any signs of change. He visibly relaxed, his shoulders loosening.

"You don't know the standard soldier wages, do you?" He asked, laughing boisterously. "You must have gold glowing from you to so easily piss it away, but I'll spread the word. That should get you at least fifty men, easy."

"Good, because I need them to report tomorrow

morning for training and logistics, I need to get a solid count so I can get armor and weapons ready. Not to mention several hundred tabards so people know who they'll be fighting for," I said, stressing myself out with the weight of it all.

"They'll wear the Black griffin on a field of white then, and not the insignia of House Variyn?" He asked, scratching at his beard.

I looked up and felt suddenly foolish. "Is that not standard practice?" I asked, cursing myself for not knowing all this already.

"I don't know, to be honest, the last time there was a war I fought among the ranks of House Variyn, but under the banner of the King, like all Awakened when it finally came to a head at Lynsteen pass," he said, his eyes looking far off as if reliving the memory. "It wasn't a time I'd want to revisit. Vast armies of the undead, each one requiring a good smack upside the head to finish off."

"My father fought in that battle," I said, trying to imagine him fighting against waves of undead that had been imbued with the powers of Chaos.

"Your father turned the tide of that battle, but he fought more powerful foes than I've ever encountered. I spent years wasting away at the bottom of a mug after that battle, my progression gone stale. Even now I'm only a level higher than what I was that day. Seeing all my friends, even some family, be pulled apart limb by limb and being unable to do a thing..." He went quiet suddenly and I let him recover. "But this is different, a simple war of the

Houses, a common thing really. You will do your damnedest to keep my people alive, won't you?"

"I will," I said, clasping his hand and shaking it.

He left then, heading back towards the front of town and I lingered in the square to give him some space, eventually heading out of town and joining Ares as I waved the guard's goodbye.

The next morning came swiftly and the air, while still cool, was warm when compared to the last few days. So much so, that I heard the chirps of insects moving just out of sight and spotted wildlife moving here and there among the trees. I'd ordered the troops to be assembled at the edge of the forest, not far from where we'd hid, all those months ago when first coming across Blackridge Keep.

Emory and Alayna had stayed in town to get a bite to eat, but I didn't walk alone. At my side were my most trusted and respected guards; Mick, Raphael, Gabriel, and Michael—whom I respected for his rank as an elite guard, but I knew very little about him. I'd considered taking a few more guards that I had my eyes on to be leaders, but I'd leave that work for Gabriel. I'd pulled him aside and tasked him with telling me who he could lose and who would be best leading troops, one of the reasons why he was with me now despite not having any plans of going to war with us.

The crowd of three hundred looked smaller than I'd

expected in my mind, but I wasn't great at visualizing groups of people. There were five distinct groups, each of them splitting up based on race.

"I want the three of you to line them up in proper lines and teach them to stand at attention," I said, seeing the mayor walking over. The three Elite guards went to work, yelling and calling people into line. It was obvious all at once that the orcs, trolls, and goblins had no clue what they were saying, but as the dwarves and humans fell into line, they took notice and began to line up as well. All but the goblins had formed up really well.

The goblins, most wearing scraps of clothing or looking extremely malnourished, sat around or stood purposely out of the straight lines they tried to form. Gabriel narrowed in on them and with considerable work managed to get them all lined up.

"We had one hundred and three men try to sign up when I told them the wages offered," Valestein said, his low voice turning to a rumbling laugh. "I picked you out the best we have to offer, half of them are rough men used to rough circumstances. They will be effective soldiers if you can work them into listening to you."

"I'm sure they'll do just fine," I said, looking over the humans that had been gathered. "It was a ragtag lot of various ages, even a few men with graying hairs."

I turned to the mayor and gestured at a few of them. "Bit old for soldiering don't you think?" I asked, trying to mask my disappointment until I heard his reasons.

"Those three older looking gentlemen will be the best

soldiers you have, not a single one of them is below level ten in their proxy levels for being a soldier. I think they said they each earned their perks and levels as men at arms, so they'll be naturally faster and have skills with a spear more than these green horns. Trust me, you are getting a bargain with them. Those proxy levels of theirs have made them easily the strongest men we have in the town, it was a great loss to me when I saw they'd signed up."

My look of disappointment faded into something new, appreciation. I knew many of the orcs, trolls, and perhaps a few goblins, had proxy levels relating to wartime, but their structures were vastly different, or so Cron told me. The dwarves had very few soldiers left alive, but their men were a hard people and quick to pick up training, again, this was according to Cron's word. I trusted him though, even if he did talk up his own people.

"I'd like to speak with them," I said, starting to walk towards the group but the mayor held out a hand.

"Best let me grab them and bring them here. You're a Commander now, let them do the walking," Valestein said, his large form moving swiftly through the grassy earth.

The sun was out in full force just over the horizon and I was reminded that my armor didn't have the comfort enchantment I was used to. Though the leather jump suit and the metal plates that went over it that made up my armor were hot, my high constitution had a way of dealing with it and making it only mildly discomforting. This armor was likely strong enough for multiple enchantments at item level 40, so I'd see about adding my favorite enchantment when I got back to town.

While I waited for the old timers to come over, I went over what else I needed to do when I returned. I'd have to visit an enchanter and see what other items I had that could take enchantments, any little improvement would be welcomed. I also needed to buy better attribute increasing gems for my armor. I'd put in the best I had to offer, but I knew that if I was willing to pay, I'd be able to slot +10 per Dual-Aligned Gemstones instead of just the +5 that I could personally craft. If I had the time to figure it out, likely a few weeks minimum, I'd do it myself, but I didn't.

I'd also need to get with Lance and see if he could recommend someone to work as an assistant and quarter-master for the coming months. I had too much to do to remember and take care of myself. We needed armor, weapons, supplies, and more that I likely wasn't remembering. There was also a need to organize the *Awakened* in my service to act as supply lines with the help of dimensional storage. War would be a different beast without storage containers that could literally store enough supplies for an entire army for weeks.

I remembered back to when I'd had a hand in the slaughter of the goblin camp, something I'd made my peace with long ago, and how I'd been able to store away so much just by using extra-large containers that only took up a single slot within my dimensional storage cube. It still bounced at my side whenever I walked, its square shape not ideal, but I'd not replaced it yet. My ring of storage that I'd gotten had been a lifesaver many times over, as I could easily pull weapons from it without much trouble.

"These are the men I was telling you about." The mayor's voice rumbled from behind me, I'd taken to staring back towards the keep while I thought on matters. It was truly a sight to behold now that work on all but one tower was complete, large spires set atop the tallest of the towers reached up into the sky like fingers wanting to grab down the clouds.

I turned and regarded the men. Up close they looked even older, their skin weathered and wrinkled. But I held off my judgement, I knew by experience, that age wasn't always a defining factor in one's ability to do hard work. Ferdel's consistency outworked the younger men that we employed, age having no luck slowing him down. Perhaps his proxy levels as a soldier had something to do with that? It was an interesting thought and made me wonder why more people didn't seek out proxy levels as a soldier if it could have such long-term bonuses.

Being a guard or a soldier, it would seem, were the best proxy levels you could get as they stayed with you no matter where you went. My proxy levels as an orchard farmer were tied to my farm and without some specific system permissions from those over the town or kingdom, it was hard to transfer them to another place. It was one of the reasons travel and relocating like what Mayor Valestein had done was so uncommon.

"Give me your names, soldiers," I said, trying to

channel my inner 'Commander'. It seemed to work, they straightened and stood at attention, answering me left from right.

"Man at arms, proxy level 14, Victor Brecken."

"Man at arms, proxy level 11, Otto Caldwell."

"Bowman, proxy level 26, Silas Boden."

It was a struggle not to whistle at the last one. I gave him a proper look and it was clear he was the strongest of the three. He had all gray hair, his face mildly wrinkled, and piercing orange eyes that I'd only seen on Delvish before. He wore leather armor, all three did, and it was well cared for, it had the shine of a recent oiling. Looking at his neck I saw muscles that would make a young man jealous, then seeing how his armor ended at the elbow I saw he had massive forearm muscles, much bigger than the other three.

I imagined his back must still be muscled from years of drawing a bow as well. Warbows were not an easy thing to draw, and it took a lot of time and practice to get to the point where you could use the most deadly ones. Obviously, his proxy levels had been at work in keeping him fit, but I would bet a small fortune that this man continued to practice the bow.

"Silas Boden, you have kept up your skills and are ready to serve?" I asked, raising my chin as I walked around all three inspecting them. Their uniforms were truly immaculate, and I noticed that each of them had a belt knife with a House insignia pressed into it, House Variyn.

"Yes, sir," Silas said, raising his own chin into the air and staring forward.

"All three of you at ease, tell me of your experience Mr. Boden," I said, each of them relaxing but still standing at attention as far as I could tell, perhaps just a little less stiff. Whatever training they'd received it was ingrained into them and these three would be a welcome boon to my troops.

"I served in more conflicts than I can recall, I stood against the undead hordes, and I am ready and willing to answer the call," Silas said, bringing his fist up to his chest and hitting it twice in salute.

I nodded, and asked the same of the other two, getting similar answers. These were men that had seen war and come out the other side ready to do it all again. I hoped that the men I was taking to battle would turn out half as well adjusted as these three seemed. Though, of course one didn't wear one's weakness on their sleeves, so who knew how close my views were to the truth.

"You three do what you can to get those boys ready for war," I said, looking into each of their eyes and seeing determination enough in each of them. "We've got a tough road ahead of us, but with soldiers like you I don't see how we can lose."

They each stood a little taller and I saluted them before dismissing them back to stand in line. I could tell the other humans were a bit nervous, many were barely old enough to be considered adults, but I trusted Valestein wouldn't send anyone he didn't feel was ready for what lay ahead. I turned back to the mayor just as he addressed me.

"That was kind of you," he said, smiling gruffly. "That should help lift their spirits and maybe they'll help the greener troops. Have you had a look at your Commander tab yet? I've never led troops myself, but I'm told that when you do the system assists with that, similar to how the Settlement tab works."

I did a quick check, focusing my mind and accessing the various menus I'd acquired over time. Sure enough, at the very end was a new one called 'Commander Tab'. Focusing on it I was greeted with all sorts of information. Currently, I was a Rank 1 Commander and that, combined with my level of 20, meant I could command a total of 2,000 troops. Currently it had me set as having 521 out of 1,000, it must have already considered the Runeforged that I declared would serve as part of the troops, interesting.

I had my choice of a few perks, marching speed, increased proxy leveling rate, and a perk that lowered the food required per soldier to keep them at a 'Satisfied Status'. There was also a place that showed troop morale, it was currently at 'Neutral', whatever that meant in the context of morale. It listed every soldier, first and last name, proxy level and assigned position. I found Silas and saw that he was assigned as a Bowman already with his corresponding proxy level. There were a number of others with proxy levels, the orcs for instance had the most, but almost all of them were tagged as 'Men at Arms' and they all were under level 10.

I saw one more interesting section that drew my attention. I had access to a few different 'Auras' that could be activated and affect the troops under me within a fairly great distance. At Rank 1 I had two choices that weren't grayed out and unable to be read. Aura of the Turtle or Aura of the Wolf. One added to the physical resistance of those under my command, as well as reducing morale lost from losses. While the other increased attack speed and troop ferocity, making morale loss halt completely while in effect. Each one could be activated once every half hour and lasted only five minutes.

I didn't make any selections and closed the tab, focusing on the troops. There would be time to fiddle with the menus and make those choices during our training, which I hoped included telling me what the hell I was supposed to be doing.

Stepping up to the troops, they quieted, and I readied myself to speak to the biggest crowd I'd ever spoken to. What was even more unsettling was the fact I would be asking these men to go out and risk their lives for me. Well not for me, I reminded myself, for Lord Variyn and his war. But I'd come to peace with it as much as I could. This war was happening and complaining about it would only weaken my resolve, possibly resulting in the death of those below me who put their trust in me. From this day forward, I was a hundred percent in.

"I am your Commander, Caldor Miles," I said,

projecting my voice as loud as I could while keeping it under control. "I am an Arcane Knight, Defender of the weak, Knight of House Variyn, Vassal Lord of Blackridge Keep, and I am asking for you to put your trust in me."

A few murmurs rippled through the crowd, but the three elite guards quickly brought them to order, the silence returning.

"I'm not going to give you a big speech or try to inspire you. War is not easy, battles that you will endure will test you to your limits, but I will stand as a shield against those that would do you harm. To the best of my abilities, I will see you all return home."

I let my words wash over the crowd and I watched their faces. I'd say a few of the humans enjoyed what I had to say, standing taller and perhaps even being inspired. However, the orcs, trolls, and goblins looked as confused as they had been at the start. I needed to get translators and begin mandatory lessons in learning common, at least enough to follow orders. The dwarves were a hard people to read, with their mighty beards and stern faces.

"We are going to practice marching from Valestein to Blackridge and back here again. Once I feel you've all learned to walk properly in formation, you will be free to go home. Every day until called upon, you will report here for additional training. Is that understood?" I asked, not expecting any answers. Many of the humans, the previous soldiers were the loudest, and many of the dwarves called out some manner of 'yes' or 'aye'. Then a second wave of grunts followed as the non-Common speaking races caught on.

I motioned Raphael over. "I'll leave the training to you. I'm going to depart for Variyn at once and send word of when you should report. Get me a list of guards from Gabriel and have it sent by messenger to Variyn at the fastest possible time. Have it brought to Miles Manor and given to Lance Terook.

"Yes of course, Lord," Raphael said, inclining her head ever so slightly.

With that taken care of, I returned to the keep and sought out my friends.

"Emory, I hate to do this to you, but I need to leave, and I'm going to take Ares and fly back to Variyn. Are you alright staying here for a bit, or do you feel comfortable traveling alone?" I asked, the burly armored man was eating a chicken leg off the bone while I talked to him. He wiped the greasy meat off with a sleeve and took a long pull on his drink.

"Alone? What about Alayna?" He asked, gesturing to her sitting beside me.

"Ares will be able to carry her with me, as long as she can let Vash return to the astral plane," I said, she nodded as I suspected, and Emory looked at me with a sudden devious grin.

"I'll be alright. Might stick around here for a bit and see what there is to see," he said, his grin still as wide as ever.

"Don't go distracting one of my few elite guardsmen,"

I said, seeing where his thought process must be going.

"You mean guardswoman," Emory said waggling his eyebrows.

"She's coming to war with me, so don't get any ideas about pissing her off," I said, glaring in his direction. "I'll chop it off if you can't keep it under control."

"Oh yeah," Emory said, half standing and drawing a few inches of his own blade. "You better get a bigger sword if you want to cut mine off!"

I burst into laughter and slapped my thigh. God I was going to miss having Emory around all the time. "You shit eater better visit me when I'm off way in the West," I said, dropping the pretend anger I'd been playfully directing his way.

Alayna was rolling her eyes so hard I swear I could almost hear it.

"If you keep hotties like Raphael around, I'll be at your side forever," Emory said, reaching out his arm. We clasped them together and squeezed, each of us powerful enough to nearly break bones. I felt like I won, despite his larger size, but I'm sure he felt differently as I released first. I just didn't want to actually break his arm, and I had several times more strength I could have called upon.

"You ready to go?" I asked Alayna, she gave me a look that said, 'you are such a boy sometimes' but I just smiled back with childlike chagrin.

"If you boys are done, then yeah I'm ready."

We said our goodbyes and before I knew it, we soared above the trees, heading back to Variyn city.

CHAPTER 25
COURT FUNCTIONS

Ares went to rest, shifting into a figurine that I stored away. Alayna said she had research she wanted to get to and disappeared towards her favorite library, leaving me to my own devices. I had plans to grab a bite to eat but first I needed to seek out Lord Variyn to find out when the troops were meant to be gathered together.

I went to the room that I found him at the most, a sort of office suite, but the door was locked and no one answered. Next, I asked guards if they knew where he was, but all the guards I crossed paths with refused to give me any information or didn't really know. So, I headed for the kitchens, I figured Merlin the chef ought to know if he were required to feed the man. I made it about halfway to the kitchen that I'd last encountered the old pub owner turned chef, when I was pulled around roughly.

Non stood before me with a bored expression on his

face. He had white gloves on and when he spoke, I felt a measure of his power infusing his voice, forcing me to follow his command. "Follow me."

I was helpless to resist, so I followed him.

"You don't have to compel me, I'd have come without it," I said, the compulsion not enough to stop me from speaking. I felt at it with a tender touch of mana, pushing and feeling its limits. From what I could tell, he'd used a weaker version and if I focused enough, I was sure I'd be able to break it, so I did.

It shattered against my force of will, but I continued to follow him, not losing a step. If anyone knew where Lord Variyn was it would be Non.

"Well done," Non said. "Follow me or I will use a compulsion that you cannot resist. I must speak with you in private."

"Like I said before, you just had to ask," I said, scoffing a bit at the extreme measures Non liked to take. "Can you tell me where Lord Variyn is?"

"Not out in the open, be quiet and through here," Non said, walking up to a statue and pushing it inward, a section of the wall beside it slipped open. With eyebrows raised I followed him in, not sure what to expect. It turns out it led into a winding passageway that eventually led out right in front of Non's little hidden section of the keep. When we were in his study with the door closed tight behind us, he turned to me and stared.

I waited for him to speak, but he didn't, so finally I gave it a try. "So, how's the weather been these last few days? You see any entertaining plays or hear any new tales from the bards?" If he wanted to waste time, I could do the same.

"Tell me how you came across the discoveries you are making a fortune from," Non said, sitting at his desk and pulling out one of his little black notebooks.

That is what he wants to talk to me about? Not really any of his business, so what should I tell him? Would it hurt to just give him the truth or should I just be vague about it? I decided to go for the vague side. "Just hard work and studying," I said, giving him nothing and he knew it.

"Did Tim or any of his cronies ever tell you their war plans and if so, why did you not inform me?" Non asked, he looked up and his eyes looked straight through me before returning to his notebook.

It was as if this entire ordeal was a boring task given to him that he had to reluctantly perform. I wondered suddenly if that were the case, had Lord Variyn put him up to questioning me?

I realized I was just staring at him and hurried to answer. "You know all I do, they invited me to join House Attra and planned to escape at their earliest convenience. I have nothing to hide, Non, so if you are done, perhaps you can answer a question of mine?"

"Perhaps," Non said, holding back the hint of a smile twitching at the side of his mouth.

"When am I expected to have my troops report for duty and where? I was promised information to be sent to me, but I've yet to receive anything," I said, since I hadn't checked in with Lance in a week or more I realized that might not be entirely true. Damn, should have checked back at the manor first.

"Details have been sent to your little establishment," Non said. "Lord Variyn is concerned with how many Runeforged you've collected, I'd advise you to act wisely in the coming months. War has a way of making people dead and you don't want to give others reason to accelerate the process."

"Are you telling me Lord Variyn wants me dead?" I asked, sputtering out the words in surprise. I wouldn't have thought he'd go that far or that he considered me any kind of threat to him or his own.

"What?" Non asked, actually showing some surprise. "No, what I am saying is you appear to be gathering a force around you and Lord Variyn has noticed, which means other lesser Lords will have as well. They might think that you intend to fight for more territory after the war and will decide to be done with you before you are a true threat. Have I spoken plainly enough for you?"

"Yeah, I got it," I said, rubbing at the back of my neck. "Are we done here?"

"One last item on the agenda," Non said, looking up from his notebook. "There is a ball tomorrow and you've yet to attend a single one. You have certain duties that you are meant to attend to as a Lord and going to court functions is one of them. I would suggest you go tomorrow and meet with the Master General, Busard. He is on loan from the King and will be in charge of training the commanders and overseeing the troop training before deployment."

"Master General, Busard. Got it. Is the ball like a dance or just a dinner?" I asked, actually interested in the idea of going if I could have Alayna come with me.

"Both," Non said flatly. "Good luck in your future endeavors and I truly hope you make it through the war alive."

"Me too," I said, standing and leaving Non behind in his office.

Alayna had quickly agreed to go with me to the ball and even helped me pick out some formal clothing. I had my outfit provided by House Variyn when I first appeared before the Court, but I wanted something a little less standout-ish. So now I found myself dressed in the latest fashion, or so I was told. I wore a white long shirt with a tight collar that went halfway up my neck and a ruffled sort of tie made of green silk tied around it.

Over that I'd been given a vest that buttoned up just as tight, fitted to press against my muscular midsection and restrict my breathing. She said it looked dashing, but I worried I'd stop being able to breathe soon. The vest was black in the back and an emerald green with reflective bits of silk the same color that looked like burning flames when the light hit it just right. Over that, I wore a black overcoat that hung down to my knees and had a large collar that stuck up in the back a bit.

My slacks were pretty straightforward, black all over except for a matching green strip down the outside of each leg. My shoes shined from a recent polish and tapped loudly against the ground as I walked. Though it wasn't necessary there was one final item I'd bought at the shop she'd taken to dress me, it was a cane with a green gem atop it that turned out to be a gentleman's sword hidden within. It clicked along with my shoes as we approached the door to the keep's larger ballroom.

Alayna wore a dress to match the accented colors I had on my clothing, or more accurately I wore clothes that accented her dress. She had her hair put up in a way that several curls cascaded down the back from atop her head while the front was pulled tight. She accented her look with emerald earrings, a necklace and a ring. In a word, she was beautiful.

"Step forward and be announced," said a well-dressed man who I had seen since the day I'd first been announced to the court.

We did as he instructed and first, he introduced her, with her many titles, then my own name, with more titles attached to it than I remembered from last time. A few had me wanting to look at my titles tab to see if he was pulling them straight from there or if someone had told him a string of fake titles to tell him.

The ballroom had a large area set for dancing, currently at least a dozen couples spun and dipped doing one dance or another. While there were several dozen round tables decorated in various ways, from blacks and blues to golden and rosy reds, hardly anyone sat at them. Instead, they'd formed dozens of smaller conversational circles. I felt completely out of my depth, whereas this was my first ball, it was not Alayna's. She grabbed hold of my arm and led me out to the dance floor.

Few things are more terrifying than going to a dance without knowing how to dance. Luckily, I knew a few, and a simple waltz was among my repertory. We began to dance and it seemed like all eyes turned to us, but I hardly noticed as I stared into her beautiful eyes. The moment stretched and it felt like I got to hold her in my arms for an eternity, until all too abruptly the song ended.

"Let's sit and order some food to snack on before we get hounded by gossips," Alayna whispered, all the while, smiling and waving over to another couple not far off. They approached before we could escape and Alayna introduced them.

"Caldor," Alayna said through pursed lips. "This is John Matsinger and Kendra Melillo, they are distant cousins. Oh, and their fathers will be joining you with their legions in the coming battle." She added the last bit as an afterthought.

"Must we speak of such dreadful events," Kendra said, wrinkling her nose. "My father is upsetting the locals to the point of rebellion trying to raise his stupid legion."

"Have some commonsense girl," John shot the words at her like arrows. "I'm sure your father wouldn't want you spreading such rumors. My father for instance has had no trouble gathering his troops."

"That's funny," Alayna said, tapping her chin. "I heard that he placed a rushed order on Runeforged to meet his number, and that he will still fall short."

"That's only because one of the other damned Lords saw fit to add those damned creations to his army, now everyone is trying to get some as not to be left behind," John said, scoffing and shaking his head.

"I'm that other damned Lord," I said, raising my hand just a bit. "However, I just had them on hand for security, I didn't purchase them for the sole purpose of war."

Kendra leaned in suddenly and said in a whisper as loud as her normal voice. "I heard that Gilfoy's is working on a new type of Runeforged specifically for war, like a Warforg-" She was suddenly cut off as I cleared my throat, a dryness there I hadn't noticed.

"Sorry we should really get some drinks and a bite to eat," Alayna said, excusing us from the little circle of conversation we'd created.

"I've not eaten yet either," Kendra said, grabbing hold of Alayna's hand as we tried to depart.

"I could go for a drink, something stiff, eh Cal my boy?" John said, despite not looking much older than me.

It was truly surprising to see how many young Lords and Ladies were around Alayna and mine's age. I'd assumed from the only other celebration I'd been a part of that they were all middle-aged old men, but perhaps these were their children come out to enjoy the balls and parties of noblemen and women.

"A legion of your own then?" John said, putting a friendly hand on my shoulder. "I'll be serving as a Knight in my father's service, leading a company of his best men." He said the words with a measure of pride, however I didn't know what a 'company' of men was so I just sort of smiled and nodded along.

The moment we sat down a servant appeared asking us if we'd like the chicken or the fish. After gathering our orders, she took our drinks. John ordered a premium scotch, or so he told me a second later, Alayna and Kendra ordered wine.

"I'll take a beer or some ale, I'm fine with anything cold," I said, smiling ruefully up at the finely dressed young woman taking our order.

"Right away, your Lordship," she said, her accent one that I hadn't encountered yet, she drew out the L in Lordship a bit longer than normal.

My eyes washed over the crowds, trying to pick out which older gentlemen must be the Master General that Non spoke of. There was a distinct Silver haired gentleman with a strikingly deep scar on his left cheek, but I thought I might have seen him during my first court celebration, so it couldn't be him. I saw Bagard Veslmy and Dunst Alvera who'd cornered me for information all those months ago, each of them looked several measures more haggard and stressed than they had been before.

I half expected to see Mah'kus make an appearance

and found myself searching the room for where the servants had set up drinks, finding it but no Mah'kus. I looked up to see the skinny form of Bagard Veslmy heading towards our table and I groaned.

John noticed and looked up to where I'd been looking. "Oh, Lord Veslmy the slime ball is coming over to pry for gossip about my father's recruiting efforts no doubt." Then turning to me he added behind his hand. "Father sends me to these events because he is much too busy, so I get the attention of a full Lord here."

"Caldor Miles," Bagard said, out of the corner of my eye I saw John's face fall a measure. "I would speak with you in private, perhaps you can join Lord Alvera and I at our table when it is most convenient for you?"

This was a much different tone than the questioning interrogation-like conversation I'd gotten from the pair last we spoke and it immediately made me suspicious.

"We'll see," I said, then gesturing to the table I added. "I'm about to enjoy my meal, so another time."

Lord Veslmy didn't seem deterred at all, simply nodding and smiling. "Very well, please at your earliest convenience." With that, the skinny man in his overly tight vest disappeared back into the crowds.

"That was odd," John said. "I've never seen that slime ball so pleasant, have you something over him?"

"I don't think so," I said, shrugging. Our food arrived and conversation lulled as we ate, the girls managing a few words between bites but John and I remained quiet.

Drinks followed and I enjoyed a nice cool beer, the

bitter hops playing flavorfully across my tongue. Having finished eating, our plates were collected, and I ordered another drink. They'd served it in a narrow tall glass that gave me about a fourth of what I normally enjoyed drinking with my meal. No sooner had I stood, that another servant approached me, his attire slightly better than the ones serving dinner spoke of him being more important.

"My master bids you join him at his table, alone," he said, his voice like a groan of agony spoken through his nose.

"And who might your master be?" I asked, taking a long pull on my glass of ale, finishing its contents.

"Master General, Lord Marco Busard," he said as if announcing the King himself. I'd needed to meet this Busard fellow, so this worked out perfectly.

"Lead the way," I said, then turning to the table but more specifically Alayna I said, "I'll be back in a few." She smiled and waved at me. Meanwhile, John looked confused and struck at the same time, perhaps meeting with this Lord Busard was something of an honor?

The crowd parted for the servant that led me through the room as if he himself were a noble and I saw many a shocked looks on the faces of those who saw me following behind. It made me wonder if something else was going on, but I had no way of knowing and soon decided to let it be and stop being so paranoid.

We walked towards a table toward the back with a single occupant, sipping on a wine glass. He was noticeable for many reasons, the least of which being the armor he wore in place of evening attire.

It was as elegant as it was simple. A plain flat chest-plate, with blackened leather underneath and silver chain-mail hanging down from a mail coif he wore over his head. He wore no helmet, but the mail coif covered everything but the front of his face, which was strikingly young. I wouldn't put his age even a few months after my own, if I didn't see the look about his eyes as he locked them against my own.

That timelessness that came with suspended aging was the strongest here than I'd ever seen. It appeared as a still-ness and a few stretched lines about the eyes. It was easier to tell on older men, as most I'd seen sat in a suspended age from their mid-forties. But this man must have leveled and taken the highest of ageless perks at an early age to have frozen himself so thoroughly in time.

His eyes were the color of amber and a single stray lock of black hair curled from out of his mail coif. The servant presented me, speaking my name but no titles. I hardly heard him as the heavy gaze of this incredibly powerful man searched through me. It was like a weight being pressed upon me and I knew he was learning as much as he wanted about me, whether from an Inspect ability or through keen observation I couldn't say.

"You're an honorable man, like your father," Busard said, his voice as smooth and sharp as his chin line and masculine features. "I can see much of him in you."

"You knew my father?" I asked, the question feeling like a phrase I'd uttered one too many times in my lifetime.

A fatherly kind smile spread over his lips and despite his youthful appearance I felt he gave off a very fatherly vibe. "Most knew your father," Busard said. "I had the pleasure of being his friend and on several occasions, a partner in battle."

"My father didn't fight in any wars; I mean, other than the battle of Lysteen pass?" I asked, posing my statement as a question.

Busard's eyes narrowed in on me as if searching for something and then suddenly he relaxed, and I knew he'd found whatever it was he had searched for. "You are right of course, but I have not always been a general," Busard said, smiling.

"Of course," I said.

"Your father and I handled many threats in our time, but never did he mention his family, very secretive man your father," Busard said, he'd gone completely conversational.

"Then perhaps you weren't as close as you thought," I said, realizing a moment too late how rude I must have sounded.

"While I appreciate brashness, you'd do well to control yourself," Busard said.

"You called me here for what reason?" I asked.

"I wanted to meet the child of the famed Elkor Miles and soon to be a Commander under my service," Busard said.

"That's me, I said, it is a pleasure to meet you, Master General Busard," I said, inclining my head in his direction.

"It is a shame you swore loyalty to just a House of Newaliyn and not to the King himself, I have it on good authority that he'd have welcomed such a formidable adventurer such as yourself. And if it was land you sought, the title of Duke within the grand city of Newaliyn carries with it much more land potential than a simple House Vassal. But we must all walk the paths we've chosen," Busard said, smiling knowingly at me.

"I agree with that," I said, staring hard at him. "We must all walk our paths."

"Be sure young Caldor, that despite having such a famous father you will not be getting any special treatment during training or deployment. All who are called to serve must accept the terms to which they agreed upon and are ordered, is that clear?" Busard asked.

"Yes, it is clear," I said. I nodded at Busard and stood to leave.

There was no more that I wanted to hear from this man. He had the power and strength to make my impossible mission possible and it seemed like he'd simply ignore me, and for what? Because of a blind faith in the arbiter or the path of Order? I was young, that much was true, but even I saw the advantages of teaming up. Hadn't he just bragged about going on adventures with my father?

The rest of the night passed in a blur as I kept mostly to myself and my thoughts. I took Alayna to dance several more times and did my best to ignore the rest of the people at the party, however a rather persistent fellow came over to speak for the third time, so I finally decided to speak with him. The times prior I'd just gotten up and walked away, that was only going to work as long as I didn't mind being rude, and two times was my max.

"Name's Mitchel Fitz, Lord Fitz if you're into using titles or just Fitz," Fitz said, he had a nervous way of speaking where he sort of mumbled every other word.

"Caldor Miles, Lord of Blackridge Keep," I said, extending my hand and then raising it up to signal for another drink to a passing servant.

"So, Cal, I hear you are a new Vassal like me, pretty daunting, isn't it?" Fitz said, his nervous tic becoming less noticeable the more he spoke. "I mean raising a thousand soldiers has been nearly impossible, but my father, the late Lord of Dentridge Keep, kept the peasants well fed and they've bred like rabbits, so it isn't really a matter of having enough of them, just no one seems to have any patriotism any longer."

"I've raised five hundred troops, two hundred of which are Runeforged, I told Lord Variyn I'd not be able to do a thousand," I said, speaking for the sake of conversation and searching the crowd for the servant that was fetching my drink.

"And he didn't strip you of your titles and lands?" Fitz asked, looking genuinely surprised.

"He'd do that, you think?" I asked, if he had there would be no change, he'd have even gotten the five hundred from the lands out by Blackridge Keep. There might be more villages close by, but they were so small as to be worthless for recruiting more than a dozen or so soldiers. Still, perhaps I should have tried, an extra hundred troops would have helped me stand out a bit less.

"That is the rumor going around, if anyone who doesn't gather their legion will have to answer directly to him and if you believe what you hear at the court events he is not the forgiving type," Fitz said.

He really seemed to like to talk, but I wasn't sure what he expected me to say. It wasn't like I could provide any decent gossip on the matter; I'd had my conversation with Lord Variyn, and he seemed rather understanding, not threatening at all. "I didn't get that impression at all."

"Is it true," Fitz asked, lowering his voice suddenly and leaning in.

"Is what true?" I asked, leaning slightly away from him.

"That you are courting his daughter?" He asked.

I looked at the man and he waggled his eyebrows at me. "I don't see why that is any of your business, but it's no secret," I said, hoping that was actually the case. If we were meant to keep it a secret, then someone had forgotten to tell me.

"So, you admit that you are getting preferential treatment in the troop requirements because of a relationship with Lord Variyn's heir?" Fitz said, straightening and deepening his voice slightly. It was like his prior speech was a childish game. "I do say that would be dreadful gossip if it got to the rest of the Lords in his service."

"I highly doubt that," I said, dryly. "If you've so easily come to this false assumption than I am sure the rest of them will settle on it as well. Leave me be, Fitz, I don't want to be a part of your stupid gossip mill."

"Tell me why you've been buying up so much food stock, armor, arms, and Runeforged?" Fitz asked, his eyes narrowing in suspicion. "You knew before all of us that this conflict was coming, didn't you? What are you two truly up to, has he set you up to marry his daughter and take over his seat as High Lord? Surely, he knows we won't fall in line behind you when our forces could easily force a splintering in the House."

I hated politics, it was so easy for them to see assassins in every shadow when really nothing malicious awaited them. Not knowing how else to rid myself of him I decided to play along.

"You caught me," I said, holding my hands up in surrender. "I am the new heir to House Variyn. In fact, I'm thinking of changing the name to House Miles, scourge of the Lordship. That last bit will be more like a motto than anything else, but you get the picture."

Fitz stared at me for a long couple of seconds before huffing out air and storming off. Surely, he knew I was joking? I was really good at making friends among those I'd soon be on the battlefield with, I decided.

The rest of the night moved as if in a blur and soon Alayna took me from the ball to a carriage awaiting us. We fled to my Manor where we spent the night together, enjoying every minute that we had left.

CHAPTER 26
MAKING PREPARATIONS

L ance put in the orders I requested, and they'd been filled, but a part of me really wanted to visit Gilfoy's Emporium, as it had been a while. Despite now having people to do this sort of thing for me, I went shopping.

The marvelous and elaborate building didn't have the same awe-inspiring effect on me as it had the first few times. I still didn't know how they did so much of what made it special, but having been exposed to it and greater magics had a lessening effect The Runeforged at the door was missing, perhaps the entire stock had been purchased by Regina? Or maybe another Lord has begun to drain their stock with all available funds they could muster.

"Lord Miles, how may I assist you? My name is Candace Catreese" A stern female voice sounded from just ahead. I looked to see someone I'd not met before, with brown hair pulled into a bun, a slightly more elaborate company uniform with silver embellishments here and there, and a fake smile on her face that was basically a trade mark of Gilfoy employees.

"I'm actually just here to browse," I said, my eyes flicking across some merchandise behind her. "Anything new and exciting?"

"We receive new items daily," Candace said, putting a hand on my shoulder and guiding me to a nearby display. "For instance, this contraption is a new invention based off your own patents. We are calling it a 'Mobile Collector', you can pick one up for only a million gold each. The King has made a special order for several dozen recently."

"What do they collect?" I asked, studying the fist-sized sphere.

"Essence," Candace said, her voice barely above a whisper.

The ball was made of a stiff silver metal lace of inter-twining webs laid atop each other. Even as I stared at it I could see the inner sections moving, each having a direc-tion of their own.

"There must be a gem inside capturing the essence, right?" I asked, a knowing smile on my lips.

Candace didn't react at all at first, but slowly a fake smile returned. "It is all so technical; we have another item you might recognize. These arm bands we purchased from your estate to resell here. Each of these Bands are able to collect essence as well, but far less than a 'Mobile Collec-tor'. In fact, one might call them inferior if it weren't for your compact design."

The essence bands I'd had a hand in creating were

being displayed and with a price tag that made my anger surge. I'd instructed Lance to begin the sale of the arm bands at a set price of materials plus a thousand gold, while that would be a lot to some, most adventurers could save to get that amount without much trouble. Meanwhile, Gilfoy had marked them up to one hundred thousand each.

"That is quite the mark up you've added," I said, shaking my head. "Don't expect to be able to purchase much more inventory from us if that is the price you wish to sell them."

Her smile faded. "We have a contract to be supplied with a hundred thousand units over a period of five years, are you telling me you plan on going against it?"

"I signed no contract, and I am one of the primary inventors of those essence bands," I said, more out of surprise than malice.

"Feel free to contact our legal department and I'm sure they'll be able to help you Lord Miles," Candace said, her smile back once more.

I'd talk to Lance about it, but I was not happy to hear that the essence bands were being made so inaccessible. My dream of every adventurer who needed one was slowly being shattered, but that could be a worry for another time. Crude business dealings aside, I came here to find something fun to add to my array of items or armor. I wouldn't let them ruin the fun of shopping for me.

"What else do you have?" I asked, and Candace led me

down further to show me a variety of other items, nothing that interested me until we came upon the last item.

"What is this," I said, holding my hand out towards the items. There were two being displayed, one open and standing about six feet long while the other just appeared to be the handle.

"Aw this here is a new line of items we've been working on, this spear starts out small enough to sit on your belt, but when fully extended it can reach lengths of twelve feet long, depending on the setting you press. Here, have a look, but be careful not to activate it beyond a few feet," Candace grabbed hold of the foot long handle and passed it over while indicating a dial with a number wheel and a button below it.

It was currently set to zero, so I thumbed it over to two and pressed the button. I felt a surge of mana and a swish. The spear extended so fast as to be nearly unobservable.

"Convenient, aren't they?" Candace asked, then took the item from my grasp before setting it back to zero. "We imagine that soon we will be able to do this with most weapons, creating an entire line of easy to obscure weaponry."

"I would like two hundred of those spears," I said, a completely different plan in mind for their use.

Though I wouldn't tell her, Gilfoy had just created a weapon of war that I imagined could help turn the tide of a battle. If the enemy force marched against a wall of my troops and suddenly spears six feet along shoot out with magical force, they'd be stopped dead in their tracks, quite literally. I looked at the price and cringed a little.

"Can I get a bulk deal?" I asked, each unit was labeled at four thousand gold. It wasn't like I couldn't afford it, but honestly, I didn't even know the state of my funds anymore. I had stashed away close to a half a million in gold in my father's 'Arcane Asylum' but that was for emergencies. Something tickled at the back of my mind, something obvious about my father and his situation that I'd failed to confront. I pushed it away for now, not willing to think about it yet.

"I think we can arrange something," Candace said, her fake smile turning into a devious little grin that seemed all too natural on her face.

Business done, I left and found Lance back at Miles Manor.

"We have a contract with Gilfoy to allow them to sell our essence bands for five years?" I asked, eyebrow raised.

"Yes, sir," Lance said, nodding as he pulled out several papers from seemingly nowhere. "I've got it here if you'd like to review it. It is one of many items that still require your signature, though I gave them leave to begin to sell the items."

"Before I will sign that, I need a clause added," I said, channeling my inner 'Regina'. I explained my terms, that they be limited to a two hundred percent markup. At first, I suggested only a one hundred percent markup, but Lance convinced me that at the price we were selling them we needed to allow more in order to make profit and be able to continue making improvements on them. It would make the items well within a price range that most adventurers could afford or work towards affording, so that settled things with me.

I thanked Lance and headed to my room to deal with the thoughts that refused to leave me alone.

I'd been so willing to believe that my father could be alive that I missed something so obvious. A fact that proved, at least to me, beyond a shadow of a doubt that my father was in fact dead. The system had passed the 'Arcane Asylum' to me and said something while doing it.

'This Arcane Asylum belonged to 'Elkor Miles'. As he is no longer able to access it and you are his approved successor, would you like to claim it?'

I blinked, the system message in its entirety had played back in my mind when focusing on it, that wasn't something I realized I could do. Making a mental note to remember that in the future, I went over the words. Now that I saw them again it was just barely vague enough that maybe, just maybe it didn't mean he was dead.

If that were the case, then what would make someone unable to access their system given perk? Could perhaps he have been stripped of his powers like that wretched Chaos Knight was doing to Warrick? It was a possibility, but the more likely scenario swirled in the front of my mind. Elkor Miles, my father, was likely dead and no amount of wishing for a different outcome would change that. So why didn't I really believe it when I let those thoughts form? Was I so blind to the truth that I was unable to accept anything outside the realm of how I'd like things to go?

Then there was the Chaos Knight, still alive, still free to do whatever it is she was doing, probably looking to corrupt more Prime Mana Shrines and further the destruction of the Ley lines. Surely, she knew that without the Ley lines working, her own power would fail. From personal discussion with Warrick, we'd both been puzzled by her actions and why she hadn't done what so many before her did, merely turning the Shrine from Order to Chaos.

Warrick had explained that the Ley lines were meant to be without influence either way, neither towards the side of Order or Chaos, merely being raw power ready to be harnessed. Now that Chaos corruption had seeped into the very lines of power that connected the world, the consequences would be dire and planet shaking. But so far, other than news from dungeons of limited power reaching them, I'd seen few other effects.

Warrick explained it was a slow poison that would only be sped up if more Prime Mana Shrines fell. When I asked about normal Mana Shrines, he explained that only the Prime Mana Shrines ran all the way to the deepest Ley lines, where the Mana Shrines we used operated on the higher to the surface web of lines fed from the deeper ones. Infecting the surface level ones would be even slower but would worsen the trouble if she took the time to corrupt them.

So, the Wyrd was being poisoned to death and I was going to war. No, I can't think like that. I had to stay focused on one task at a time. To deal with the Ley line threat I needed allies, possibly an army to deal with the threats I'd encounter, so I'd hold to my oaths and fight in this war. Plus, if I couldn't get there, which I couldn't, there was nothing to do but grow stronger and there was one thing war was good for, it would be getting me stronger.

The daily influx of essence, even the low amount given off by the death of soldiers, would be enough to swell my level. I had mixed feelings, but I squashed them down. I had a duty and I'd see to it.

Lance passed on the information regarding troop expectations and when to report. It wasn't long, so I decided to check in with Kora about the Runeforged she was training. Regina had been told by Lance that I'd be taking two hundred of the Runeforged with me, news he said she took, 'alight', but wouldn't elaborate further. I hadn't much contact with her, she remained busy with her work, and I gave her the space she needed to make me more money.

"How goes the training?" I asked Kora, she turned from speaking with one of the dozens of Runeforged that no longer looked as they had before. Each one was unique, even their coloring, which had hints of her white metal look, were varied enough to make you think each one was created uniquely.

"I won't have two hundred converted in time, my powers are limited at how fast I can convert them, but I have enough to be assigned both Captains and Lieutenants over twenty squads, each consisting of ten Runeforged," Kora said looking proudly at her modified Runeforged.

"Is it necessary to convert them all?" I asked, she'd told me they were weaker when converted, at least at first, but how much weaker I wondered.

"They enjoy a freedom of mind and spirit when I alter them, is that not better than enslaving them?" Kora asked, raising her gaze up to me as I stood close enough that our height difference was noticeable.

"We are going to war, Kora," I said, simply. Pausing to let out an exaggerated breath. "I need them to be strong, not free."

"I see," Kora said. "Perhaps you'd like to spar with one or two and gauge their strength for yourself?"

Luckily, I almost always wore my armor, and the new enchantment was working well to keep it clean and me cool inside of it. So, I cracked my neck to the side and said, "Sure, let's see what they can do."

"Ventus come show Caldor what you've learned. Ignis, you are on deck so be ready," Kora said, her words carrying over the din of their continued sparring. At her words they all stilled and formed a wide circle, in which Ventus stepped forward wearing simple leather armor and carrying a spear with a small leaf like blade at the end.

He twirled the spear around with incredible speed before locking it under his arm and pointing it towards me with his back arm out. "I am ready," he said, inclining his head towards me.

I decided I wouldn't risk cutting him up with my sword, despite his metal form, my cuts were deadly to opponents much stronger than him. Instead, I pulled out the spear handle that I'd just purchased, I had to get one for myself. Setting it to a length of five feet I pressed the button, and it extended in a satisfying whoosh. Michael had taught me a bit about using a spear, so it wasn't a completely foreign weapon to me.

Swirling it around I gripped it tightly when it stopped, getting a feel for the weight. With my increased attributes it might as well have weighed nothing, but it was sturdy enough for what I wanted.

I stepped into the ring of Runeforged and got into a ready stance. Ventus immediately charged forward, swinging his spear around for a downward slash of the sharpened edge. I wondered momentarily if he would be trying to kill me as part of this sparring session. As if to leave nothing about his intentions unclear, he somehow switched from an overhead slash, that I was all set to block, to a thrust in a flicker of movement.

I rolled to the side, letting the spear pass by me harmlessly, but if I'd been any slower it would have gotten me. If I didn't know better I'd have said he activated Swift Strike to redirect his momentum. The blows didn't stop, he slashed to the side, I blocked with my spear and used my greater strength to send him stumbling back.

But unlike most opponents I'd faced, he didn't pause

to readjust his strategy or even take a moment to breathe. Instead, he rushed back towards me, thrusting forward with deadly accuracy. Each time I knocked his blow aside, until the very last one I felt something building inside of him. A rush of air slammed into me, lifting me from my feet and throwing me backwards.

Abrupt pain flashed across my face as one of his continued thrusts hit me, I hadn't bothered putting my helmet on and suddenly I was regretting it. As soon as I landed, awkwardly on my feet somehow, I kicked off and slammed my weight into Ventus. He went flying backwards, end over end onto the ground. Blue energy flickered around me as I realized that instinctively I'd added a bit of essence into that attack.

Ventus stood, air swirling around him like a mini tornado. It was almost like the elemental inside of him was showing through. Mistakenly, I looked over at Kora to question her about it, when the full force of a spear thrust hit my gut. Luckily, my armor's redistributing power saved me, despite him hitting the leathered area and not the metal chest plate. The blow skittered off harmlessly, leaving only a blunt pressure where it had struck.

My attention was immediately back on Ventus, and I slammed the tip of my spear forward. The air elemental infused Runeforged dodged it with ease, but I activated Swift Strike to redirect my momentum of the attack and slapped the side edge against his head. He slammed to the side, his entire body lifting off the ground and hitting among several other converted Runeforged.

"I've seen enough," I said, and Kora stepped through the circle.

"Ventus, stand down," Kora said.

But Ventus stood, and though his capacity for facial expression was limited compared to mine, I swear I saw anger there. He took a step forward, snapping his arm forward and twirling the spear. I thought he might rush forward and attack again, but his aura of wind dissipated a moment later. He bowed his head before speaking.

"Yes, Kora," Ventus said, then turning slightly to face me he bowed again. "You are my better, for now."

A chill ran up my spine as my mind ran over the dangerous potential these Runeforged were going to have on the battlefield. No soldier could hope to match arms against these converted ones, much less the standard model that was said to be stronger but lacking elemental abilities.

"I would like you to spar with Ignis as well, she is far weaker than Ventus and has yet to show more than a small bit of her elemental potential," Kora said, waving forward a Runeforged I hadn't met as an individual yet.

She had the usual white metals, but it was mixed with strands of orange and red that came together in swirls on the surface of the metal. Oddly enough, as I watched those swirls they seemed to still be moving and shifting like sand being blown by the wind. She didn't even have leather armor on, instead she wore no shirt, showing her metallic chest of varied colors, and a loincloth. Around her waist was a long section of rough tan cloth tied into a belt that covered halfway up her Runeforged stomach with a section at the end hanging down.

Ignis took her place where Ventus had stood and placed her hands together as if in prayer, bowing her head. I waited to see if she'd look up, but she didn't, so I looked at Kora who just smiled and left the circle.

I gave her another few seconds, but she still didn't look up, so I stepped forward to attack. As I neared her, I lashed out with my spear, not wanting to let one of them take me off guard again.

At the last moment, she snapped her head up and punched in my direction, but whatever was supposed to happen, it didn't. Instead, her fist glowed a very faint orange and my spear blow took her right in the chest. Metal against metal sounded in an ear-splitting screech and crunch. Ignis was sent flying backwards, caught by her comrades.

Unlike Ventus, Ignis took her time to get up and wobbled a bit when she finally stood. She looked at me then down at her chest, the plate over her left chest muscle had a good size dent in it. She closed her hands together again and bowed her head.

I decided to slow it down a little bit and let her have a chance to strike out. She didn't have a weapon, so I reduced mine to its foot long length and put it away. Hand to hand combat it would have to be.

Running forward at half speed, I threw a punch for her face. Ignis reacted, her eyes flaring orange and a punch of her own connecting with my chest. Instead of a small flash of orange light, it ignited into a ball of fire that threw me backwards a moment before my punch would have hit.

The heat was intense, but my defenses were more than adequate to keep me safe against it. I slid on my feet; arms crossed out in front of me at the last second. Another ball of fire ripped through the air and suddenly I was moving, avoiding each one as I closed in on her.

Moving at full speed, I was able to dodge and duck my way to her, slamming a fist against her face. She went sprawling and as she struggled to get up, I slammed my foot atop her back. While physically weaker than Ventus, Ignis had a burning potential in raw power that would be best kept in check.

"That's enough," I called out, and Kora stepped back into the ring.

Ignis, when I stopped pushing her down with my heel, stood and took the same hands together and head bowed pose. Kora came up to her, placing her hand on her chest and it began to glow. The damage that had been very noticeable before was gone, all signs of it washed away by whatever powers Kora used.

"You've done well," Kora said, putting a hand on the Runeforged and gently pushing her back into the circle. She went, raising her head and letting her hands fall to her side. She didn't acknowledge me or thank Kora, just simply walked away.

"That was a bit different, but if all of these converted Runeforged have these abilities, you will be a force to be reckoned with on the battlefield," I said, letting myself get excited by the idea of having the strongest legion in the army Lord Variyn called together.

"Yes, I imagine they will kill very effectively," Kora said, her eyes running over them and her hands on her waist.

I passed on the information about when we'd be leaving and asked her to practice having them march in formation to prepare for our trip. She agreed and I left her to her work.

Going to the common room that doubled as a pub inside the manor I found all my friends gathered, Ismene, Emory, Creed, Fred, and Fran. I ordered a drink and a plate of food from a cute brunette that Lance had hired to run the pub, before sitting across the table from Creed.

"What did you decide?" I asked, seeing from his expression he knew exactly what I meant.

"I leave in a week to join my father," Creed said, he looked more confident now than I'd seen him in a while, so I just nodded my head. "I got a second letter saying my surname would be restored so I will once again be Creed Nefrah, son of Lord Nefrah."

I sensed a shift in his tone as he said his name. "I'm happy for you, but always remember that you have a home here as well. If you ever need a place to go, my doors will be open to you."

"Thank you," Creed said, then slipped into a silent

stare that I'd found him when I arrived, sipping his ale and picking at a meal but barely eating anything.

"What about you, Emory, you great bastard," I said, shifting in my seat to face the table that he and Ismene were at. "Are you coming to war with me? Apparently, I need Adventurers to carry goods and clear monsters, maybe even dungeons, as we march. You up to it?"

Emory made a show of thinking about it, then said, "I'm finally catching up with you all, thanks to that band you gave me. I doubt I'll get more essence playing war with you instead of running dungeons. Sorry man, but I'm staying behind." He must have saw my face fall a bit as I pretended what he said didn't sting because he added, "I'll still visit, maybe talk to Lance and see before I go out if I can carry some supplies. Just not full time or anything."

"I understand," I said. I didn't, but in part at least I knew he wanted to keep progressing and, in his mind at least, war wasn't the place to do it.

"I'll go with you," Ismene said, smiling over to me. "I don't think I can bring myself to go out and kill the other army, but I can clear monsters, and do dungeons while carrying those supplies you mentioned."

I saw Emory's reaction, he seemed surprised, and a bit deflated by her words. In a moment of either stupidity or ingenuity, I made a decision.

"Ismene," I said, smiling. "You stay with Emory and you two grow as strong as you can. After this war is finished, we have a very dangerous quest ahead of us, so I need you both in tip top shape."

"What quest?" Ismene asked, her face looking more confused than upset that I was telling her to stay.

"We need to go to the Isle of Avalon," I said.

This time her expression did change, from one of confused curiosity to outright utter surprise. "You can't possibly think we are strong enough to go there yet! Just talk to Merlin and he will tell you as much. Hell, why not just ask him to take you and then whatever you have to do will be easy. That guy is insanely strong."

"I wish I could," I said, sighing. "Apparently Merlin has taken an extended vacation to places unknown."

"Really?" Emory asked. "Every time I visited, he seemed to be having a grand time washing the same mug over and over."

Emory snorted and Ismene just shook her head at him.

Emory and Ismene began to chat about what dungeons they would do, it hadn't been hard to convince her to stay.

I moved over to where Fred had his nose in a book and Fran looked on at our conversation from afar with a sour look on her face. Her freckled cheeks turned a similar shade of her wild red hair when she caught me staring.

"I'm not staying behind," Fran said, as soon as I sat beside them. "We made an oath, and we meant it. I don't like the idea of war, especially between Houses, but I'll kill any soldier who tries take a swing at you."

Her fierce loyalty had me rethinking what I was going to suggest for them, but I held to my first thoughts. "You and Fred need to stay behind so that you'll be ready for the

Isle of Avalon as well. I am going to need every ally I have as strong as they can be, to accomplish that impossible task."

"No," Fred said, looking up from his book. "Besides, based on just my rough calculations we are likely to gather more essence, Bands or not, if we join you where the most essence will be released."

"Book for brains is right," Fran said, picking it up where her brother left off. "We know that even with all the downtime there is at war, that clearing monsters has to fall onto someone, why not us? It'll be like running a dungeon or more every day."

I honestly had considered what she said, so it wasn't hard to resist her logic. How would that make Ismene feel, if I told them they could come when I asked her to stay behind with Emory? Ismene knew me well enough that she wouldn't take it personally, I hoped.

"Are you sure?" I asked, directing my question to both of them. Fred looked at me from over the top of his book but said nothing, instead letting his flat stare do the talking. Fran, meanwhile, had a much more verbal response.

"Yes, you big idiot. We are coming whether you like it or not. But about those essence bands we keep hearing about," she said, letting the words sit in the air as I looked at her.

"Didn't I give you both one already?" I asked, trying to think back if I had. Life had been so busy that I literally couldn't remember. "Here these are the latest models." I pulled out two from my Dimensional Cube and handed them over.

"Oh fascinating," Fred said, actually setting his book aside. Fran smiled wide, little dimples appearing in her cheeks. She was strikingly beautiful when she wasn't being a sarcastic ass.

With all that settled I passed on the information about our departure and bid them to gather as much supplies as possible. Then, I took Ares on a day trip, speeding through the sky to deliver the message for my forces at Blackridge Keep to begin their march. If they began now, they'd still be at least a day behind, but it was the best we could do.

The forces were ready, I caught them out doing marching training and they said they'd be able to begin their march first thing in the morning as their troops would need rest. I gave the go ahead and checked with Cron for any news, nothing but a few monster attacks. All the former bandits were behaving and had been armored and armed. My bands of *Awakened* were ready to march as well.

Returning to House Variyn, I arrived just as night fell on the city. Flying by the light of the two moons gave enough to see by that I set down right inside the front courtyard without worry of being mistaken as an intruder. Pulling out a bear steak I threw it to Ares and told her to find some rest in the stables, where she'd get pet down and pampered. She happily obliged; she'd been getting along well with the stable boy that Lance had picked out to help run the stables.

Our stables were small, holding three horses—two purchased for use by Fred and Fran as war steeds that they'd be bonding with during our trip—and one used by the staff to pull a wagon for supplies to the manor.

However, I had purchased and would be having two hundred horses delivered to the front to act as cavalry horses. I'd bought them through an intermediary by way of Lord Variyn for use in war, as had all other Lords. It surprised me that so many horses could be found, but they assured me, after taking my gold, that they'd have all two hundred head ready for delivery.

The next day we gathered the Runeforged and began our march out of the city. Alayna greeted me just outside the gate atop Vash.

"You going someplace?" I asked, I'd just seen her the night before for a dinner, but she'd been distracted and busy with research, so we didn't spend time together afterwards.

"I'm marching out with you for the first day or two," Alayna said, speaking very loudly and clearly. She looked at me with eyes that told me something else was up.

I thought I had an idea of what she might be up to but didn't want to blow her cover if she felt secrecy was necessary.

"Ares wanted to fly for a bit, and I was going to go with her, but maybe I can get on one of the spare horses and walk with you," I said, watching her expression for any hint that my suspicions were right.

"That's alright," Alayna said. "Fly ahead. Flying is on

my mind as well. Did you know elven armies have cavalry made out of stag riders? Much more effective than traditional horseback cavalry I'm told." She winked at me as she spoke.

My suspicions were right. She was going to go to the elves or do something to further our agenda with flying ships. I could be daft some days, but I had to be understanding it right.

"If I'm not riding with you, perhaps you would like Fred, Fran, or even a Runeforged to ride alongside you?" I asked, trying to be cryptic enough that whoever might be listening wouldn't understand my meaning.

I knew my earrings blocked someone scrying me directly, but I couldn't remember the range. Anyone among my retinue could be a spy, I had about thirty different helpers and they'd all been appointed by Lance. There was no telling if any of them had come at the behest of someone else.

"Perhaps one of the new Runeforged could offer me some interesting conversation," Alayna said, nodding along to the idea.

I smiled, happy that she'd be taking some protection. I flagged down Kora, dismounting Ares in the process and whispered to her.

"Give me your strongest Runeforged to accompany Alayna. They need to protect her at all costs, regardless of risk to self," I said, trying to stress that last point.

"I will fetch Ventus for you," Kora said, nodding.

I groaned internally but said nothing. If she thought

he was up for the job of protection, then I'd go with it. However, he'd shown signs that made me worry, like aggression. Perhaps a little aggression wasn't so bad as long as he kept to the mission.

Ventus approached; his head held high. "Ventus," I said, getting his attention. He bowed his head in my direction but said nothing. "I need you for a special mission and it is critical that you be prepared to fight to the death, no matter the threat."

"I will do as I am asked," Ventus said, standing with a stiff back and raised chin.

"Stay with Lady Alayna and protect her, that is your quest and your purpose until she releases you. Do you understand?" I asked, whispering despite only Runeforged being around for a few dozen feet.

"I understand," Ventus said, following me as I came back to Alayna. Calling over one of the stable boys, the one Ares liked, I had a horse brought over for Ventus. He mounted it with a fluid confidence of a lifelong rider and once again I was amazed at how swiftly they picked things up.

"This will be your riding mate, his name is Ventus," I said, introducing Alayna.

"Nice to meet you Ventus, you can call me Alayna," she said, smiling at the Runeforged that rode beside her now on a black horse.

"I am ready to serve, Alayna," Ventus said, inclining his head.

With that taken care of I wished Alayna safe travels by

giving her a kiss and whispering three words in her ear. Meanwhile, I told Fred and Fran that I'd be flying ahead and above, but I'd check in every hour. Fred was riding atop a brown horse, but his eyes were locked in the direction of the small army of Runeforged that marched with us, more specifically towards Kora. She'd been busy keeping track of the Runeforged and they hadn't talked since we'd left. Fred would need to talk to her soon or risk hurting his neck for how hard he was staring.

CHAPTER 27
REPORTING FOR DUTY

The skies were clear, and we flew high and far. Despite the cold blasts of air, I stayed warm, my enchantment providing just the right temperature no matter the temperature outside. Or at least to a certain extent. I'm sure the armor had its limitations, but as we flew, I didn't encounter any. I wore a new pair of goggles on my eyes to avoid bugs and debris from hurting my ability to see. I was sure they made me look odd, but they were so practical that I didn't mind.

It was because of this clear ability to see all around and my attunement with Ares's own sight as we flew, that we both saw the black dot in the sky around the same time. We didn't change course at first, wondering what would be in the sky among us that was that big. It wasn't until it turned direction towards us that we got a good look at the black wyvern that flew freely over House Variyn.

This wasn't the same one as before, as that one had

been dealt with by Lord Variyn himself, but somehow there was another!

Ares wanted to engage but I wasn't so sure. But regardless of my feelings, the will of a griffin isn't so easily turned aside. I braced myself against her back as she shot towards the black form with incredible speed. I realized then that she'd been holding back with how fast she could go for my sake.

I sent her a reassuring mental message and readied my spells for a fight in the air. We flew just below the cloud layer, Ares occasionally dipping into a dive to build up even more impossible speed.

The black wyvern was noticeably smaller than the last one we'd encountered, perhaps a third of the size and much skinnier. I tried Inspecting it, but as with all Chaos infused monsters my efforts were in vain. It had caught sight of us from a great distance, but now its mouth began to glow yellow, and it opened its maw to let loose a stream of fire.

Ares easily dodged the long line of fire and I let off my first spell, aiming for the wings. My Lightning Strike cracked the air and smashed into our flying opponent's wings right where the left one connected to its powerful shoulder muscles. It left no noticeable mark, but it screeched in frustration at me. I'd heard this screech attack before, and with how close we'd gotten, my mind swam as I struggled to remain conscious.

Ares was in control though, and she dived down putting enough distance between us, that the weaker but still powerful screech attack wouldn't knock me out. The cry died off and Ares swooped wide, just as the wyvern came for us in its own dive. Weaving back and forth they made shots at each other with their claws. Ares was obviously faster but each time she raked her claws against the wyvern's wings, it didn't even penetrate the flesh, instead leaving lines of red irritated scales.

I shot out Firebolts, Arcane Missiles, and more Lightning Strikes, but we did little damage. Finally, I summoned my sword and tried my hand at throwing it into the creature's wings. Activating Power Strike and Swift Strike together I threw it end over end. Luck was with my ridiculous idea, and it stabbed through the wing, but stuck there, not putting more than a blade size cut in it.

I summoned my blade back and tried again. This time, the blunt end hit, and my sword fell to the ground. Before it got far, I summoned it back and then let it fade away so I could hold onto Ares with both hands. She had enough of these games and landed on the wyvern's back. It was just about our same size, and she clawed and ripped with her beak, but it was slow work, and the damage was minimal.

I knew what I had to do. I infused essence into my next spell, letting it fly loose the moment Ares detached. First, I cast Restoring Light, hoping that perhaps I'd pull some of the Chaos taint from it, but where my spell hit, the scales just shimmered as if it were deflected. Next, I cast Lightning Strike filled with extra essence turning it a dangerous blue green. It struck the wyvern's back and sent it spinning. The attack left a bloody scorch mark, but after a few seconds it recovered and was back on the attack, sending fire into the sky all around us.

"Ares lets head back, I have an idea," I said the words aloud, but she heard them as if I spoke them into her mind.

She resisted at first, but I explained my idea and she changed her mood. "We have two hundred armored and armed Runeforged that will swarm this thing like ants on prey. We did our part weakening it, let's go finish it off."

Diving to gather speed, Ares showed just how much faster she was than the wyvern. At one point, I had her slow down, so we didn't lose it. The small force of Rune-forged appeared below us and I checked behind us to make sure the wyvern was still on our trail. It was, but it must be getting tired because it had slowed down.

Landing a bit harder than normal, I yelled out for everyone to be ready. Alayna and Ventus were nowhere to be seen and I guessed that they'd already left. I got the Runeforged to form up with the servants behind them just as the wyvern made its appearance.

Fred's eye went wide, and Fran laughed like a lunatic.

"Attack!" I yelled, and what came next was nothing short of a brutal massacre.

First, a wave of elemental attacks showered the wyvern, doing limited damage by themselves but the sheer force of them all had it flinching away. Next, came over a hundred and fifty Runeforged built to match a level 40 adventurer in battle. Stabbing, piercing, slashing faster than even I could follow in the mix of it all. The elemental attacks ceased as so many Runeforged attack that you could no longer see the wyvern as they ripped into it.

What was left was a bloody mess that took us over an hour, with Runeforged help, to harvest all its useful parts. The body was easier to purify after killing it, and the scales remained resistant, but I collected them anyways.

The next few days passed without incident. I flew back and forth between the two parts of my army, my Blackridge troops marching much faster than I anticipated. Soon, a day before we were meant to arrive, our forces had gathered together into one main army. In total, we were just a hair over five hundred strong, but we had another hundred in *Awakened,* servants, and a few family members that decided to tag along.

When we finally marched close enough to see the other forces, my jaw dropped in the shock of it all. Thousands of tents in neatly formed lines were put up, each section belonging to a specific vassal. Banners flew and soldiers marched. A scout found us as we approached and directed us into a spot at the far end, to which we marched and began the work of putting tents up. Wooden pegs had been placed where main walkways were to be observed and I did my best to make sure we matched the neat lines that the other legions had been able to achieve.

I spoke with Fred and Fran while the Runeforged put our tents together.

Fran looked excited. "There is a dungeon not far from here and these mountains are loaded with wild monsters. Should we go get first pick of killing some before someone calls you to a meeting or something?"

I chuckled. "I'm sure I'll be called to meet with the rest of the vassals eventually, but until then, sure, let's go kill some monsters," I said. Then I had a thought. "What dungeon is it that is close? Does it have a theme or just floors?"

"Just floors, but they go all the way to level 24, so it might not be possible to do a full clear, just several floor clears," Fred said, knowingly.

"I bet we could clear it," I said, a wicked smile on my lips as I mentally went through what other *Awakened* we had in our service.

While I considered it, a messenger arrived.

"Lord Caldor Miles of Blackridge Keep?" His tone implied a question, so I nodded and answered.

"I am Lord Miles of Blackridge," I said, looking over the messenger.

He wore a large tabard over armor and looked more soldier than messenger, except for the odd fluffy hat he had on. His tabard had a sigil I didn't recognize, a golden eagle on a field of black.

"Your presence is requested this evening in Master General Busard's tent for dinner and debriefing. Please limit your entourage to a single steward," he said, turning his horse and riding away as soon as I inclined my head, acknowledging I'd heard his words.

"Must be in a hurry," Mick said, walking up on the three of us. "Tents are coming up nicely, only a bit of complaining, but we'll sort it out."

"You're a good man, Mick," I said, slapping his shoulder with a bit more force than I meant to and sending him stumbling.

"And you're a strong man, no need to show off to the pretty lady," Mick said, inclining his head towards Fran, who went redder in the face than normal.

"We are going to go hunt a few monsters, but we'll be back before dark, I have a dinner to attend after all," I said, ignoring his remarks.

We left, just Fred, Fran, and myself, to seek out monsters to kill. I had Ares fly above as a spotter and she would inform me of when she found something. With her help we found and killed six monsters during our hunt. From Dire Bears to something called a Night Spawn, that moved within shadows and required magic to hurt it. In all, I was able to gather a good bit of essence and made a mental note to visit a Mana Shrine to go shopping for new abilities to add to my repertoire.

Busard's tent was a massive affair that was as big and nicer than the house I grew up in. They'd even laid out tiles that clicked together and put out a full-length table to seat nearly fifty if I had to guess. Men all in armor, like myself, walked beside more casually dressed folks who I assumed rightly were their stewards. Most were older gentlemen and I instantly felt out of place with the young brown haired teenager that I'd taken with me. She'd been a direct recommendation from Lance, my steward at Miles Manor, but now I wonder if he didn't do this as a spot of fun against me.

Not for the first time, a younger of the vassals approached me and asked after the name of my date. Going so far as waiting for me to actually respond, to which I explained as gentlemanly as possible that they ought to go find a cliff and throw themselves off it. A hand touched my shoulder and I prepared myself for yet another tirade of stupid jokes at my expense, when I saw Zander in his pale white armor.

"Glad you showed," Zander said, in his usually snide tone. Even when we were on good terms it seemed like he was angry at me for one reason or another.

"You doubted I would?" I said, more as a casual response than any true inquiry.

"My uncle did," Zander said, raising his eyebrows at me to enunciate the point.

Perhaps I'd been too free about my thoughts around Alayna, Zander, and Lord Variyn. He knew me so little as to think I'd dishonor my oath, that surprised me.

"I keep my oaths," I said, not meaning to sound harsh but it came out with a touch of wrath.

"I know," Zander said, putting his hands up in mock surrender. "Did Ismene travel with you? I haven't seen her yet."

"She didn't come," I said, then seeing a hurt look pass over his face I added, "She'll visit, but her and Emory are going to focus on catching up with us."

"Didn't you tell her there is experience aplenty to be gained here? I offered to pay to have her power leveled just last month and she refused me, stubborn girl," Zander said, his tone serious.

"Ismene likes, whenever it is absolutely possible, to earn what she gets," I said, thinking back to how she'd become a *Sparked*, no doubt the idea of someone power leveling her, when so much after she had that handed to her, just annoyed her.

"She can be stubborn," Zander said, shaking his head. "Looks like dinner is starting."

I saw what he meant; everyone began to sit so we followed suit. A servant directed us each to chairs a few away from each other and we sat. The murmuring came to an abrupt halt as Busard entered the tent and sat at the head of the table. Chatter resumed a moment later as plates were deposited on the table, and everyone began to eat.

I leaned over towards Zander and asked, "Is Lord Variyn not going to be here?"

Zander answered me with a simple shake of his head, no.

That seemed odd to me, why wouldn't the person who started the war not be in attendance to the very war he started. That wasn't to say he might not make an appearance later, but it set the wrong impression I believed.

The food was good, but not great, which surprised me. I thought I heard a few other vassals complaining about the quality of the food, so I knew I wasn't the only person to notice. Looking around the table I came upon an obvious realization. Each and every one of these, mostly youthful faces, were all level 20 or above. This room represented over thirty powerful *Awakened* fighters and suddenly I wondered what capabilities each of them had. Were they fighters, casters, did they prefer attacking from a distance or close up?

Plates were cleared and the point of the meeting, Busard speaking with us all, began.

"31,000 Troops were meant to be marshaled by you all, who wishes to offer the first excuse why only 25,500 have arrived?" Busard asked, his voice hanging over the crowd of now quiet vassals.

We were over five thousand troops short, that meant more than just me had trouble getting troops together. If averaged out it would seem that every vassal was short about a hundred and fifty soldiers.

"I thought not," Busard said, breaking the awkward silence that filled his question. "It is good then that Lord Variyn and I have recruited from the major cities, mercenaries, and prisons. In total, we, through our own singular effort, have recruited an additional 30,000 men. Let that sink in for a moment. We were able to recruit so many where you failed to make your minimum requirement.

"Furthermore, I'd like to speak on behalf of Lord Variyn in expressing my utter frustration in how long it took you to muster your troops. Though you were told to arrive by today, it is always expected that you should arrive a day early. You are meant to lead these men and you will show a proper example," Busard said, looking over the gathered vassals.

"Each of you Commanders will receive one thousand and five hundred men," he continued. "Those with quick wits will realize, that leaves roughly nine thousand troops in reserve. This is intended and they will remain under my direct control and training, becoming a reserve force able to turn the tide of battle when I'm through with them.

"Now tell me, who flies the banner of the black griffin?" Busard asked, but his eyes had already fallen on me, so I knew he knew it was me.

I stood and spoke. "I do," I said. "It is the banner of Blackridge Keep."

"And you thought it wise to bring a force of two hundred Runeforged with you, Lord of Blackridge Keep?" Busard asked, his voice somewhere between sarcasm and boredom.

"I did," I said, deciding confidence was the best option here as I didn't know what Busard was playing at.

"You may have a seat," Busard said, smiling in my direction. "I wish you all had the commitment of Young Lord Miles. He has gone to a great expense to ensure that his legion is the strongest gathered. Despite his failing to recruit the full thousand men, he has come with the Runeforged able to slaughter ten men with ease and a retinue of *Awakened* that makes even my own gathered groups to be small. This is a man ready for war, a man who understands the commitment required of him."

This is a man confused, I thought. What was Busard playing at calling me out in front of everyone? Surely, he knew he was making me an enemy of everyone present and putting a target on my back. I'd gotten the message loud and clear from other sources, war was dangerous, and I needed to make friends, not enemies. But here I was on day one, being called out by the Head of all the army, congratulated, while everyone else was scorned.

"Lord Zander Variyn," Busard said, and he had my attention once more.

"Yes, Master General Busard?" Zander said, he didn't stand, and his tone was one of annoyance, more than concern at what he'd say.

"You arrived with the smallest force, a mere two hundred and fifty men. Is your commitment to this conflict mirrored in your recruiting efforts?" Busard asked, staring hard at the pale faced youth.

"Not at all, I merely didn't have proper resources or time to gather from the eastern dominance with how poorly it is maintained and populated," Zander said, his lack of respect in the way he addressed Busard made me cringe. Being the nephew of Lord Variyn meant he didn't likely have to worry about repercussions, but Busard didn't seem like a man you'd want to cross.

"I get the feeling you have lessons to learn," Busard said, nodding his head as he spoke. "Perhaps I will allow you to continue to use just your gathered troops as we engage in battle with far more superior and well-trained forces? Would you feel confident that your men will perform well?"

Zander just glared at Busard for a long moment before letting his gaze falter. "I will require additional troops. Though I failed in gathering the correct amount, I will not fail in battle, Master General Busard."

"I believe it is too early to tell if your statement is truthful, but you are right. You will receive troops, like the rest of the Commanders, and with a bit of training, we will win this war," Busard said, lifting his glass in a toast.

Busard left after his toast, but his steward remained, explaining a few key details. He started with the basic command structure we were expected to follow and assign within our Commander tabs.

A squad would be led by a Captain and a Lieutenant. These consist of ten men each and are the main fighting body and structure of war. Ten squads make a platoon or one hundred men. Each platoon is led by a squire. Five platoons make up a company that consists of five hundred men. Platoons are led by Knights who report directly to you as a Commander. The legions will consist of three platoons, or one thousand five hundred men.

We were instructed to assign four types of ranks within our tabs, Captains, Lieutenants, Squires, and Knights. Doing a quick count, I determined I needed one hundred and fifty Captains and Lieutenants, fifteen Squires, and three Knights.

Without much thought to the matter, I assigned Mick,

Raphael, and Michael as my Knights. They were my two elite guards and Mick, so it made sense. I'd leave it to them to decide who they felt should take the role of squires under them, five each. And then let the squires pick their Captains and Lieutenants. I didn't know how the system recorded that information, but I'd have them make reports if needed, so they could manage the work later.

He went further to say how important it was going to be to let them name their squads, platoons and even companies. That we should let it become like sport where they compare and push each other to do better. Then he shifted topic to morale, saying that it was just as important as fighting ability. Some scoffed at this, and he gave them the stink eye, saying that if we treated our troops poorly, they would perform poorly. And poorly performing legions would be the ones wiped out by the enemy.

The next topic was one I paid special attention to as he spoke.

"The role of an Awakened in battle is a precarious one," he said, letting out a deep sigh. "It is well understood on both sides that a single *Awakened* fighting in the battle can change the entire dynamic of battle. As a courtesy rule followed by most is that you never allow yourself to be the first to have an *Awakened* engage, but once one does, you must counter with the full force of your might, lest you be overtaken by the force of their own.

"As you all know, all of the *Awakened* under your service cannot be called to war under the rules of the Adventurers Guild, however, if they choose to fight on their own, we will not stop them. Beware being known as the one who always brings his strongest to battle." His eyes rested on me. "You will soon become a target among the enemy. I do not envy that poor soul."

I suddenly felt less excited about the force I'd brought with me.

"Most, if not all, *Awakened* you've brought will need to be used to maintain the supply lines for your army. Lord Variyn and King Newaliyn are subsidizing the cost of supplies to tend to the gathered armies, but you will be required to handle the logistics."

"Back to the matter of *Awakened* and a spot of advice to those who might find themselves with an overabundance of such volunteers willing to do battle. Tell them to mask their strength and hold back. For only the keenest of eye will be able to spot them, but having a near unstoppable soldier among the ranks can do wonders for morale." Again, he looked at me and I swear I saw him wink.

"As for a Commander's duties, one that I like to remind them of, is the clearing of monsters and mandatory dungeon clearing when we encounter one. This is a tradition that has been followed for many hundreds of years, but if you wish to break tradition it has become acceptable to appoint other *Awakened* to do this duty in your stead." The last bit quieted many rumblings from some older Lords, though older was a bit of a misnomer as most present had the timeless look of one who'd been alive a bit too long.

And with that, the meeting ended. But I found myself

confused by the lack of mentioning a certain technology that Alayna had been so worried her father would be using. I pulled the steward aside before he could disappear and waited for the rest to clear out. He seemed content to wait and leveled a curious stare in my direction.

When the tent was cleared, I asked my question. "There was no mention of air ships, are we not going to attack using that method after all?"

"And where did you hear such rumors as these?" He asked, but before I had a chance to respond he sighed and said, "Ah you must have spoken with Lord Variyn himself. I do hope he hasn't made it common knowledge as no one knows what the ears of spies will hear. To my knowledge the ships, or platforms really, are not ready. However, when they are you can be assured, young Lord Miles, that this conflict will swiftly come to an end."

I nodded and another thought came to my mind. "Thank you for the tip about adding Awakened into my ranks. I will use your advice as wisely as I can."

The steward just nodded and turned, leaving me alone with my thoughts.

CHAPTER 28
LEARNING HOW TO WALK

I entered my tent, a sizable structure with three rooms. The main room had a commander's table with a map, troop placement figures, and several reports laid out for me to look over. Standing over the table was my assistant, Verena, and my three newly appointed Knights.

"I'm a level 1 Knight," Mick said, as soon as I entered.

"As we all are," Michael said, his voice gruff. Even in his mannerisms, his eyes darting here and there as if he was ready to jump into action at any moment, were different than the cool and calm Michael that currently taught my siblings. Seemed like a common enough name, but it was throwing me off, so I decided to fix that.

"Michael, do you mind if I call you Mike?" I asked, his eyes going a bit wide at first but settling a moment later.

"As you wish," Mike said. That would make it a bit easier for my brain to keep track of. Can't have too many important people in my mind with the same name, that'd be insanity.

With that settled, I stepped up and glanced at the first of the papers I needed to review. This one was just a summary of the meeting we'd attended, so I set it aside a moment later and grabbed the next.

"This is the training schedule for the next few weeks," Verena said, her voice as peppy as ever. I really ought to have found an older man to do her job like the rest of the Lords. But she did her job well, so it was hard to take the thought that seriously.

I looked it over and asked a few questions, before setting it aside. We'd be required to separate the army into squads, platoons, and companies, but first we had to place them into one of the three types of soldiers Master General Busard had instructed through his steward. Being either, Cavalry, Men at Arms, or Bowmen. Each type would fulfill other require-ments, such as some bowmen squads would be required for scout duty, and from the men at arms we'd recruit sappers if we attacked any keeps, engineers for the same siege warfare, and all manner of special weapons training as I saw fit.

In my mind I saw a force of two hundred trained to be front liners wielding the spears I'd ordered, but I had no idea how long it would take them to fulfill that order. I trusted Lance would bring them at his first opportunity though.

"Do any of you have an idea who you will call as your squires yet?" I asked, putting down one of the reports detailing the basic training meant to happen over the next week or two.

"I've got my eye on Sam, Barney, Robert, Todd, and Jase," Mick said, speaking quickly and smirking at Mike and Raphael as they both opened their mouth to speak. "I know each of those boys well enough. They'll do their duty and put good men in charge of squads."

"You know Jase and think he ought to lead other men?" Raphael said, her voice doubtful. "What about the incident with Darion, you think that shows leadership quality?"

"I've his word he won't be touching the drink, he can't control himself on it, so I've elected to provide him with a nice numbing weed that he's been smoking since the...uh... incident. Nothing to worry about now," Mick said, smiling a bit too wide at me.

An insect buzzed in front of us, a nasty big black thing and before I could shoo it away, Mick pulled his too-large knife. He skewered the insect with his knife, slamming it against the table. Lifting it up to his face he reared back. A moment later it puffed into blue smoke.

"Someone thinks to spy on us," Mick said, looking around suspiciously.

Damn. I hadn't taken the time to add any protections on the wooden poles of the tent or written out a single non-scrying rune, my earrings were making me lax.

"I'll get wards put up tonight," I said, going through my head which books I had on hand and which ones I'd moved into my Arcane Asylum. I'd need to summon the door and find the ones on warding.

We finished going through reports and I bid them all goodnight, though I had much work to do before I turned in. I summoned my door and retrieved the books I needed. It was tempting to stay in the space and use it as intended, a small study. But I'd found myself hesitant to spend too much time inside, it was too easy to feel disconnected from it all when inside. Plus, it had been my father's space, and spending time inside, necessitated that I make changes. The more changes I made the less it became a place that reminded me of him.

I enlisted the help of Fred, Fran, and Kora to place the complex runes. It required that we take each of the thirteen largest support poles and carve directly into them. There were more temporary measures we could do, but I imagined my tent would remain the same through the conflict, so we might as well get the work done. Kora was by far the fastest, but she left the infusing and activating to me, saying her magic was just different enough to cause problems.

A few times she offered suggestions in ways to improve the wards, I took all of her comments and made sure to make notes. Fred hung on her every word and more often than not, they worked close beside each other.

"Come check this sequence out," Fran said, she'd been struggling the most but so far, she'd made no mistakes big enough to dampen the field I was creating.

"It looks good, just remember to leave this bit open so

that it connects to the rest of the formations. Here, like this," I said, reaching to grab her hand and gently change the stiff line to an open swish instead. "See, not so hard."

"Something feels hard," Fran said, a silly smile on her face.

I glanced down and saw that my armor's cod piece was pressed into her back. I went red and backed up with my hands raised. "Sorry about that, I'm not used to having an armored cod piece. It's a bit awkward and bulky," I said.

Fran stared at my crotch, biting her lower lip and said, "Yeah, I can see it is a pretty big cod piece. Does it get in the way or are you used to having big problems down there?"

"Shut up, Fran," Fred called out from across the room.

I was still wholly embarrassed, and a bit thrown off by Fran's odd comments. I wasn't so dull as not to recognize a bit of friendly flirting, but the way she was staring at me unsettled me as much as it stirred a deeper hunger within myself. There was no ignoring Fran's beauty and I liked her well enough that had I not already been with Alayna, I might consider taking a roll in the sack with her, but there was more to consider now.

I was a commander now and technically she worked under me. Any relations we might have, could be affected by that, as well as potentially ruin our friendship. There could always be one involved that decided the sex wasn't just sex and meant a deeper connection.

I shook my head to gather my wits. Fran had stood and basically pressed herself against me while asking a question that I didn't even hear. Blood was rushing to all the wrong places, and why was I even considering the ramifications of something that shouldn't happen. I took a breath and stepped back.

"What was that, sorry I had a buzzing in my ear," I said, taking a few steadying breaths and finally gathering my wits together.

"I was just asking if you could show me a few more rune formations later tonight, maybe in private?" She asked. The smirk on her lips made it hard to tell if she were being serious, but the look in her eyes told me she definitely wasn't joking.

"I think Alayna will be joining us, uhm, at any time, and uhm, you remember Alayna, right? Well, we are sort of courting and well, maybe I can show you something right here with everyone else around?" I asked, finally getting the words out.

"Oh, Caldor, you are no fun," Fran said, hitting my arm with a playful punch. "One of these days I'll get you in the sack and we will see if it's all Alayna claims it to be."

Now I knew without a doubt I was red in the face. Had Alayna talked to Fran about us having sex? Had this been some kind of test organized by Alayna to test my faithfulness or was Fran seriously interested in having sex with me? All these questions were too much, and I went back to the cool focus of carving runes into the stiff wooden poles.

It took longer than I had hoped, the sun peeking over the horizon by the time we finished, but it was work that needed to be done. I bid farewell to my friends, thanking them for their time and went to lay down to catch a few hours of sleep before attending to my duties.

I had just laid my head down, when a loud trumpeting was sounded from all around. Then I heard voices outside the tent a few minutes later. Groaning from the lack of sleep, though really it didn't bother me so much to lose a single night of sleep, I headed out to the front of my tent.

Ignis stood barring the way to my three Knights and Verena.

"Master Miles is resting now, please return later," Ignis said, her voice sweet and melodic, when compared to the robotic voice of non-converted Runeforged.

"It's alright, Ignis, let them in," I said, stifling a yawn. Kora had mentioned in passing that she'd assign a Runeforged to guard my tent while I slept, but I hadn't known it would be Ignis. I found myself more worried about the tent being set ablaze than anything else.

"That trumpeting was announcing the need to gather our troops. We each are being assigned a man by Busard to train our troops in the proper way to walk. Or so they said," Verena said, a coy smile on her lips.

"What of the additional troops to be added to our ranks?" I asked, as they stepped inside and stood around the table.

"They are joining us in the field, might be a good time to make some introductions," Raphael said. I noticed the three of them wore matching armor, plate not very dissimilar to mine, but with tabards that covered their chest and hung just above the knee. They were white, Mick's already had a touch of dirt on the edges, with a black griffin on the chest raised up as if to strike.

"Fine idea," I said. "Let us go meet the troops."

The Runeforged stood like statues on the open grassy field that we'd been given to teach how to march. The rest of my forces, not so much. My Blackridge troops were in a semi-loose formation, that perhaps started out in a line and orderly, but had devolved a bit while they awaited my arrival. They stood out against the newcomers because of their matching armor and tabards. The final item that made them stand out was the height and race differences. Short Stout dwarves were lined together, next to tall, muscled orcs, who had been placed next to even shorter goblins with scrawny arms, and then a mix of trolls and humans. The trolls tended to be close enough in height, but the tusks, varied green and gray colors of their skin, set them apart from each other.

Meanwhile, the entire one-thousand-man group we'd been given were humans. They also had no end to the mismatched types of armor and a few smaller sections even held banners of hog's heads, or bear heads. What that meant I did not know yet, but I was sure to find out.

"Have you picked out your squires yet?" I asked my knights. Each of them gave an affirmative. "Gather them together and we will get these men lined up and organized into squads. Start with temporary lieutenants, no captains. Stress that this appointment is temporary."

They agreed and entered the mass of troops, pulling out their squires. I got each of their names as they came and assigned them in my interface, giving them the titles and ability to level up through proxy levels. If I focused, I could see the specific perks they'd be given to choose from, but I'd been informed that it was best to instruct them all to pick the same perks, allow for a synergy between our forces.

We started with our own troops, having them gather into ten-man groups, then assigning a Lieutenant from one of the ten. In lines of ten, as they were formed, I ordered them to begin to march out and send a few squires to adjust their march as needed. We didn't know what to expect yet, but I wasn't the type to sit around waiting to be told to do something.

We made it through our group of five hundred troops, including the Runeforged who marched so well in synch that it was a bit mesmerizing, before the man meant to train our troops arrived. He announced himself as Knight Gadwell.

"I'm glad to see such a valiant, if not piss poor, effort from you, Lord Miles," Gadwell said, wiping his hand across a stuffy nose. Despite his apparent sickness, he had a very rough voice like he spent his free time screaming so loud that he'd permanently damaged his throat. This was not an elegant man and his features fit the personality I was seeing so far. His nose had been broken at some point in his life and not set back in the right direction. Both his ears were puffy and lumpy in a way I'd never seen, but I guessed was due to damage of some kind. He had an ugly scar that ran from his lower jaw down into his neck, disappearing into his armor.

He wore a tabard, as all soldiers seemed to now, it was familiar, but I couldn't place where I'd seen it. It showed a winged white horse on a field of black. A Pegasus perhaps? I stared at it for a moment longer before it clicked where I'd seen it before. Outside of Busard's tent this banner had been flying, he must be one of his Knights.

"We've got one third of the troops assigned to squads, the rest are troops given to us from the reserve units," I said, letting him know where we are in the process.

"Ah good, well those walking piles of shit are already organized into squads, and you should have gotten or soon will, a list of their captains and lieutenants. Feel free to fuck around with those appointments, they weren't done with care I can promise you that," Gadwell said, spitting a nasty brown liquid from his mouth in front of us. I noticed a bulge in his lip and suspected he was chewing some type of herb.

Before I had a chance to answer him, though what I'd have said to the crude man I didn't know, he walked off and began yelling orders at the troops we'd received.

Soon, and with the help of my own knights and squires, we had all the troops gathered in their squads and marching in formation. Gadwell had acquired a horse and was charging all over the place, screaming orders. I decided to call down Ares and join him to see if I was meant to do something.

Ares arrived a few minutes later from whatever monster she'd been hunting, blood still staining her beak. I mounted her and trotted over to where Gadwell was screaming at an orc who looked very confused. We'd made sure every squad had someone who could speak common well enough, so one of the other orcs said something in orcish and finally the orc stepped into line.

"What the fuck are you looking to him for, do you not speak my language you maggot! For the love of fucking order and the holy Ordu, you better fucking learn," he continued to scream at the orc, going red faced.

When he looked away to get a translation, I thought Gadwell might jump from his horse to strike the poor orc warrior. But he managed to stay mounted and when the translation came through, the orc's face actually paled a bit. I couldn't help but smile, but as Gadwell straightened to look at me I hurriedly wiped it from my face.

"Fucking fuck Lord Miles where did you find these worthless Southlanders?" He asked, then did a double take, looking at Ares. "For the love of all that is holy, you have a fucking griffin mount? Of course, you do. I'm going to need to speak with Busard, fucking hell on toast, I'm not suited to train a damned griffin rider. Do I look like I have fucking wings? Wait, no shit. Miles, you are fucking Elkor Miles' brat, aren't you?"

So many questions, some that I couldn't help but feel

insulted from, hit me at once and I had to take a moment to gather my wits before responding.

"You are a crude man," I finally said, shaking my head.

"Nonsense, I'm a fucking soldier and I'm also your damned best friend and you know why?" Gadwell said, he was practically shouting at me now.

"Why?" I asked, through clenched teeth. Not a single soldier was looking our way and I could understand why. Gadwell was akin to a monster.

"Because I'm going to teach these shitstains and you, you fucking griffin rider, how to properly kill the enemy while not fucking killing yourselves. So harden your skin, boy, because Lord or not, this is war and war ain't no damned game." Gadwell practically growled as he spoke.

I was at a loss for words, but I made a mental note about possibly requesting a different knight, as the one they sent me was an absolute lunatic.

We trained in a massive valley, each legion separated by less than a quarter of a mile. I hadn't ever imagined seeing sixty thousand troops gathered together, but it was breathtaking. I'd moved away from Gadwell, letting him do his work of teaching the troops how to walk while screaming like a maniac. He set the men to rest after a few hours, but pulled all the Captains and Lieutenants together, it should have been three hundred men, but as we hadn't assigned captains yet, it was closer to two hundred.

Then he went to work teaching them how to march and respond to stop commands. The knights and squires were a part of this, needing to learn all the commands as well. I elected to listen from afar, not wanting to engage Gadwell in conversation just yet.

We broke for lunch, and then dinner, but Gadwell required everyone to return after. Under the light of two moons, we trained into the night. All other legions hadn't returned after dinner, so I wondered what Gadwell was up to and decided to ask him as much.

"Why are we still out here?" I asked, between his shouting. It seemed his voice had no end in its ability to be loud and obnoxious.

"You go leave and go to your posh tent, sit your Lordly ass on a cushion while we fucking get this right," Gadwell said, still shouting.

"I've had enough of that," I said, my breathing increasing. "You can talk however you want to the troops; I understand it is a part of the training. But if you fucking raise your voice to me again, I'll teach you the meaning of respect."

I hadn't meant to, but my sword appeared in my hand and sparked from gathered essence. Gadwell spurred his horse to the side, and I followed him until we were out of earshot for all but *Awakened.*

"About time you speak up for yourself, Lord," Gadwell said, his voice lowered to a normal speaking level for the first time since meeting him. "These shit-bags need to know you're in charge, so here is what you'll do. Put that damned sword away and punch me right across the chin. I'll be a respectful shit after that, and your men will have learned a valuable lesson. The asshat yelling at them all day is no match for their Commander. Be a pleasure to receive a right hook by the son of such an honorable man. Riding a griffin, and the son of Elkor, you've got the gods own luck with you boy."

My sword faded away and I sat for a second staring confused at Gadwell. What was he playing at with his request? Sure, in a sick way it made some kind of sense, but did he really want me to strike him? Oh well, here goes nothing.

I reared back and struck him across the chin, not holding back. The sound of my fist connecting echoed through the near empty darkened valley and Gadwell was lifted from his saddle and thrown to the ground, rolling several times and cursing all the while.

The entire army seemed to gasp at the same time and a few even shouted joyfully. I dismounted Ares and she was confused, but I sent her calming thoughts, before she tore into Gadwell as if he were an enemy. Walking over to him I held out a hand to help him up. He took it and pulled himself close to whisper a few words at me.

"Damn good right hook, now push me away and don't help me up this time," he said.

I sighed and shoved him hard. He went flying backwards end over end and I could have sworn he was purposely making himself fly farther than he would have normally. This was a weird way to get my troops' respect, and I doubted it would work, but after all the abuse they'd suffered under his hand even more cheered as he fell. I had a sudden idea and stepped forward to shout out to all the troops.

"Training is over for the day," I shouted. "Return to camp and extra ale rations for everyone!"

Now the entire army cheered. I caught a grin from Gadwell as he stood, taking his time as if I'd really hurt him. Whether or not Gadwell was an *Awakened,* if he was a knight under Busard he had proxy levels enough to survive a little tossing about by a level 21 Adventurer.

My knights joined me, standing by my side as Gadwell slowly walked over to us. After checking that all the soldiers, save my knights and my assistant Verena, were out of earshot he spoke.

"You hit like a girl, but you earned my respect," Gadwell said, saluting me with his fist to his chest.

I saluted back and he gave me an appreciative nod. "Now about these Southlanders and them not knowing Common," Gadwell said, before launching into an idea of several key phrases they could learn, in order to do well enough to obey orders. Verena took notes and I got all three of my knights to agree to begin working with the captains of the southern squads, but I added that I'd prefer they begin to learn Common as well.

After that, Gadwell went over various plans he had for the next few days, having the troops go through different stations while we observed their weapons skills. It would be wise to get a good look at all their capabilities before assigning each member into a type of soldier, which might involve switching around squads, but he'd prefer they stay together as they'll start building their camaraderie, which was important, he assured us.

"Lastly, about those Runeforged of yours," Gadwell said, shaking his head. "I'd save them in battle and allow them to work as a footed cavalry of sorts. I imagine if they got running at full speed they'd work just as well. It isn't uncommon to have a few golem types fighting in a war, but they are mostly treated like *Awakened* forces to be deployed when you need to shift the type of battle you're waging. Leading with those metal men will likely make you a focus of the enemy, one that they'd set an ambush for the first chance they got to take you off the board."

"I appreciate the advice," I said. "I honestly do, but I have plans for the Runeforged. They will be our front line, a shield between the death of my troops and the enemy force."

"What of the lives of the Runeforged?" Kora asked, startling every last one of us as we turned to see her approaching, as quiet as a field mouse.

"Soldier, you were told to return to your fucking tent," Gadwell said, looking unnerved as he got a closer look at her. "Damn you are a freaky looking thing aren't you. Almost human but not in all the ways that matter."

"I am more alive than you could ever hope to be, meat bag," Kora said, before turning to me and giving me her 'are you going to answer me' stare.

"Runeforged aren't easily destroyed, and they can be repaired," I said, giving her my full attention. "I'm not being careless, and I won't be sending them in alone, I just want to use my most durable units to be where the most potential of death will be. When we die, we are dead, but if one of the Runeforged fall we can repair them."

"Can *you* repair them, or do you mean I will have to? I doubt my newer designed Runeforged are something you'd want Gilfoy getting their hands on. No, if a squad of Runeforged are placed in the front lines, so will a meat bag squad. Fair is fair," Kora said, I'd never seen her so passionate about something.

"I'll consider it," I said, putting my hand on her shoulder. "Go see to your soldiers, they did good today."

Kora stared at me for a long few seconds before turning and running off into the distance. Why she chose to run, I don't know, but I guess if you had somewhere to be, might as well get there fast.

"Are we going to talk about that?" Gadwell said, looking dumbfounded by the entire exchange.

I sighed and figured he'd need to be in the loop. I filled him in on what she was and how she was basically the Knight that would be over her troops, I just couldn't assign her in my interface or her troops. He took it all rather well, calling me a fucking moron for trusting it, but said it was my choice. I held my tongue and wondered if punching him again would be appropriate.

All in all, it was a successful first day of training. Despite sitting on the back of Ares most of the day, I was finally feeling the effects of being up for two days and fell asleep the moment my head hit the pillow.

CHAPTER 29
OLD FRIENDS

"Grab the bow and get your ass moving!" Gadwell yelled, he'd taken the lead on one of the dozens of archer lanes that had been set up. We were testing squads together to check for proficiency in horseback riding, archery, and spear wielding as well as testing to see how many could use a sword if their spear failed them.

I watched as a man I suddenly recognized stepped up to the plate and put arrow to bow. Dan Lion, the dark-skinned man with handsome features and piercing blue eyes that had worked for my Farm, was drawing back the bow and readying it to fire. Looking at the ten men gathered behind him in a loose huddle I saw Cam Castle as well, the married man with short blonde hair and deep brown eyes.

Staying out of the line of fire, I walked over to the group. Dan released his arrow, and I cringed as it went wide. He was the third to go from his group and not one had gotten close to the target yet. These were looking like they'd be men at arms or cavalry for sure, I thought.

"Dan Lion," I said, and he looked up surprised as he lined up his next shot. It went wide and nearly hit a surprised Gadwell—which was saying something as he stood midway down the lane and far off enough that it would have to be deliberate if he were hit.

"Sorry," he said, seeing Gadwell go red in the face and begin screaming obscenities.

"We got placed in your legion just by asking," Cam said, stepping up and shaking my arm. "I told the rest of them that you wouldn't let him beat us down all night, and then you laid him flat. We are so happy to have made it here and the pay is twice as high as our last unit. We are getting six silver a week."

"Not bad," I said, clasping his hand and shaking it. "How are you adjusting to military life?"

"After that long night, we were beginning to wish we hadn't transferred," Dan said, handing the bow off to the next squad member, a burly bald man who looked to be in his thirties.

"You still think that?" I asked, grinning as Gadwell began screaming at the next guy to hit his mark or he'll be marching the entire length of the valley.

"Nah we're alright now, plus," Cam said leaning in. "They made me Captain and Dan Lieutenant."

Dan frowned and suddenly Cam laughed. "What's so funny," I asked, seeing them poking fun at each other.

"They just picked the first two people in line and Dan

had me switch because he didn't want to be at the end, so he made himself a lieutenant," Cam said, still chuckling at the turn of fate.

Gadwell yelled something that didn't sound as angry and I saw that the bald man had hit all his three shots, nearly making a bullseye. Cam and Dan turned to look, and Dan whistled appreciatively before saying, "Good job Hank, you weren't lying about being a crack-shot after all." Hank just grunted and passed the bow off to the next person.

So far, Hank was the only decent shot among the bunch. "Have you tested with the horses yet?" I asked, wondering if they'd be any good at riding with how little I saw them ride back home.

"I'm pretty good atop a horse," Cam said, then thumbing over to Dan he added. "But Lieutenant Dan here, couldn't stay atop the one they gave him for more than a second."

"It was out to get me," Dan said, cursing under his breath.

"So, you'll be a man at arms then," I said, smiling. "You any good with spears or swords?"

"As good as the next man, just point and stick the sharp point into the enemy, right?" Dan said, shrugging.

"Basically," I said. "Maybe I can show you all a thing or two after you get your official assignment. I might even have a tip or two about which perks to pick when the time comes."

"We don't get to pick our own perks," Cam said, knowingly.

"You don't?" I asked, wondering why I wouldn't know this as the Commander of the entire legion.

"Squires said they are told from up top what you will pick so that the legion will be synchronized. You'd think you'd know that?" Cam asked, a grin on his face like he was about to laugh at something extremely funny.

"I'll figure it out, but if it's true, then I will definitely have a say in what perks you get, and you'll get good ones. I promise," I said. "I'll see you all later, perhaps tonight I'll take your squad to do some special training. I've got a new spear I want you all to train with and see how you handle it."

Walking over to Gadwell, he called out to me just loud enough that no one ought to be able to hear. "You know those worthless slobs?"

I ignored his insults towards Cam and Dan, nodding. "Yeah, they worked for me back home. Orchard farmhands. Cam has a new wife and little girl and they're both real hard workers."

"Too bad they can't shoot to save their lives. With that amount of uncoordinated skill, I'd wager they won't do well as men at arms either. I'd set them to front line duty and let the waste burn itself off," Gadwell said, spitting his dark juices into the fresh green grass.

I was over letting his suggestions and words get to me, but it really took me off guard hearing him so casually mention the death of my friends. If I had soldiers that were struggling, the last thing I'd do it stick them in the front lines. It would be a death sentence. Of course, being in the front lines was likely a death sentence period and with Kora giving me so much flack, I would be hard pressed to change that fact.

"They'll learn and you watch, those two will go far," I said, nodding along as if I knew what the future held. I had faith that two hard working men who wanted nothing else but good wages to help their futures, could succeed. Life wasn't always fair, but if these two could come out on top it would mean something.

The training continued for the next week until all the squads had been assigned an area of focus and Captains. I left all the formerly assigned Captains with special instructions to the squires to watch out for those that seemed to be failing in the role and to report directly to me for what to do. I didn't want to admit it, but I wanted Dan and Cam to stay in their positions and give them a chance to learn.

Our nightly trainings had turned into a bit of a routine where I taught them both spear and sword techniques I'd learned. Then on the fifth day of training, another squad came, and I taught them too. After about a month, our entire force of men at arms was being trained nightly for only about an hour, going over specialized techniques and drills. It got to the point where even Gadwell joined us every sixth session to give tips and formation techniques.

Soon, two months had passed by, and while other legions had seen battle, mine had yet to be called into service. We were well trained, even Gadwell said that we were 'better than most shit stains out here', so I had faith that once the call for battle came, we'd do well. Our camp had moved as well, further into the House Blalor lands as the front line of war changed.

CHAPTER 30
FIRST ENCOUNTER

I'd leveled up twice—getting to level 23—and gotten a few new abilities, as well as picked my combat perk and auras after some discussion with Gadwell. I brought my Constitution over its threshold, adding the remaining two points into Concentration. Because of my armor, my health pool far outstripped my Mana pool, now at 2,631 to 1,954. However, my Strength and Intellect values were in sync and that mattered more to my class.

Just from training I'd gotten to Commander Rank 2, which enabled me to pick two auras. I took Aura of the Turtle and Aura of the Wolf, both seemed like they had amazing use cases. The combat perk I picked was a bit more difficult to decide. I only could pick one so far, as I unlocked a new one every other rank, so I wanted it to be the right one. I ended up going with a perk called, Prime Morale 1, which had the effect of increasing the general morale during battle and lowering the threshold for when the men would retreat because of low morale, effectively meaning they'd fight longer than they normally would under harsher circumstances.

It was the perk Gadwell suggested, I personally wanted to go with a perk that buffed their performance or gave them better innate defensive ability, but he argued that morale was more important and won more battles than skill or protection alone. Looking over my new abilities I thought back on how effective they were while Fred, Fran, and I fought a level 17 Dire Bear.

Fred put himself in another precarious situation and I reached out my hand to use one of my new abilities, a spell called Mana Shell. Charging it with 10 mana it erected a blue translucent shield around him with 50 hit points. The bear slammed against it, cracks running over its surface.

I activated my other new abilities, a skill named Speed Burst, and for the cost of 100 Stamina, I closed the gap and struck the bear three times before it wore off. The world coming back to its slow reality a moment later.

But it was too late for the bear, it slung down dead just as my barrier shattered away under its weight. We'd been encountering loads of monsters in the area as the front line moved forward, but a part of me remained eager to get our first battle over. So, when I saw the flare go up, an orange one that meant deploy orders for one of the legions, I hurried back to camp, Fred and Fran struggling to keep up.

As we arrived out from the distant hills, I could see a force gathering and it was mine. Excitement, mixed with anxious trepidation, washed over me, but I pushed it all down. Now was the time that all our training had been leading up to.

Our first battle.

I arrived and met Gadwell as the troops finished lining up.

"There is a force of eight hundred men marching to reinforce a keep, but if you march double time, we will catch them before they add their might to that keep," Gadwell said, his armor was in place but something he said caught my attention.

"You aren't coming?" I asked, surprised that he wouldn't want to see us in action.

"Can't," Gadwell said. "I'm too important to die in battle with you." He winked and I knew he was joking, but it still stirred some of my deepest doubts. I'd grown accustomed to having Gadwell around and he'd really toned down his profanity around me in recent weeks.

"Very well, where do I go?" I asked. He gave me the intel and suggested I get my troops marching while I do some recon with my flying chicken. Ares wasn't fond of being called such, but I had stopped trying to correct him after the fifth time he referred to her that way.

I relayed the orders to my knights and Kora. The march began, each company marching separate and ready. Our cavalry were our weakest when it came to training, as learning to be a mounted spearman wasn't easy, but overall I felt in my bones that we were ready. That's when the rain started. I took flight atop Ares, watchful for a shift in the weather towards lightning, as we'd be forced to land.

The rain made it hard to spot what we sought, but after about half an hour we found a large force of men marching out in the open. To the east, was a keep, but it was such a small dot that it would take them an entire day at their current speed to reach it. I doubled back and landed among my marching troops, joining my knights at the back of the columns.

"Enemy is northeast from here, if we push our march, we can come behind without them noticing," I said, rain soaking us all through.

"Men are complaining at the speed already," Mick said, seeming hesitant. "Wet feet make grumpy men and this legion's feet might as well be swimming."

"I recommend we hold our current pace, perhaps even slow it, for the sake of morale," Raphael said, looking to Mick and nodding.

Mike shook his head. "Push them harder, they are ready for it. They've trained all these months for a chance to earn their pay, give it to them."

"Let's push hard for now and we will slow down as we get into position, giving the men time to rest," I said, going with what I thought was a good compromise. "Kora, your troops aren't as affected by these conditions. I'm afraid I'm going to need as many as we can to take the front line positions, otherwise we might buckle on contact."

"I understand, but I'm not happy about it, meat bag," Kora said, surprising me with how quickly she accepted my orders.

The rain had turned the grassy fields into mud filled

slosh. It came in torrents now, just warm enough that it didn't become snow, but cold enough that I knew my men must be chattering their teeth. I had no perk or aura to deal with these conditions or spells that could warm an army, but at that moment I wished that I did.

Our scouts kept me apprised of the situation as it evolved. The enemy troops had increased their march, so the idea of slowing before battle or taking a longer route to come up behind them wouldn't work. Instead, I ordered an adjustment that would take us right into them, head-first. It was sure to be a deadlier encounter, but hopefully for them and not us.

"I think I will fight among the troops, morale is low and they need to know I'm ready to stand at their side," I said, nodding along to my own words.

"That's not a good idea," Raphael said, her voice a bit harsher than I'd heard it before.

"Nah, that's a terrible idea," Mick said, adding his opinion to it.

"I agree with them this time, Gadwell has been very clear about when to have your *Awakened* engage, and I think in this circumstance it would include you," Mike said, his words making far too much sense.

"Fine," I said, looking to see if Kora had an opinion, but she remained silent atop her horse. "Maybe I'll just do a few Lightning Strikes, with all this rain they might not even know its me."

That got an eye roll from Raphael and a snort from

Mick, but no one told me I shouldn't, so I filed the idea away for later use.

I needed to be smart about this, it was important that I keep my men alive, but I'd do no one any good if I got killed myself. So many emotions threatened to take center stage, but I found a calmness that I latched onto as we neared the enemy. And they were the enemy, I had taken Gadwell's advice on that matter. He said that it was important that I and those under me understand that these weren't men we were fighting, they were the enemy and that was all.

I knew he did it to help shift us away from seeing them as people, making it easier to kill them, or even bear the thought of taking their lives, but it worked all too well. A part of me couldn't wait to strike our first blow against the enemy and ride home victorious.

"Give the order to charge," I said, we were within sight of the enemy, and it was finally happening. I got ready to activate Aura of the Wolf a moment just before they smashed into the enemy, but not a moment sooner.

"Lead Platoon, charge!" Mick yelled. Horns that acted as a signal for what he'd just said, sounded, piercing the thick sheets of rain.

Our first platoon, made up of all men at arms and Runeforged, charged forward in a mass of 500 units.

"Bowmen form up, cavalry stand up," I said.

Mick repeated my words and the horns blared.

My archers formed up and were able to let off two full volleys into the enemy before our men at arms arrived, spears ready. I activated Aura of the Wolf and felt a surge of violent energy infuse me.

"Holy hells," Mick said, shaking his head. "I feel like I could rip the enemy apart myself."

I ignored his remark, focusing on the troops clashing in the distance. My improved attributes made it just barely possible to make out what was happening in clear-ish detail. The Runeforged were as deadly as I'd hoped. The entire forward march of the enemy army had been halted. Runeforged literally marched directly through their lines, cutting to the back and started attacking a group of riders.

With their army already split in two, the battle that had started only minutes ago seemed to be winding down already. We outnumbered them three to one, but it might as well have been ten to one, with how effectively the Runeforged killed. I felt small pops of essence being released and then suddenly several larger washes of it. I focused on the back line and saw that the Runeforged had just killed the riders, likely their Commander and several *Awakened*.

So fast had we appeared and attacked that the enemy hadn't even formed up to loose any arrows, either that or this army had been made up of men at arms only, because besides the Commander and those around him, none had been atop horse back.

Just as I took a breath and felt that sweet release of victory, I heard a rumbling from behind us. We stood behind our third company, the one with our cavalry in it and for a moment I thought they'd begun to charge, but it wasn't our cavalry, it was the enemies! They'd circled us, likely thinking they'd turn the tide of battle, but what they didn't realize was that they'd effectively lost already.

"Third platoon, turn and charge!" I yelled, holding out my own hand and summoning my sword. They couldn't fault me for fighting now, the enemy had literally come running at me.

I had Ares kick off the ground and spring in a low gliding run. Water stung at my face as we charged right into a hundred cavalry. The enemy might think my actions reckless or perhaps foolhardy, but I was a griffin rider.

They never stood a chance.

At the last moment before we smashed into each other, Ares launched herself upward and I released the Fireball I'd been building. It smashed into their ranks and men died alongside their horses. I felt bad for the horses, but there was little I could do for them now. I struck out with Arcane Missile, knocking three riders off their mounts. Following it up with a Lightning Strike that missed but blew up so much debris that two horses bucked their riders.

My few attacks had thrown their charge into chaos, and they had no time to recover as my own troops smashed into them as they'd been trained. Screams filled the air as our men went to work. I had Ares land behind their charging cavalry, and I charged into the fray.

Suddenly I wasn't alone, Fred and Fran appeared, covered in mud.

"We knew you'd find a way to enter the battle," Fran said. "We will stand with you whether you like it or not."

I smiled but said nothing. I cut down a man whose back was to me, while Fran slashed the leg free of a horse and stabbed its rider as it fell. Fred chanted and fire swirled around him, striking out at the backs of the enemy and turning them into blackened corpses.

As we slaughtered from behind, our army pressed them against us, and the enemy died.

I heard a yell from the middle of the battle and a man appeared, jumping completely over the horses and spraying water out as he faced us down. I knew without sensing him that this was an Awakened soldier, but I felt bad for him. He was surrounded by three deadly adventurers, and he didn't even have armor on. Instead, he raised his fists, wrapped in tan colored gauze, like he meant to brawl.

"Have you no honor!" He screamed and I chuckled.

"Says the guy that attacked our backline, don't speak to me of honor," I yelled back, then added. "If you surrender now, I'll spare your life."

The cloth wearing man with no weapon or armor laughed. I was about to laugh back as one of our soldiers charged him from behind and was about to spear him through. Except he never got the chance, the enemy shifted ever so slightly and grabbed hold of the spear, smashing in the soldier's face with it and kicking away his body as he fell limply at his side.

I didn't know if he was dead, but I wouldn't risk it.

Focusing I cast a heal on him and then I realized what we were dealing with. This man was a monk, a specialized class that didn't need armor or weapons as their bodies were trained to be hardy and deadly. Their skin able to turn away sword slashes and their punches infused with enough force to shatter stone.

"He's a monk, be careful," I called out to my comrades.

They both nodded through the rain and Fred lashed out with his fire snake that coiled around his form. To my utter astonishment, the monk grabbed the flame snake and with a flash of green-blue light it went out, the sudden change in brightness causing me to blink. That was all the monk needed to close the gap, likely using a speed burst ability to reach me.

A powerful blow caught me right in the chest and blood flew from my open mouth into the monk's face. Despite the pain and surprise of the attack, I activated my own Speed Burst as my body flew backwards. My feet dug into the mud, and I sprinted forward, infusing my blade up to the second tier with essence. It sparked blue and green energy as I slashed downwards at the surprised monk. He dodged with ease, and I found myself about to be punched in the face for overextending.

Fran was there, slashing at his neck, forcing the monk to dance backwards if he wished to not die a painful death. I thanked Fran with a nod of my head, and we attacked together, slashing and stabbing. The monk dodged and even turned away a few attacks with his bare skin, though he quickly learned not to do that with my sword strikes after I my sword dug into his left forearm.

As if being fast and hard to kill wasn't enough, he placed his hand over his wound and radiating a greenish glow, it was healed. His skillsets weren't that much different than mine it would seem, at least in the sense that he could heal and do physical combat skills.

Fred was back in the fight as the battle all around us began to quiet. Firebolt after Firebolt rained down on the monk, and I added my own to the mix a second later. He did some sort of dance like fighting moves that sent the attack smashing into the ground all around him, but I saw where he paused before moving into the next rotation and decided to take my advantage. As soon as I saw him pause in his movements, I hit him with a Lightning Strike.

He went rigid and fell over, the puddle he stood in magnifying the effects of my lightning-based attack. Before he hit the ground, both Fran and I had put the tips of our swords into his chest. Fran's made it about three inches deep, but mine went through like a hot knife into butter. The light left his eyes as he fell, and we were infused with his essence.

Looking around I saw our soldiers, bloody and hurt, but alive. The battle was won, and I'd gotten to fight after all. I let Fran pick at his gear, while I sought out my Knights for a battle report.

It took them about an hour to get a full count and report of what had happened. Mick had a nasty gash on his cheek that he wouldn't let me heal, saying he needed a good battle wound. Mike and Raphael were covered in blood, but not from any injury someone scored on them. Mick described them like wet cats battling for their lives. Demons set loose among children, slaying ten or more each without issue or worry of injury. Their proxy levels and skills as elite guards were coming in handy for sure.

Meanwhile, Mick said he'd taken down two men and seemed proud of his accomplishment.

"We have three dead, fifty-two wounded, and one slightly damaged Runeforged, her name is Ignis, and I guess she got tangled up against this Commander and lost an arm," Mick reported, and my heart fell.

"Three dead?" I asked. We'd done so well and still we lost lives.

"What are their names?" I asked.

"Flodis Fan, Eric Letcher, Brad Gibson," Mick said, he knew them without having to ask and I knew he'd be toasting to their sacrifice tonight among the men.

"We will honor their sacrifice with a drink tonight and learn from our mistakes here," I said, looking each of my Knights in the eyes to ensure they knew how serious I was on the matter. "Every life here matters, no matter where they've come from." I added, seeing an orc walk by with a gash on his arm.

Kora appeared from the rain and raised a hand in

greeting. Our soldiers were still looting the dead and stacking the bodies for burning before we could leave.

"You meat bags die easy," she said. I cringed a little at her poor timing but said nothing in response. "I've repaired Ignis, but it is as you promised, none else were seriously damaged at all. We fought with such vigor that I hadn't summoned but one of my beasts before we broke their lines, and they began to run. I am sad to report that two of the horse riders fled and escaped to the east."

We took no prisoners, as our blood lust from the Aura of the Wolf had ensured no time for such actions, but it was unfortunate that word of the battle would be spread. I'd hoped to hide the fact we fought with Runeforged so early in the campaign. House Blalor had the means and if he could get them constructed, he could possibly raise an entire army of just Runeforged. Would Gilfoy do that and risk the ire of the King? I knew about as much about commerce as I did political maneuvers, so I let the thoughts die without any resolution.

"Let's finish here and report back to camp," I said, then speaking louder for all that could hear. "The enemy will mark this day as one to remember. This is the day that Blackridge Keep entered the fray!"

A general cheer went up, but I knew my words lacked. I wished I was better at speeches or at least public speaking, but I did what I could. After another hour of preparations, we set the bodies ablaze using Fred as our source. The rain had died out enough that once large wood pyres had been lit, they would stay that way until the end. I had several

Awakened goblins out among the field of battle with Dimensional Spheres picking up everything that wasn't tied down, which included unfortunately, stripping down the soldiers to the skin. Every bit of cloth and uniform would be collected and repurposed.

"I've read the initial report," Busard said, I sat across from him and only our assistants were present. "But I had a few questions I wanted to pose to you."

I straightened in my seat, ready for whatever was coming next. "What can I answer for you?" I asked.

"Why did you not take prisoners?" Busard asked, but before I could answer he spoke again. "We rely on the intel we can gather from those we capture. In fact, many that we capture can be turned to our side as they are merely mercenaries. What excuse do you have for me?"

I swallowed, and though I was prepared to answer such a question, I wasn't prepared for the look he gave me, like an upset father who was more disappointed than angry.

"I'd activated an Aura that led to a swift victory and no prisoners. I will endeavor to take prisoners next time," I said, speaking the words I'd practiced.

"I'm sure that you will," Busard said, looking down at a piece of parchment his steward handed him. "You allowed several of the Knights of Vanlong's army escape. There will be consequences for that in the future, believe me. But for now, celebrate. You've won your first of many victories, I'm sure."

Vanlong, this was the first I had heard of the Commander that I'd faced. He hadn't stood a chance against my overwhelming force and my victory was ensured the moment we were sent out against him, but I admired his tact in trying to flank us with his cavalry. I just wished my Runeforged hadn't enjoyed killing 'meat bags' so much, we might have captured him alive.

"Thank you, Master General Busard, I plan to," I said, standing.

I left, Verena by my side, out into the muddy field that was our army's campsite. The rain had done a number to any grass that had once been here and now it seemed we camped in a bog. Water and mud up over the ankle as far as the eye could see. I wondered if there were any talented wizards or sorcerers in the art of ground manipulation, or perhaps even one talented with moving water so that we could have something done about it, but I knew casters of all kinds were in short supply.

"That went rather well," Verena said, her leather long coat swishing in the wind as a few drops of rain began to pour on us once more.

She had dark hair and eyes with a deep tan complexion, and not for the first time, I wondered what part of Newaliyn she'd come from. I hadn't asked, wishing to keep things as professional as possible.

"Yeah," I said, something bothering me, and I had just realized what. "He didn't ask about the soldiers who fell in battle. I thought he'd care more about that or at least give me some pushback from my losses and injuries."

"Three dead is fantastic and all the injured have been healed by the camp healers already. Or at least those willing to be healed," Verena said, smiling.

"You mean Mick, don't you?" I asked, shaking my head. He'd been poking at the gash on his face all the way back and I nearly healed him several times.

"He had it sewed up and treated with cleanser, despite the healers telling him if they healed it, there would still be a scar," Verena said, rolling her eyes when I looked away. My peripheral vision being just as strong as my normal sight ever since increasing my thresholds.

We'd made it halfway back to our camp when I walked across Zander, his tabard torn and bloodied. He didn't seem to see me at first, so I called out to him. Turning, I saw his face had a haunted expression on it and it almost made me reel back in surprise.

"You okay?" I asked, walking up to him and shooting a glance at Verena to stay back. She took the hint.

"I'm heading back to camp," she called out, leaving us alone.

Zander looked like he was in some sort of shock, he tried to speak but his breathing increased, and he closed his eyes tight. Finally, he pulled himself together enough to say something.

"I lost so many men," he said, his words filled with a hollowness that I wasn't used to hearing. Normally his tone had the assumed feeling of being better than everyone else hearing it, but not this time.

"You were deployed as well?" I asked, realizing he must have went out shortly after us because I hadn't seen an additional flare or horn get sounded.

"Just got back," Zander said, looking up at me with confused eyes. It was almost like he didn't quite know who I was at first, but then he focused and blinked at me several times. "Caldor, Busard is going to have my hide. I've lost over half my men, and we had to retreat."

"You lost over seven hundred men!" I shouted, cursing myself a moment after as he flinched back like a child expecting to be beaten. "Sorry, I just, that is a terrible blow to our forces. Tell me, how did it happen?"

Zander licked his lips and looked around to ensure we were alone. "It started off so well, I used an Aura and we cut into the enemy line from the side, causing chaos. I committed all three of my platoons, you know, I thought I could end it before they had a chance to organize a counterattack."

"And then you were attacked from behind?" I asked, feeling like I needed to highlight this harder in my report to Busard so he knew the tactics these Blalor armies were using.

"Yes!" Zander said, shaking his head. "But it's worse than that, they had another force just as big as the one we'd attacked, and they came at my three platoons from all sides. Our back line was in tatters just as I got charged by Cavalry. They nearly captured me, but my knights fought violently to the end, giving me a chance to escape. If not for my scouts and a rescue force deployed, they'd have harrowed my army all the way back here."

"So, this new force, you pushed them back?" I asked, trying to find a silver lining in a disastrous first conflict.

"Yeah, didn't engage, the enemy retreated when they saw the force coming," Zander said, and I thought he might start to cry.

I did something that I never imagined in all my life doing, I reached out and pulled Zander into a side hug and reassured him. "War is never going to be easy. Stay strong for your men and learn from your mistakes. Besides," I said, releasing him and looking him in the eye, "there was no way you could know they had such a large force. We rely on the intelligence we get and when it's wrong, we are destined to fail. Don't let Busard get you down, this wasn't just your fault."

Zander looked up, but my words seemed to have little effect on him. He gave me a halfhearted head nod and a 'thanks' before walking through the mud alone to meet with Busard.

He'd lost half his army and all of his knights by the sound of it. I did not envy the thoughts he must be thinking or the words Busard would have for him. The morale after such a blow would be hard to recover from.

I couldn't get Zander's situation off my mind as I watched a space be cleared for our celebrations. It wasn't going to be anything too over the top, just extra food and drink brought out and a few bonfires set. Word had been spread to the entire legion and I expected spirits would be high. Despite having only lost three soldiers myself, I couldn't bring myself to feel happy about our victory.

Such mixed emotions surged through me but when I attempted to squash them down, as was becoming my norm, they resisted. Thoughts such as, what if you'd been deployed to where Zander had, would you have lost as many? I wanted to say that I wouldn't but the way he described the sheer number of forces that came his way, made me realize some mistakes I'd made of my own.

Gadwell had warned me against overcommitting my troops early, but as soon as I had a chance, I threw my forces against them as hard as I could. You'd think with all the reading I'd done in my life I'd know something of war and strategy, but I found myself severely lacking in terms of large-scale battle strategy. Perhaps I could set Verena to finding me a book that went over common battle formations and stratagems.

With renewed effort and promise to improve I finally set aside my feelings, not getting over the losses or my experience with Zander but getting it out of the forefront of my focus at least. It wasn't healthy mentally this much I was sure of, but it was the best I could do now, considering the responsibilities I had to attend to.

Verena had drafted three letters of death, meant to be

sent out to any next of kin along with a death payment. I had the payment doubled when I found out how little it appeared to be, then signed the letters after reading each one. It mentioned nothing of the men or their lives, but I had an idea for honoring them. I'd set Verena and my knights to finding those who'd known the fallen and gotten at least a few to agree to share one or two stories about their lives.

By the time I made it to visit the wounded, they'd all been discharged to rest in their own tents. I'd visited one or two that Mick had told me were the closest to death and found them in good spirits. One such lad told me he'd never fought so hard in his life, and he grew up a street urchin. I gave them all my thanks and asked a few questions about their lives to show my interest.

With all events considered this had been a successful day.

The bonfires lit up the night and the buzz of insects were barely audible over the noise of the soldiers. A surprising number still wore their armor as they moved about eating and drinking. We'd set several hundred long tables up, it was amazing what you could fit in a dimensional sphere, but most chose to walk about, sharing conversation with their fellow soldiers. I walked up on Mick at a table set for twenty, much smaller than the massive, long tables we'd store for occasions such as this.

Mick had a red and angry line on his face, sewn together by the healers. He caught my eye as I made it to the table and shoved one of his squires over, gesturing for me to join him. I did so and moved aside the plate of half-eaten pig to the squire beside me.

"Get the Lord Commander a plate," Mick shouted out into the crowd. Despite the crowd's size, someone must have heard because a younger boy appeared with a plate seconds later. It had large portions of pork, some mashed potatoes, and roasted vegetables. I didn't know if they were saving this plate for me, but everyone else just seemed to have meat and ale.

"While I appreciate the effort to get me more than just meat, I can survive on meat and ale along with everyone else, you know." I gave Mick a look, but he just winked, then cringed in pain as the winking eye he'd chosen was on his wounded side.

"Damn cut stings," Mick said, and I sighed.

"Let me heal you, I promise that you will have a nice scar just like you want," I said, digging into my meal.

"It isn't about the scar," Mick said, holding his ale close before taking a drink. "I took lives and I deserve to feel the consequences of that and since emotionally I'm honestly not too bothered by it, I figure a little physical pain will do me good."

I turned to the guard captain turned Knight and really looked at him. From his sun-bleached hair to his baked skin, he really was a good guy. Light blue eyes stared back at me with a hint of humor, always ready to ease any serious conversation.

"You're a good man," I said, slapping him on the back before going back to enjoying my meal.

On the opposite side of me, Kora sat down.

"Good evening," I said when she didn't immediately speak.

"When those new spears arrive, I would like them for my people," Kora said, leaning forward as she spoke.

I knew she'd seen me showing off the spear to a few of the soldiers, but I hadn't realized she knew I intended to train our front line with them. Though I hadn't meant for the Runeforged to use them, they had all sorts of advantages as it were. I shook my head and was about to answer when something she said struck me. Had she referred to the other Runeforged as 'her people'? That was new.

"The spears aren't meant for you all," I said, deciding now wasn't the time to broach the subject of Runeforged and them considering themselves as people.

"We will be able to use them most effectively. And we have decided that we will be your entire front line, which will prevent more of your kind from falling in battle," Kora said, then pausing she smiled. "But only if you give us the spears."

"Deal," I said. I didn't have to think long on that, because she was right. With them taking the entire front line it would mean less death on our side, but far more death on the other side. I imagined the battle if they'd gone first and held a straight line while arrows rained down, unworried that the Runeforged would be damaged by such strikes. We could hold back our men at arms all together until the Runeforged got surrounded or just flank the enemy.

I needed more Runeforged I decided. Searching behind me, I found Verena standing off to the side as expected and had her lean in. "Tell Lance to buy all available Runeforged and send them to me on the front. Also have him confer with Regina to see how few Runeforged are needed in the Manor's defense and send the rest of those here as well. Money is no issue, but time could be."

My latest income report had showed an additional surge of platinum as Regina finished signing some deals with the King of Newaliyn, the Queen of the elves, and various other smaller factions who apparently had gold to burn. She'd also made several new discoveries tied to our initial one that were being sold and marketed all through the kingdom. Business was good, but it was almost entirely because of Regina.

"I'll draft a letter right away and send a rider," Verena said, nodding. She disappeared into the night, likely going to see to it at once. I felt a bit guilty taking her from the festivities, but being around drunken soldiers after battle might prove to not be the safest place. I'd worry about Raphael, but she was such a ball buster and several times stronger than any soldier here that I'd almost wish to see one try anything so I can watch her put them in line.

Kora had gotten up and left while I spoke with Verena, so I turned back to Mick to see who he was speaking with.

"I heard they lost half their legion," Mick said, shaking his head. "I hope someone is getting brought up on charges for such a terrible loss."

"What do you mean charges?" I asked, not sure if I

understood what he was implying. Did he really think Zander would be held responsible as a Lord and nephew to Lord Variyn?

"Well, a blunder like that, someone has to be at fault, right?" Mick asked, turning back to me and away from Mike who he'd been speaking with a moment ago. "Probably an issue with the scouts reporting incorrect numbers but mark my word. If nothing is done, they're going to have a lot of very angry soldiers on their hands."

Ah, so he hadn't meant Zander after all. I guess it shouldn't surprise me that the Commander, as vassal Lords, wouldn't be the first person you'd pointed the finger at.

Time passed and it got to the point in the night where the fallen soldiers' friends shared stories of their misadventures with them. Only a few hundred around the poor half-drunk men could even hear their words, but I got a front row seat. Each one spoke, telling wild tales of chasing women or getting in trouble doing stupid things. I let the words sink deep into my mind and tried to scorch the names of those I'd lost into my mind. These three wouldn't likely be the last, but I'd do all I could to make them so.

CHAPTER 31
THE TOLL OF BATTLE

Gadwell congratulated me on a victory well won, before ripping into me about my use of troop formations and putting the command structure of the legion at risk by engaging in battle. I understood where he was coming from, but it wasn't like I really had a choice when the cavalry charged at us. According to Gadwell I did, I was meant to call for the third platoon to charge and withdraw behind them.

I played out his version of the events in my head and saw many more losses due to an *Awakened* Monk having taken the field of battle, telling Gadwell as much didn't help. He assured me that when and if he showed himself in battle, I had more than enough *Awakened* of my own to deal with the threat. When I reminded him that he was high enough level that it took our combined forces to take him down, he merely scoffed.

I finished that back and forth with a sour taste in my

mouth, but I knew he only did it to help me better myself. After a week of waiting and by the good graces of Verena, I received half a dozen books on battle strategy, one even got the approval of Gadwell who said that general's insights were extremely well thought out. I decided to start with that one.

The training of the men continued, lots of marching from place to place and drills with squads fighting squads. A few times we'd participated in a mock battle against another Lord, which we lost, but I wasn't sure I understood the point of it. It ended up being more about position and strategy, both of which the other Commander excelled at, whereas my strategy was a bit more straight forward. It also didn't take into account that my Runeforged wouldn't have been 'killed' by merely two strikes as the mock battle's rules stated.

But it was a learning experience, and I got an earful from Gadwell about how he thought I was reading some of the books. He even went so far to ask if I was just holding on to them to keep my hands warms or did I like people thinking I was smart, because he hadn't seen any benefit from my apparent learning. All in all, our relationship was growing closer, and I really valued his opinions.

I walked up on Jase, one of Mick's squires that I didn't know all too well. He was over Dan and Cam's squad, and I'd been meaning to ask him what he thought of them. He happened to be watching them right now, so I made my approach.

"Lord Commander Miles," Jase said, saluting me.

"Relax, how are they doing?" I asked, gesturing to the squads. Two squads worked on drills together, the other squad's captain doing callouts while the rest responded.

"Two of the best I'd say," Jase said. "Are you here to check up on them or me?" He chuckled a bit but when I did laugh in response he straightened and became serious.

"Don't relax too much," I said, suppressing a laugh. "Should I be here checking up on you, Squire?"

"No, sir, uhm Lord Commander," Jase said, then stealing a glance at me he added. "Mick already spoke to me and made it clear the consequences if I step out of line again. The broken leg was healed right up, and I don't intend to speak out of turn again."

Now this was something that hadn't made it into the report. I wondered if Jase always told on himself when he got nervous. Surely, he could read my expression and know I didn't have the slightest clue what he was going on about. I firmed my expression, ready to learn more from this squire who might be losing his position soon.

"Tell me, Squire Jase, who broke their leg?" I asked, he stole a glance at me, and I think he realized suddenly that I hadn't known of the issue yet. He grew even more stiff as I imagine he cursed his flapping jaws.

"My leg, Lord Commander," Jase said.

I sighed. "Am I going to have to go to Mick for the entire story or you going to enlighten me?" I asked, trying to use a not so intimidating voice. I must have failed because he paled a bit at the prospect, and I thought for a second, he might suggest that I go speak with Mick.

"It was really nothing Lord Commander," Jase started to say, then saw my look of frustration and continued quicker. "I merely tried to woo a beautiful red head and when her brother told me to sod off, I punched him in the nose. I was drinking and not thinking the best. I've since apologized and been thoroughly spoken to."

"You came on to Fran and she broke your leg?" I asked, now I was smiling and really close to laughing.

"No, her brother broke my leg, kicked me clear across the courtyard," Jase said, then chuckling to himself he added. "Didn't think the skinny man had it in him."

"You do realize they are both *Awakened* adventurers, right?" I asked, looking at him now and trying to figure out if there was any way he didn't know that, but failing.

"I did, but I didn't think he was the strong type, and I wasn't thinking straight," Jase said, blushing a bit when he saw me start laughing at him.

"Let me give you a tip, soldier," I said, patting him on the back. "Stay away from any *Awakened* and you'll be alright. He might look like he's nothing, but even if he didn't kick you across the yard, he could have fried you from the inside out and I'd have little to do about it once it was done."

"Yes of course, Lord Commander," Jase said, saluting me again.

I saluted him back. "Tell me about the squad led by Captain Cam and Lieutenant Dan."

"Strong group, good leadership as far as I can tell," Jase

said. Pointing to Dan he said, "That one just about lost his legs but the healers were able to work a miracle on him."

"What happened to him?" I asked, seeing Dan perform an admirable strike that I'd worked with him personally during the night time drills the men at arms did.

"I didn't find out, but I can if you wish?"

I shook my head. "Nah, that's alright just keep a special eye on that group. Those are boys I know from my hometown and I want them to be the best trained soldiers we have. Did everyone in these two squads level up to men at arms level 2 or greater?"

"I believe so, some even managed to get to level 3, so we'll need to work out their level 4 perks soon enough before they decide they know better than we do," Jase said, then added a 'Lord Commander' at the end.

I hadn't ever saw myself as someone who could make someone nervous, but I sure seemed to be having that effect on Jase.

"They've all taken the Hardy perk as I instructed?" I asked, and Jase nodded. "Good. Gadwell was insistent that it nearly doubles the strength, endurance, and constitution of a soldier. If that ends up being true, then I see it as the easier way of doubling our fighting power with a simple perk choice. That, and just getting them leveled up enough to match strength against some of the career soldiers they'll encounter."

"Yes of course, Lord Commander," Jase said.

"I'm going to interrupt their training and have a bit of fun, go fetch me a spear, will you?" I asked, waving to Cam as he pivoted toward me in his fight. He saw me and paused mid-fight, getting a staff in the face for his trouble.

They all practiced with wooden staffs that had a blunted end on each side, as we didn't have the healer resources to be fixing minor cuts all day. They were weighted well enough that the practice was still worthwhile.

I took a spear from Jase and let him return to where he stood before I approached, watching the training. I spun the spear in my hand, my increased agility and focus making it easy for me to do so without risk of dropping it. To me, it felt like I was slowly flipping it in my grip, but to all others it would appear to blur as the speed increased faster and faster. I was just showing off at this point, so I stopped it, slamming the end into the ground. It stayed while I addressed the crowd.

"What do you do if you find yourself facing an *Awakened* person on the field of battle?" I asked, projecting my voice to the twenty-soldier strong group.

No one answered at first, so I waited until they did. About fifteen seconds of awkward silence followed until some spoke up.

Cam spoke up. "Personally, I'd put as much distance from him or her as I possibly could."

"Good answer, but what if that isn't an option," I said, raising an eyebrow at Cam.

Dan answered saying, "Then I'd kill him or at least try."

That got a round of 'yeah' and 'stick him with the

pointy end' which despite what I was trying to teach them, got a smile on my face.

"Cam and Dan, would you like to spar with me?" I asked, lifting the spear from the ground and cracking my neck to the side.

They looked a bit dumbfounded, but both of them stepped up to fight after sharing a look. These were brave soldiers that would learn an important lesson today.

"A single strike from an *Awakened* will likely mean death, nearly every time, so if I strike you, then you are out. However, you will need to strike me at least...let's say ten times or twice in the head," I said. I could tell they weren't excited about their prospects, but they got into formation anyways.

"Oh, and if I manage to pick up some mud and throw it at you that is also a kill, because you know spells will kill you too," I added, reaching down and grabbing a handful of mud.

"Start whenever you feel ready," I said.

They rushed me, trying to close the distance. I used one hand to bat away each of their spears, tripped Dan while he charged, and gently placed the mud on Cam's face all while slipping between them and not using any speed enhancing abilities.

"Well done," I said, twirling my spear. "Now two more."

I continued the display of power until I was fighting their entire squad. I managed to avoid each strike, but it took focus. Breathing hard but nowhere near at the end of my Stamina I called for the other squad to join in.

"Remember, you just need ten strikes or two to the head," I said, then added, "I'll do my best not to injure you all, but I'll need to move full speed, so be ready for a bit of pain."

With twenty opponents I felt like my point would finally come across. I may be faster, stronger, and infinitely more powerful, but I was just a single man. With ten men, I'd barely dodged the strikes and even taken a hit to the back, glancing though it may have been, I'd still have counted it.

I readied myself, staff in one hand and mud in the other. Throwing the mud, I knocked Dan out immediately, he stepped aside, and the rest of the squads rushed me. I activated my skill, weaving through the strikes and ending soldiers one tap at a time. But even with my increased speed, I felt strikes begin to land. Twirling around my spear I activated Swift Strike to parry three attacks at once. Then I felt a bonk on the head and looked up to see Cam smiling. I put my staff across his face a bit harder than I need to, but it cost me, another strike to the head.

"And it's over," I called out, really breathing now. I'd killed all but four of them in those short seconds. "You did it. See, we aren't invincible, and it might take the lives of all those around you, but if you run you will die. If you stay and fight together you have a chance. Remember this lesson and you will do me proud."

There was a round of cheers as they congratulated themselves. They'd done well, but I worried a bit as I was certain that if we went again, I'd be able to adjust to such a large crowd by merely moving away and thinning them out. I needed the army to not fear *Awakened,* so that they'd stand a chance, but it was a hard thing to ask, because they should be feared.

Walking over to Jase I gave him instructions to equip each squad with two or three sturdy nets. If they could slow down an *Awakened* with a net or something, perhaps they'd have better odds. He agreed that it was a fine idea and I left to speak with Gadwell. He liked my idea about the nets and said he'd organize training for every one in ten men to be proficient at netting.

I sat at dinner, days later when the horns of battle were sounded. Looking across the table at Mick, I stood, ready for war.

We marched out to face the enemy. The ground was solid beneath our feet, a pleasant chill in the air, and plenty of light to see by as both moons gleamed in the sky. The conditions were perfect for a battle and if I had to make a bet on the outcome, I'd wager we would crush the enemy.

Fitz marched his legion just behind my own but rode next to me in the middle of the two legions. This was to be both of our first time fighting a joint battle where the enemy was said to be a force of nearly two thousand, meaning we'd outnumber them, but not significantly. I'd been reading so many of those strategy books and all of them recommended favorable odds for every encounter, one going so far as to say that battle of a lesser force against a greater force was a gamble and retreat should be the only option.

"I'm just saying, that perhaps you should fight the enemy yourself and I'll hold back my legion to surprise them when the battle is nearly won," Fitz said, twinkling his fingers like a complete lunatic.

"That has to be the dumbest idea I've heard from you so far and you've been saying some doozies," I said, Fitz was purposely trying to get under my skin I felt, so I tried not to waste any effort on him.

"Fine, we march in together, but you should lend me a hundred of your Runeforged," Fitz said, then seeing my face he added. "I saw that you got more, so don't pretend that you can't spare a few, you rich bastard."

"I'm the rich bastard?" I said, having to mentally restrain Ares from ripping at Fitz's exposed neck. "You are literally wearing armor plated in gold, like how tacky is that?"

Fitz wore a full suit of armor, one unlike I'd seen anywhere before, but only in old fashioned depictions of knights going to battle. Each joint and connection up to the neck was enclosed. But the cherry on top had to be the golden plated color and the griffin style helmet. It had an undersized beak and feathers carved into the surface being swept back as if blown by a high wind.

"It's pretty glorious, right?" Fitz said, then leaning on his horse towards me a little, he cupped his armored hand around his mouth as if whispering and said, "It's a family heirloom and is made from Mythril beneath the surface."

So, it was tacky and worth a huge amount of platinum, no surprises there.

"You shouldn't tell everyone that if you want to keep the armor," I said, flatly. "I'm sure there are several Lords that would love to accidently acquire the armor if you died. Not me of course, but you get the idea."

"Nonsense, I'm perfectly safe inside this armor," Fitz declared.

The inane conversation continued for a good time longer, until a scout came to give a report. He reported a disturbing bit of news that the enemy force was nearly twice as large as we'd been told. One of our scouts, Fitz's man, had died getting the information and the other escaped in time to report it to us. It was a trap and we'd be ambushed if we continued our path forward.

"We should turn around, looks like this battle is lost. Oh well," Fitz said, already waving his Knights over to give the order.

"No," I said, shaking my head. "Give me a minute to think, we might still be able to accomplish our mission. If we don't stop this force, then our troops at Laris Keep will be overwhelmed, we have to hold the force off."

Fitz considered and held up a hand to forestall his knights.

"I'm listening," he said.

I called out for Fred, he marched not far off with my Knight, and he came running when I called, along with Fran.

"Yes?" He asked as he approached.

"I'm going to let you ride Ares back to camp, deliver the scout's report to Busard and request additional troops be sent immediately. I know we have a force big enough in reserve to swing this battle. Return as quick as you can with news," I said, dismounting Ares and giving her a comforting wash of emotions as I proposed my plan to her.

She looked Fred up and down, screeching at him. He looked apprehensive, but approached with a hand held out. Ares snipped at it, and he looked at me eyes wide.

"She's just messing with you, hop on, she's agreed to take you," I said, smiling. Ares would be laughing right now if she could, I felt her humorous emotions rubbing against my own.

Fred mounted her up and she took off with a whoosh. I'd told her to go as fast as possible, but not to lose her rider. I heard Fred's screams into the distance as he disappeared into the horizon.

"As for our troops, we will march double time, send out twice as many scouts and surprise the force meant to surprise us. Surely, we can deal with a smaller force while we wait for reinforcements?" I posed it as a question to Fitz, but he didn't seem convinced.

"Or, and bear with me now, I take my troops, we leave, and you go do what you said," Fitz said, smiling wide.

"While I can appreciate a healthy dose of fear, you seem to be overflowing with it. Are you a coward Fitz?" I asked, mouthing the word coward as the barest of whispers in a vain attempt not to embarrass him in front of Fran and the gathering Knights. It didn't work, he turned red, and his nostrils flared.

"I'm no coward," Fitz said. "I'll have my men march in front and we'll do all the killing. You just wait and see."

And with that, Fitz sent out signals for his men to do a double time march and passed up my three companies. Scouts were sent out and we readied ourselves for battle.

Fred appeared less than an hour later with news. Two additional legions were being dispatched on a double march. Based on the distance, Fred guessed we'd have them catch up with us within an hour. I told him to stay with Ares, going back and forth to report our new positions until the battle started. I took up a steed, a fierce looking black horse named Fiend, and readied myself for battle.

The battle came swiftly and with a bit of surprise. Our forces had just made our way through some densely packed forest and reformed up when the enemy was upon us. I could only watch as cavalry swiftly cut through one of Fitz's companies. But we moved quick, Fitz and I both sending our own cavalry to be in position to strike if they should charge again, while our archers attempted to shoot where the horse would be, but they failed to kill more than a dozen or so.

The rest of the enemy force crested a hill and I saw how truly outnumbered we were. It was worse than the reports had said, there had to be at least five thousand men in total. We had a force of three thousand with another three thousand coming. Perhaps retreat was the move here, but we'd be slow to retreat against the thick woods and with how fast the enemy approached, they had to have gotten a perk or two in movement.

Retreat meant huge losses, but so did staying. I felt my mind locking up as every option I had meant death, and nothing I could imagine would stop that.

Fitz rode up on his horse breathing hard. "We need to retreat, there are too many!" He yelled the words, but I barely heard them. I just looked at him as our forces clashed with the enemy and men began to die. Fitz's forces were already being decimated and my Runeforged company were readjusting their position, ready to block a cavalry push.

While I watched, suddenly three huge fire balls flew out from the enemy towards my Runeforged, and I reacted. Reaching out my hand, I pumped Mana into my Mana Shell, and tested the true range of the spell. It turned out the further and wider I wanted to spread the shell, the more mana it took. I had just barely pumped enough, a little over 300, before it formed over my battalion, blocking the fire balls just in time.

I activated the Aura of the Turtle, hoping to save lives, and wished I'd taken the perk to reinforce their defenses more, instead of the Increased Leveling 1 perk I'd recently chosen.

The air ignited as they exploded and shattered my

barrier. I had no time to get locked up, they were using *Awakened* right off the cuff and so would we.

"To battle, Fran, gather the *Awakened* and push into the fray!" I shouted and she moved. I had four entire groups, each one made of dwarves, orcs, trolls, and goblins. With a single group of humans that used to be bandits awaiting my call. Why had I brought so many? I'd anticipated lots of loot to be collected and we'd run low on larger crates to effectively store items, so we just needed to have Dimensional Sphere holders.

The enemy cavalry charged full speed towards my Runeforged, but Kora had not been idle. First, a huge sandworm appeared, smashing into their ranks, next fireballs, wind funnels, ice spears, and blasts of lightning struck out into the group. By the time they reached the non-converted Runeforged that stood in the front, the cavalry had all but been decimated.

More balls of fire rained down and this time I wasn't quick enough. I don't know how many Runeforged we lost in that strike, but I heard screaming, so some soldiers had definitely died.

I ordered my companies of men at arms to gather in tight and try to punch through to the *Awakened* in the back line, meanwhile my archers showered their position and I saw several barriers being erected. One of the wizards, an older looking man, hadn't been attacking the entire time but I could feel him building up a spell. Then, as the air in front of me shimmered, I realized what he was doing.

"Fran!" I called out but she and the other *Awakened* had already joined the battle and were out of earshot. I sent the signal for them, three short bursts of the horn, to return, but it wouldn't be fast enough.

"Ready yourself for battle, Fitz," I said, wishing I'd asked what kind of *Awakened* he was before the battle had started.

"What's that?" Fitz asked, turning his steed he saw the portal forming and a dozen soldiers rushing in with nets, tridents, crossbows, and two younger wizards following after them.

I heard a gruff voice behind them yell through the portal. "Kill them and bring me their heads!"

Before even I could act, I heard Fitz dismount and his horse neigh as it went running. He walked forward, seemingly unafraid suddenly. I Inspected him, to hell with what was proper, and saw why he wasn't so worried.

Mitchel Fitz, Paladin, Level 39.

I dismounted as well, not confident in my ability to fight on horseback. My horse stayed at my side though, kicking its hooves at the enemy and seeming to snarl at the approaching soldiers. This was a badass horse I decided, and if we made it out of this alive, I'd see about buying him and learning to fight atop a horse, as well as mounted atop a griffin.

Nearly thirty men had come through the portal now and they attempted to surround us. Fitz acted first, chanting a few words that lifted my spirits and made me feel like I'd be able to do anything, before slamming his fist down into the ground. It seemed to crack with light, and I felt further uplifted, even giddy as I awaited the enemy to make the first move.

I could tell the opposite was true of the soldiers we faced, they sagged and stumbled suddenly as if in incredible pain. Figuring I shouldn't let Fitz do all the work I reached out and struck out with my Lightning Strike spell. It slammed down from above, hitting a soldier who'd just barely stepped through the portal. I followed that up with a Force Wave, right down the middle.

Being that I normally fought with powerful monsters, I expected them to take the hit and keep coming, instead my Force Wave bisected a man and mortally wounded three others before the force was only enough to push another dozen backwards. I heard Fitz laugh a bit maniacally as he swung out with a hammer made of translucent light. Nets hit him, but he ignored them, the dozen men unable to hold him down.

I thought the battle was going pretty well as I unleashed an Arcane Missile, killing three more soldiers with ease, when it all changed. A net was thrown towards me, I could see it was actually metal and had weights, but I activated Power Strike and cut right through it. At the same moment, I heard and felt the air split. Powerful arcs of lightning shot out from the two young wizard types.

I threw up a quick Mana Shell over myself, but I hadn't been the target. Fitz screamed in pain, and I saw his body go rigid. But the attacks didn't stop, they were both using a spell that allowed them to channel powerful lightning right from their hands. I couldn't help feeling envious of such a spell as I pumped essence and mana into a Fireball.

By the time I was ready to release my spell, Fitz was on all four and his entire form smoked, and his skin was beginning to char. I unleashed my massive Fireball, being careful to throw it right behind the casters as I knew the blast would be immense. One of the wizards cut off their attack and formed a barrier over the two of them, blue light springing up just as my Fireball passed by, striking it.

Kah-voosh!

I extended my own barrier over Fitz as the blast ignited, red, blue, and green flames incinerating everything in its path. Perhaps I'd done a bit too much, I thought, as my barrier shattered, and flames overtook us. But we were lucky, it was just the trail end of the flames and did minimal damage. I used Restoring Light, followed by a Mending Touch, nearly tapping out my massive mana pool to bring Fitz back from, what I thought had been, the brink of death.

He was laughing and coughing now.

"You pack a punch little sword-wizard." His voice was scratchy like he'd scorched his throat, but still he laughed. "I didn't need those heals; it was merely a flesh wound."

"'Tis but a scratch, I'm sure," I said, laughing.

I wasn't so sure, but I nodded, while pulling out a mana potion and downing it in a single gulp. A coolness spread through me as my body and mind realigned resources. An array of scorched bodies, over thirty, laid out all around us posed in place from their final moments. Several held hands in front of them, while others still held swords scorched black by the terrible heat.

Luckily, my brave horse had bolted at some point, and I heard him neighing behind me some distance away. I searched the scorched bodies to find the wizards and was surprised to find one still alive. His robes had been burnt off and his body had been blackened, but he walked slowly towards the portal, each step looking painful.

As I watched, Fitz started walking towards him and the wizard noticed. His body began to glow all over from Runic symbols and he turned to face Fitz. Not wanting to be outdone, I fired off a Lightning Strike, it came down and cracked into the enemy wizard's shoulder, but he barely seemed to notice. Raising a hand at me he fired off three spurts of Arcane energy, blue and glowing.

They smashed into my Arcane Armor, and I felt it shattered under the blows before feeling the heat scorch my chest, throwing me back. I Inspected him and got limited information.

Teldari Makem, Runecaster, Level 44.

I wondered how high or low level his companion had been. As I stood, a single thought occurred to me. Fireball infused with loads of Mana and Essence was a truly over-powering combination that was likely as deadly for me to use as it was for those I faced.

"Allow me to retreat, my brother has fallen and my will for battle has gone with him," a voice said, and I looked up to see it was Teldari speaking.

Fitz's voice was back to normal, and he taunted the Runecaster. "You've come to fight us, why not finish what you started? Decorum in battle has truly changed from when my father took the field. He told me tales of honor and soldiers fighting to the death while we got to enjoy the show from afar."

"You broke the unspoken accord first, we received reports of the massacre at Gelfand valley by that dangerous fool," Teldari said, pointing at me. "He uses such force of magic beyond even he can control."

"Watch out Fitz, he's powering a spell!" I yelled. I could feel Teldari moving Mana around in preparations for a spell of some kind.

"What's that?" Fitz asked, actually looking away from his opponent to look back at me, a stupid smile on his face all the while.

The strike came just as he turned his head back. A spear of frozen ice slammed into Fitz's chest, and he went flying some twenty feet back from the force of it. I activated Speed Burst and was upon the Runecaster within seconds. I struck out, my blade arching downward and filling with essence. In shock, he raised his arm, his runes flashing. I'm sure it was meant to block the attack, perhaps with some sort of skin hardening, and if my sword had been normal or if I hadn't just activated Power Strike, it might have worked.

Instead, his skin made a shattering noise, followed by my blade passing right through his forearm. His arm just below the elbow fell to the ground and blood began to pour out of it. To my surprise, he reached down as quick as I moved and jumped through the portal. The elderly wizard on the other side shouted a few words of power, lightning flying from his hands just as the portal closed. I took the strike square in the chest and lost half my health in a single attack.

I spit blood, my hair stood on end, and I could feel steam rising from my ears. My regeneration swiftly took me back over the top of my half health, ticking towards two thousand. I had so much health because of my sword and gear, but if I had been unarmored and unarmed, that strike would have killed me outright. Why hadn't they just sent that guy through, because he was an absolute beast.

"We aren't done yet," Fitz said, finally making it back over.

I stood, my body still shaking, and saw what he meant. Without us, our knights had been calling the battle maneuvers and we had lost any advantage we'd had. My Runeforged fought with armored figures that I soon realized were other Runeforged in the middle of a chaotic sea of soldiers and banners. I couldn't even tell which were ours at this point and wondered if they could.

In the middle of a melee that was slowly moving our way, I could just see Fran fighting along with the other *Awakened*, they were circled up but fought foes that were either highly leveled in proxy levels or *Awakened* themselves. We stood on a slightly raised hill that gave us a good view of the battle, but we'd need to decide what to do in a hurry.

"Shall we join the melee or retreat and hope our horn bearers aren't dead yet so we can direct this mess," Fitz asked, his eyes still had that playfulness that always seemed to be there, but he was looking to me for answers, and that was surprising.

"You retreat back enough to direct the battle, focus on gathering our forces together again. I'll go see if I can find the knights to send back to you. Be smart," I said, nodding my head to Fitz and running straight for the melee. Right in front of me, a black shape slammed down and suddenly Fred was there, jumping off Ares and summoning a torrent of flame around him. Ares, on my command, retreated back to Fitz where she could be safe until I needed her.

With a precise surgery, his flames struck out in front of him, killing and burning enemy soldiers while leaving our own forces alone. It was truly a sight to see, such control and measured use of power. Where I could bring amazing force to bear, I didn't have anywhere near the precision that Fred was showing here.

Soon, with me sort of just walking behind him, I came upon a bloody Mick. He'd taken a sword wound to the leg and stomach, his movements slow and jerky. I didn't wait to ask him, I hit him with a Mending Touch and watched as a bit of his color returned.

"Get back to Fitz and he'll direct the troops, gather any Knights and horns bearers you can find, oh and just in case you don't find one," I said, pulling out a horn that I'd stored away but only just remembered.

"Thanks mate," Mick said, rushing past me towards Fitz.

I followed the path to where Fred connected with his sister. She fought against another swordsman, and while she was clearly the better fighter, his immense strength was nearly knocking her sword from her hand with each blow parried. I rushed forward hoping to help, but Fred already went to work. His fire serpent wrapped around the fighter completely and lifted him into the air.

It almost seemed unfair, as Fred roasted the man alive while he couldn't do anything but squirm and scream.

"I'll never make fun of you again," Fran said, running up to Fred as he finished off the fighter with a flash of fire.

"That's a funny joke," Fred said, smiling slyly at his sister.

The battle wasn't won yet, but I heard the horns of war sound, then they were answered by another blaring. Reinforcements had arrived!

I worked with Fran, Fred, and the *Awakened* to cut down enemies left and right. The ememy's morale broke, and they fled before us. Just as I was starting to think that the battle would go our way, a force of six Runeforged arrived before us. At first, I thought they were mine, but as one ran straight up, grabbed a goblin and ripped it in half, I realized they weren't. They moved with terrible speed and another three *Awakened* died before me as I lashed out with my spells.

My Lightning Strike dropped one, but only for a few seconds, so I followed up with a Firebolt, then an Arcane

Missile, until finally readying my sword as another two ran for me. Side by side, Fran, Fred, and I fought with tooth and nail. It was clear how powerful these base units were as my arm broke from a punch after I'd disarmed the Runeforged. Their techniques were basic, but their strength, ruthless.

Fred was doing the best, his spells throwing the heavy Runeforged around like toys. My arm healed enough to put weight on it, and I cast Mana Shell, saving an Orc from a cut from a Runeforged. It was after ten of our weaker Awakened had fallen when I saw Kora step into the fray.

Moving slow and calmly she walked behind a Runeforged and placed her hand on its head. It lurched backwards, the lights in its eyes flaring before falling face first in the dirt.

"Silly of them to send us more soldiers," she said, grabbing hold of the two Runeforged Fran and I fought, their eyes flashing and then falling to the dirt. One by one, she touched each of them, and at first, I'd assumed she'd somehow killed them, but they rose up and saluted her in a way I'd not seen before, by putting their straight hands against forehead and straightening their backs.

"How'd you do that?" I asked, limping on a leg that was still healing from a destructive kick from a Runeforged.

"I just rewrote a few Inscriptions and gave them a choice, they decided they'd prefer to follow you now, well, me but I follow you, so," Kora said, smiling as if we weren't in the middle of a deadly and bloody battle. Her own armor looked barely touched by the fight and besides a single scuff on her arm she appeared undamaged by it all.

Just as casually as she'd come, she disappeared back into the mix of soldiers. I marveled at the sight until suddenly, the sky darkened, and I looked up to see a hail of arrows coming down on our general position.

"Shields up!" I yelled, all our troops had been given a round shield they wore on their backs during marching, while training with their use in battle.

Very few stopped to raise shields up and I realized my voice just wasn't high enough for how much noise the battle was generating. So, I did what I had to do. Raising my hands up and letting my sword fall to the side I cast Mana Shell as wide as I possibly could, using all but a hundred of my remaining mana.

I could feel the small dings as arrow after arrow broke against my barrier until it was too much and the barrier, thin as it was, shattered. Arrow bits and a few dozen unimpeded arrows hailed down on us. I dodged them easily enough, but poor Fred took an arrow right into the shoulder, dropping him back from surprise.

"Shit," Fran said, producing a potion and rushing to his side. She painfully ripped the arrow out, Fred screamed from the pain, and she forced him to drink the potion.

Seeing that they'd be alright, I ordered our retreat. We needed to get back to Fitz and see where we'd be most useful. By the time we did so, I saw that the battle had changed immensely. The enemy force was being harrowed;

their morale broke by the sudden pressure brought on by newly arriving troops. Fitz's forces were hard to make out, so many of his bannermen had fallen, but I recognized at least two of my companies forming up around a small force of Runeforged led by Kora. She got to do what I yearned to do, fight right alongside her troops each battle.

"It'll be a bloody long list of losses," Fitz said, actually looking, for a moment, like he cared.

I didn't answer, instead a feeling a dread settled over me as I realized he was right. I'd alone witnessed the death of over fifty of my men, soldiers and *Awakened* alike. There was no telling how many Runeforged were lost or how well they could be healed by Kora. I think it was safe to say that without her and the immensely strong force of Runeforged we'd have not won this battle.

I almost wanted to request that she stop converting Runeforged into their elemental weaker forms. I'd battled with them and could match strength and technique, but these basic Runeforged had an entirely new tier of strength that made them deadly effective. We needed that more than we needed ones that could potentially get that strong, given enough time.

"Here comes the Commander they sent to lead the forces," Fitz said, gesturing to a small group of men on horseback. I was surprised to see Gadwell there in blackened armor with silver accents.

"Truly a lesson in idiocy," was the first words he said, looking at both of us. "Why engage a force so large when you had reinforcements on the way? Had we attacked together and with my skill as a general, this could have been a simple victory."

Fitz didn't even seem to hear him or chose to ignore the critique of his battle strategy. "I see that you arrived with four thousand men and not the three that we were told?" Fitz posed his words as a question.

Gadwell looked Fitz over and raised his brows while taking in his armor. "Aye, we came across a Lord returning with their remaining forces, took a heavy loss again. Isn't that right Lord Zander Variyn?"

Zander's horse stepped forward from behind several others, but he didn't look nearly as distracted as he had before, in fact, I'd say he looked rather proud of himself.

"We won our battle and will help to win a major victory here," he said, his chin raised in pride. "I would say that I've had a successful day indeed."

"Enough jabbering, we will chase down their retreating force and take a few prisoners. But whatever we do, they will not be allowed to regroup and enforce any keeps," Gadwell said. Commands were given, horns were blown.

The rest of the battle went without much issue. A sizable force of the enemy threw down arms, the Commanders were captured by the Runeforged, Kora managing to not kill them this time. The troops that fled were cut down or captured until Gadwell was sure that no sizable force had escaped. What surprised me most, was the ancient looking wizard who'd nearly done me in, had surrendered as well.

Gadwell later informed me on our way back that the wizard was a mercenary and specifically hired to kill me, though his force that he sent against me failed, it was a story that Gadwell actually seemed to enjoy. He admitted that I had no choice but to fight when portals appeared in front of my face, but he did ask me if I'd studied any portal magic, as formations can be halted if you catch them early enough. I of course hadn't, but I added it to the long list of magic that I'd need to learn about one day.

CHAPTER 32
AFTERMATH

I arrived back in camp and was given a general breakdown of losses for my Legion. The numbers were what I expected, having taken the time to gather our dead and store their bodies away for later burial. But still, it shocked me to see the full extent of our losses. Five hundred and forty-eight men. There was also a note that eight regular Runeforged that had been damaged beyond repair, but that Kora says they'll be ready again as soon as she can find suitable cores, whatever that meant.

A heavy dark weight fell on me as the next list arrived, I'd asked for the names of every man who fell under my command and I spent the next hour going over each one, trying to commit it to memory. I imagined a little about every man's life, though I didn't know any of them well enough so far for my imaginings to be anything more than a vain attempt to connect with those I'd failed.

That was, until I came across a name I did recognize.

Dan Lion. His cause of death, only one in fifty had one listed, was trampled by horses. I quickly scanned for the names of his other squad members, finding all of them listed except for one. Cam Castle.

"Verena come here," I called out. "Get me the status of Cam Castle right away. And do we have any lists of the injured or have they been tended to already?"

"No list," Verena said, jotting notes down. "The healers are slowly making their way to the most injured, but we have hundreds still awaiting healing."

I stood, setting my lists aside. "Show me where," I said. There was work still to be done and moping over the dead wasn't likely to see it accomplished.

When she'd said hundreds, I hadn't really imagined the amount, nearly a thousand groaning, bleeding, and dying men lay out in massive triage tents.

"Find whoever is in charge and ask them where they need me," I told Verena, but didn't wait to heal, instead kneeling down at the closest injured and casting my most efficient heal, Restoring Light. It had no Mana cost, I didn't know how exactly that worked, but I could cast it every 5 seconds for free and I did so. Using Rank 1 Lesser Heal and Mending Touch to preserve my mana.

I'd healed over a dozen people before a healer came over to direct me to the most severe cases. She asked if I had experience with wounds or just a raw healer. I didn't know the difference so said I must be raw. She explained quickly as we walked that the more you knew about the healing required for specific wounds the better your mana could be directed and thus healing faster and more efficiently. I decided I'd add, study of the body and medicine, to my ever-growing lists.

I wasn't a healer, that much was easy to see when I saw the others at work. Their wounds closed with minimal scarring and much swifter. But it also seemed to take more out of the patient than themselves, something that when I asked, I was told that is the proper way to heal outside combat, allowing the natural energy of the patient to bear the load, if sometimes only partially. Meanwhile, my body took a beating as I healed and healed. Though my mana ticked upward, and I took mana potions I felt a draining beyond that. After four hours, I was forced to take a break to eat an enormous amount of food and water.

I spoke with a healer as I ate, and they rested. "Has Alayna joined the healers yet on the front lines?" I asked, curious if she'd finished her task with the elves.

"She hasn't, but I am told that she is meant to report any day. Are you new to the healer's legion, that's what we like to call ourselves. Ours is a battle that takes place after the real fights," she said, a kind of sad smile on her face. She was haggard looking, but I could tell that she'd been beautiful at one point in her life. But age, and likely this intense healing, were taking a toll on her, stretching her features and sinking in her cheeks.

"My name is Caldor and yeah, I guess I'm new, today is the first day I've done any intense healing like this," I said, not wanting to give myself away as a Commander of the legion they worked on, but not willing to lie about who I was either.

"I'm Sheri, nice to meet you Caldor," she smiled, but her eyes showed a heavy weight there, then suddenly she got a confused expression on her face and turned her head to the side. "Wait, not Caldor Miles, the Commander of the legion we're trying to save?"

"That's me," I said, unable to keep the sad tone from my voice. The weight of the loss, and continued loss as more soldiers died from their wounds, was almost too much.

"You are a healer, or a fighter?" She asked, her eyes began to water up just slightly and I wondered if she was about to cry for some reason.

"I've picked up a few healing spells, but I'm basically a spellsword, a fighter that relies on magic and weapons," I said, smiling but not feeling any joy behind it.

"You know, many of these Commanders leading these Legions are powerful healers, but not once have I seen one or even Lord Variyn himself, enter these tents and try to save the lives of those who fought so hard under them. Good for you boy, now get back out there and fight for your men one last time." Her words broke a little at the end as tears rolled down her cheek. She stood, brushing herself off and wiping away the tears, ready to go back to work.

I stood as well, no tears coming to my eyes, but a new steely resolve to push myself beyond my limits to save as many as I could burned in my chest. The battle was not yet over, and this was one fight I could be on the front lines for.

It was morning the next day when the last of the men had been healed. All my mana potions had been used and I'd pushed myself to the very limits of exhaustion. During my short time, I'd learned much about healing, the body, and wounds. By the time I finished healing the last man I could do it with a quarter less mana and twice as fast as when I began. It truly was amazing how knowledge could adjust the effects and outcomes of magic, healing or otherwise.

I'd left soon after, wishing all the healers the best and thanking them for their hard work, before falling into a deep sleep. I dreamt of Mah'kus, but so terrible was my exhaustion that whatever warning or words he thought to bring to me were lost, something I felt he realized at some point as my dreams ceased.

I was awoken by a shaking and a voice I recognized. "You're late for a debriefing with Busard, you must hurry," Verena said, finally pulling me from my sleep.

I got up, I wore the same dirty clothes I'd changed into after the battle. My own armor sent off for repair. Throwing off my shirt and pants, a surprised Verena turned a shade of red and turned her back. I muttered a quick apology while splashing myself with a bit of scented perfume and putting on a quick change of clothes. I left the vest off, no time to struggle with the buttons, but I did grab a dark blue overcoat that hung loosely around me. It had a high collar and Blackridge Keep's sigil on the chest.

Feeling mostly put together and hopeful that Busard would be forgiving, as he expected people to report on time and in armor, but I had no time to get into a spare set of armor. I strolled out, thanking Verena as I went and downing some water that sat on the command table.

There was no way to tell how long I slept, but I felt refreshed and ready for the day, until I remembered the battle and my mood went sullen almost instantly. All the eager energy I had from waking vanished in a moment. I remembered the faces of those dead on the battlefield, the names I'd struggled to memorize and worst of all I saw Dan's face. I hadn't seen him dead, but I imagined well enough that it wasn't a pretty sight. But I saw him alive, which somehow was worse.

It felt like I could just reach out and grab him, whole and healthy from my memory, but I just lacked the ability to do so. I knew I was foolish to let myself think like this, but I couldn't help it and I decided I'd refuse to sleep until I'd memorized the names of the rest who'd died. Not because they were just some name on an ever-growing list of dead for a this House War, but because each one of those men had families, friends, perhaps even children. But no, they were dead and I had been in command of them.

"You feeling okay?" Verena asked, likely seeing the aguish in my face.

"No," I said, curtly. I had no intention of spreading

my sorrow to others, but I couldn't help but feel a bit angry at it all.

"Here are the reports, just in case he asks for any details," Verena said, not at all put off by my curt tone. "Oh, and good job last night. You really should be proud of how many you saved."

She had always been so straightforward and on task that it surprised me to hear her mention my actions last night, much less congratulate me for them.

"I did what needed to be done," I said, still no emotion in my voice, but I managed to keep any anger out of it.

The tent appeared over the rise we walked and I slipped in to find Gadwell, Zander, and Fitz already present and Busard talking to them.

"Sorry I'm late," I said, stepping next to the three, all in their armor and me looking like a finely dressed servant.

Busard looked over me for a long second before his eyes flicked back to Gadwell. "How'd you know he'd be late?" Busard asked, a smile on his lips that seemed out of place there.

"Damn fool spent hours in the healers' tent trying to be something he's not," Gadwell said, shaking his head and shooting a look that I couldn't quite discern.

"You have healing spells?" Busard asked, he looked surprised. "I can't recall if your father had many healing spells. Evoker based I'd wager?"

"Yes, that's right," I said, standing at attention. Busard was the only one sitting and I wondered if they'd been waiting for me to sit. However, no call to sit happened.

"And you saved many lives I'd wager," Busard said, nodding. "A true Commander if I've ever seen one. I hear you are to be congratulated and given credit for the success in repelling the enemy. Fitz here, says that without your quick thinking your forces would have been over run. And Gadwell tells me that if you hadn't engaged the enemy when you did, the battle at Laris Keep would have surely been a defeat. Instead, we are one keep closer to toppling House Blalor's grip on their lands."

I looked first at Fitz then to Gadwell. This hadn't been the reaction I excepted. What had changed for both of them to give me any kind of credit? Had I really made a difference in any way that truly mattered?

"I lost so many men," I said, dumbfounded and only able to see the battle as a failure. My mind just couldn't accept what I was hearing.

"Acceptable losses," Busard said, and it was like someone punched me in the gut. I stuttered trying to say something but failed to get any words out, so I just looked to the ground and wished for the meeting to end. Acceptable losses...the words echoed through my head.

"You'll receive a commendation; it won't be a big ceremony, but I'll expect you in armor when I give it to you. And well," Busard sighed. "I suppose I'll be needing to give you a special commendation for helping the healers as you did. I know them well enough that I'll hear no end of it if I don't. You did well, boy, be proud."

I nodded along to all of it and gave half answers when they were required, but I'd checked out of the meeting and my mind reeled as I settled into my new normal. Zander tried to speak with me afterwards, but I just smiled my fake smile and nodded along, not hearing his words. There was something wrong with me, and I didn't know what. I thought perhaps I ought to go to the healers and see if I'd been broken, but I didn't want to ease the pain or whatever it was that buzzed in my head and made thought impossible. I deserved the pain, didn't I?

I could have done better, I could have been stronger, focused more on dungeons and monster hunting. Or even used the essence I'd gathered, I had only a hundred thousand right now. What if I had just leveled and stopped obsessing about attributes? Perhaps I'd have unlocked powerful high-level perks or spells that could have turned the tide? Why oh, why had I not just been stronger, stopped the battle somehow.

At some point I got back to my bed, and I held the updated list of the dead and repeated the names until they were seared into my mind. Sheen Masto, Val Sheck, Dan Lion, Brayton, Jahn, Tanith, Mike...Michael my knight.

I'd lost one of my knights and he was someone I'd relied on heavily. An elite guard willing to follow me out into a keep so far out in the sticks that only the coin it paid could convince a man. But I'd known him well enough over these last few months to know it wasn't about the coin for him. He'd wanted to be an adventurer, just as I had, and I'd almost decided to give him the gift he wanted by taking him out monster hunting after the war. But there was not going to be an 'after the war' for him.

Michael, who I called Mike because I'd known too many Michaels, was dead.

Dan Lion was dead. So many more were dead. They are dead. What can I do? Who is next? How many will die before it's enough? Death is...death is life and life is death.

CHAPTER 33
DEATH IS LIFE, LIFE IS DEATH

I t was days later, and I was at dinner with Mick and Raphael. I'd yet to pick another Knight, but I would have to, soon. Silence ruled the dinner and it seemed I'd finally snapped enough at them both to keep them from trying small talk. But just as I'd accepted that this was the new normal, Mick opened his mouth to speak. I tried shooting him a glare to stop him, but he spoke anyways.

"I've a list of Squires for you to consider, we ought to pick one soon, as we are up next for deployment after Zander," Mick said, keeping his gaze low and not willing to look me in the eyes. I'd said a few choice words at him that I knew I couldn't take back, but a darkness filled with blistering anger slept within me now. I often found myself repeating the names of the dead that I'd memorized, probably looking like a mad man.

"What does it matter, they'll all die in the end. Just pick whoever the hell you want," I said, my words filled with venom and like every time I spoke like this, I immediately regretted it, but I refused to apologize. I had too much anger inside of me to even try.

"Men die every day!" Mick yelled suddenly and I looked him right in the eyes, surprised at his sudden angry response to my words. "If not war, then something else. We live in a world of monsters and men as strong as gods. You have a chance to save more than you lose, but if you let this darkness rule you, then we are all dead. We are dead the moment we are called back to battle. You think those five hundred are a heavy weight? Add another thousand and then you'll see where you're heading. I'm out of here, find me when you get some sense."

Mick stood and stormed out of the tent, throwing his drink against the tent wall.

Like a million needles, I felt Mick's words, but it made no difference. The darkness couldn't be dispelled by a few words, but he did have a point that I could latch on to. If something didn't change soon, I'd have more names to memorize. I didn't have to be the same cheery person I had been, but I had a duty to see to.

"Make Jase the new Knight, he's changed much since getting his leg broke," I said, catching Raphael's eyes and she nodded curtly. "I'd like a list of new squires and captains. Make the choices and I'll stand behind them. And Verena," I said, turning in my seat. "Gather a few men at arms squads tonight for a drilling session, there is much to learn still."

"Very well," Verena said, making a note and disappearing out of the tent.

I met the men she'd chosen an hour later and much to my surprise, Cam was there. Damnit Verena. I wasn't ready to face the boy just then, but there was something in his face that stirred emotions inside of me. He didn't seem to have the same darkness and hate that brewed within me, no, his face shone with pride and resolute determination as he began the drill. As I finally got within earshot they all stopped at his command and saluted me.

It was hard to feel anything after what had happened, but the smallest bit of stirring occurred then and I felt a bond grow deeper with my men. I saluted them back and held the salute for several seconds longer than was normal, making sure to look each of them in the eye. These were the men that survived, the ones that fought hard and, by the luck and chance of the gods, made it out in one piece.

"We've suffered some losses," I began to say, feeling like I owed these men an explanation. But before I could finish Cam spoke up, speaking with fierce determination.

"And we gave as good as we got!" He yelled, the men cheering along with him and slamming their hands on their chest in a continued salute.

I smiled and for the first time since I memorized the names, it felt real. "That's enough," I yelled, matching their fierce tone. "Time for us to train so that next time they face us they'll piss themselves and run off like scared cats before the first drop of blood is even drawn!"

Another cheer went up and we broke into groups. I sparred among the men, pointing out ways they could improve. These training sessions were meant to teach one-on-one combat, as opposed to the drilling we did during the day where they learned to fight as squads. And I knew that it helped, because all too often, lines would break, and it would come down to a man and his spear against another man and a spear. And when it came to that, I wanted my men to excel.

We finished the training, and I pulled Cam aside to speak with him as the other men left.

"Thank you for that," I said, trying and failing to smile.

"I meant it," Cam said simply. Looking me in the eyes, he clasped his hand on my shoulder. "It's a damn shame that we lost Dan in that battle, along with my entire squad. I feel a weight that threatens to crush me, but then I think of you. You're responsible for the entire army and if you can stand strong despite all you've lost, so can I."

By the gods of the Vanir, he thought I was holding it together and that gave him strength? I made a promise to myself while I held back tears and looked into this young man's eyes. No matter the darkness that swirled within me, I would put up a front, because they needed it, not me.

"We all do what we must," I said, "Have they gotten you over a squad yet, captain?"

"The lot I came with lost their Captain and Lieutenant, so I'm filling the spot. I was worried they'd say something about having a Captain that failed his men, but they've got a healthy respect for you, so when I told them I used to work for you it helped," Cam said, releasing my arm and shrugging.

"A healthy respect, eh?" I asked, wondering what he meant.

"Yeah, from what I've heard they were all severely injured in the battle and most of them were healed by you. Is it true that you spent an entire day healing? They make it sound like you were some kind of sentinel against death, pulling men back from the brink. One of them swears that you had an aura of blue that sparked around you as you worked."

Had I been using essence while healing? My memories of the time healing had become erratic, like a fever dream as I struggled against having enough mana and healing all those around me fast enough to stop them from dying.

"I healed as many as I could," I said, averting my eyes. "Not everyone made it, but the healers legion worked miracles that night, I was the least among them."

"I wish I had the power to do more like you," Cam said, almost as if an afterthought.

"You want to be *Sparked*?" I asked, then added. "We lost a good many *Awakened* during that battle. We aren't invincible."

"But you can heal, cast magic, and move as fast as a god," Cam said, obviously in awe to what he imagined *Awakened* could do.

"Can you keep a secret soldier?" I asked, looking about to make sure we were alone. We were.

"Not according to my wife, but I think so," Cam said, laughing.

"I can make you *Sparked* but it's more likely to kill you than this war is. Would you trade your life for a sliver of a chance to be greater?" I asked, watching his expression as I told him. It went from surprise, to consideration, to something I couldn't quiet mark.

He didn't answer for a long while and I think at first, he was trying to decide if he believed me, but eventually he spoke after nearly a minute. "I get it," he said. "I'm happy to do what I can as a soldier, and I know *Awakened* have it hard as well. But to answer your question, no, I wouldn't trade a near certain death for the chance at power. Being a soldier is enough risk for me."

"Why even risk being a soldier?" I asked, suddenly curious why he'd pick one risk of death over another.

"Because my family needs a future, and the money I've already earned is making it possible for us to purchase some land, now I just have to survive long enough to enjoy it with my wife and our new baby girl," Cam said, chuckling though there was a sadness in that laugh that I felt.

This man wanted to better his situation and was willing to fight for it. He missed his wife and his child, fearing that perhaps they'd seen the last of him. What hurt the most was the realization that Cam wasn't alone in his situation. Each soldier, even those that died, had families, had plans for the money they'd never be able to spend themselves. Sure, we had our fair share of mercenaries in the army who did this kind of work no matter which house was at war, but even they had lives and plans for the future.

"What if I gave you five platinum and released you from service, honorably," I said. "You could walk away and go see your family. I'm serious, just say the words and you are free to go."

Cam looked like I'd struck him, staring at me he shook his head. "Don't do that," he said, shaking his head and closing his eyes. "I've made an oath and my word is my bond. If you want to give me extra gold, give it among all the men instead. I'm just one soldier among thousands, do not tempt me to break my honor. I have to see this through."

"But what if you don't survive?" I asked, raising my voice as the desperation rose. Just take it Cam! Take the chance I'm giving you and be with your family!

"Then take my body back to my family and give them that money, as I'll finally be taking you up on the offer to return home," Cam said, almost jokingly as he looked up at me with emotions I couldn't quite understand.

"I'll do that," I said, fearing that before the end I'd be doing just that.

"What is this dungeon called?" I asked as we approached the entrance. We'd pushed the front line far enough that we'd taken in a new dungeon, and I was going to do a dive with Fred, Fran, Zander, and Daniel Marteese the warlock.

According to Daniel he had the ability to summon a demonic pet that would act as our tank, but either way I wasn't worried, as this dungeon had a max level of 12 for the final boss.

It was almost not worth the amount of essence, but I needed some time killing something that wasn't technically alive. Though if I posed that idea to Kora, I'm sure she'd overrule my thinking with some crap about how the summoned creatures are very much alive, but I had no time for that, so I'd left her behind. She didn't mind though, as she was so busy converting and growing her army. She'd hunted and recovered half a dozen more monster cores to bring her fallen Runeforged back to life. As long as we recovered all the parts, she seemed capable of returning all her lost troops to life, though she claimed it was more like getting new troops, as the monster cores used are destroyed when she lost a Runeforged.

"Kobolds," Fred said, "The final boss is the weakest dragon you'll likely ever see in a dungeon. Officially, I think it's a baby dragon, a red one."

"Good, I've always wanted to kill a proper dragon," I said, ignoring the baby dragon part, a dragon was a dragon.

I noticed several dozen people in the dungeon staging room, each of them standing over orbs that I recognized. Gilfoy's essence collection devices I'd seen at their storefront.

"What are you doing?" I asked a uniformed man wearing Lord Variyn colors.

"Bugger off," he said, then turned and saw who I was,

he must have recognized me because he went a little white in the face and stuttered to correct his words. "I-I mean I'm just collecting essence as instructed, Lord Commander Miles."

"Yes, but why here and not in the dungeon?" I asked.

"We aren't on the schedule for a while, but there is a good bit of latent essence in the staging area and Lord Variyn has commanded we collect as much as possible," he said, then lowering his voice to a whisper he added, "You know, for the device."

"I don't actually know," I said casually, before turning to follow my team into the dungeon proper.

The dungeon started off easily enough, we entered and slew of a bunch of short little lizard-like humanoids that couldn't survive more than a hit or two. This continued on for another hour, until we cleared the first floor. From what we were told it only had three floors, so this was going to be the quickest dungeon run of my life.

The traps were easy to work around without a rogue type. Daniel summoned a large rock elemental looking monster that barely fit in the dungeon and glowed a demonic green. It just lumbered through and triggered all the traps before smashing against the foes in the next room. We continued along like this for a while until finally reaching the second floor boss, where we encountered a 'Dragon Blessed Kobald Champion'.

The room was lit by fireplaces cut into the stone room and a red and gold carpet covered the floor. The Champion stood nearly five feet tall, a couple feet taller than the biggest kobold we'd encountered so far. It wore golden armor, or at least a few armor pieces. It had pauldrons but no chest plate, armor on his hip but no leggings, only boots. Then to top it off, he had a helmet and gauntlets that ended in sharp claws.

He almost looked like a formidable foe, until you Inspected him. He was only level 11 and had 950 health points.

"I'm going to take this one by myself," I declared, cracking my neck to the side and ready to have a good time.

"I don't need to remind you," Fran began to say but her brother cut her off.

"Boss mobs are stronger than they appear, be careful," Fred said, and Fran punched him in the arm, earning a hurt glare from Fred.

"I was going to say that," Fran said, rolling her eyes.

"You are a weird bunch," Daniel said, eyeing us suspiciously.

"They really are," Zander said, smirking.

"Quiet down," I said, stepping forward to face the boss.

I was going to see if I could trigger his different phases before just outright killing him. He looked like he should be a fierce combatant and suddenly I wondered how many people had died under his claws. Then another thought hit me, was he weaker than he'd normally be because of the Ley line corruptions? I guess I would find out, we were a way's away from where the initial infection had occurred, even farther than the previous dungeon.

"Do you want me to heal you?" Zander asked, calling out over a sudden roar from the kobold.

"No, I'll be fine," I yelled, dodging a slow attack from the Kobold Champion. His little gauntlets glowed a bit as he moved, but he was much slower than me.

Weaving through his attacks, I just drained my stamina for a bit while parrying attacks. Then when I began to get bored, I removed one of his arms. The look of surprise on the kobold's face almost made me laugh out loud. This was such a pointless dungeon run and I shouldn't have let Fred and Fran talk me into it. I'd thought doing some monster killing would lift my mood, but it wasn't.

The kobold began to glow red, and fire filled its maw. I threw my sword aside and grabbed its elongated snout, forcing the mouth shut. With one hand, he clawed at my armor, but it repelled his weak attacks without any issue. I wanted to see just how fireproof this kobold was, and I wasn't disappointed. The monster struggled and squirmed, black smoke coming from its mouth until I was sure it had swallowed the fire.

Letting it go, it scurried away and I swear it looked afraid of me. What was wrong with me? I dashed forward and took off its head, ending the suffering. Turning back to my group they all had different expressions. Fred looked almost bored, Fran had a wide-eyed expression of surprise on her face, Zander looked like he enjoyed the show, while Daniel looked absolutely terrified at my show of power.

"This, ahh, normally how you all do dungeons?" He asked, taking a step back and nearly stumbling. "I think I've had my fill for today."

"We are going to do a full clear," I said, venom in my words, though I hadn't meant there to be.

"Yes, ahh, yes of course," Daniel said, looking at the others for support but getting none.

The rest of the dungeon progressed even faster as I no longer wanted to play around, so almost by myself I cleared each room using all my abilities to speed the process. When we finally got to the dragon, it fell from three essence infused attacks, much to the disappointment of everyone else.

"That wasn't even fun," Fran said, looking at me with a defeated look. "Let's get back to camp, Fred and I want to do some monster clearing later tonight and you aren't invited."

Her words didn't hurt, and I honestly didn't know how much was sarcasm so I just shrugged. This was my life now, and I had lost joy for the one thing I truly loved doing, clearing dungeons. If I couldn't enjoy this, then what was left for me in life? Plenty, I heard a small quiet voice say in my mind, but I pushed it further down. I'd do my duty, save my men as much as possible, and get this war over with. How many more men needed to fall beneath my blade before the end? I wasn't sure but I'd all but decided to settle into the commander role more firmly and stop fighting on the front lines unless it made sense tactically.

I leveled to 25 over the next two months of battles, monster clearing, and dungeon diving. My actions against monsters had become more reckless and I wasn't really sure why, but I killed them now, with a ruthlessness that scared me at times. With my attribute points, I'd risen my Endurance over its threshold and put the rest into Concentration, leaving only Concentration and Core attributes to be pushed over the next threshold. The Endurance changed me in ways I didn't expect. I no longer needed to sleep every day, in fact, I literally couldn't. Now it only made sense and felt right if I slept one day in three.

I hadn't picked up any new abilities, though I had some cool options open up when I hit level 25, or when I unlocked most of my attribute thresholds, I didn't know which ones triggered the new abilities, but I ignored them all the same. My spells had been working fine for me and until I increased my mana pool further, I couldn't even think of upgrading my spells to the next tier, as they already limited me to about five or six spells before I was dangerously low.

I could always use the first-tier spells, but it took a bit of extra focus to do so and it wasn't always practical in battle when moments mattered. I'd been attacked again by more *Awakened* mid battle and survived just fine. It was odd to me that the enemy seemed to be spending so much time targeting me, and it was just me. I'd spoken with a few of the other Lords, and none of them had been targeted by *Awakened*, only regular soldiers on occasion. What made me so special in that regard, I couldn't figure out.

Sure, I'd won every engagement I'd been in so far, and my Runeforged usually made quick work of the opposing force, but that was more Busard than me. He was in charge of when I was deployed and against how many. In the last two months, I hadn't gone up against any force with greater numbers than my own, and when it was an even legion versus legion, it wasn't a fair fight as my Runeforged literally could be counted as a squad each, and I had nearly two hundred and fifty.

We hadn't yet come across another force willing to oppose us with Runeforged again, word must have gotten around that we had Kora and she could turn them to our side. Kora had converted nearly half of all Runeforged into some form like her, some of the new ones had almost bestial construct forms, instead of the normal humanoid look. Kora explained that she'd not been able to find elemental cores, so she used bestial types, and they preferred these forms better.

I fell asleep reading the names of the soldiers we lost, but I kept up appearances everywhere else. Training them nightly, praising them and handing out commendations of my own. They truly thought I was a beacon of light in a dreary dark war, when really, I felt like an endless void that sucked in everything that came near. Those closest to me knew I was suffering, but like Mick, they chose to be rough with me in an attempt to snap me out of it, but it wasn't so easy.

I'd repaired a bit of my troubles with Mick, at least getting us back on talking terms and I'd even drank and gambled with them a bit. I laughed and smiled, but inside I felt empty. I was getting so good at showing people what they wanted to see that it frightened me a bit.

After all that had happened, a single truth repeated in my head. Life is Death, Death is Life.

CHAPTER 34
A DIFFERENT WAY

The horns called out for us to go to battle and, as I'd been doing the last few engagements, I sent for Verena to gather additional intel before we marched. We got the basic orders, where to go, who to engage, but Verena had a way of pulling together gossip and other rumors about the enemy commanders that had been coming in handy lately. I'd gotten her used to Ares and Ares with her, so she rode on her back while I rode, Fiend, the black war horse I'd bought after that fateful engagement.

I knew it bothered Ares that I used her as an information runner, but I'd let her go hunting whenever she'd liked and even let her disappear for two weeks at one point, so she could just deal with it. A part of me wondered where she went during her extended trips, but there was no way currently for me to find out that mystery. Alayna still hadn't made an appearance and when I asked the Healers Legion, I just got excuses.

"Remember, the general I told you about a few weeks back, most call him old Ironfist, but his name is Aldrik Ironfist, a surname he gave himself some years ago when he took on being a fulltime mercenary," Verena said, going over her notes and flipping from page to page while we marched.

"Does he actually have an Ironfist?" I asked, making a look to match how odd I felt it was to give yourself a silly name like 'Ironfist'.

"No, I do not believe he does," Verena said, making a notation with her pen.

"So, what do we know about him, other than he likes cheesy names and thinks of himself as stern," I said, wanting to roll my eyes but restraining myself.

"Well for starters, he is the one I told you about that throws up the white flag of peace during engagements, always wanting to trade words before the battle. I think it allows him to get a full look and rundown of the enemy troops, but he's never used the situation, not yet at least, to ambush enemy commanders."

I scratched at my clean-shaven chin, my hair had been trimmed as well and I was looking rather presentable, I thought. "Perhaps I could ambush him and end the fight before it began," I said, trying to work out if I thought his men would still fight with their commander dead. "Why does he call the commanders together again? To offer them a chance to surrender or something?"

"No, actually. He gives the commander a chance to duel him one-on-one to decide the fate of the battle, offering to withdraw his troops if he loses or is slain during the engagement. Three Lords have taken him up on the offer and all three have lost, one dying, a Lord Fitz I believe, just last week."

I shot her a look. "How did I not know Fitz had died? I swear I just saw him at one of those dinners Busard throws," I said, shaking my head in disbelief. I was truly losing my grip on things if I hadn't realized the only Lord, besides Zander, that I knew well enough to not fully dislike. Fitz was dead, and this guy had killed him.

"You've missed the last two dinners and been officially censured by Busard," Verena said, raising an eyebrow at me. "I told you this just yesterday and you even took a report detailing how you are being fined by him until you arrive at one of his dinners."

"We are paying him for missing a few dinners?" I asked, shaking my head at the ridiculousness of it all.

"That's correct."

"Well don't let me miss the next one," I said, fully intending to actually go this time.

"I will do my best."

"So, I'm going to offer to duel this man then, do we know his level?" I asked, trying to picture someone who could kill Fitz. I'd have been able to kill Fitz, he was bulky as a Paladin, but with my ability to infuse essence into myself and how practiced I'd become with it, I had no doubt that our level gap meant absolutely nothing now. I figured by my own math that I'd be a challenge for someone twice my level.

"From gossip I've heard, he is said to be level 50," Verena said, frowning. "Do you think it wise to challenge such a formidable foe?"

"Leave the actual fighting to me, will you Verena," I said, my tone sarcastic.

"Yes, Lord Commander," she said. She only used my title when she was miffed at me, so I did what I'd been doing for the last few months when I angered people, I distanced myself. In her case I just rode ahead a bit and put physical distance between us. She was used to it, and I knew she had thick enough skin that she'd not mind.

Riding forward put me up next to my Knights as they rode just behind their squires, who rode just behind the companies.

"Looks like we won't be fighting today after all," I told them, getting a surprised head turn from all of them but Mick, he didn't even regard me.

He did speak however, his tone natural. "And why is that, our witty Commander?"

I grimaced at his question and tone. I'd done some damage when speaking to him that still hadn't been recovered, it didn't help that I continued to be an ass when opportunity presented itself. Despite doing a fair job with others I always seemed to be overly critical with Mick. After a few games of cards, I thought we were good, but then I opened my mouth and said more stupid stuff.

"This commander is named Aldrik Ironfist, perhaps

you've heard of him?" I asked, seeing if anyone else were keyed in on rumors and gossip.

Raphael cursed and I looked her way. "You can't be thinking of dueling him? He's deadly enough on the field with his troops, but to challenge him to a one-on-one is suicide," she said, increasing her speed to get beside me. "You should request reinforcements now. Even with our advantages we won't be his match. His troops have never lost a battle and he's never taken serious casualties."

That last bit stung and she realized it, backing off a bit. But I didn't lash out, instead, I looked around to gauge everyone else's reaction. Jase was the quietest of the bunch, so I targeted him.

"Tell me Jase, is it suicide for me to go against this commander and prevent the deaths of my troops by defeating him one-on-one?" I asked, and Jase, to his credit, didn't flinch or turn away, as was common among people I spoke with lately.

"I've seen you do some impossible magics and feats of strength," Jase said, his words confident. "And I've heard this Ironfist fellow is a strong one, but I doubt he can match you if you go all out. I say go for it."

Mick shot Jase a cutting look, but Jase ignored it, giving me a head nod.

"At least one of my Knights has confidence in my abilities," I said. "If I'd known that requesting duels before a battle was a legitimate way to prevent battle, then I'd have done this from the start. I will face Ironfist, and I will kill him."

"You don't think his troops will just withdraw, do you?" Raphael asked, her expression dumbfounded, as was her tone.

"They'll be without a commander, so if it comes to it, we will defeat their army as well. I still think it is worth a chance, and that is enough for me," I said, my tone indicating the conversation was over.

A rider approached on a brown horse, wearing Blackridge Keep colors and a bowmen's armor, so a scout report most likely.

"Urgent news from the scouting team that just returned," the man said, I didn't know his name, as most my time was spent learning the names of those who'd fallen already in battle.

"Out with it," I said, motioning with my hands.

"The reports of troop sizes are inaccurate, this commander is leading a force of just over two thousand men, mostly men at arms by the looks of it. Also, they've marched into a large open valley and have stopped their march."

"They aren't pressing forward to the keep any longer, have they abandoned their attempt after all?" I asked, not that I expected an answer from this scout.

Mick gave an answer. "This is on brand with what I've heard of him. He knows we are close so he will set up in a place that is most suited for battle and wait for the enemy to come to him. Then he'll run up the white flag and kill you."

"Or I'll kill him," I corrected. "Report received, go

inform Verena to send for additional troops but we will not slow our approach. Make sure she informs Busard I intend to challenge the Commander in single combat."

"Yes, Lord Commander."

I looked over my shoulder as I sensed Ares take flight and watched her while she disappeared into the distance.

Fred and Fran galloped up to me as I let myself fall back away from my knights and bannermen. With them, they had Daniel and his crew of four others, each on a horse they'd bonded.

"Daniel just returned with the scouts and has news," Fran said, gesturing forward the dark-haired young adult.

"They've got nearly five dozen *Awakened* in their ranks, they are dressed as normal soldiers, but I sensed them. Also, that commander of theirs is level 51 and has a massive health pool, I was surprised I got any information regarding him really. And his class is Iron Knight, I've never heard of such a class before," Daniel said in his usually 'know it all' tone.

"Iron Knight?" Fran said, her forehead scrunched up in concentration as she thought. "I had access to so many physical based classes, but I don't remember an Iron Knight being offered. What about you Caldor?"

"Nope," I said, shrugging. "It doesn't matter his class though, well, it would if I knew what it meant, but I'll beat him all the same."

"You aren't worried about his class?" Daniel said in shock, by the exaggerated look on his face.

"It's probably a tanking class, so I'll just have to cut him real hard to get past his defenses," I said, shrugging.

The ground disbursed after that, Fred and Fran wanted to talk strategy, so they stayed behind, despite me not seeing the point.

"If the duel isn't going well, I'll attack first," Fred said, nodding to his sister.

She nodded back and added, "And I'll try for a surprise attack from behind."

I sighed and pressed my eyes closed for a second to try and banish a headache that was beginning to form there. You'd think with so many thresholds passed and attributes added that headaches would be a thing of the past, however, that couldn't be further from the truth. Whether my recent increases causing it or the general stress of being a commander, I found myself with more headaches than I ever remembered having before.

"You will not interfere with the duel, even if I fall in battle," I said, making sure to keep my tone hard so they wouldn't mistake me.

"We have oaths that say otherwise," Fran said, smiling.

Fred cleared his throat before adding, "I doubt we'd physically be able to stop ourselves. You'd have to send us away if you don't wish us to interfere."

Fran shot him a look and I smiled.

"Fred and Fran, I order you to return to camp. See to it that reinforcements are on their way and I will meet with you after the battle," I said, thankful that Fred had given me the idea.

"You idiot," Fran said, and I honestly couldn't tell which of us she meant. Fred looked a little stunned and turned his head to the side.

"Oh shoot," he said, realizing what he'd done.

"What if we refuse to leave. It isn't like we don't know what you plan," Fran said.

"If you wish to continue in my service, I'd suggest you learn to follow some orders. That or take an oath that you won't interfere in official one-on-one combat, despite what the outcome looks like?" I posed my final words as a question.

"Won't those oaths interfere with each other," Fran said, looking at Fred for the answer.

"I believe the newest binding takes precedence and would cause an alteration of prior ones. Plus, we made the oath without prompting and he's repeatedly told us we could break it, which makes new oaths more binding. It isn't an exact science, but from what I've read, I would say it is sufficient," Fred said, saying more words than I'd heard from him all week in a single breath.

"Do it and stand by my side," I said, honestly wanting them close by as they were slowly becoming some of my best friends. Emory and Ismene had visited twice now, each time they'd showed how much stronger they'd gotten, nearly catching up with me. They complained about dungeon dives being taken over by House collectors—people set out by House Variyn to collect essence in essence collection orbs. But otherwise, they'd made decent progress, saying that the monster populations seemed to be thriving lately.

Looking at each other, they stopped their horses and quickly dismounted. I stayed atop my beefy black horse and watched them as they took a knee. They said a new oath, Fred going first and Fran repeating. Until finally, I felt a tug where it connected, and they'd further bound themselves to me. Oaths were odd and the compulsion to follow through with them even odder.

Satisfied, I motioned for them to mount up. "Fine, orders rescinded. Come with me and watch me as I defeat an Iron Knight."

CHAPTER 35
IRONFIST

Ironfist's army looked as big as ours, but with an entire extra two companies toward the back, one of which was entirely made of cavalry. It was truly a sight to behold, and I wondered how well my advantages would hold against his forces. Surely our Runeforged would do as they had been doing and throw his forces into disarray.

Snowcapped mountains sat at the back of his army, and I wondered how smart of a tactician he must really be if he made retreat so impossible for himself. Despite the late months, I saw that where they had positioned themselves also had some snow on the ground, this was surprising considering we were well into the next season by now, but the chill did stick around much later in these higher climates.

His front line of men at arms were also unique, I realized, in that I didn't see very many spear men, most of them held sword and shields, along with full sets of beefy looking armor. I'd outfitted my own men with chestplate and leather under armor, but this was a whole other level of preparedness. I could see a single man standing before their army holding a white banner, meaning he wished to parley.

Behind him, his forces flew blue banners, but they had no sigil of any kind. It was odd, even the platoon banners were absent. My own legion had banners that slightly differed down to the squad, giving each group within the legion a chance to feel a part of something, more theirs than mine. It seems that old Ironfist wanted them all under a single banner with no exceptions. That told me something about him, but whether it meant he wanted all the focus on him or perhaps a focus of mind on the battle and army being as one, I couldn't know.

Either way I did as I had planned. I got on the back of Ares; she'd returned with news of reinforcements being dispatched and orders—that I pretended not to hear—saying we were to await reinforcements before engaging and under no circumstance engage in one-on-one combat with the enemy commander.

Ares kicked off the ground and in a show of strength, I flew low over his army, but not a single one of them flinched or even looked up. Instead, like statues, they held their gaze forward, looking toward their commander. Ares screeched mightily and we landed with a skid in front of the Commander Ironfist. She tilted her head to the side while looking at him and screeched into his face. He had a helmet under his arm and smiled at her in a very fatherly way.

"Return for now," I told Ares as I dismounted. I had to press the orders upon her two more times before she listened, continually stealing glances at the enemy commander. She felt something from him but what it was I couldn't tell. She took flight, doing another pass over the enemy army before returning to Verena, Fred, and Fran. Through her eyes I saw that she saw they were all worried, but I pushed the distracting thoughts away.

"You seem to know why I've run up the white flag," Iron-fist said, his voice was as firm as iron and filled with power.

He looked to be in his late thirties or early forties, but his eyes spoke of many more years. The timelessness of an *Awakened* who takes the right perks were visible as the slight wrinkles around his eyes. He had a fatherly tone in his voice that made you want to listen to him, and his light brown eyes invited you in. He seemed so kind just by the look of him, yet he was built like Emory, thick in the shoulders, neck, and thighs.

He wore intricate armor inlaid with gold on the edges and designs on his pauldrons and chestplate. He wore no tabard, and neither did I. His sword, currently put away in its scabbard at his waist, was massively thick, almost comically so. I knew the extra weight meant nothing as an *Awakened,* but I imagined it might be a bit unwieldy. However, it had done its job well enough, killing poor Fitz.

"How do I know that your troops won't just attack

after I kill you?" I asked, meeting his eyes and feeling as if I were staring down my own father. He gave me a disappointed look and a part of me wanted to shrink from it.

"Death is not what I wish here," he said, shaking his head. "It was an unfortunate overstep that ended with your fellow commander dead. This is a House War, and we are the commanders, but that doesn't mean we should want each other dead. Our men are just as precious, and we can save lives by participating in a friendly duel. No one need die."

"You didn't answer my question," I said, flatly. I didn't like how I felt, but I planned on fighting to the death. I would end this threat of a commander and House Variyn's campaign against House Blalor will be all the better for it.

"You plan on killing me, I've heard much of your honor, Caldor Miles. And that of your father. I daresay, he'd been worried about you, seeing how hardened you've become," Ironfist said, again his fatherly tone chastising me and drudging up emotions I wished to keep locked away.

Before I could repeat myself, he held up a hand.

"To the death is acceptable," he said. "My men have sworn an oath to withdraw if I were to ever lose. It hasn't happened yet, so they may be slow to act, but the oaths they took will bind them to it. I require no oath from you, but I would expect that you've told your Knights your wishes if you should fall?"

"I have, but I have no intention of losing," I said.

Ironfist squinted his eyes suddenly and I knew he must be Inspecting me.

"An Arcane Knight like your father, so the rumors were true. However, young man, you are far below my level and thus not much a threat to me or even some of my Knights. Do you have a second you wish to fight in your place?" He asked with audible concern in his voice, and I hated him all the more for his genuine worry for my life. What kind of enemy commander was this!

"I am capable, and none will fight in my stead," I said, holding out my hand and letting my sword appear.

"Neat trick," Ironfist said, putting his helmet on and drawing his sword.

It was a massive thing that only had one sharp edge that ended in a sharpened point. More cleaver like than sword, I thought. I cracked my neck to the side and began to slowly fill my body with essence, as well as infusing my blade up to its first, then second, and finally third tier.

Fulgar'vi'lectus, my sword, sparked with potential energy and I decided Ironfist wasn't going to be an enemy that I should hold back on, so I cranked it up to its fourth and then finally for the first time its fifth tier, moving my base damage potential from 35-53 to a whopping 79-120. Furthermore, my Strength and Intellect attributes rose from 20 each to 45 each, giving me additional Mana and raw strength.

My passing of my second threshold in Endurance and Constitution meant I could pack more Essence into my very muscles, so I did so, and I felt them bulge. Energy, wild and sparking, traveled through me and I knew that this fight was mine. All the while, I stared down my opponent, first confirming that he was in fact what he said, however, I didn't get any health point values as Daniel claimed to get, instead I saw his name and his class, Iron Knight, along with a level.

"That is a neat trick," Ironfist said, raising his sword into the air and walking a circle around me. I moved my feet, keeping our distance the same and circling him as well. Round and round we went. When his arm went up again, his Army cheered, so I rose my sword into the air too, a gesture I hoped my men could see from such a distance.

Both forces were far enough away that I wasn't in any immediate danger from his men nor he from mine. As my sword was thrust up into the air, blue sparks fired off straight up and I could feel the blade seemingly calling to me to be used. Even from the distance that they were I could hear my men cheer and I felt a warmth grow in my chest.

Locking my eyes forward, I awaited my opponent to make the first move, but it seemed he had the same idea, as we continued to circle. I decided I should respond to his words and perhaps taunt him to get him to attack.

"It is no trick, but rather a sign of your doom," I said, my words seemed to come out sharper and louder than I meant, while under the influence of essence. Mentally I went through my preparations that I'd made. My Arcane Armor was in place, though under the bright sun of the afternoon it was hard to tell, as it was transparent, though solid. My sword shone with a faint light from my Light Blade, giving me my +6 to base damage since upgrading it to tier 2. I'd done my daily task in adding my sword as my Preferred Weapon, giving it an additional +5 to damage output. My Blade Ward was in effect, giving me another bump in base weapon damage of 30, my Physical Resistance spell had taken effect—reducing physical damage taken by 11 percent—and would last another hour at least.

All these things working together to keep me alive and make my damage potential far above my level, but still, I didn't see him coming.

Like a crack of Lightning going off, something hit my chest plate and I went flying. In the air, I twisted and turned until my feet made contact with the dirt. Sword raised before me and straining my Perception to its limits, I noticed him standing where I'd been a moment ago. As my feet hit the ground, dirt flew up in an arc behind me and I went still. It had to have been a tank ability to get to me that fast, I thought, but why hadn't I sensed his activation of it or anything for that matter.

I poured more essence into my muscles as I ran toward him, moving nearly as fast as when I activated Speed Burst. I poured essence into my eyes, and I could feel them bristling with energy. It was a good thing I did, because he blurred and I barely saw him coming, when I activated Speed Burst. The additional speed boost brought me up to his speed, but I struggled to control my muscles under such an increase. His sword appeared going for my chest again in a downward chop, I activated Swift Strike, and smashed my blade against his in a dangerous parry.

All the while, I focused and activated my Instant cast of Lightning Strike right atop him the moment I was clear of his blade. My sword pushed away from his as Lightning Struck down on him, scorching the top of his helmet. His cloak, more like a cape than anything else, flared out behind him and the lightning seemed to travel through him and out the cape, sparking behind him.

Some sort of magical release cape perhaps. He hadn't been affected otherwise, by the Lightning Strike that normally left my opponents' muscles seizing up. I slashed out, releasing Force Wave at Ironfist, just as my speed boost ended. The arc of force moved at the speed I had been at the time and struck him hard in the side, but he didn't even react to it. Instead, he turned and slashed downward, forming his own arc of energy that shot towards me through the small distance. It hit me full on in the chest and sent me flying backwards. If it hadn't been for the force distributing effects of my armor, it might have cut through the leather section of my gut.

Rolling to my feet, I raised my blade, ready for his charge. He moved towards me, this time slow, really slow. It was almost as if he were mocking me now. It would take him at least a good five seconds, if not longer, to reach me, so I cast Arcane Missile, taking up two and a half seconds, then cast Firebolt with the other two and a half seconds. Each spell tier two and infused with extra essence to give it a better kick than Lightning Strike had done. Down just under 400 points of mana already, I was glad for the extra my increase intellect provided.

Arcane Missile lashed out first, sparking with the additional essence I'd poured into it. I sent them wide to slow them down, all three shooting off either up, left, or right in a big arc, so that my Firebolt could streak right down the middle as it went off. With my timing perfect, and Ironfist still walking comically slow, my attacks hit with devastating sparking effect.

He was still a good five feet from me when the strike hit. I saw much of the power get redirected into his cloak, and it spit arcs of arcane energy and fire, but not all of it made it to the cape. The sparks of greenish blue struck him right into the chest and left a blackened mark as he was lifted from his feet and thrown back a good twenty feet. Not one to waste an advantage I activated Speed Burst and ran the opposite direction. When I was a good one hundred and fifty feet away, I began channeling my Fireball spell, Essence and Mana pouring into it.

I knew better than to use it close up, but I also had to be careful not to make it too big because its blast wave was dangerous, and I doubted my Mana Shell would save me if I put too much into it.

Capping it at a hundred mana and half that amount of essence, I lifted the fist-sized ball of green and orange burning fire, sparks of blue crackling all around my body, and was about to throw it when I realized he was gone. Suddenly a force hit me in the stomach so hard that it took all the breath from me, but instead of flying backwards I felt an armored knee take me in the back of the head, my helmet going flying off my head.

That blow sent me flying forward and I released my Fireball way too close. The blast sent me tumbling through the air as it landed below me, and at Ironfist's feet. He yelled out a series of words and I swear his entire body went gray just before the ignition of the Fireball. With a muttered phrase I sent the Mana Shell around me infusing it with a fast bit of mana, so fast that it hurt, and I knew I risked doing damage to myself. It shattered, along with my Arcane Armor, a moment later, but it was enough to save me from the initial blast. The shockwave of fire burned at my skin, and I screamed in pain while I flew ever higher into the air.

This landing was going to kill me I realized, and I activated Speed Burst to give my mind more time to think. The world seemed to slow down for the three seconds it gave me, during that time I started to arc down towards the ground like a speeding rock from the sky above. Not knowing what else to do I did what I knew I shouldn't. I began to infuse even more essence into me, my bones, my muscles, my tissue, every bit of me. And for good measure I managed to get off a Restoring Light in the final seconds as I fell.

Miraculously, I hit leg first, one knee coming down and the bones shattering, while my front fist hit the ground, also breaking, but I managed to stay off my back. I lived, despite being so high up in the air that I thought I should have just tried to call Ares to pick me up on my way down. I'd created a crater all around me, dirt and debris still clung to the air around me, obscuring my physical vision. I sensed that Ironfist was still there, somewhere out in the cloud of dust, but I could do nothing but wait for my healing to mend my bones. I used a Mending Touch on myself, just as I heard laughing from in front of me, some twenty paces.

"You truly are your father's son," Ironfist said, but his words just pissed me off as I stood. I was tired of everyone knowing my father, everyone expecting something of me because of what he did. My emotions raged inside of me, and I realized that sparks as big as my Lightning Strike attack shot out all around me. My body was over saturated with essence, and it was not good. There was a reason why your Core was meant to hold this volatile energy and not your tissues. I knew without seeing it, that pieces of my cheek had flaked away, and light showed from beneath. But even as it showed, my healing closed the wounds.

I released a good measure of the essence, using how I'd practiced with my sword to syphon it back into my core. It worked, and I felt my body begin to slack, surprisingly my emotions cooled with it.

He hadn't attacked again yet, and I needed a moment, so I responded looking towards his silhouette in the cloud of dust. "I am proud to be my father's son, but I am Caldor Miles, Lord of Blackridge Keep, and Knight protector of the House Variyn lands. By my own accomplishments I will be known."

"Your father was a great man, Caldor. A true hero," Ironfist said, stepping forward and through the dust.

"I know that, Ironfist," I said, my voice filled with conviction. "I am proud of him, but I will be known for my own deeds and not just as Elkor's son!"

"Very well," Ironfist nodded slowly. "Well then, I see now what you are capable of, Caldor. It is time for me to show you my true potential."

He shot forward, his blade thrusting out and barely cutting the surface of my cheek. I activated Swift Strike to move my blade up to catch his and we locked into place. The essence in my sword sparked and lashed out at him. His strength was terrible and overwhelming. I infused more essence into my body, and I could feel it buzzing out of my eyes so much of it filled me. It was while we stayed locked sword to sword, that he spoke to me and his words nearly made me give up.

"I've used a single ability against you to test your speed and limits. I admit that Fireball was enough to have seriously wounded me, but I see where your limits are now. Normally I'm able to use a single ability to defeat most foes, you've already forced me to use my other class ability. I feel comfortable telling you that I will now use all that I have at my disposal, so be ready. If you choose to give up, I suggest you make it clear, otherwise I'll likely kill you without meaning," Ironfist said, his fatherly voice filled with concern and conviction all at once.

I cast Lightning Strike with a thought and kicked off his blade. It did next to nothing, despite having infused a small bit of essence into it, his cape taking care of the magical damage. The strike shot more dust into the air, and he was a silhouette once more.

All the dust and debris still in the air around Ironfist, suddenly blew away as the very ground cracked around him. Energy, a grey color, perfused his body as he began to yell. It was like his entire body was hardening and becoming Iron. He began to step forward again, each step leaving an indent in the hard ground.

He moved slow and plodding, but before he made it more than a step or two, he lifted his hand in a throwing motion and suddenly a section of earth behind him lifted up and came flying in my direction. A great shadow followed below, and I saw that there was little chance I'd be able to dodge in time.

I set my sword up and readied myself for a significant Stamina drain. Using the combination of Power Strike, Swift Strike, Force Wave, and releasing my Light Blade, I waited until the very last second that I thought it could possibly work. My attack released, the Stamina drain enough that I felt my knees buckle a little, but I stayed standing through it all.

Slicing through the air, dirt, dust, and rocks smashed all around me as the chunk of earth rained down. But I'd done it, my attack had cut a big enough line that I hadn't been buried. Although I wasn't exactly free to move around much, so I took a second to catch my breath then launched myself upward until I stood atop the biggest piles of newly churned dirt and rocks.

"That was impressive," I called out to a grinning Iron-fist. "But it is going to take more than a little dirt to take me out."

That was when the ground around me opened up and I fell into the earth. It pressed hard all around me, suffocating and terrible in its completeness. With powers like these why only use them when whatever his first power had failed him? I hadn't even figured out exactly what his first ability was, going fast and then really slow? What did it matter. My mind raced, looking for options.

I finally came up with an answer with Mana Shell, attempting to form it around me, I failed several times before I got it right. I started with a thin shell just outside my skin and pumping mana into it I was able to expand it outward, while thickening the walls to hold back the dirt. Several cracks appeared, but I found if I focused, I could add more mana before the destruction became too much and repair it.

Now that I was able to breathe and move around a small amount, I needed to figure out how I was going to unbury myself. Sure, I could do it the slow and boring way, but another idea came to me, and I smiled to myself as I let my Mana Shell shrink around my form. I practiced expanding it as quickly as I could, having to take a break and downing a mana potion, before trying what I planned. The quartermaster had seen to it that all *Awakened* that were mana users took five each, same with health potions, and though I thought it a silly expense at the time, I was thanking him now.

Getting ready to expand my Mana Shell as large as I could, I infused essence into it and saw it begin to spark. Then when I was ready, I poured mana and essence into it, exploding the dirt out in all directions in one swift expansion. Sunlight greeted me from the darkened hole I'd been stuck in, and I breathed a sigh of relief as I was free once more.

"Impressive," he said, walking towards me slow and plodding. His whole form had a kind of greyness to it and his skin, where I could see it, had a sheen like polished metal.

I used Stamina Surge, chugged a mana potion, and summoned my blade back to my hand from the ground where it had fallen. It was time I got some strikes in if I were going to end this fight. As I charged in with Speed Burst, I noticed that a single part of him remained in color and unaffected by whatever ability he was currently using, his brown cape.

Every time I'd used mana-based attacks on him, his cloak had taken the brunt of the attack and released it. Perhaps he wore the cloak because of an inherent weakness to magic based attacks? It was the best bet I had going forward, so I set my sights on a new target.

His movements remained slow as I came in with my sword, striking his chest. The blow ran across his armored form without so much as a scratch, but I used my momentum to take me around the now sluggish Ironfist. I slashed for his cape, infusing essence into a Power Strike. He must have guessed what I was doing, because suddenly his color returned, and he moved like Lightning.

A punch to my exposed face sent an awful crack through my jaw and sent me flying. I wasn't sure but I could have sworn that my blade cut fabric before I was struck. As I rolled to a stop, twisting back to my feet in an awesome display of dexterity and agility, I thrust out my hand to cast Lightning Strike. The spell answered my call, being infused with Essence it rumbled louder than normal before striking out.

Blue lightning, sparking and dangerous, slammed into Ironfist as he charged me, his speed no match for the mechanics of my instant cast spell. It was hard to miss when moving something as fast as light itself, but my hope for a quick victory was shattered when my spell struck, and he kept coming. Sparks flying out from behind him in a wilder manner than before, his cape had been cut, but not severely enough to deplete down its durability and ability to do its job.

I took a defensive stance, not ready for the speed in which my opponent was approaching. Lucky for me, depending on how you look at it, the moment he came into view of me he went gray and slow. My sword strikes hitting every exposed spot I could see but finding no purchase on him. He slammed into me with his sword, slower than before, but with a lumbering strength that caused me to abandon my parry and twirl out of the attack's path. It was like it wouldn't stop, no matter the strength I put against it.

"You are a powerful foe," I said, already beginning to pant. My strikes continued, but over and over I saw how useless they were against him while he was like this. Even if he hadn't used this ability, I began to worry my strikes weren't enough to penetrate his powerful armor. Doubt trickled into my mind, and I began to realize that perhaps the level gap between us truly was too great, despite the extra attributes I'd put in and my ability to infuse essence.

His abilities, abilities with such powerful results that I did not have access to, were proving to be too great a challenge. As if he wished to push this point further, his color shifted as I went for another strike on his cloak and suddenly, I hurt all over. He'd moved so fast that I hadn't even seen him this time, but I'd been cut deep on my cheek, and bruised several places on my chest. His blows staggered me back a few feet, but I managed to stay standing.

"I am truly impressed," Ironfist said, his color remaining normal. I couldn't tell if it were wishful thinking or not, but it sounded like he was panting a bit. Perhaps this battle wasn't over with yet, if he could be tired out, then he could be defeated.

My Speed Burst came off cooldown and I shot forward under its effects. I used an Instant cast I hadn't used for some time, hoping it would give me the opening I required. My Light spell flashed as a globe of light appeared just behind him. He reacted turning and cutting at the light, perhaps thinking it was some attack I'd saved. I smirked at the clever use of Light and slashed a Swift Strike and Light Blade combo, right at the tattered edge where my last strike had hit his cape.

With a satisfying sound of fabric being cut free, a sizable section fell to the ground and a moment later I was struck. First a fist to the chest, then a blade across my neck that cut deep and would have likely taken my head off if he hadn't pulled his strike. Even so, I clasped my hands to my neck as I flew through the air, desperately casting Restoring Light. I barely got the cast off as I hit the ground hard. Before I could gain my bearing, rocks the size of my fists smashed into me, over and over again keeping me from doing much more than curl into a ball as I waited for my ability to speak to return.

The moment I felt the blood stop pouring from my throat I cast Mana Shell, thrusting a heavy chunk of mana and essence into it as fast as my pathways would allow. Moving mana so quickly felt like my blood turned to fire, but I clenched my teeth against the pain. Each rock was taking a decent chunk from my health, and I was getting dangerously low at only 655 health left. As soon as my barrier was up, I worked on healing myself, first taking a health potion and drinking it, then casting Mending Touch. The healing potion spiked me up an impressive 250 health, while my heal hit me with an additional 300 as well as slowly healing another 300 over the next 15 seconds.

I didn't have time for anymore healing, as my barrier vibrated and cracked against a flurry of blows from Iron-fist. It lasted a second longer than I'd have thought against his might, perhaps the essence adding more strength to it than I previously thought possible. But no matter, I had already begun a new spell and I'd be ready for him. My Fireball spell, easily my most overpowered and dangerous spell, charged with mana and essence.

What made Fireball so potent was how it worked, taking in as much mana as you could give it. What made it so deadly when I used it, was my infusion of essence increasing the destructive power several times. This was likely to hurt me just as bad as it would hurt Ironfist, but I had to try something now that I'd negated his ability to turn away magical strikes.

My barrier shattered just as I finished making a Fireball, ready to end this fight. Ironfist was in a rage, something had really set him off, with incredible speed he swung his sword at me, but then at the very last moment he noticed my Fireball. It hit him just as he went gray all over and I activated Speed Burst, kicking off the ground and away as the Fireball detonated in his face. I hit some upturned dirt from his big earth attack and rolled over it, casting another Mana Barrier and at the same time sending essence and mana. I made sure to keep a line to the spell, ready to feed it more mana as needed to keep myself alive.

With an explosion big enough to level my family home, my barrier simply shattered upon impact with the blast wave and I dug down low against the scorched earth, casting Lesser Heal on myself as my skin began to burn all over and my armor turned black from the heat. Mentally I checked and saw my armor had been taken to roughly twenty-five percent of its durability. I'd dropped my sword but knew that it would be safe because of our bond.

Summoning the blade to my hand, it hurt to press my fingers around the grip, my skin skill struggling to heal. I'd managed to stay alive, but I was hurt bad. The cooldown came up on my previous Mending Touch and I let it wash over me, followed by a Restoring Light. Every part of me wished for a proper strong heal from either Zander or Alayna, but I did as best as I could, remembering what I'd learned from the Healers Legion.

I focused not just on casting the spell, but what I wanted it to do and pictured the ruined flesh becoming whole again. It worked, my heals knitting my flesh back together much faster than if I just cast the spell and forgot about it. However, it took focus, and a sudden yell of frustration broke that focus.

"You are insane!" The voice screamed, it sounded scratchy and raw. I looked up to see a blackened figure standing amid a crater on scorched earth.

Ironfist had survived and he was standing!

"How are you still standing?" I asked, slowly making my way over the small ridge of dirt I'd hid behind. It had likely saved my life, keeping my precious few health points above zero.

"With great difficulty, I assure you," he said, then closing his eyes I saw his aura flare as he began to turn gray again. But something happened this time that hadn't happened before, it flickered and went out just as it started, returning him to normal color.

He fell to a knee gasping for breath, his sword clattering onto the ground beside him. It wasn't good form, but I had to be sure. I cast Lightning Strike, not bothering to infuse it. The spell struck him on the back with enough force to flatten him the rest of the way. He was still breathing but he had to be close to death at this point.

As I approached, he rolled to his back, slipping his helmet off. His face was a ruined mess of burns so bad that his ears had all but melted and his hair, despite being under a cover, had all burnt away. His lips trembled as I approached but he didn't beg for mercy, instead, I saw a glint of defiance in his eyes. Suddenly I dodged to the side as rocks the size of my head came whirling through the air at me. They weren't nearly as fast as they'd been in the past few times he used the ability, so it wasn't a great challenge to dodge them.

A total of eight hunks of earth passed me before even that was too much for him. His breathing became ragged as I came and kneeled by his head, my blade ready to end him.

"You are so strong," I said, panting as my own health slowly ticked upward. "I feel like you could have matched yourself against an entire legion and likely come out ahead." I meant my words, but I didn't know why I wasted them with a soon to be dead man. He had been easily the most powerful opponent I'd faced and I'd found a way to beat him. What did that make me? Someone half his level who had the power of far greater opponents.

If it had been anyone else, Fred or Fran for instance,

they'd be dead long ago. Fred unable to counter his anti-magic cape, and Fran unable to do damage to a foe that could somehow harden himself against harm, while also being able to increase his speed at ridiculous rates. But I was an Arcane Knight. A Defender of the Balance. Words I had spoken so many months ago repeated in my head.

I'll protect the weak, be a shield against the darkness, when I am needed, I will answer the call.

But I'd won, right? Did I need to take this man's life as well? A powerful *Awakened* warrior that might aid in the battles to come, assuming this petty House War ended. I'd protected my soldiers. I'd been a shield against the death that would have surely fallen upon us if we'd battled this mighty army. I did as was needed; I answered the call.

Lifting my sword up over my head I prepared to strike downward. I locked eyes with Ironfist and saw that he'd resigned himself with his fate. It was plain to see that he expected death. He spoke what might be his final words then.

"Honor the results of this duel, allow my men to go free," he said. His words were like iron, he spoke through the pain and damage of his throat to deliver a final plea for his men. This was a man of honor, of power, and a man worthy of respect.

My blade came down, swift and deadly, burying itself into the dirt beside Ironfist's head. I released the grip and offered a hand to the fallen warrior. I could see relief wash over him and he took my outstretched hand.

"You'll withdraw then?" I asked, knowing he'd hold to his promise, but wanting to hear it regardless.

"I'll withdraw and do one better," Ironfist said, I could see his skin slowly healing with his natural *Awakened* recovery. It was slow but eventually he'd look mostly normal. "I'll make it a point to not accept any engagements against you. A few of those Fireballs and my army would be a flaming wreck. I don't know how you survive your own abilities or how you do what you do at such a low level, but if you ever want to run a dungeon or get some training by an old sword like me, you look me up after this War. Hell, any chance you'd consider switching sides, you might be the tilting point of this war. House Blalor is doing much better than House Variyn is, even with the King's support."

I let him talk, his voice sounding better as he did so, but I just nodded without acknowledging the offers. He knew that I wouldn't switch, and though I might take him up on his offer of help in the future, now wasn't the time for that.

"We will see," I said, turning and putting my back to him. A part of me screamed that it was foolish to expose myself, but I'd battled with this man and knew him to be a man of honor. As I suspected, he did not strike out and when I checked over my shoulder as Ares arrived, I saw that he was walking back towards his army, favoring his right leg.

I had done it. I'd found a way to keep my men safe and prevent countless deaths. If I could beat this Ironfist in single combat, surely, I'd be able to challenge others and save more lives? I could feel the winds of change settling around me and I could almost let myself feel happy, almost.

The next three months passed in a blur of activity. Alayna still hadn't surfaced and now the Healers Legion said she'd been called off to other duties and another high-level healer was set over the legion. I'd been doing far more dungeon runs and monster killing, pushing myself hard to gather essence required to level up in hopes of unlocking new powerful spells and skills. It was during this period of hard work that I made it to level 30.

It triggered an event that really turned the tide in my battles and duels I had against other *Awakened*. Having all my attributes, including my Core over my second threshold, gave me an awareness of my body, mind, and soul that was unprecedented. No longer did I feel any sluggish response of a single part of my body of general functions, I was whole, and I couldn't imagine what the next threshold would bring. That was far in the future I knew, but it would mean a drastic improvement that I could hardly imagine.

Very few the last month would accept my challenge for duels to settle the battle, likely because I'd won several dozen using the tactic. A few times, the enemy commander attacked anyways, but a few well-placed Fireballs in front of their army reminded them of the power I could bring to bear, and they left. In fact, we'd only had another two battles in the last three months that got bloody, but even then, the losses weren't as big as the first terrible time.

I'd stayed aloof from my men but kept the trainings going. They progressed wonderfully and the longer we fought the more powerful they got with increased proxy levels and better perks. I'd received more commendations, handed out some of my own, and generally excelled as a Commander. Life had fallen into a rhythm and despite rarely seeing my friends, Emory and Ismene, I knew they were leveling at a rate they found acceptable. Not quite as fast as me, the arm band and my Paragon Core Affinity meaning few, if anyone, leveled as fast as me. Life was different now that I had other options to war. Though few had taken advantage lately of me dueling them, I found shows of strength like an infused Fireball in front of their lines, proved to be just as effective.

Fred and Fran had been gone for nearly a month, a dungeon giving them a quest, that because of my responsibilities I couldn't attend. They'd grown a good bit, getting levels, new abilities and more. I'd increase nearly all my abilities to tier 2, but still hadn't decided on any new abilities, holding out for something spectacular. Time passed and battles were won, but still my mood didn't improve.

CHAPTER 36
FLIGHT BARGES

"What do you mean they are recalling all forces, but a few of our weaker legions?" I asked, Gadwell folded his arms and gave him his signature 'shut up so I can tell you' look. I did as his expression suggested and shut my mouth to hear what he had to say.

"They've finally finished the Flight Barges and we are going to end this War in a fortnight," Gadwell said, his smile broad and knowing.

I sat down in my chair, pulling a book out from under me and setting it aside. My tent had begun to be pretty messy, as the front line had shifted very little and whole legions were being sent out further and further as we won key battles or lost key keeps to House Blalor. I'd emptied a number of books from my Arcane Asylum as I became cozier in my own tent and assured of its protection. Six Runeforged watched guard at all times around my tent, three converted and three unconverted, including Ignis who'd gotten much better at controlling Fire.

I didn't know how to feel about the news I'd just heard, and I opened my mouth several times to speak before I finally managed words.

"Why did it take so long?" I asked, thinking about how many long months had passed since the conflict began. Surely it would have made more tactical sense to not start the conflict until your means of victory was ready.

"The barges have been operational for months now, but Lord Variyn was working on another tool of war that he assured Busard would be worth the wait, I've only just been briefed but I can't imagine what terrible instrument of war he's procured," Gadwell said, shaking his head.

For months? This news hit me even harder than I expected, and if I hadn't been sitting down already, I would have. My mind went over the more recent names I'd memorized, those lost in the last three months. I knew each name, but I couldn't put an exact number on them, hundreds at least.

My resolve firmed and I took the news for what it was. "Good," I said, nodding my head as my thoughts gathered. "Let's end this conflict and send these soldiers home. When do we report for duty?"

Gadwell held a hand up. "We've got a few steps first. Lord Variyn will address the troops and right after they'll march onto the barges, assuring no spies have a head start on us. Everyone in the camps will be required to come, we won't leave any behind, and those legions we've left in the field will not hear of this news until the key capture of several keeps has occurred."

"Fine, fine," I said, already thinking about what would be required to break camp and get my men ready.

"First, you come with me and let's get the official debriefing over. Act surprised, I wasn't meant to be telling you any of this," Gadwell said, laughing.

I followed along until we reached Busard's tent, and I was surprised to see him sitting to the right of his normal spot at the head of the table that was brought in for such meetings. At the head of the table was Lord Variyn, but he looked older than I remembered, or at least my perception of him had changed. He had stress lines around his eyes and a forehead filled with worry lines. But on his face, he held a look of proud confidence as he addressed a nearby lord's questions. Lord Variyn saw me and motioned to a chair that a lord was already sitting in, to his left.

"Sit here, Lord Miles," Lord Variyn said, the lord sitting there looked put out, his eyes shooting a glare in my direction, but he moved regardless.

I took his spot, Gadwell sitting a few seats down, and I smiled kindly to Lord Variyn despite the growing pit in my stomach whenever I thought of him. He wore armor, shining and polished silver and gold. His beard and hair had been recently trimmed and everything about him spoke of his last six months not being filled with war, like the rest of us. My armor had been mended several times, but the camp armorers were unable to work the magic that

Gilfoy's could, so my armor was down several dozen Durability points and looked nice, but well worn.

"I've received many reports of your victories on the field of battle and Busard speaks highly of you now. That is a rare thing indeed," Lord Variyn said, shooting a look to Busard who didn't appear to notice.

"My soldiers have done well," I said, smiling politely.

"Soldiers do not win these battles, their commanders do," Lord Variyn said, as if to censure me.

I looked at him hard and tried to imagine how he'd fair in a duel. I didn't fool myself that I might have a chance against him, no matter his level he was a powerful healer and could likely heal himself faster than any damage I could dish out. Nothing short of a surprise death blow, like the one that killed his brother, would be effective, and I didn't have that kind of burst power short of my Fireball. There was no doubt in my mind he'd just put a shield up that would negate any swift killing damage.

"As you say, Lord Variyn," I said, inclining my head respectively.

"You've learned some decorum as well. I think I like this new Caldor Miles. My daughter sends her regards, by the way. She's been caught up in projects and I've set her to rest for a while and recover her strength," Lord Variyn said, his keen eyes watching me for any emotional reaction.

The only hint that I gave was surprise and confusion, as I genuinely was both of those. What projects had she been working on? The last I'd heard, she was going to the elves to share...oh no. Had he found out about her trying to share the information regarding flight and put her under some kind of house arrest, keeping her from joining the front?

"I've missed her greatly, but my duties as a commander have kept me busy," I said, quickly coming up with the best response I could to deflect his attention.

"Yes, being a commander is dangerous and busy work, however I'm sure you find time for your friends. I've heard you have gathered a sizable force of *Awakened* around you, friends from your adventures?" Lord Variyn asked, sipping at his wine.

A drink was set in front of me, along with drinks for the rest of the table. I watched, waiting until someone else had drank theirs before taking a sip of mine, never could be too careful. Of course, it occurred to me that if someone wanted me to be poisoned, they could have easily only put it in my drink, but I could only do so much without looking paranoid.

"Most come from Blackridge Keep," I said. "In fact, it would appear goblins, orcs, trolls, and even dwarves have a higher chance to become *Awakened,* so it swelled our ranks a good bit. Something to do with how warlike they are and normal members of their race killing monsters in large parties," I watched Lord Variyn's expression for any reaction and when I didn't get one, I continued. "Supplies have not been a problem and I'm thankful for their help."

"Yes, the Southlanders are turning out to be quite the boon to us," Lord Variyn said, nodding.

What did he mean, us? Had he taken advantage of a

population of them in some way as well or did he mean Blackridge Keep and my soldiers? I decided to ask as tactfully as I could manage.

"Yes, as soldiers they are very brave and useful," I said, my eyes flicking from his to Busard's, who was not listening in. "Have you encountered more Southerners in House Variyn in recent months?" I knew the tribe I'd encountered with Creed had made their way to Blackridge Keep, because they'd sent soldiers to join the battle some months ago, so who else could he have encountered?

"Oh, very often," Lord Variyn said, sipping at his wine. "You see, we've discovered portals that lead to underground caverns way below the ground. A tribe of goblins led one of my enforcers to its location and we've since ended the incursions into our land, but I am very sure that the rest of the Houses are open to such invasions, should they not act as I have."

So, he found the old roads they spoke of and closed some? I wondered what it'd take to get him to tell me where they were so I could study them. If there was fixed portal magic, then that would be worth more than just keeping a few goblins out of the area. Certainly, he could see the benefits of such a useful magic.

Before I could speak again, he continued. "I wanted to thank you specifically Caldor, some of the research you and your gnome friends are doing has come in quite handy in recent months. When mixed with research Alayna has done, you will find I have many great surprises to reveal in the coming weeks."

"Like what?" I asked, downing the remainder of my wine and holding my glass up to signal to the servant to fill it. I was surprised when a familiar face, wearing servant clothes, stepped up beside me and poured my wine. It was Mah'kus.

I turned in my chair ready to stand in surprise, but he gave me a look that seemed to say, not now, so I let him fill my glass and turned my attention back to Lord Variyn. He was staring at Mah'kus with a confused look on his face.

"More wine?" Mah'kus asked, smirking.

Lord Variyn nodded, but said nothing, tilting his head to the side as he looked at the god-like man who seemed to be able to appear and disappear at will. Finally, Lord Variyn spoke, but it was with a voice and tone bereft of the confidence and pride that normally perfused his voice.

"I know you but from where?" Lord Variyn asked.

Mah'kus continued on smirking and answered him. "You are mistaken, Ceon. Enjoy your wine." Then he turned and disappeared between two servants. Lord Variyn actually stood and held his hand out as if he were pointing at something but said nothing, and a moment later sat awkwardly, his eyes on the wine, which he poured out onto the floor beside him.

What interaction between Mah'kus had Lord Ceon Variyn had that left him so shaken by the man's appearance? I knew well enough that he could bring dreams of marvelous and frightening things to you, but I never felt as if my life was in danger from him. I sipped at my wine, confident that it wasn't poisoned. Lord Variyn regarded me as I did and cleared his throat before calling a servant over to fill his glass, this time Mah'kus wasn't the one to answer, nor did I see him walking among the other servants anymore.

"My research, Lord? You said it had helped you and I was wondering in what way?" I asked, not wanting to let the subject die just yet.

"Oh that, no point worrying about that, in time I hope to reveal its use to the entire Kingdom, but not yet. Suffice it to say, we have made great leaps in our knowledge and a good measure is thanks to you. I am considering giving you a more suitable land holding and passing Blackridge to a lesser vassal than you are proving to be," Lord Variyn said, his shaken demeanor shifting back to the one of confidence and pride.

"I don't want more land, I am happy with Blackridge Keep and what I've been able to do there," I said quickly. I didn't want to sound desperate, but I wasn't about to give up on the land I'd worked so hard to make a place worth living.

"Even if I were to give you control over the keep that rules over your hometown, Creeshaw?" Lord Variyn asked, raising an eyebrow.

"Even so," I said, without hesitation.

"Very well," Lord Variyn said, then clearing his throat he spoke to the whole table. "It is time we begin, please quiet yourselves."

The room fell silent, and Lord Variyn began to drone on about responsibility, pride of House Variyn, and all manner of useless speech that said nothing, but used many words. The point of it accumulating up to his announcement of the flight barges and the immediate deployment of all legions into the back line of House Blalor. He spoke of new methods of keep penetration and how it has been a greatly guarded secret.

I almost wanted to laugh at that, as not a single Lord seemed surprised by the news and had likely heard whispers, if not recently, then several months prior. It made me wonder how prepared House Blalor would be for us if it wasn't as big of a secret as Lord Variyn hoped? Would they have put measures together to deal with flying barges? What could they do, besides using *Awakened* to try and burn them out of the sky? I hadn't seen them yet, but I assumed they'd be bulky wooden things that were slow and lumbering in their movements.

CHAPTER 37
ATTACK FROM ABOVE

The talks ended with Lord Variyn inviting us to gather our troops and prepare to depart while the barges landed. I followed the other lords out, keeping my eyes up to the clouds, looking for any sign of the barges. It wasn't until my troops' tents were all but cleared that a blackened mass caught my eye, and I watched one, then two, then a dozen and more massive platforms soar from above the clouds to the ground. They moved incredibly fast, and the entire constructions were painted black, perhaps to hide our approach at night.

What was more interesting as I focused on them and saw details with my enhanced vision, I realized that they were made of metal and not wood at all, or at least from the bottom. However, they weren't straight rectangular barges like those that ran on a river, instead, they were more square in shape and had dozens of circles cut into them. I couldn't imagine what for yet, but I didn't see any sign of what gave them flight and I wondered how such an achievement was being done.

"I told you I saw something on the way in," Fred said, walking up beside me and shooting a look at Fran who appeared on my other side.

"How was I to believe," Fran said, pausing to huff out a breath of air, "that you'd actually seen flying black squares? You know how weird that sounds, right?"

"You're back!" I said, my excitement at seeing my friends a welcome wash of relief.

"We accomplished a quest and made friends," Fred said matter-of-factly.

"So, are you finally going to tell me the details of the mysterious quest you both got?" I asked, having been in the dungeon when they'd gotten it, well Fred had gotten it and shared it with Fran, but claimed he couldn't share it with me since I wouldn't be going. That it was very important but also meant to be kept secret.

"I suppose," Fran said, shrugging. "No point in worrying now as that pesky Chaos Knight can't stop us anymore."

This caught my attention, and I turned fully on Fran, grabbing her shoulders. "You fought with a Chaos Knight?" I asked, flabbergasted.

"More like we ran from one," Fred said, nodding with a large smile on his face.

"It barely got close to us," Fran said, sighing. "Anyways," she looked around to make sure we were out of earshot of anyone. "I think you'll want to hear about this. We were sent on a quest to help heal the Ley lines. We found an old crystal in an abandoned ruins and fought off golems built by the Ordu but were damaged over time. Then we had to go on a journey deep into these caverns connected by portals and drop the crystal down into an infected area of the Ley lines. It gave us a massive essence boost when we finished the quest, I wish you'd been able to come."

"Me too," I said, and I meant it. They'd been directed by the dungeon to do the exact kind of thing I should be doing. I knew, or at least guessed, that what they'd done had only slowed the spread of corruption, otherwise why was my quest still active?

"I can answer that," a familiar voice said that I recognized the moment I looked at him.

"Mah'kus," I said, giving him a surprised look while Fred and Fran both jumped in surprise as none of us had sensed his approach. He wore the same servant's outfit, black and white neat pants and shirt, with a tight black vest around his middle.

"Good job on your little adventure," Mah'kus said, looking toward Fred then to Fran. "And don't worry about the hermit, he got out in one piece."

"How'd you know about that?" Fran asked, stepping forward and looking suddenly hostile.

"Relax, Fran," I said, putting a hand back on her

shoulder. "He's a friend, if a bit of a weird one. What are you doing here?"

"I've come to witness the start of the end, after today, there is no turning back," Mah'kus said, frowning. "You will have to unite them, against the force that travels here even now. Just remember when the time is right, choose to unite and not break asunder. I do not envy the path you must follow, but it is necessary, so hold fast and remember who you are, Caldor Miles."

I looked away for a moment as several more of the barges began to land, just plopping right into the dirt and muck that used to be a clear and grassy valley. When I turned back, he was gone, and Fred's eyes were as wide as I'd ever seen them.

"Did anyone else see that?" Fred asked, his voice shaking a bit.

"No, I looked away at the barges," I said. Fran said she'd also looked away.

"He stepped through a tear in the air and inside of it I saw...well I don't know what I saw but my head hurts now," Fred said, putting his hand to his forehead. "I'm going to go sit on our hippogryphs while we wait."

"Your what?" I asked, turning to see two hippogryphs, one totally black and the other completely white, standing some ten feet away. They had the bodies of horses with the top half covered in feathers and a bird head not unlike Ares, but instead of claws on all feet, they had horse hooves in the back and bird talons in the front. Their faces were also more elongated, like a horse's, with the thick neck of a war horse. Each of them had a mane of feathers down their head and connecting to the wings.

"How did you?" I began to ask, and Fran answered cutting me off.

"We rescued them in the ruins, and they bonded with us," Fran said, a huge smile on her face. I'm sure she'd been dying to show off the fact they'd both gotten flying mounts.

"That's incredible, what'd you name them?" I asked, walking over cautiously, remembering that they could be skittish if they felt threatened.

The white one flicked its talons against the dirt and kicked up mud. "Easy girl," Fred said, grabbing hold of her reins. "Her name is Hip, and he is named Griff."

"Hip and Griff, like hippogryphs? You two are impossible," I said, chuckling.

"I thought it was a fun idea, better than Fred's idea," Fran said, shooting him a look.

"What'd he suggest?" I asked, figuring it would be some academic reference.

"Biscuit and Gravy, like his favorite meal," Fran said, shaking her head.

I looked at Fred, who still looked wobbly on his feet, but he merely shrugged. Mentally reaching out, I called Ares from where she was hunting. She informed me in no simple terms that she was eating, but I urged her to hurry as I had a surprise. This piqued her interest and within ten minutes she landed before me, just as troops began to be ushered onto the platforms, one company at a time.

At first, I felt feelings of hostility from Ares towards the two new flying mounts, but after a little back and forth she eased and decided to ignore them. She stood right in front of Griff and went low, so I could easily mount. I looked at Griff and Hip, but I didn't see the same fierce intelligence as I sensed with Ares and wondered if Fred and Fran shared a mental bond with their mounts but didn't ask.

"Looks like we are up," I said. My battalions, by the commands of my Knights and Squires, were marching forward toward one of the blackened barges.

The top surface was made of dark oiled wood planks; the closer we got the more details I could make out. There was a rail built on the sides, but not by the circle openings spread over the surface. I saw large spools of rope by them and a long series of chains that seemed to be bolted into the ground through circular rings set into the floor. As troops got into place, there were attendants on the barges already that showed them how to attach a length of short rope, attached to the chain, around their waist. Some sort of harness to keep from falling perhaps?

What I didn't see was how the heck they were flying these contraptions. It wasn't until I noticed a few attendants appear in the back from a lower deck that I realized there must be an internal section, but the troops were just being placed atop the barge. I saw that Busard, Lord

Variyn, and the rest of the lords had gathered, so I bid Fred and Fran farewell for now, walking over.

"You will not be permitted to bond the Pegasus, however, they can be used for the duration of the conflict," Busard was saying loud enough that all within earshot could easily hear. When he saw me riding over, he added, "Though I am aware that a select few will not have need of the King's mounts, you should still follow the same procedures and stay on the barge with your prospective Legions."

That was when I noticed the horses, they all had wings, so they were Pegasus, not horses after all. Busard had the only one that wasn't white, instead being a striking black that shone beautifully and had a mane of tightly braided hair. Their shoulders and backs were extra muscular, likely from the need to lift themselves and a passenger into the air, but it made for a fearsome looking bunch of mounts.

Of course, none of them held a candle to Ares and her majestic qualities. I made sure she felt that thought strongly and she let out a screech of acknowledgement that almost sounded like a challenge. Several of the Pegasus backed away, one even opened its wings and startled his mount. Busard's mount didn't so much as move, instead, looking at Ares with an intelligence that surprised me for a Pegasus. I'd heard they were smart creatures, but this one seemed to understand Ares's challenge and didn't much agree with it.

"There is no time for reluctance," Lord Variyn said, he

held a war mace that glittered silver and gold like his armor. "Three barges will assault each of the keeps Busard outlined. Your job is to get your men down those ropes and kill the occupying forces. This will enable us to take their ten most key keep locations behind enemy lines. With the supply of Pegasus provided by the King we will keep our supply lines fresh. This conflict will be over in a fortnight!"

The lords cheered in unison, but I kept my silence, waiting for further instructions. They never came, but Gadwell filled me in on the way. We were being sent to a keep to invade from above. Our arrival was timed perfectly with nightfall, and we will be traveling under the lowest layer of clouds. Apparently, they tested how high the barges could go before breathing became difficult and found that while some clouds are higher, most were around the level of being able to breathe.

So, standing atop Ares I waited while the barge slowly lifted off the ground and we floated towards battle. Once we'd gained enough height, our speed increased and a general murmur came over the soldiers, but everyone remained calm. Our cavalry was all at the very end, their horses tied down and their riders standing beside them to help calm them. I didn't know how useful horses would be if they meant for us to literally take ropes down to the enemy from above, but I imagined they'd land afterwards to release some ground troops.

An attendant came by and told me they'd be going through the troops, issuing orders so they knew when to start going down. She asked if she had my permission to proceed, which I found odd, but gave it to her all the same.

Night fell, and soon I saw the tiny dots of light that indicated the presence of a keep below us. Three other barges had stayed close to us and together we'd be attacking the keep. It was one of the bigger ones, with a good-sized town around it, also with a gate. From what I had been told, the plan was to lower a legion into the town, the keep, and just outside. The inner force would fight to open the gate and allow more troops in, while the keep force would be pitted against the keep's garrison.

Our legion had been given the bloody task of going against the mass of troops that likely waited for us in the garrison, but Gadwell seemed unworried.

"They are operating with skeleton crews, all available men have gone to the front, a place far from here now," Gadwell said, gesturing out to the surrounding sky. "It'll be up to us and a few of those fucking useless *Awakened* teams you've gathered, filled with goblins and the like. I imagine that a few *Awakened* hold this keep currently."

"I've only brought two teams, one of which is made up of bandits and the other orcs, the rest were off rotation, so I sent them back to Blackridge Keep," I said, shrugging. "But I'm sure the four of us will be more than a match for anything we encounter." I gestured over to Fred and Fran atop their mounts and Gadwell chuckled.

"Aye, she is a fine little fighter that Fran of yours, though her brother is a bit odd. If not for his fiery magics he'd be all but useless," Gadwell said, holding tight to his Pegasus as the barge shook and we began to descend.

"Here we go," I said, patting Ares and readying her for battle. She needed no prompting though and hunched down ready to launch us upward on my command.

The barge moved fast, my stomach lurching as the descent increased in speed and suddenly slowed, giving me another lurching feeling. More than one person could be heard retching their lunch all over the place. Shouts rung out from atop the barge as suddenly we got too close to one of the others and a force pushed us violently to the side. Several men screamed, but one louder than the others as his harness broke and he tumbled through one of the holes next to him.

Without giving the command Ares acted on my instincts and we launched into the air and over the edge. I could see him, a speck in the night, and Ares could make him out even better. Swooping into a deadly fast dive I lurched in the saddle as we approached him. It was going to be close and if he didn't stop flailing, she might not be able to scoop him up.

I sent her a message to grab as best she could, but not worry about hurting him, as I could heal the damage. She took my suggestion and claws out grabbed hold of the falling soldier. He screamed and began to swing at Ares.

"Easy soldier, we got you, stay alive and be still!" I screamed the words, but they were lost in the wind. However, we managed to make it to a high tower balcony where we dropped him, and she landed. I hit him with a heal, his armor had been dented and ripped. As soon as the heal hit him he began to scream again and suddenly falling wasn't our only problem.

Two guards opened a door not far off, light poured out and they pulled weapons. They wore expressions of utter confusion, but looked well trained judging by their stances, perhaps elite guards? One of them struck forward, looking to impale the wounded soldier, but I activated Swift Strike and parried the attack, before striking back with my own thrust. He yelled in pain as I cut his leather armor open across the stomach, his insides becoming his outsides. The other guard turned and fled.

I didn't have time to waste chasing him down, so I finished another heal on the soldier and got him to climb onto Ares's back, before kicking off and joining the battle. Streams of long sturdy ropes were lowering troops into tower platforms, courtyards below, and even rooftops. I spotted a Pegasus and two Hippogryphs landing in the courtyard below, where several hundred troops began to form up.

Before landing I scanned the area for resistance. The troops in the most need of help appeared to be those set out on balconies and rooftops, guards were pouring from upper rooms to defend their keep. I decided the ground troops could wait, as I noticed at least one of my Knights down there giving orders, Raphael by the looks of it.

Bringing Ares low over a rooftop where three soldiers faced off against three of the keep's guards, with two more on the way from a ladder leading to the top of a balcony. I had her claw out at the two climbing, before smashing down behind the trio of guards. In one lithe motion I pulled myself free and let loose a Force Wave into their backs. I thought to just stun them, but they all went down hard, and my own soldiers jumped out of the way just in time to miss getting hit by the force I'd unleashed. Whoops.

I checked the guards, but they were dead, nearly sheered in half. Blood poured from the slight tilt of the roof, and I signaled for my men to get up so they could get onto solid ground. They followed my motions and soon I had them at my back as I got onto the balcony.

"Clear the rooms to the ground floor, don't kill unless you have to, we aren't here to purge the place," I said, feeling as if I needed to say as much when looking at these three, blood thirsty, young men. They weren't part of the groups from Blackridge Keep, I knew that much at least. Mercenaries most likely, but even they'd fallen into order after months of serving under me.

"Yes Commander," they said in unison, all three saluting and disappearing into the dimly lit room beyond. I let my sword dematerialize and summoned my bow from my ring inventory.

I had enough arrows stashed away for half an army, but only about fifty that weren't in containers to save space. I climbed back up on the roof, the cries of battle all around me, and I mounted Ares. We'd be more effective clearing out troops on the go. Between my bow and spells, I should be able to stay mounted as well, thus helping more troops in a shorter period of time.

"Keep it steady and swoop right by those four," I said, directing Ares to our next target. Over two dozen guards had marshaled against a small force of four, two orcs, a troll, and Cam from Creeshaw. How he'd ended up being side by side with the Southerners was anyone's guess, but he wouldn't survive the encounter without help.

The larger force was in no hurry to engage, they looked rather green with how they huddled together with weapons out instead of spreading wider. A bigger guard, with slightly finer armor, was calling out orders and the force began to move forward, he would be my first target. I let loose an arrow, but the wind took it and it hit the neck of a guard on the far left. The arrow left with such force that it shot completely through his neck instead of staying there, blood gushing from the now open wound.

Adjusting for the wind as we glided overhead, my next shot smashed against his chest, penetrating his breastplate and sticking fast. It was lower than I meant to hit, but still a damn good shot. My time training with this more powerful bow had been well spent. I trained with all the weapons I could, as Michael had taught me, but there was a relaxing quality to practicing with my bow. It reminded me of simpler times when I used weapons for hunting and not the killing of soldiers.

With their leader out of the way, the larger group had lost their confidence. Whether because they faced orcs and trolls or I was raining death down on them, over half of them started to run. I decided to help the others decide what they wanted to do, casting Lightning Strike Rank 1 down on them. My attack struck with deadly accuracy, throwing one unfortunate guard right off the edge.

It was amazing how little I needed to use my Rank 2 versions of my spells, and while it took focus to downgrade the casting to lower ones, it was worth it when I wanted to save Mana and Stamina. Now that I'd fully upgraded my abilities, spells and skills to Tier 2, and had just over 2,000 Mana and nearly that much Stamina, I found myself in an odd situation where my increased resource pools still emptied just as fast as when I had smaller amounts and Tier 1 abilities.

I refocused as my four soldiers charged into battle. Using Arcane Missile Rank 1, I spent 50 mana to take down another three just as my soldiers charged, evening the odds. As they engaged, spears moving in practiced thrusts, I realized I shouldn't have been so worried. Even with five against four, the advantage was wholly on the soldiers' side. Whether from higher proxy levels, time spent fighting over the last six months, or sheer dumb luck, I didn't know, but they took down those five in a matter of seconds.

Cam alone pierced the throat of one, spun into a parry and used a thrusting proxy skill I recognized as the power thrust, I'd ordered all the soldiers to choose. It punched right through the chest plate and came out the other side. He let the spear fall and pulled out an arming sword in one smooth motion, but it wasn't necessary, the battle was won for now. All the enemies either dead or fleeing.

Cam looked up and I raised a fist in salute to him, he answered with a fist across his chest, before retrieving his spear and inspecting it for damage. I looked away from my townmate as he continued inside the keep, and I scanned for other soldiers in trouble.

I was able to save or assist in some way another dozen groups before our troops had all gathered together or gone missing. Landing on the ground I saw a bloody Cam running alone from the inside of the keep towards the formation of troops in the courtyard. I swooped low and hit him with a Mending Touch just as he arrived, his larger gash on his forehead sealing.

"There's a group," he paused to breathe hard and tried to catch his breath, "of *Awakened* inside killing us all," Cam said, falling to a knee, exhausted from whatever fight he'd been in.

"Get this soldier with the wounded and keep them safe," I called out to a squire that had rushed up to my side. "Fred, Fran, Daniel, and," I struggled to remember the name of the orc *Awakened* that I saw standing about wearing shamanistic gear. He wasn't a newcomer, but he had a particularly long name, and, in my head, I'd gone to calling him Gak, but I knew how sensitive their pride was, so I just pointed until he saw me. "Come here! We are going to go clear out *Awakened* and save any soldiers we can."

"Righty-o boss man," Daniel said, sounding unusually

perky for some reason. Then as if to answer my questioning look, he leaned in and said, "I just got enough essence to hit level 17 which means I'll finally be able to get demon armor. You have really changed my life around, thank you." He clapped his hand against my arm, but I just gave him a head nod. Now wasn't the time for this shit, we had to go.

"Gakoranderonason reports for duty," Gak said, standing proudly with his head raised. He had leather armor made from the skin of Dire Bears, his fist covered in bear paws that I imagined would work as effective weapons, but I'd only seen him fight from a distance. I only knew what I'd read in reports, he was some type of shaman class that specialized in melee styles of fighting called an Enhancer.

"Let's get rolling before Fred leaves to find Kora," Fran said, rolling her eyes.

I hadn't noticed any of the Runeforged inside the keep yet and wondered where they'd gotten off to, as I saw none in the courtyard either.

"Where are they?" I asked, looking at Fred who wore a worried expression, though why I couldn't understand. Runeforged could fend for themselves several times over.

"They joined up to take a force to help break the gates. There is an inner gate into the keep and a gate in the town below," Fran said, wiping muck from her blade before sheathing her sword into its scabbard.

"We have an entire legion in the town, Kora should have stayed here to help clear guards," I said, shaking my head in frustration but unable to do anything about it now.

"You didn't see?" Fran asked, her eyes suddenly wide. "We lost a barge to ballista fire, it fell into the town, see look," Fran said pointing down at the fires burning in the town below. I'd noticed the fire and just figured it had to do with the townsfolk fighting back, but I'd been so focused I hadn't seen the black silent barge get taken out of the sky. How many soldiers had that Commander just lost or were most down already?

"We can worry later, let's clear this keep," I said, then turning to Raphael I yelled. "Clear the keep grounds and march into the town. Leave a token force here to guard the wounded and secure the area after its clear!"

She nodded that she'd heard me, and I ran towards the keep where Cam had exited, a path of blood making it easy to follow where the action would be. Behind me, Daniel began to chant and suddenly three little red demons ran alongside him, small things with long snouts, pointy ears, and thin bodies. I knew from experience that they packed a punch, each one throwing powerful Firebolts.

Gak had begun to chant as well, but it was a rhythmic sound that brought up feelings of nature and power. I felt like I could breathe deeper and run harder. Turning to him as the chanting ended, I nodded my appreciation for the buff. The hallways of the keep were wide, with ceilings twice my height that arched and connected to partially exposed fluted columns.

The blood led into a double doors that had been

closed and the sound of battle could faintly be heard on the other side. But as we approached and I put my hand on the door, it fell silent. I pushed it open, ready for anything. What I found made me want to wretch.

The room was a ballroom of some sort, the vaulted ceiling twice as high as the hallways and massive fluted columns supporting the load every twenty paces or so. It was decorated with banners and colorful murals, but I saw none of the beauty. Instead, my eyes ran across the two dozen soldiers, maybe more, that had been torn to pieces by a huge ugly dog thing. Except it wasn't a dog or even a wolf, it was a creature that I'd only read about in monster books and suddenly my mind latched onto its name. This was a Dire Hyena, a creature that was common in the vast plains of the lower elven lands.

Behind the blood-soaked creature was a white robed elf, sweat beading on his forehead, and his blonde hair tied up in a bun. His robes had been ripped, exposing his chest and a red mark that I knew meant he'd been healed recently. Beside him was a diminutive man who I recognized as a Gnome, probably a rogue by his gear. On the other side of the giant hyena was a human of middling years, his black hair with a single streak of white in it and wielding a staff that glowed with a blue arcane light.

Somehow our soldiers had happened upon most of an adventuring party, it seemed. What was the next move, I wondered, as we all stared each other down, neither side acting first. I could feel my anger growing over the loss of my soldiers, but another part of me tried to speak sense, that perhaps I could talk to this group, maybe even pay them to our side as they'd likely just been working for a sum of money for house Blalor. There was also the chance they'd just been staying in the area while running dungeons, I realized.

However, my choice was made for me when the Hyena growled suddenly, and Daniel's demons threw out a round of Firebolts at it. The room burst into combat, and it was time to act.

I hated to fight an elf, I was friends with most I'd met, but it made tactical sense to take out the healer first. So, I struck out with a Lightning Strike, it cracked down from above him and flattened him to the ground, leaving a nasty blackened mark on his exposed chest. Three Firebolts struck the fallen elf, and he stopped stirring completely. I became aware of loud chanting that abruptly cut off and each of the three demons took an Arcane Missile, or some similar spell, right to the face.

Gak had engaged the Hyena alongside Fran, between them they kept it at bay, scoring hits here and there as they weaved in battle. Gak's punches crackled with lightning and twice I saw him swipe his bear claws with an intense green energy that extended the claws into near sword-lengths, to dig deep into the snapping hyena.

Meanwhile, their gnome rogue had disappeared, and Daniel was throwing purple demon fire at the dark haired wizard, cursing him for killing his demons. The wizard had summoned fire into both his hands, both blocking by hitting away Daniel's fire and attacking by throwing small bolts of fire in between attacks. Fred was working on something big, but he paused every few seconds to wave a hand and push the other wizard's fire spells off target.

As I watched him build up his spell, I saw the tiniest shimmer of air around him and I reacted instantly, cutting out just behind Fred with a Force Wave combo-ed with my Light Blade spell. It hit a target, breaking his invisibility just as he was about to hamstring Fred.

Rushing forward with Speed Burst, I was upon him before he could recover, slashing downward. But in a poof of white smoke, he was gone again. I heard a chuckle behind me and whirled, but it was too late. A painful stab hit me right in the gut, almost as if it were ignoring my armor, and then he twisted the blade. With my left hand, I grabbed his arm, holding him in place, then activated Swift Strike and Power Strike, bringing my blade down on the little trickster.

I half expected him to get away or use another trick, but instead, my sword strike cut him wide from shoulder, straight through to his crotch. Blood went everywhere as he fell into two distinct pieces. More gore added to a room already soaked in the blood of my fallen soldiers. My rage abated a little, but the battle wasn't over.

A screeching roar that sounded more throaty than any beast I'd ever heard, filled the room as the hyena went wild. It had locked its gaze on me and now glowed with an orange aura. Ignoring the wounds given to it by Fran and Gak, it charged me. Its eyes blazed with hate, and I readied my sword. With my left hand I let loose a barrage of

Arcane Missiles, each one singeing flesh and nearly knocking the hyena off its course.

Flushing enough essence into my sword to reach its third tier of bonuses I cracked my neck to the side and stepped into a slash. Might jaws came down on me, but I moved faster, cutting right along its open mouth and extending its smile up towards its ear on one side. It screamed in pain, but I wasn't finished. Putting my left hand against an open wound I cast Firebolt, singing my hand, but sending a magical bolt of fire directly into the hyena.

It began to thrash about, but I kept at it, slashing and piercing it with every opportunity. Fran and Gak joined me, while Fred and Daniel finished off the dark-haired wizard. I saw flashes of fire and heard screams of mercy, but they quickly died out as whatever Fred had been working on finished its cast. Meanwhile, with a final slash to the neck, blood pouring out, the Dire Hyena began to shift and change.

A moment later a completely unwounded and furious elf stood before us, wearing green robes with vines and even twigs in some places on his armored robes. He had striking yellow hair, tall ears, and piercing blue eyes. Despite the anger that I could see smoldering in his eyes, he held up his hands in surrender and spoke quickly.

"I surrender, please, we wanted no part in this war, but those men wouldn't listen and now...my dear companions...," he spoke softly at the end, and I almost thought he'd changed his mind about surrendering when he clenched his fists and I felt power stirring, but a moment later he released it with a defeated sigh.

I gripped my sword tightly, but the blood spilt had eased my rage enough that another life, especially one who'd surrendered, wouldn't do me any good.

"Fine," I said, reaching out and taking his weapons. A dagger and a gnarled wand in a belt made of vines. "But if you resist us, you will die. I hope you are able to pay reparations for the deaths of these men, because if not, you have long years of service to render."

"It's not so bad," Daniel said, clapping the man on the back. "I was a bandit and now I'm leveling every month. Best prison sentence I've ever gotten." He winked at the elf, but he didn't seem enthused by the idea.

"My family will pay whatever is needed for my return," he said, as if it weren't a matter worth discussing.

It was easy work after that to secure the keep and town below. I learned that the barge wasn't a complete loss, they even managed to get it to fly again, despite having been on fire. The enemy having ballista was a surprise, but our intel hadn't known that this town was a manufacturing hub for such weapons. Lucky for us, so deep into House Blalor lands, there hadn't been a need to set any up, so there was only one, a display model of sorts, that had been ready to fire. It hit a vital corner of the armor and one of the contraptions providing lift failed.

However, we'd suffered more losses than we ought to have, considering our strategy. The legion sent against the town lost half of their forces in the crash, burning down several of the large warehouses used to manufacture siege weapons. I hadn't gotten the final report of soldiers lost, but I knew it was at least a hundred, a quarter of which had been dispatched by the adventuring group. Cam made it out alive so there was a bit of a silver lining. I really hoped to be able to get that young man back to his wife and child, I could do that at least.

CHAPTER 38
KEEPS WILL BURN

The next two weeks progressed in a haze of activity. We did nonstop night raids, taking keeps and fortifying them until we'd captured two dozen or half of all the keeps House Blalor owned. However, the time of sky barges was at an end, only a couple weeks after when reports came in that the enemy had figured out a way to counter whatever measures were being used to give us flight. I was lucky enough not to be a part of that raid, but all three barges went down with all hands killed or captured.

It was a mighty blow against our forces and Lord Variyn decided that until they could figure another work around or means to protect themselves, the barges would remain grounded. However, that meant we had a large force that had created two front lines of battle and we had to push to maintain it. House Blalor still had a sizable army that pushed into House Variyn land and pushed against the keeps we'd taken.

Lord Variyn announced that we'd make an advance for the capital, taking key keeps along the way, so that is how I found myself readying for battle outside one of the biggest keeps I'd seen so far, called High Mountain Keep. It wasn't actually on a mountain, but it was built into the oddest rock formation that seemed like twisting fingers reaching out of the ground. It had a single approach point, unless you felt like climbing the sheer back rock face or repelling from a barge, risking it being lost.

I'd suggested that perhaps we might be able to miniaturize the flying mechanisms to make them faster and harder to hit targets, but Lord Variyn explained—extremely vaguely—that a certain distance between the mechanisms was required to make it work and that at least three were required to work it. I didn't understand, but he wasn't forthcoming in his secrets, even keeping a special force of his own that maintained the barges and were mingling with the general army.

But the barges did us no good sitting on the ground, not being used for battle. They'd still gotten some use ferrying troops back and forth to battles, saving them from marches, but they stayed low barely above the ground. When asked if we'd be getting a troop resupply, Lord Variyn said he didn't want to risk losing any more barges and they could only go so high and maintain air for soldiers to breathe.

We used the parts of the siege equipment we salvaged

from the first keep my legion had a hand in taking and set them up to be used in battle. Siege warfare wasn't something I was familiar with, but we'd been given five legions total to take it, with myself being set over the campaign. My orders were to take it in less than a week or flee before a relief force arrived from House Blalor. I had several teams of scouts, as well as Fred and Fran in the air searching for any larger bodies of House Blalor troops, but so far, we remained safe from a retaliatory force.

Seven days was a stupid amount of time to give to take over a keep, and I think Lord Variyn knew this, but if we were going to keep pressing forward, we couldn't leave such large targets uncaptured or allow ourselves to spread too far apart. I'd tried everything from running at the walls with ladders, to throwing Fireballs at the wall, but the enchantments used repelled everything. Even the siege weapons did us little good, shattering on the walls or doing minor damage to the structures inside.

Each time I'd tried to throw magic beyond the wall, it proved too high and required me to get too close. I still felt a phantom itch from where the arrow took me across the cheek, it had been fired by an *Awakened*, there was no doubt in my mind, but luckily the spreading effect of my armor had taken a shot to the eye and turned it into a glancing blow. I was finding more and more reason to be grateful to that dungeon and its gifts.

"We need a way to get inside and open that gate, because without that, we aren't getting through those walls," I said, sitting at my desk inside my tent surrounded by my Knights, Squires and several *Awakened*. I'd just come from a pointlessly long and useless meeting with the other Commanders where nothing of note was accomplished.

"We could try sappers again?" Mick suggested, he'd grown used to my new mood and our relationship of friendly banter had recovered.

"I've had Fred look at the enchantments we found on the rock and he's not any closer to breaking them, if he does, it will become an option, but not a fast one. I need something that will get us inside and get this siege over by the end of this week," I said, rubbing at my temples as I strained to gather any and all ideas I had.

If the enchantments weren't so damn good at disbursing the magical energy I threw at it, I'd throw the biggest most powerful Fireball I'd ever created, but according to Fred, it just funneled away to be used elsewhere. He thought it was used to further the defense of the main gate, but I wondered if they hid a weapon that would be unleashed upon us if we gained entrance. This was a keep that dated back to the times of the Ordu and it was proving to be an impossible foe.

"The answer is simple," Daniel said, smirking. "Get those black sky machines up in the air and drop as many soldiers as you can before they fall. Throw enough men at the job and I bet we win the gate, then the rest can walk right in."

"And lose all our barges," I said, looking at him pointedly. I wasn't in the mood for games.

"At what point is it necessary?" Raphael asked, looking at me hard. "We can't leave this fortress standing and give the enemy a rallying point where they can harass our troops from behind. The closer we get to the capital, the more the battles will turn into chaos, citizens attacking, soldiers setting fire to our camps and escaping into the night. I've already read reports of such activities from the force moving ahead of us. It'll only worsen if we don't take this keep and put our own force in it. I think Daniel's plan holds merit."

It was my turn to look surprised. How could she think such a massive loss of life would be worth it, even in the long term. There had to be an alternative that I wasn't seeing, something that involved more risk but less loss of life perhaps. My mind came back to a plan that had been completely shut down at the beginning of the week.

What if I went into the keep myself, atop Ares at the dead of night, fought my way to the gate room, and just opened the gate? Sure, it was risky, and I knew I wasn't invincible, but who else could accomplish what we needed? I knew that they'd station an Awakened, or several, in the gate room to prevent covert operations like the one I'd suggested, Gadwell had told me as much, but still.

Fred gave me a glimmer of hope that perhaps it wouldn't be so much a suicide mission after all. I turned to him, only having half heard what he said.

"Say that again," I said, giving him my undivided attention.

"I've broken down the enchantments on their sewer system. It had damage from, uhm, overuse," Fred said, looking uncomfortable. I guess he didn't like that he'd had to root around in their waste, but this could give me what I needed.

"This gives us access," I said, slamming my hand down in excitement and almost knocking my glass of ale over.

"Who in their right mind would go in through their poo shoot?" Daniel asked, looking positively mortified.

I looked at him and smiled. "Perhaps a small elite group of adventurers that are familiar with skulking about. Anyone come to mind, Daniel?" I asked, satisfaction growing as I saw the look on his face shift from repulsion to outright horror at the idea.

"You can't possibly mean me? There isn't incentive enough in this world for you to get me anywhere near that foul smelling area," Daniel said, standing and brushing off his robes as if he could feel himself getting dirty already.

"What about the enchantments I paid to have added to you and your crew's armor?" I asked, smiling even wider. "It will clean you up just minutes after taking a swim in it, surely this is repayment enough if you do this small thing for me."

"No chance, stick us back in a cell, because there is no way," Daniel said, shaking his head.

After another five minutes of discussion, he'd agreed and left to get his men ready. All it took was their promised freedom from any form of required service, they'd be welcome to stay on but each of them could be free men after this mission. I could see my Knights didn't agree with my liberal offer of freedom from their oaths, but I saw no other way to get this situation finished.

They were adept at cloaking their form and hiding, and each of them had grown strong enough at this point that I figured they'd stand a decent chance. What they didn't know, was I fully intended on being there with them, just not from below. I told no one, but I would come in from above and aid them in taking the gate room, all the while my Knights would think I was flying above out of reach but watching over the flow of battle.

Ares didn't like the idea, but I told her that she'd be safe if she stayed up high enough, but that wasn't what was bothering her. Apparently, she thought my idea was stupid too. Perhaps it was, but a thought occurred to me when Ares sent a mental nudge to me. A picture of Kora. Ares was trying to say that she could carry more than one person and it gave me an idea.

"You can keep a secret, can't you?" I asked Kora, walking into the Runeforged section of the tents.

They were by far the neatest and well aligned. No fire pits burnt here, just cold metal Runeforged and their fragile but tough looking leader, Kora. Looking around, I saw that almost all the Runeforged had been converted now, but still, losses remained low for them and they had over two hundred Runeforged still functional. I knew she had a tent stacked with a few dozen dead or as she put it, too badly damaged, Runeforged. I imagined they kept them around for spare parts, but I couldn't be sure, as I spent little time around Kora as of late.

"You know that I can," Kora said, staring at me with the single-minded focus that Runeforged had so keenly mastered.

"Good," I said, then went about telling her my plan.

She listened without interrupting or nodding along, just staring at me with that deadly stillness. "And you want a Runeforged to go with you to keep your meat from expiring?" Kora asked, finally inclining her head as if she understood.

"Not exactly, I was actually thinking maybe you'd want to come and help," I said, my smile wasted on her as she just frowned at me.

"My responsibilities have grown too great here, but Ignis is fond of you, she shall go if asked," Kora said.

I considered her words, Ignis was much weaker than me when we'd last fought, but I suspected she'd grown, as many of the converted Runeforged had. Both in level—or their equivalence—and in overall power.

"That could work," I said, deciding that she'd be worth bringing along. If nothing else, Kora claimed she was fond of me, which meant she might be more inclined to keep me alive.

"I will fetch her and give her proper stealth gear," Kora said, turning and leaving to do as she'd said.

Meanwhile, I watched the camp where the Runeforged walked about, doing one task or another. I noticed as I scanned the area, that several seemed to be standing about and just talking. It was odd for me to think of the Runeforged as I once had, mindless automatons. They had changed into their own people it seemed, filled with life— though different from what others might consider normal life but still real.

"Good evening, Lord Miles," Ignis said, her voice as sweet and innocent as I remembered it from before. "I'm to accompany you on a," she paused to look around conspiratorially and dropping her voice to a whisper, "a secret mission?"

"That's right," I said, "if anyone asks, we will be saying you are taking up a position as my personal guard and must be with me at all times."

She tilted her head to the side before speaking and sounded a bit confused. "Is that not the truth, I was told I will protect you. Is there another use you had in mind for my time?"

I cleared my throat and tried explaining in simpler terms. "We are on a secret mission, you will be protecting me during it, but if anyone asks just tell them about protecting me and not the secret part, got it?"

She nodded. "I got it," Ignis said, her face contorting into an odd approximation of a smile. Her features weren't nearly as flexible as Kora's, so it looked more like she'd raised her cheeks and her lips stayed where they'd been before. I understood the gesture and couldn't help but smile back.

The plan was to happen this very night, so I prepared by using a spell Fred guided me through from a book he had, to darken my armor. As Fred was Fred, he asked why I needed to darken my armor, the spell put a layer of mana over the armor making it appear all black and gray. I was sure to get it added to the others as well, Daniel's party grumbled but overall were grateful for any additional barrier between them and the sewage they'd be traveling in.

I pulled Daniel aside before he left and told him that he should expect help from above. He saw my armor had been blackened as well and I didn't need to say any more, he smirked and nodded his understanding.

With the legions and commanders informed and ready to gather and storm the gate at a minute's notice, the bandit crew went to work. I took Ares and Ignis, flying off into the distance first, then going as high as I could stand, we circled back towards the keep. We'd need to give them enough time to get in and find a way out of the sewers. I would meet them near the gatehouse, or as near as I dare without setting off any alarms.

To accomplish this I, using Ares's near perfect distance vision, instructed her where she should land, a way's away from the gate where very few light still burned this late into the night. It was well into night and the moons were hidden behind cloud cover, giving me the perfect chance to get behind enemy lines.

"Ready," I told Ares, and we dove. The air ripped at my face and I was glad for the goggles I'd begun wearing while riding atop her. Ignis held tight around my midsection, her metal form cool against my back. She'd opted to put on dark leather armor and a dark black cloak, it flapped noisily in the wind behind us.

As we dove, I could make out guards atop the wall and on towers inside the wall, each of them stood near ballista that had blunted arrows as big as a man loaded within them. If we weren't shrouded in black, I'd be worried they'd see us, as their eyes were all looking up and searching the sky, not on the land in front of them. House Blalor had adapted so quickly to our use of barges against them that it almost made me think they had foreknowledge. Not enough obviously, as we'd dealt a devastating blow against them by taking so many keeps. The war had truly turned a page and now House Variyn was the clear leader when it came to victories.

Ares skimmed the top of a roof, slowing herself but, unfortunately also sending a few tiles tumbling to the ground, making significant noise in the dead stillness of the night. Mentally I commanded her to get to the ground but down several streets, she glided perfectly quiet until we landed softly.

"Okay girl, now get out of here and stay high enough that they can't bother you," I said, stroking her head. "I'll be safe, Ignis has my back," I added. She was sending me worried emotions and bucked her head into Ignis a few times before staring her down. I'm sure Ignis didn't understand, but Ares was telling her to keep me safe, or else.

Then Ignis surprised me by reaching out and petting Ares on the head. "I will keep your human safe," she said in her innocent sweet tone.

I looked at her and then to Ares. "I'll be fine, now go and be safe. I will call when we are ready."

Ares gave me a resolute nod and pushed off, blowing dirt and debris up as she gained altitude. I heard voices calling out and I was afraid if it was from her getting spotted, but they stopped a moment later and she was gone, safe for the time being.

The streets inside the massive keep town were quiet, at least in this part of the town. We moved, Ignis staying covered as best she could, and my own cloak hiding my armor well enough that I hoped to pass as just another town goer out and about, if caught. The streets were cobblestone, and all the buildings were made of white bricks with the faintest lines of enchantments glowing on them. This truly was a keep from the time of the Ordu.

As we moved through the town, everything was going good, until I heard voices ahead. We'd nearly made it to the most eastern corner, where I planned to follow the wall towards the gate room. As I approached the noise, cautious to stay in the shadows, the winds shifted, and I caught scent of a foul smell. Relaxing a bit, I was sure I'd just found who I was looking for.

Sure enough, I recognized the hushed whisper as I turned a corner.

"We won't be sneaking anywhere smelling like this, Todd," Daniel was saying, but from where, I couldn't tell at first. Then suddenly, a grouping of shadows shifted a little and I realized that they didn't look quite natural.

"Daniel," I said, the shadows whirled, and I leaned to the side to dodge a dagger flying past my head.

"Damnit Greg, that's Lord Miles, go get your dagger and pay better attention next time," Daniel said, then switching his tone to a lower one he mocked the words, "Oh sure I'll watch our back duh duh duh."

"How was the trip upward?" I asked, in a hushed whisper. I decided to keep my distance, as their smell was foul to say the least.

"It smelled like freedom," Daniel said, the shadows dissipating enough that I got my first look at him. Everything he wore was covered in small chunks of, something, and I didn't want to know what.

"Still waiting for the enchantment to do its job?" I asked, seeing that slowly but surely the grime was going away. The enchantment worked slow but it worked well. Give it another ten minutes and it'll smell like the day it was enchanted.

"Let's move closer while it works, the place seems mostly deserted in here, I haven't come across a single person," I said, growing confident that we'd be able to accomplish our mission easier than I'd worried.

I had suspected that there would be a limited number of troops, but it would seem that even the guardsmen are few and far between. On the walls, I'd counted perhaps two dozen total and our spotters hadn't counted more than thirty during the day. Perhaps getting the gate open would be all we needed to do, as soon as they see the force we are bringing against them, they'll surely surrender.

They grumbled but we moved forward, I took the lead. Mostly it was to keep them down wind, but I also had much keener eyes than any of them since passing over my second threshold. It was because of this keen eyesight, that I saw movement ahead, and held a hand up to stop the approaching bandits turned adventurers. They came to a silent stop, invisible in the dark night, and I slipped out of sight with Ignis into an alleyway.

Whoever was coming, they were walking straight for us and stumbling. After a moment, I realized what the man was, a drunk. He stumbled past the alleyway and onward. Instead of letting him pass like I'd hoped, I heard him cry out. Looking back out to the wall side of the road, I saw Daniel had sunk a dagger into the drunk's face.

"That wasn't necessary," I hissed, regretting choosing these low life thugs to do this mission. "We aren't here to kill random citizens. Have some damn sense!"

"I do," Daniel whispered back. "Drunk or not, he saw us as he passed. There was no helping it."

"No more killing citizens unless I say so," I said, returning to our trek forward.

We encountered a patrol of guards halfway down, but simply hiding in another alley as they passed worked fine, and we avoided killing anyone.

"See," I said, to Daniel, who looked upset to have not taken out the guards. "We can do this without all the extra killing."

Their stink had all but gone when we reached a stairway that led up into the parapets and connected into the upper gate room. Based on intel we'd received, the top area was where you'd find the gate release, and if I triggered that and then somehow fused the metal, it would give our troops plenty of time to make the march up the single approach into the keep.

The night was filled with the conversation of two guards as we moved as swiftly and silently as we could towards the gate house. However, a pair of guards from behind, ones that must have just come up the stairs a minute behind us, called out.

"You two! Stop! You can't be up here!"

They hadn't spotted Daniel and his crew. A mistake they wouldn't live to regret. I stopped and turned, Ignis keeping her head low and our hoods down over our faces. They stopped shouting, but their weapons were pulled as they approached. Suddenly, one of their heads ignited in green flame and it looked like he wanted to scream but no sound came out. Meanwhile, the other just ahead of him took a dagger to the throat by Todd.

Before I could tell them differently, they threw the bodies over the wall and sank back into the shadows. I shook my head but turned to continue on, hoping that the guards keeping their eyes to the sky would prevent them from noticing the falling corpses of their companions. It was no good, an alarm went up less than a minute later and calls went out all around us.

We were so close to the guard house that I turned and yelled, "Run for it!" as quietly as I could, given the circumstances. Their shadows faded and we ran for the door. Two guards appeared just outside it, but I summoned my sword and took his head from his body, while Ignis simple punched the guard in the face.

It didn't just knock him out though, her fist sizzled as it made contact, and she caved in his face before he could make a sound. She'd grown in strength for sure, and if I had to guess, she'd also added fire or heat rather, to her punch, cooking a section of the dead guard's face. Springing through the door we saw what awaited us.

An empty room. A door set into the other side of the wall where the gate continued and a trapdoor in the ground, open. I saw a massive chain coming up on both sides but no mechanism to open the gate like we'd been told. It must be down below after all, and I guessed that the trapdoor must be the only way in or out. A scan during our approach showed no bottom floor exterior door or windows.

Going to the massive chains, I tried to peek down below. I heard voices, a good bit of them, joking and laughing. We had a fight on our hands, but were they guards or *Awakened* soldiers? There was one way to find out, but I didn't like it. So, I made a choice that I hoped turned out to be the right one.

"I'm going to throw a Fireball down there, but not a very big one," I said, even more unsure about the choice as I announced it.

"What if it ruins the mechanism to open the gate?" Daniel asked the question I was avoiding thinking about.

"You're right," I said, sighing. "We'll have to go down

quick and be ready for a fight. You all prepared? I will go first, and I need you right behind me."

I got a number of weak nods and noncommittal grunts, so, basically what I expected from this bunch. Moving to the edge of the trap door I smelled deeply, someone was smoking a weed of some kind and the smell of ale perfused the room just as completely as the weed smoke did, wafting here and there. That could be to my advantage, depending on the type of effects the smoke had on them.

Taking a deep breath of the fresh air above, I stopped stalling and jumped down the ten feet, not bothering to use the ladder. I held out my hand the moment I landed and released an essence filled Lightning Strike into a surprise group of ten *Awakened*. It hit a cloth-wearing caster type with rich blue robes, and scorched his chest, leaving a crater where my attack had struck. Before they could react, I let loose an essence infused Arcane Missile and took a healer, who just began to chant over the caster in blue robes, with all three strikes.

Another healer, wearing golden armor and lifting up a massive mace, stepped forward, chanting. I Essence charged a Firebolt into his chest, but he got his chant off before my attack struck. Healing light washed over the wizard and the priest, only the priest stirred. One down, nine to go.

At my back, I heard several thumps as I was joined by Ignis, Daniel and his crew. Ignis wasted no time, her cloak fluttering around her as she let loose a stream of fire on the nine of them. It was intense heat and I worried we'd damage the internal mechanisms, so I raised a hand for her to stop. She did, the paladin's barrier that he'd managed to get up shattered as she rushed forward and punched it.

A large muscular demon with long claws appeared, running into battle behind Ignis, and the battle was on.

The attacks from this group were weak when put against Ironfist, but their combined might was nothing to scoff at. I dipped, dived, and dodged through the melee with my sword singing a song of death. In the end, we'd lost all bandits but Daniel, who stayed protected behind demon armor, and Ignis had lost an arm again. Walking through the death and carnage, I searched for the mechanism that would raise the gate.

Above us I heard a slam as the trapdoor was pulled shut, and a thud as the bolt fell into place. We were trapped, but we had a job to do before I could worry about that.

"Give me a hand," I said to Ignis before remembering she'd lost one and wasn't going to be much help. Daniel snorted and tried to hand over Ignis's crushed hand. "Daniel, just get over here and help me figure this out."

There were three levels, each one attached to a cog that attached to other cogs. I imagined that one would open the gate, the other close, but what possible use could a third have?

"Might be a kill switch," Daniel said, responding to my unspoken question as I stared at the three levers. "Whelp like my mum always said, choose the right."

Daniel reached out and tugged on the right most lever. There was a clunk sound but nothing else happened. "Left it is," Daniel said, reaching for the left one. I grabbed his hand and glared.

"Why not the middle?" I asked.

"Far as I can figure this right one just tried to close it, and If I were making this gate, which I didn't, I'd put the kill switch in the middle, if it is a kill switch and not just a level to hold the gate into place once raised," Daniel said, adding little bits of useless information into his speech.

"Left it is," I said, considering his words. He had a point; it could just be a holding mechanism or even a quick drop method.

The gate began to groan and a steady 'tick tick tick' could be heard as the chains moved and the gate opened.

We'd done it! Now how were we going to get out of here in one piece? I wagered we'd likely taken care of most, if not all, of their *Awakened,* so we could always wait it out. I saw no holes or ways for them to get to us other than the trapdoor, which in that moment swung open. The feet of guards, one after another began to come down, shouting and yelling for the gate to be closed.

Before I could stop her, Ignis acted. Flames hit the lowest of the guards, the spurts of flame then traveling up the wooden ladder out the top. Guards screamed as they were burnt to death and my stomach turned at the smell and sight of it. My first reaction was to let the guards see the fallen adventurers and give them a choice, but that wouldn't happen now.

Ignis, one armed, stepped forward and with a wave of her hand put all the flames out. Daniel hurried to the ladder, looking up. "We should hurry before they close it," he said starting the walk up. He was halfway up when a spear came screaming down the ten-foot ceiling, striking him right in the eye and exploding out the back of his head. He was dead before he hit the ground and no amount of healing could fix an injury like that.

"Shit," I yelled, rushing forward and casting Lightning Strike at the guard that leaned over the open hole. However, it wasn't a guard, the armor looked far too intricate. Whoever it was, took my essence infused Lightning Strike to the back of the head and came tumbling through the hole onto a pile of burnt corpses.

With a wave of his hand as he fell, three spears appeared and launched towards the two of us. It was in impressive show of skill, especially while falling. I dodged the attack with ease after activating Speed Burst. Ignis, side stepped the one heading towards her and rushed forward, her fist glowing red as she went for a punch to his head.

Despite his bulky silver armor, he rolled to his feet with the agility of a practiced fighter. Ignis's punch squelched into the group of bodies and before I could erect a Mana Shell, she took a spear to the shoulder. The metal on metal let loose a screech and she was thrown backwards. I couldn't tell what kind of damage had been done, but I didn't wait to find out, releasing a Force Wave with a downward slash and charging my new opponent.

While closing the distance, I activated Light Blade and

wished I'd had the sense to activate Arcane Armor after we'd entered the gate house. Sending a rush of essence into my sword, I put it all the way to tier 5 and felt my muscles bulge in response, as well as the surging of my Intellect, enabling me to add additional power behind my spells.

My opponent, wearing a hawk faced looking helmet, summoned a spear in his hands and caught my sword as I slashed downward. Sparks flew and so did he. The force of my attack was too much for him and he slammed against the back wall, the stone cracking from his impact. I was on him a moment later, this time slashing with Power Strike to end this fight.

His spear glowed a faint white color and pulsed, hitting me with a beam of energy that took me off my feet before I could finish my slash. My skill wasted and my head jumbled, I made it back to my feet in an impressive roll and tuck. I shot off an essence infused Firebolt, ready to end this fight. It whistled through the air, sparking blue and green energy. He dodged, and another chunk of rock went flying.

"You were foolish to come here yourself, Commander Miles," a middle-aged man's voice said. I couldn't see any of his features because of his armor, but if he wanted to start monologuing about my mistakes, that was fine with me. It gave me just enough time for my cooldowns to wind down.

"I tend to be a bit foolish," I said, three seconds to Lightning Strike cooldown. My strike to the back of his head must have done some damage to him, but he didn't look particularly dazed or slowed, maybe I'll aim for a limb this time. Perhaps try to hobble him? I cut my thoughts just as Lightning Strike came off cooldown, but not before he began to speak again. I didn't bother infusing it with essence as it added a bit of time to the build up before I could cast it.

"Do you even know who I am?" He asked, a moment later a Lightning Strike hit his arm holding the spear and it fell away as he yelled in pain.

I was surprised he'd gotten the entire question off before I got my spell off, but not so surprised as to not immediately begin casting a follow up Arcane Missile Rank 2 infused with essence, making the two and a half second cast nearly three seconds. It was fine though, because the armored spear wielding knight bent over to grab his spear just as my arcane missiles arrived.

Thud. Thud. Thud.

Three hits in quick succession, one on the same spot I'd just hit, and one on each knee. His armor was heavily scorched, but I hadn't really broken through it, so it was hard to tell what kind of damage I'd done. Running forward, just as he shakily got to his feet, I activated Speed Burst. For the next four seconds I hit him as hard as I could, bending and in some places sundering his armor with the help of Power Strike, Swift Strike, and just as I disengaged, a Force Wave combined with Light Blade's arc of energy.

He took each hit, unable to get to his feet or bring his weapon to bear, however, his armor might as well have been airtight, as there were no exposed areas for me to draw blood. Arcane Missile came off cooldown, so I unleashed it as a plan formed in my head.

The heavily armored knight was coughing now, and I wondered once more how much damage I'd been able to inflict. Ignis still hadn't gotten up and I was beginning to worry this bastard had done her in. Just as I'd given her up for dead, I heard the scrape of metal on metal as she pulled free the spear in her chest and threw it aside. Looking over, I saw her eyes flicker and she struggled to sit up.

"Take it easy," I called out to her. "I'll finish this one off."

Somewhere distant I could hear the sounds of battle echoing in from above the trapdoor. Our troops must be making it close now if not having already made it inside the walls. But I still had to deal with this foe if I wanted to help them. My sword was obviously not the answer to a fully armored opponent, so I pulled back in the essence and let my sword fade away in my grip. The loss of strength and intellect was noticeable, but I was still much stronger than my opponent, that much I knew for sure.

Looking around on the ground, I found what I was looking for, the fallen paladin with his massive spiked mace. Reaching down I hefted the weapon, dodging to the left as a spear came flying across the room as my opponent finally found his feet. He was obviously hurt, but he refused to give up.

"I'll give you a chance to surrender, but only one," I said, doing a few test swings of the heavy weapon. It was a bit unwieldy when compared to the light and finely balanced sword I used, but the weight didn't begin to come close to bothering me. It actually gave me an interesting thought that I'd have to run by the crafter that made my sword.

If she could make me a massive sword, several times heavy and larger than normal, I bet I could really do some damage to opponents like this guy here. I mean, I have strength beyond anything that I could have ever imagined before, lifting as much as ten or perhaps even fifteen men. Why shouldn't I wield a blade with as big of heft on it and use it to cut down scores of monsters at a time. I could do the same to soldiers, my mind prodded me with the thought of how destructive a commander I could be with a larger, more deadly weapon.

Up until this point, using a normal sword made sense because of precision and technique, but there was something to say for the brute force technique. It was a thought I would seriously consider later, as my opponent looked like he was finally going to answer after several seconds of breathing hard and holding himself up at the knees.

"You won't take my keep so easily," he said, coughing hard. "I'll get those gates shut if I have to die doing it!" He must have found his second wind because he was up and charging me, another spear appearing in his spare hand. It was an odd sight seeing a man wield two spears and holding them as if he might throw them both at once.

He'd stalled enough to bring me back plenty of precious mana and stamina, so I activated Speed Burst again, then Power Strike as I slammed the mace into his running form, sending him crashing back to the same spot where he'd struggled to rise. His body hit with a meaty squelch, and I saw the spikes on the mace had pierced him in two places on the chest.

Apparently, his armor did have some seams, as blood began to leak from the inside and his final words were lost as he fell into a fit of bloody coughs. I dropped the giant mace, shaking my head at Lord He'ret. That was who was supposed to be over this keep, so if this truly was *his* keep, then I'd find a middle-aged man who'd never been much of a commander. According to our intel, he preferred dinner parties over combat. Still, he'd lasted longer than the adventuring parties he'd hired who must have only been mid-teens in levels. Such a shame that so many *Awakened* were being lost to this war.

I looked at Daniel and his crew, shaking my head but not really feeling the same sense of loss for them. They'd proven in the end that they were worth saving and died heroes. That at least gave me a sense of pride for them, and I would be sure to tell everyone how valiantly they fought to the last man.

Remembering Ignis, I turned to her to check on her condition while reaching out to touch Ares's mind to check on her as well. Ares was flying high, and I got a few impressions of a battle taking place inside the keep walls before she flew through a cloud.

Ignis, on the other hand, didn't look so good. I picked up her parts, putting them in my ring storage, then picked up her body. Her eyes glowed a very faint orange, the color of her element.

"D-did I k-keep you safe?" She asked, her voice stuttered a bit, but I understood her.

"You did great," I said, smiling down at her. "Rest now and I'll get you back to Kora so she can fix you up."

"I don't want to die," she said as I carried her to the ladder leading up to the trap door. Her words sounded scared, which threw me for a loop, as I hadn't realized they'd thought like that at all.

"You won't die, I said, then added, "I promise." It was a promise I hoped I could keep, but right now she needed comfort and I'd say whatever I had to.

Her body shook with sudden tremors and her eyes flickered. She wasn't going to last much longer, the wound in her chest must have damaged something important. Instead of trying to do the step ladder I put a touch of essence into my legs and leapt the ten feet with ease, landing hard in the upper room.

I called out to Ares as I made it to the walls. Soldiers fought down on the streets below, and I realized I'd been wrong about the amount of resistance. It looked like troops must have been stationed somewhere inside the keep and they'd come out to defend the town. It wouldn't matter, with the gates open and our legions pouring in, the Ordu defenses no longer meant anything.

Ares glided down beside me, and I got on, strapping my legs in and holding Ignis tight with one arm, I held onto the reins with another.

"Go Ares, go and find Kora," I said, flinching as an arrow zipped past my head. Glancing down, I saw the archer who'd taken the shot of opportunity and released the reins just long enough to kill him with a Lightning Strike. Off we flew, towards the back of the columns where our legion still waited in formation to get into the city.

Perhaps I'd been too quick to leave the guard room, but it looked like an entire legion had made it inside, so there was no way we'd lose this battle now, even if the gate were closed. I would have to make sure to send one of my *Awakened* to gather all the loot from the fallen allies and foes inside the lower gate room. Besides being a den of carnage and blood, it was filled with valuable loot. I could have that commander's armor repaired and be practically immune to everything but blunt damage.

Ignis's eyes were barely visible as we glided down towards the column of Runeforged. The moment we landed, Kora came running. It was like she could sense that Ignis was in trouble, she had even gathered several spare parts that she set down at my feet, I emptied her mangled arm and missing metal plates into the pile as well.

Kora took Ignis from my arms the moment she set the parts aside and her hands began to glow, bathing Ignis in a soft blue light. Kora set her down by the parts and placed parts atop her, including her mangled arm. Then with the same blue glow she held her hands over the Runeforged. I could practically taste the power pouring out of her, power that could only come from a dungeon, pure and filled with potential.

"This will take time," a voice said, putting a hand on my shoulder. I turned to see Ventus standing there in full plate armor and a spear in his other hand. "Please give her the time and space she requires."

"Inform me the moment she recovers," I said, meeting Ventus's glowing eyes.

He nodded, then paused mid-nod and asked me a question that put knots into my stomach. "And if she should expire?"

Another name to remember. "If it can't be helped and she is to die, then I'd like to be here to wish her well. It is the least I can do for what she's done for me," I said. Ignis had been a vital member of our little quest into the keep, but it was more personality and will to live that drew me to her. Out of all the Runeforged I'd met, Kora included, she seemed the most human.

"It will be done," Ventus said, turning back to monitor Kora's work.

I left to find my Knights and report the success of Daniel's crew and my assistant, that proved to be invaluable in the end. It had been risky, but I'd noticed something when fighting today. I'd been so far beyond these fighters that even in the thick of battle against ten, I never truly felt worried for my life. Daniel had been strong enough to survive to the very end as well, but surprise attacks to vital areas were unavoidable and unhealable.

If he'd had some armor on, his Demon armor didn't protect him in the end, he might have survived, but a spear to the face is a hard wound to deal with. My mind went back and forth with the feeling of invincibility and inevitability that one day I'd die as Daniel had. A lucky shot by someone of equal or lesser power, taking me down before anything I'd worked for could counter it. Passing thresholds, attributes, new abilities, none of it could prevent death completely. Though I did wonder if I could survive a spear to the face now that I'd passed my second threshold. Would my brain matter be able to repair itself if someone removed the weapon fast enough?

Perhaps death wasn't inevitable after all, perhaps if I found a way to get to my third threshold, a feat no one I'd heard or read of had accomplished. It took 150 in an attribute for it to push past the third threshold, or at least that is what the books theorized. As it would require a normal adventurer to achieve several hundred levels even if they added 2 extra attributes a level, it wasn't something that had even been recorded.

My own calculations said that I'd need to gain another one hundred levels before I reached my third thresholds. But if I focused purely on my Constitution, the main factor is strengthening the body's health, I could reach it in 17 levels but it would unbalance me to a great degree. I wondered if there were others who passed their second threshold and focused on a single attribute to be extremely good at that one thing? It would take a normal adventurer close to 70 levels to reach their second threshold, a fact that stunned me when I realized it.

Doing a bit more mental math and looking I paused in my walk back to find my Knights, Ares walking by my side.

To reach their first threshold in all six attributes most adventurers would need to reach a minimum of level 38. I was fighting people twice my level, but not twice my strength. Of course, it was only true if they stuck to the commonly accepted two extra attributes per level. Old Ironfist had obviously not, and he was near my equal in raw strength because of it. Perhaps I was wrong to assume everyone would be trying to do as I did, doing three extra per level plus the natural three I get for being a Paragon.

Surely, I had an advantage and it had shown itself tonight, but I wondered as I reached the higher levels how far the imbalance truly would be. Perhaps I should change my tactics up some more. I was getting so much essence in the last half year that I had shot up in levels, but perhaps I should be going for an even more aggressive attribute spread. If I increased my extra attribute purchases to seven that would get me to my third threshold by level 60, however, the essence required for just those four extra attributes would be massive.

I needed this war to be over so I could immerse myself in growing stronger, otherwise how was I going to survive the Isle of Avalon long enough to get the sword and purify the Ley lines, fixing the damage the Chaos Knight had wrought on the land. Of course, I doubted that I even had the time to get stronger, this war had taken away so much opportunity for growth, yet still I am much stronger than I was before. How much longer could the dungeons stay active as the Ley lines became poisoned against them?

Would they be giving quests to others like Fred and Fran to help slow the spread while they waited on me, the Defender of the Balance, to rectify the problem permanently?

And if I truly wanted to end the threat I'd need to find and deal with that Chaos Knight or what was to stop her from doing it again. Though something told me that my chances against her would be far greater if I had an artifact of the Ordu on my side, as she had. I knew something for certain, I was ready for this war to be over and for the deaths of my soldiers to stop. If we took the capital, it would be over, I reminded myself.

Without Lord Blalor's seat of power, he'd struggle to maintain his forces. All the major banks within House Blalor operate out of his city, so financially he'd be ruined, unless he'd already planned for that contingency and moved his funds away from a centralized location. So many wheels turned in my mind that I didn't notice I had begun to walk again, reaching Raphael and Mick in heated conversation.

"What's the matter?" I asked, they sounded serious.

"For the love of the Ordu!" Mick said, backhanding my chest. "Here he is. We thought you'd died." He was exacerbated and shook his head at me in disappointment.

"I told you he'd turn up and regardless, we'd have never gotten all the Pegasus to do what you wanted," Raphael said, giving Mick a hard look, then smiling friendly at me. "How'd your secret mission go?"

Of course she'd guessed I'd do something, Mick probably did too, but they couldn't do anything to stop me when I had Ares to take me anywhere I wanted.

"It could have gone better," I said, frowning as I prepared to deliver the news. "Daniel and those that went with him fell in battle. Without them, though, we'd have never gotten the gate open. They died heroes. But it was good I went and took Ignis with me. We fought tooth and nail, killing the Lord of the keep and two whole adventuring parties he'd gathered to guard the gate controls."

"You faced eleven *Awakened* and *only* Daniel and his crew died. You should be dead as well, my proxy levels should be a match for yours," Raphael said, suddenly her hard look fell on me as well.

"Levels can be deceiving," I said, taking her look in stride with a smile. Just keep smiling, I told myself, eventually this hellish war will be over. My smile faded and I found it difficult to put back.

"At level ten I'd wager he was a match for you," Mick said, nudging me in the ribs and showing an unusual amount of comradery when compared to the last few tense months.

"What matters is the keep has been taken and we can move our armies onward towards the capital to end this war," I said.

They gave me various reports and I fell into the normal swing of it as I awaited news of Ignis. It came an hour later. Kora delivered it.

"I'm sorry, but her Core was too greatly damaged, and I can only do so much if it can't retain essence. She has died," Kora said, her tone solemn. "Her frame that held her Core has been fully repaired, however, I have no Cores to bring it to life. It is well suited for a Fire Elemental; would you find another so that her memory might live on?"

New Quest Offered!

Bring New Life

Kora has asked you to find the Core of a Fire Elemental and bring it to her so that Ignis's sacrifice, and her memory can live on in some form or fashion.

Objective: *Bring an Intact Fire Elemental Core to Kora*

Rewards: *1,000 Essence.*

Accept or Decline?

Without hesitation, I accepted the quest and searched for the words to say in response to the news of her death. I'd been right, another name to add to the list. Another person, at least I considered her a person in her own way, had perished because of me. It was getting so hard to bear the weight of responsibility that came with the lives I commanded. But I was strong and if anyone had to bear it, why not me?

Ignis, the converted Runeforged that did not wish to die...

"I wanted to be present, if it were possible, when she," I searched for the right words, "left us."

"It was my fault, Caldor," Kora said, one of the few times she'd used my name so formally. "I was arrogant and thought that I could do more than merely repair her body. When I tampered with her Core, the remaining strength she had vanished in the blink of an eye. Another of my kin lost to the service of your kind."

Her last sentence wasn't lost on me, but I didn't challenge her. I understood the pain involved with loss more than I ever thought I would. On a much smaller scale, she understood what I had been going through more than any of my Knights or Squires could. Even Fran and Fred, loyal as they were, did not fully understand the weight of responsibility that came with command.

"The end is near," I said, speaking clear and resolute. "I'm sure of it."

"Good," Kora said, looking at me with her glowing blue eyes. She had such an elegant design and the power she held inside was extraordinary. The knowledge and powers of a dungeon brought to life within a Runeforged.

"Do you miss being a dungeon?" I asked, watching her as she adjusted her armor. Still the same leather armor she'd first decided to wear.

"I'm still a dungeon, but no, I do not miss it yet," Kora said, then likely seeing my confused expression she elaborated. "I'm much older than most, if not all, of your kind. So, this time spent with you in this physical form, though it may seem long to you, has been but mere moments of my existence. One day I hope to return to the earth, but now wouldn't be the time to do it."

She paused to tap on her lips before continuing. "Even without the work I am doing, with the collected Cores and converting them, now is a dangerous time to be a dungeon. The Ley lines, as you well know, are in need of tending. I only hope you survive long enough to make a difference as I know of no other called by the Ordu, not that we dungeons get many opportunities to gossip, however, we do feel the vibrations of change."

"I hope so to," I said, turning and leaving a few moments later.

Our victory was lauded as a genius move and all of Daniel's crew were given commendations from Busard. We never did get any next of kin, so we had nowhere to send them or any place to give their death earnings. I spread the earnings among the other adventuring parties under my command and I kept the commendations, another reminder of their sacrifice.

Our march continued but the other keeps didn't fall as easily. Fortunately for us, they weren't old keeps with Ordu warding's on them, so with enough bombardment, we left them in ruins. Another week passed, and then the two weeks Lord Variyn assured us it would take, also passed, until news reached the front that changed everything.

A force representing more than three quarters of House Blalor's forces were marching towards Variyn city. They'd laid siege to a number of keeps and were only a week's march from sieging the city itself. I'd never seen

Lord Variyn truly angry until that day. He burned the tent down around us in his fit, but no one was harmed, all of us being *Awakened* Commanders. Apparently, Non had arrived to share the information as our scouts had still not reported anything and he'd gone to verify our losses firsthand.

So it was then that all the remaining barges were loaded with troops, my legion included, and we made our way out of House Blalor lands, leaving only token forces at each keep to maintain them until we could return. It should be enough Gadwell assured me, saying that House Blalor had made a huge tactical error sending so many troops into House Variyn lands when we had superior mobility to answer against threats like that and they didn't have enough troops to retake their own keeps when we withdrew. This would be the final battle, he assured me, saying his own Lords would likely string him up after this failure.

We were passing the original border of House Blalor and House Variyn when the surprise attack happened. We left as a force of twenty-three thousand strong to go face a force of only sixteen thousand; we felt prepared.

CHAPTER 39
BATTLE OF TENSON FIELDS

"D o you know where Non went after reporting in?" I asked Gadwell, though my voice barely carried over the whistle of the wind, I saw that he'd heard me.

"Special mission," Gadwell yelled back.

I'd wondered where Non had gotten off to after reporting in, as I'd tried to speak with him and not gotten the chance. But what could this special mission be that he was sent on and why did he look so upset after speaking with Lord Variyn alone. I'd never seen much of any emotion on his face and the way he'd looked towards me after speaking to Lord Variyn, had put a shiver down my spine. A part of me needed to know, but I didn't know how to broach the subject with Lord Variyn, nor did I feel like he'd answer my request if I did work up the courage to ask him.

The barges flew in a loose formation, far enough away that their occasional swaying didn't cause an accident and that was probably what saved my legion's lives. A dozen or more flying Pegasus appeared, each of them with metallic contraptions that looked almost like cannons, on their backs, and gnomes operating the controls on little seats. How the Pegasus flew with the awkward machines or whatever they were I did not know, what I did know is they were up to no good.

One of them went off, shooting a glowing blue sphere at the underbelly of a nearby barge. As soon as it got close it stuck to the bottom and the barge began to free fall, dozens of men at once falling off as it went side edge downward. I undid my harness just as one of them turned towards our barge and I jumped off the edge, calling to Ares. I knew she was flying close by, and I'd told her my plan moments before I jumped.

She caught me, matching my speed, and I fell with a thud into her saddle. I wasn't abandoning my men, like it might seem, in fact, I was hoping to save them. I reached out my hand and cast Lightning Strike on the Pegasus, not the contraption, but the metal attracted the strike, and I was glad that it did afterwards. It exploded on contact with my spell, a blue wave of energy being released along with chunks of white Pegasus and gnome parts.

I had eight seconds before I could do that again, so I switched to Arcane Missile, firing on one a moment too late. Another barge and another two thousand men began to fall to their deaths from far too high a distance to survive. My strikes threw the gnome rider off his mount and the Pegasus flew off into the distance. Another rider targeted our barge and got his shot off just after I hit it with a Lightning Strike.

Shit! The barge stilled in the air and began to tilt and fall.

I sent commands to Ares to get us closer. I would blow that thing off if I could. Moving closer as the barge tilted, I saw several men fall to their deaths, but I was helpless to catch them if I wanted to save the rest. The air screamed around us as we approached and I let off a Firebolt, it struck to the left just missing.

"We have to get closer!" I screamed into the wind and Ares dove straight for the center most area where the blue metallic sphere was lodged into the surface of the under-sealing. It was an odd half circle with sharp points that dug into the surface of the metal and appeared to have fused on contact.

We got close enough that I cast Arcane Missile, followed by a quick small Fireball. Each one hit but did nothing other than scar the surface of whatever metal they'd used.

Urging Ares even closer, I got ready to do the dumbest thing I'd ever attempted. Sharing my plan with Ares I felt her resist, but I assured her that she'd be able to catch me after and we'd be safe. She relented but I got the feeling she'd want to 'talk' about how much danger I put myself in later.

Summoning my sword and infusing myself with essence, I got ready to stab into the sphere with my sword. Pushing it to full, I felt my muscles contract and my mind sharpen. It wasn't the best plan, but if I didn't act fast it wouldn't matter. Releasing my leg straps and getting my feet to her saddle I launched myself from atop her, towards the now vertical barge. I used Speed Burst a moment before launching off, activated Power Strike midair and then Swift Strike a moment before the blade tip hit the metal.

It sunk in deep with a satisfying screech of metal against metal. Then it exploded in my face and sent me end over end towards the ground. I could see the barge every few seconds as I turned and twirled through the air, but it wasn't for a solid two seconds that it began to straighten out and I allowed myself to breathe. Doing my best to even myself out with my hands, I realized with shock filled horror how close I was to the ground already. Seconds away as I neared the treetops and mountains below.

Just as I had the thought that I ought to call for Ares, claws clasped around my shoulders and mighty wings beat against the momentum I'd gained. Ares brought us to the ground in the middle of a graveyard of metal, bone, and blood. I counted the remains of at least three barges. Looking up, I saw that several more Pegasus had taken to the sky, but these ones were laden with cannons able to bring down barges. Squinting my eyes, then directing Ares to look so I could see through hers, I saw Busard atop his mount, a long spear in his hand dripping with blood.

By the time all was said and done, we'd lost just over six thousand men, bringing our total force to only seventeen thousand, against House Blalor's sixteen thousand they'd gathered. We couldn't pause to bury our dead or salvage from the wreckage, so we pressed on, each legion's commander required to fly beside their barge, ready to defend it.

Scouting ahead, we located the enemy force, they'd done significant damage to several keeps along the way, as well as set towns aflame. There was no telling if they'd gone so far as to pillage, kill, and capture citizens, but Gadwell seemed to think they might. As bad as I felt for thinking it, I was glad that Creeshaw was not in the path of the invading army. Our plan was to go wide with our barges and swing around them, putting us just inside a large valley called, Tenson Fields.

That is where the battle would take place that would decide the fate of House Blalor and House Variyn. There was a strange kind of pressure on me as I was given command of five legions, alongside Gadwell as my advisor. The commanders who I'd be leading had some of the worst battle records, but my own legion had the best. We were known and feared by the enemy, so I could understand the tactic of putting more troops under my banner to inspire fear.

And we'd done just that, the black griffin had been dispersed among the other troops under my command, even their commanders bannermen held up banners of the black griffin on a field of white. It was a clear day, the sun shining, no clouds in the sky. It was a day I'd prefer not to die on. A beautiful day filled with warmth and cool breezes.

So much time had passed that we were only months away from the beginning of harvesting season. A small part of me played out scenes of returning home to help with the harvest, Cam and I telling stories of the great men who fell in battle and the heroic deeds they'd accomplished. I'd had Fran go check to see if Cam had made it and she'd found him alive, his harness having held when dozens of others had snapped. I played with the idea of having his squad come stand by my side, only engaging in the battle when I did. *If* I did, I corrected myself, smirking at how sure I was that I'd be entering into the largest battle I'd ever witnessed.

Of course, my Knights wouldn't want me anywhere near, neither would Gadwell, Busard, or Lord Variyn, as they all assumed it was my command of the soldiers that got us victory time and time again. It wasn't, but I couldn't really get them to believe that. It was a mix of my force of *Awakened* and the efficient killing power of the Runeforged. House Blalor had ceased sending Runeforged against me, but I'd heard stories of other legions being attacked by some.

There would likely be some here and I'm sure Kora would be busy swelling our ranks with them as she worked her dungeon core magic on them. My thoughts turned to Ignis, and I wondered how many self-aware, death fearing Runeforged were nervous about the battle. Up until the point of death, Ignis had been confident, so perhaps they didn't feel fear like we did, but she definitely felt something in the end. Her trembling voice still echoed in my head some nights; her fear of death was something I personally tried to never focus on.

"They'll be coming through that gulley any minute now and form a back line. Fighting won't likely start for another hour unless Busard feels like pushing them," Gadwell said. He had a spyglass and kept watch on a wide gulley to the west. It was just flat enough to allow troops to pass and the tactician in me, however small he might be, wondered why we didn't face them there where numbers wouldn't matter as much. I asked Gadwell just that.

"Non says he has nearly a hundred Awakened and a thousand Runeforged on loan from the elves." He scratched at the stubble that had begun to form from two days of quick action and very little down time. "With your nearly three hundred Runeforged and the hundred that Lord Variyn brought, we are still outmatched by *Awakened* and they have the smaller force. The narrow gully would favor them more than us. We want them out where our archers can pepper them and the siege weapons that we've set up can blow lines through them."

"So why would we wait for them to set up, that part still doesn't make any sense. Won't they begin to put out their own siege weapons?" I asked, taking the spyglass from Gadwell when he offered it and looked to see troops beginning to arrive through the gully.

"Busard is old school when it comes to leading an

army. He wants both sides lined up and ready to face off against each other in honorable combat. As long as whoever is leading the opposing force is like minded, it'll be alright. If they slight the advantage he means to give them, then all the better for us. We are formed up and ready to strike, they'd be lucky to make it through our arrows."

I had some three and a half thousand bowmen all lined up and ready to go. Large buckets filled to the brim with arrows sat every few paces, my Awakened working hard to ready the battlefield. In front of the archers, we'd set up wooden anti-cavalry stands ready to break a charge if one came, with my own cavalry set to the side, ready to sweep through a men at arms charge. My own men at arms stood ready with spear and shield. I knew my men were proficient in their weapons, but I couldn't speak to the thousands of other I found under my command.

My knights stood ready among the bannermen, and squires rode their horses, speaking words of encouragement to captains and troops. I'd had Cam's squad put into the reserves, along with a quarter of my men at arms forces. We would need a strong force to relieve the front line when the time came, and I trusted my men to carry out the job more than any others. What that meant for his chances of survival, I could not say, but I had to think like a commander first.

"Looks like they'll take Busard's show of kindness," Gadwell said, nodding. "They are setting camp and taking their sweet time about gathering up. If I know Busard, he'll want them to make the first move. We are here to stop them after all and now that they've stopped, we are doing our job."

Gadwell and Busard had a different way of looking at war than I did, one that I could respect. They saw an objective, and as long as it was being met, they were winning. As with this action here, where I'd have attacked the choke point and started the battle as soon as I could get my troops into formation, especially since I still saw it as our forces having the advantage, instead, they chose to let the enemy regroup as it accomplished the underlining goal.

After four hours, longer than even Gadwell thought, the enemy had formed up into columns and I saw the sheer size of the force we faced. They'd stretched themselves to columns only ten men deep, which seemed very odd to me, but I was used to doing a nine-squad formation stacked two deep, which resulted in eighteen men in a row, but each squad gathered together in a three-by-three pattern with the captain fighting at the front. I felt it helped the men to see their captains leading the charge, another topic in which Gadwell disagreed with me. However, he'd become less argumentative the more I'd won battles and now we were practically friends.

I ordered the archers to stand ready, a horn went off and bows were nocked but not drawn. As soon as they were within range they'd fire in a synchronized wave of death against the enemy. Because House Blalor's forces were marching in towards us, we'd have the advantage with our bowmen. Looking out at the lines of troops, I wondered if Ironfist fought among them. There would be no duel today to decide the fate of either side and a part of me hoped he wasn't here this day.

He'd shown himself to be formidable fighter and, by reports I'd read, an even better commander. If he led these troops, I'd say the odds weren't as even as I thought, but no matter where I looked with the looking glass, I didn't see him or his banners. I ordered the first wave of arrows to be loosed.

The call went out and arrows darkened the sky. No calls for shields went up and the attacking army continued to march, steadily moving towards us. Our arrows hit a massive barrier, I could just make out the tiniest fractures of cracks running all over the barrier spell, but it held.

I called for another wave of arrows, it appeared down the line shields were being erected and arrows were ineffective. But they weren't the only side with casters. I made another call, and I readied a spell of my own, jogging to a catapult we had set up just for this type of issue. Around me three orcs, two goblins, Fred, and a troll gathered.

"Fred and I will go first, then you three and then you three," I said, pointing first to them and then to where I wanted them to stand, next to a line of catapults. These were smaller but just as effective at lobbing projectiles and getting over range issues I'd been having with my spells.

I didn't want to break the catapult, so I began my cast of Fireball nice and slow, letting it form in my hands until it was about the size of my head. Then I gently placed it into the catapult and signaled its release. Fred's went next, followed by several more. Arrows shot out right behind our barrage of fireballs launched from several scorched catapults. We'd added metal linings that prevented most of the damage, but my Fireballs and Fred's burned hot enough to char the wood outside the metal.

My strike hit first and a section of shield about twenty paces wide shattered. Arrows showered against raised shields, some finding their marks, while most filled the ground with spiny arrow stalks. Another section failed as Fred's hit, and the final few fireballs smashed into the enemy troops, exploding and causing death and mayhem.

The enemy wizards answered with arcs of lightning that blasted apart several of the anti-cavalry emplacements. The moment they'd done that, a group of horsemen broke through their lines with practiced ease, heading right for our archery. Another volley of arrows tore through them, but some broke into the line of archers, killing and wreaking havoc. I gave the order and the Runeforged, our best anti cavalry unit, rushed forward and ending the threat of the remaining cavalry before they could escape.

I looked far to see how the rest of the battle went and noticed we'd gone into a full, men at arms vs men at arms fight in several places. There was a distinct lack of Runeforged marching against my side of the battle and I wondered if the commander knew of Kora's abilities to turn them. More arrows rained death on the enemy and my attention turned back to the fight. The enemy troops' back line of archers was finally close enough to return shots, so I motioned for my casters to ready what we'd planned.

I flooded mana into my Mana Shell spells, at Rank 2 I had an easier time stretching and shaping the barrier, so I would be blocking the majority of the space we could cover. Meanwhile, the rest would create pockets of safety to save as many lives as possible. I gave the order for shields up as the arrows darkened the sky, which had a two-fold meaning in this instance, and my archers reached down, pulling shields atop themselves. The men at arms were still far enough away that it wasn't an issue.

I activated Aura of the Hare, a new Aura that increased attack speed and reaction time among my troops. My archers knew this meant fire at will, but I called for the command and the horns went out anyways. I wanted to whittle down there forces as much as possible while I had the opportunity. It worked, the enemy casters weren't fast enough to bring their shields up and the constant barrage of arrows coming at different times made it hard for the men at arms attacking to know when to raise shields. Their forward march all but slowed.

Calling the archers to retreat and the men at arms to move forward, I let off another command that triggered the cavalry to sweep through their ranks during this exchange. Our horses thundered across the open space and into the enemy forces, cutting a line through them and leaving death in their wake. This battle, at least the third that I commanded was progressing well.

It was that moment that I happened to look to the side

and see that a small force had broken through the commander to my left's forces. A band of men at arms and what I sensed to be *Awakened* moved to flank our gathered forces. I called for Kora to respond with her unit, and she swiftly pulled her forces into place. Whatever that small force had expected, it couldn't have been the Runeforged, because they tore through the 'meat bags', as they liked to call us, with ease.

The cavalry returned and I ordered my troops forward to engage the enemy. Spear against shield against spear, men died, and blood flowed. It was hard to tell now that so many had clashed together, but I thought that we must be winning. The archers on both sides had withdrawn, neither side willing to risk hitting a comrade. I watched as the archers on the enemy side took out swords and marched into the fray.

Horns blared out on the enemy side and two things happened at once. The battle shifted, the enemy came together and began to push through our lines that we'd thinned to accommodate their longer stretch of troops. Then several *Awakened* made themselves known, lightning spread through the ranks, two soldiers at a time were cut down and arrows whizzed past my head.

I gave the signal and the reserve forces pushed against this new clump of soldiers mixed with *Awakened*. Next, I ordered my own *Awakened* to join the battlefield, giving both Fred and Fran a last head nod of encouragement as they went into the chaos of battle. Fred held my gaze a bit longer than he usually would, and I thought I saw worry there, but I smiled, reassuring him that this was just a battle like so many others we'd fought. He'd be fine.

My quick response had the desired effect and the battle shifted back into our favor as their lines buckled. I saw them suddenly push back with more vigor and recognized that an Aura had been activated by the enemy to keep their troops from breaking and fleeing. If we just kept pushing, we'd create a nice big hole in their lines and we'd be able to flank the smaller force to the north.

That is when I heard the horns of retreat to the south and turned to see Zander calling for his troops to withdraw. He'd been badly flanked and out maneuvered already. I couldn't do anything to help him as I saw several *Awakened* from the opposing army break through the lines toward him. He might fall, but the battle needed to continue. I made several calls to redirect some reserve forces to strengthen our left side, but it wouldn't be enough. Already the enemy had split our forces into two distinct parts and our advantage of numbers had just run away with their commander.

I deployed all reserve forces, called the archers to arms, and ordered the last of my *Awakened* to join the battle. Several of the commanders were murmuring now, but none tried to counter my orders. I turned to Gadwell, who remained stoic during the battle.

"I'm going in and I'm going to break the flanking troops' lines," I said, putting my helmet on as I finished.

Gadwell looked at me and simply nodded. "See that you do," he said. Then smiling he added, "Those slimy bastards don't know what's waiting for them. Caldor Miles, the scourge of the battlefield, the killer commander, the rich bastard with all the Runeforged."

I chuckled, having heard a few of those names in what little gossip I overheard. Gadwell knew the stories of my battles, and the knowledge of our past victories lent to the reputation we'd gained as a ruthless killing force. My ability to kill was unprecedented. I was a good killer, and I would do what I was good at now. I cracked my neck to the side, made a signal that told Fred and Fran to join me. Signaled a final sign that would redirect the Runeforged to attack the flank with me, then turned to Mick.

"I'm going in, keep the commanders from messing this up," I said, Mick nodded before doing something a bit out of character for him, especially during a battle.

He pulled me into a quick hug and said, "Watch yourself out there, I can smell death in the air. It lingers close to us all. No one is safe."

"I'll survive," I told him. "You do the same."

And with that I was moving.

Archers wielding short swords were mixed with men at arms as they created a shield wall against the incoming force. However, lightning had a way of breaking even the best shield wall, and soon my men had been scattered. My increased rank as a Commander, Rank 6, allowed me to activate two Auras simultaneously, once per a normal engagement. I used this fact to activate Aura of the Wolf and Turtle. This would make it impossible to break my troops morale for the next five minutes.

And it was a good thing too, because right as I entered the fray, so did another powerful *Awakened*, slashing through my troops with ease. I hit him with a Lightning Strike, activated Speed Burst and met him sword to sword. His blade was easily twice as thick as mine and longer, but I had the superior strength, tossing him backwards. Rearing forward, I slashed downward with a Swift Strike and Force Wave combo. My attack found a break in his armor by his left forearm, taking the lower part of his arm clean off.

The look on his face from the sudden loss of his arm was nothing compared to the look on his face as a Rune-forged appeared above him and put their foot into his chest, bending his armor inward like it was nothing. It was Ventus, he'd grown much stronger from so much available essence over the months.

With that one down, I looked for the next biggest threat. I lost myself in the battle, moving from one threat to another, killing a total of ten *Awakened* and dozens of soldiers who made the unwise decision to attack me while I worked. I made it a point to avoid killing other soldiers, however, I wouldn't go so far as to leave myself defenseless, so some killing was required.

In the middle of the fray, it was hard to gauge who was winning, so I just kept killing. I was in the middle of trading spells with a rather powerful caster when I heard a yell for help that I recognized. An entire adventuring party seemed to be engaged in battle with a single caster, one that I recognized. As I watched in horror, I saw a knight's sword, long and sharp, pierce Fred in the chest the same moment several Arcane Blasts hit him.

His body flunked to the side like a rag doll and his eyes looked in my direction, empty and lifeless.

Before I could react, I heard a terrible scream that stilled the battlefield as everyone in earshot paused for a moment. Suddenly Fran was there at Fred's side, her first swing took the head off a caster, the next the arm from the armored swordsman, then in a sudden flurry of blows the remaining members were dead. She screamed in rage as she moved, killing a soldier that tried to attack before plunging her sword into the ground by her brother.

I turned, a blast hitting me in the back, and using an impressive essence filled combo I killed the caster that dared challenge me. Not Fred...No, no, no.

Emotions washed over me, despite being mid-battle and I fought to keep control. Sudden energy flowed through me, and I began to spark, green-blue energy surging. Essence pure and powerful flowed through me as I prepared to do something, anything. He couldn't be dead yet. My first heal lashed out like a strike against his cooling corpse. Restoring Light tried to latch on to the target, but it couldn't, I pushed anyways until the spell failed.

Somehow in the heat of battle, Kora found her way to the twins, she killed a soldier about to take a cheap shot on Fran. I released an Arcane Missile that burnt the air around it, when a caster approached, his hands burning fire and ready to strike. He was dead before his body hit the ground.

Kora was over Fred, her hands glowing. "Come on you silly fool," Kora said, her hands trembled. "Your meat is fine, just come back!"

Fran was silently crying beside him on the battlefield, her face stricken and her breathing coming in sharp rasps. I finally reached Fred's side and I pushed Kora aside. She was able to heal Runeforged, not humans. No, I was a healer now, I understood about healing and damnit Fred you aren't dead yet.

I put my hands on his chest and tried another healing spell. Mending Touch went off but wouldn't latch on to anything. I screamed in frustration at the stupid pointlessness of everything.

"You won't die this day!" I screamed at Fred. My fist slamming against his chest, over and over again. If I could get his heart moving, he could still be alright. The healers had told me that sometimes healing wasn't enough, sometimes you had to help the body know what to do. So, I did as they'd instructed me, pushing on the chest and putting my head down to listen for a heartbeat. Nothing.

Damnit Fred, no! The essence inside of me reacted to my emotions and lashed out all around me. Fran grunted in pain but refused to leave Fred's side. I put my hands on Fred's chest and I pushed, each time my essence flashed around me, and Fred's leg jerked. It gave me hope and an idea.

Taking all the essence I could into my body I focused it and began to channel it into Fred. It was slow at first, but his body took all the essence I transferred without fail until

I'd emptied my entire supply, leaving me at zero essence for the first time since I became an *Awakened*.

But I didn't stop trying, casting heal and pushing on his chest. Something had happened during the transfer I realized; his hair had turned from its normal fire red to a bone white color. His eyes, once green, now stared up into the sky a light gray, so light that it looked like his eyes were almost completely white. But as I noticed these changes, I heard something.

The faintest sound.

Almost inaudible even to my ears.

A single heartbeat.

Then almost a minute later, another.

Looking down as I cast Mending Touch as it came off cooldown, I realized something. My heal took, it hit a target.

Fred was alive.

"How did you, what did you?" Fran said, her eyes wide as she looked at her brother.

He'd just sat up and was looking around, very confused. His skin had a paleness to it that resembled dead flesh after the blood had been removed. His gaze held a power to it that sent tingling feelings of danger when he looked at me and his heart only beat twice or thrice a minute. I had no idea what I'd done, but Fred was alive and that was all that mattered.

"Fred, your alive!" I yelled the obvious, as a spray of blood hit me in the face as Kora took Fran's sword to bisect a soldier that got too close.

"I feel different," Fred said, his words came out slower than normal but despite the physical changes he still sounded like Fred. Fran took this moment to crash into him hugging him hard enough that I worried she'd keep him from one of his half minute heartbeats.

"Are you good to fight?" I asked, another soldier falling to Kora wielding Fran's blade. There was still a battle to be won and as much as I wanted to pull him out, this battle could use his power. A part of me also wondered if he was fully functioning. Whatever I'd done to him, it had obviously changed him somehow, I'd put nearly two hundred thousand essence into him.

"I think so," Fred said, pushing Fran away, though she resisted. He held his hands out and began to chant the words to his favorite spell. It answered, and fire swirled around him. But instead of the usual red orange fire, it appeared white, almost translucent, in color. And the heat was enough that I had to take a step back, Fran jumped back several feet cursing.

"Maybe you should sit this out," I said, the heat was just getting hotter, but Fred didn't seem to notice and his body remained unburned.

"It feels so cold," Fred said, his eyes flared with light as he looked over the battlefield. Then before I could stop him, he thrust out his hands and a hundred little tentacles of white fire shot out in all directions.

But instead of killing us all like I thought it might, each one found an enemy soldier, *Awakened* or not, and burnt them from the inside out. In mere seconds, over a hundred fell to the ground, a husk of burnt-out flesh. Meanwhile, I took another few steps back from Fred, he shone like the sun.

Then suddenly, he winked out, leaving white spots in my vision as I tried to look around. The battle had paused again, at least in his general area, as everyone tried to figure out what was happening. Fred was on the ground again, his heart beating a bit faster than before, at least four beats a minute. It was strange, but I thought I could just barely see a tint of red in his new white hair, but it might have just been a trick of the light.

"Fran, get him to safety," I shouted the orders, pulling Fran from her shocked position some twenty paces away. "Kora, give Fran her sword back and go lead your Rune-forged deeper into enemy lines. I want to flank the northern side."

The battle continued for another hour, each side taking losses, but we slowly pushed them back, routing entire legions until all at once the battle began to break. House Blalor troops fled in mass; their morale broken. And just as I returned to Gadwell's side, covered in blood and gore, the sky to the west flashed several times brighter than Fred had ever been. Then as I stared into the eye burning light, the ground shook and a wave of force took me off my feet.

General mayhem ensued after that, where the commanders asked each other what was going on, but it wasn't until Busard and Lord Variyn joined us that we learned what had occurred.

"It is in no small part thanks to you, Lord Miles of Blackridge Keep," Lord Variyn was beaming from ear to ear. "That we have been ensured victory not only here, but at the heart of House Blalor, or should I say the territory formerly belonging to House Blalor."

"I don't understand," I said, and I could tell by the faces of the commanders, Lords of House Variyn, that I wasn't alone.

"I've constructed a device with the help of your essence research that has laid waste to the city of Blalor, taking with it Lord Blalor and all of his bloodline. I have ended this war and prevented countless more deaths," Lord Variyn said, he seemed proud of himself, but I still didn't understand.

"You destroyed an entire city just to kill Lord Blalor?" I asked, thinking about how many people, women, men, and children, would have been in that city that he claimed to have destroyed.

I looked to the west, a pit in my stomach that threatened to make me hurl. In the distance, a cloud resembling a leafy tree filled the sky over the spot that Blalor city must have been. What destruction had he wrought? The deaths of so many at once and power that even this far made the ground shake? I threw up all over the ground in front of me, adding my bile to the mix of blood that soaked our feet.

I was to blame.

My arrogance and blind trust. I'd put out knowledge that had remained hidden for who knows how long. And not once had I asked myself if there was a reason such knowledge had never been worked out or revealed to the mass public. I couldn't feel my face and the words of those around me just sounded like a ringing in my ears.

I vaguely remember turning to Lord Variyn and wanting to strike him, but instead I walked away. Away from the battlefield, away from the soldiers, the blood, the death, the pain, the responsibility, the injured. Ares found me and I took to the sky. The last thing I remember was thinking how I'd like to never come down. How great it might be to stay here among the clouds forever.

Name: Caldor Miles | Classification: Arcane Knight | Species: Human

Level: 30, 97,650 Essence to Lvl. 31 | Essence: 283,522 | Reputation: Rank 4, 31%

Health: 2,650/2,650 | Mana: 2,080/2,080 | Stamina: 1,892/1,892

Health Regen: 130 Per Minute | Mana Regen: 55 Per Minute | 92 Per Minute

Constitution: 130 (50 Base) | Intellect 148 (53 Base) | Endurance: 92 (50 Base)

Core: 60 (50 Base) | Concentration: 50 (50 Base) | Strength: 141 (52 Base)

CHAPTER 40
VICTORY, BUT AT WHAT COST?

I t was the love of my men and the sacrifices they made for me that brought me back. Ares landed and I slipped off to the first healer tent I could find, expending all my energy and time in healing those that I could. Raphael found me at some point, but I ignored her. She shared a few updates on our men, letting me know that Mick had fallen in battle, along with several of his squires. I heard her and added the pain to my already impossible container, then tried to lock it away.

It didn't work, so I cried as I healed, doing my best to ignore everyone's request that I take a break or try to rest. I was a machine of healing and let myself only think and do that. I almost went to search out a Mana Shrine to pick up all the spells I could find for healing but remembered my little store of essence had gone into Fred. He was alive because of me, I tried to remind myself, but nothing would bring me back from the despair that threatened to overtake me.

I was done being a commander, that much I knew for sure. Oath or no oath, honor meant nothing when you were a monster like me, responsible for the deaths of women and children on mass. I was a mass murderer, a fiend that should be expunged from this world. Suddenly, I truly hoped that my father was dead, otherwise he might learn what a terrible creature his son had become. He was right to keep me from being sparked. This life and the deadly potential it holds, changes you.

The healing came to an end, twice because I passed out myself, but finally because all that could be healed had been healed. It was over and now I needed to find something else to do. I searched out Verena and requested my list of the dead, callously telling her not to include the entire city of Blalor as my memory wasn't that good. She didn't laugh and I couldn't really understand why I'd tried for such dark humor. There wasn't a single thing funny about what had happened.

Cam had survived. A glimmer of hope in a field of darkness. I had Verena take me to him, he was in a healer's tent apparently.

Standing outside the tan-colored massive tent, I could smell death inside. But outside the moons lit up the sky and the wind blew in a warm breeze. Anyone not involved in this war might think tonight was a wonderful night. A time filled with joyous pleasures of drinking with friends and walking out in the beauty of the night. But I knew the truth, life was a lie. A fake façade waiting to be pulled away at any moment and reveal the truth of it.

I finally got myself to enter the tent and when I found Cam, I wasn't even surprised to see how bad his injuries were, because of course they were going to be life changing. He lay unconscious, but alive. His arms were missing from below the elbow on one and nearly to the shoulder on the other. His right leg was a wrapped and bloody stump, while remarkably, his other leg was whole and undamaged. His chest had massive scarring, the kind that would make moving difficult, and it traveled up his neck and onto the bottom half of his face.

His hair had been burned away, but the scarring there was minimal. Even the worst scarring could be reduced with ointments and special healing I thought, but of course he wouldn't have the gold for that. I could use the blood money I'd been living so freely off of, but spending that money now made me sick to my stomach. I had enough riches of my own to help Cam. I just hoped he had any sort of comfort of living ahead of him.

No arms and a missing leg meant work would be impossible. I continued standing over him for over an hour, my mind going over ways I might be able to help him. I was interrupted by a healer who arrived carrying a severed leg.

"What are you doing with that?" I asked, looking mortified.

"His leg is in good enough condition for a transplant," the healer explained as if it were just a commonplace thing.

I stepped back and let her work, the bloody bandages finally making sense.

I'd wondered why they hadn't healed him completely and I had almost healed him myself, but luckily, I didn't. The very thought of casting another heal made me swoon as if I'd pass out.

She connected the leg, using an incredibly sharp knife to cut away some ruined flesh before healing them together. She claimed that it only worked one out of ten times, but his healing looked promising. When I asked about the arms, she said it was still possible, but he wasn't an ideal candidate, so they were seeing to those who needed them the most. I argued, she didn't give in, but said she'd see about what she could do.

She didn't return and I accepted that unless I found my own arms to give to him, he'd probably remain this way. He woke up six hours later while I sat beside his bed, ignoring my duties.

"Caldor?" He asked, squinting at me in the candlelight.

"How do you feel?" I asked, putting a cup to his lips so he could drink as the healer had instructed me to do.

"Like I don't have hands," Cam said, chuckling.

How could he laugh at a time like this? He'd just lost his ability to do basically anything, and there wouldn't be a easy life ahead of him. When I didn't say anything next, he struggled to sit up a little, checking out his leg. It moved when he tried, and he shook his head, a look of satisfaction on his face.

"They told me when I first woke up that I might get a new leg," Cam said, searching my face for something.

"I'm sorry," I finally said, no words seemed strong enough or appropriate, but I gave them all the same.

"It isn't your fault that swordsman lopped it off like it was nothing. Like I was nothing. Couldn't even get my proxy skill off before he had me in pieces, then his caster friend burnt me up while I held my hands out in front of me," Cam looked at his scarred stumps and then his chest.

"I'll get you ointment that will help with the scarring, after a time it'll be barely noticeable," I said, offering words of encouragement.

"I'll manage," Cam said, somehow managing to successfully wiggle himself to a sitting position. "I'm alive and that is what counts. They tell me it's over, that we won. Like, won the war?"

"I guess," I said, shrugging. "I've not been around the commanders, but after what Lord Variyn did, I don't see how the war, any war really, will continue. The world changed the moment he used that weapon."

We continued to talk for a bit longer, but I found that I preferred his presence when he was sleeping and left to find a quiet room. Unfortunately, as soon as I made it to my tent, I was summoned by Lord Variyn to appear. Before leaving I found Raphael and gave her orders to return with any remaining Blackridge citizens as well as the Runeforged. I told her I'd be leaving soon, but to inform Cron to resume his role as Regent of Blackridge Keep unless told otherwise by someone with more authority than myself.

When I appeared in front of Lord Variyn, it was just him and I in his tent, I immediately began to talk before he had a chance to.

"I wish to formally resign my position in House Variyn, as a vassal, as a knight, and a commander of your forces. I am requesting you release me from the oaths I made and allow me to leave in peace," I said the words as firmly as I could, my emotions still a wreck and ready to overtake me at the smallest breeze.

Lord Variyn's expression changed to one of mild annoyance, then he smiled and spoke.

"No," he said.

"But I-," I started to say, but he waived a hand and continued speaking.

"I'll release you from military duty, for now. But I can't imagine why you'd want to be released from your position as a Knight and Vassal," Lord Variyn said, stroking his beard. "What of Alayna? She cannot just court anyone, could you set her aside so easily?"

I hadn't thought of Alayna for weeks, my mind so preoccupied with the war. She'd been missing from the front for over six months. My mind settled into a decision, and I shook my head. "Yes, I am fine with that. Release me, I can pay you a great sum for Blackridge Keep, allow them to live in peace and let me find my own peace."

"I will not release you!" Lord Variyn shouted, his sudden volume and the fury behind the words catching me off guard. He took a measured breath and stood, walking over and putting a hand on my shoulder. "Tell you what I can do. I will give the accommodations planned to your last living Knight, Raphael, was it? She can receive them in your place, and you can leave. Go relax and enjoy being an adventurer once more. After a time, when you are ready, your duties will be here waiting for you. The life you've agreed to take on will not be so easily shrugged off."

I didn't answer Lord Variyn. Instead, I stared into his eyes and wondered if I'd grown strong enough to take his life. Perhaps a surprise blow to the head and I could kill him in the same manner as his brother? Instead of committing the murder of the father of the woman I thought I loved, I turned and left.

Ares answered my call, and I took to the sky once more before anyone could stop me. I didn't give her a direction, but she seemed to know where she was going. It wasn't until we came down below the clouds that I realized where she'd taken me. My armor had cleared all of the grime away by this point, so when I landed outside my family home, I didn't worry about disturbing my family with blood and gore. A part of me thought perhaps they'd see the blood that I imagined dripped from my hands. Thousands killed.

I struggled to get through the door, breaking the latch as I pushed it in. It was still the middle of the night, so I walked to the kitchen and sat on a chair, content to wait out the night. A figure appeared and a blade came to my neck.

"Identify yourself lad or loose your head," Michael

said, his voice recognizable even after so long. I purposely pushed my neck against the sharp blade, feeling the tingle of pain but it was laughable compared to what burned within me. "Caldor?" His questioning voice made me look up at him, tears slowly descending my cheeks as bits of emotion forced its way through.

"My boy!" Came another voice, as a lantern lit from across the room. My mother, the sweet and loving Emilia Miles, came rushing into the room.

"Mother," I said, standing as Michael withdrew his sword. I took her into my arms and any pretense of holding back emotions failed. Everything I felt hit me then and I wanted to pass out, to somehow end my life and the pain, but the warmth of my mother's hug held me together.

"It's okay, Caldor, it's okay," she kept repeating, but I couldn't stop myself from weeping like a child. Killing monsters, killing those that deserved it, I had done all that without much worry, but this was so different as to shatter any view of myself as a hero or a man of honor. A part of me spoke about how it hadn't really been my fault, that I couldn't control the actions of others.

I latched hold of that thought and began to build myself around it. It wouldn't push away all the pain and horror that came with what had happened. But the true monster, the man that needed to answer for the crimes of mass murder, I knew who it was now. Lord Variyn needed to die, and I was going to kill him.

LEAVE A REVIEW

Thank you for reading. Please leave a review at, My Book.

If you really liked the book, please consider reaching out and telling me what you enjoyed about it at, Timothy. mcgowen1@gmail.com.

Join my Facebook group and discuss the books at: https://www.facebook.com/groups/234653175151521/

Join my Patreon at: https://www.patreon.com/ TimothyMcGowen

ABOUT THE AUTHOR

 Timothy McGowen was born in August 1988 in Modesto, California. His journey into books started with reading the Goosebumps books. Later he read a novel by Terry Brooks and became hooked into fantasy/scifi almost instantly. Shortly after that he was given a school assignment to write a 5 page fiction story, and 25 pages later his story was half done. He hasn't stopped writing since.

His debut novel Haven Chronicles: Eldritch Knight has sold over a thousand copies of both ebook and audible so far. He writes Fantasy that contains a splash of scifi and Litrpg/Gamelit stories. Consider signing up for my newsletter for news on book releases as they become available.

LITRPG GROUP

Check out this group if you want to gather together and hear about new great LitRPG books.

(https://www.facebook.com/groups/LitRPGGroup/)

LEARN MORE ABOUT LITRPG/GAMELIT GENRE

To learn more about LitRPG & GameLit, talk to author and just have an awesome time by joining some LitRPG/Gamelit groups.

Here is another LitRPG group you can join if you are looking for the next great read!

Facebook.com/groups/LitRPG.books

List of LitRPG/Gamelit Facebook Groups:

- https://www.facebook.com/groups/ LitRPGReleases/
- https://www.facebook.com/groups/ litrpgforum/
- https://www.facebook.com/groups/ litrpglegends/
- https://www.facebook.com/groups/ LitRPGsociety/
- https://www.facebook.com/groups/ AleronKong/

Made in the USA
Thornton, CO
08/03/23 21:57:21

4d513984-24e6-4467-9378-8332c322288fR01